NANO-MAGIC

E.S. MARTELL

Adriana D'Apolito, 3P Editing – Editing
Aleksandra Klepacka – Cover Artist
Melissa Stevens, *The Illustrated Author* – Interior Typesetting and Design
Kelley York, X-Potion Designs – Cover Designer & Typesetting

ISBN-13: 978-0-9989805-6-0
Printed in the USA
Second Initiative Press

DEDICATION

This book is dedicated to the following people whose services changed it from a raw manuscript into the book you are now holding:

Adriana D'Apolito, 3P Editing – Editing
Aleksandra Klepacka – Cover Artist
Melissa Stevens, The Illustrated Author – Interior Typesetting and Design
Kelley York, X-Potion Designs – Cover Designer & Typesetting

CAN HUMANS FIND A PLACE IN A WORLD FILLED WITH SELF-REPLICATING, AI-CONTROLLED NANOBOTS?

Sophie understood the problem better than any other cyber-sorcerer. She'd been there at the beginning. The benign AI, Hippocrates, has never spoken to any other humans besides her and Michael and is now missing. The other AI, Wiindigo, means nothing good for humans. The rogue intelligence intends to dominate the world and all that it contains, humans included.

In the world after AI, nanobot mediated spells can be performed by knowledgeable humans, leaving those who don't have that ability as a permanent underclass. Spells can be used for DNA manipulation and, as a result, many species of were-creatures exist. Chimeras, animals with human DNA, have developed the ability to speak. Brownies exist, and Fairies fly over the meadows.

All is not well in the new order. Wiindigo's nanites have scattered over the countryside and blindly seek to regroup. Local concentrations of the rogue AI's nanites form horrendous threats, taking the semblance of mythological monsters.

The "Good Powers," Sophie and Michael, must contend with other sorcerers in their struggle to keep humans from becoming Wiindigo's puppets. Wiindigo's nanites are everywhere and pose a constant threat.

They will need all the assistance they can get, from every source-no matter how strange.

CONTENTS

ACKNOWLEDGMENTS

I rely on my wife, Sally, for critique and feedback. She also makes sure I eat while I'm writing and that makes things convenient. Without her help, the stories in my books would never make it out of my head.

CHAPTER 1
ACCUMULATION

There were only a few of the microscopic machines in that part of the forest. They had arrived in various ways. Some had been blown there on the wind. More had fallen, encapsulated in drops of rain. A few had been transported by a bird that had succumbed to a respiratory disease before they could utilize its life energy.

The nanobots were aware of each other. Although the signal was feeble, each of the units broadcast periodically on the same radio frequency. The broadcasts were strictly short-range, but they relayed the messages so that each of the nanites knew the location of all of the others.

It took many hours, but they gradually drew closer together, converging on the most robust set of signals. Their movement was interrupted by a brief rain shower. The raindrops hit the tiny nanites like bombs, scattering them and burying many under a layer of muddied dust.

Despite the setback, they gradually worked their way out and continued moving together.

Eventually, there were several thousand of the tiny robots grouped together. They clung to each other, the close contact reducing the need for a more powerful coordinating radio signal.

The individual bot's limited processing ability was linked to that of the others. The overall intelligence level composed of the minute processing ability of each nanobot acting in concert with that of the others in the group spiraled up until it reached a point that was comparable to that of a common arthropod—a tick. As such, it had a vague idea of finding prey.

The linked nanobots formed into a small body. Gradually legs were extruded built by some of the tiny machines clinging to each other. The units acting forming the legs flexed in unison and the accumulation climbed slowly. The available energy was strictly limited. The body gradually moved up a thin, woody stem belonging to a clump of sumac. It moved to the tip of one of the branches and then clung there resting and hanging with no movement, although its senses were alert.

THERE WAS A period of time broken only by the slow arrival of new nanobots. They were immediately absorbed into the mass, each adding its small processing ability to the group mind, bringing the overall level up slightly.

After an undefinable time, there was a stirring in the brush. The combined sensors of the mass of nanites focused on the sound. Some of the tiny machines extruded visual sensors and combined with their neighbors. These rudimentary eyes picked up a slight motion in the grass.

At first, it looked like it might be from the occasional breeze, but then a red squirrel moved into view, searching for cones from a nearby pine. It stopped some feet away from the sumac bush to pick up and efficiently shred a pine cone, discarding the unwanted parts and eating the seeds.

Dropping the shredded cone, the squirrel moved nearer to the sumac. The tiny nanite ball dropped off its perch at precisely the moment the squirrel passed below. It fell, drifting on the wind a little. Mainly by chance, it landed in the animal's back fur.

So far, the nanite ball had done no more and no less than a common wood-tick. Ticks have a built-in elementary program. They climb bushes and then wait to drop onto warm-blooded hosts. The nanite ball had done the same.

The squirrel didn't notice. It continued to the next pine cone, then stopped to shred it. It's sharp incisors cutting through the cone and releasing the hidden seeds. Meanwhile, a malignant transformation was happening unsensed on its back.

The nanites weren't a tick. Rather than finding a likely spot and burying its head to suck blood, the group separated and climbed down the fur shafts to spread out on the animal's skin. Each nanite located a pore in the squirrel's hide and passed inside. Their size was so small that their entry caused no sensation. The squirrel continued to feed.

Once inside the pore or hair follicle, the nanites bored into the nearest capillary and entered the bloodstream. The drilling operation activated some nerves in the squirrel's skin, and it stopped eating to scratch. It was used to that since it always carried some fleas.

The scratching had no effect other than moving the nanites further along the capillaries. The red blood cells were invaded next, and the nanites began to replicate, using the chemical energy stored within.

At a replication rate that doubled their numbers every five minutes, it took almost an hour before the squirrel's body was overwhelmed. The nanites' collective intelligence was now on the approximate level of the squirrel, and it made sure that the animal was entirely under its control.

From that point, the squirrel's behavior changed radically. It quit looking for cones and climbed a tree to scout out the area.

There was a gray squirrel on the tree. It barked at the intruder and quickly raced down to defend its territory. Under normal circumstances, the smaller red squirrel would have retreated, but it charged the gray squirrel, and the two grappled for a moment. The gray squirrel bit the red one and suffered a bite in return.

The gray's behavior changed in seconds. It stopped fighting and allowed the red one to cling to it tightly. The two bodies slowly blurred and gradually merged into a larger amorphous mass that gradually assumed a somewhat squirrel-like shape with features that would have amazed a biologist.

After a period of consolidation, the new, more massive creature climbed to the ground and began to hunt.

A rabbit was the next victim. The knowledge it brought led to a fox, then several more foxes and a coyote. All the while the growing mass of nanites boosted their collective intelligence level upwards.

The coyote aspect tracked a deer, and that led to a more substantial period of consolidation. A large part of the mass of flesh was disassembled into its chemical constituents and converted to energy over the next few days.

The result was a creature that looked somewhat like a cross between a pit-bull and a Komodo dragon. However, it was more intelligent than either, not to mention more deadly.

It located a hiding place in a cave where it rested, consolidating its structure and forming what its growing intelligence considered a more efficient form. One designed primarily to hunt and capture prey. It devoted more resources to legs with the intent of increasing its speed.

Since the basic bilateral structure made sense, it retained four legs with a central linkage ending in a head filled with large spiked teeth.

With its new size, it could cover far more range. This allowed it to discover a flock of sheep in the next valley over. It took several of the woolly animals, one at a time. It absorbed the individual sheep then used the additional energy to capture the next.

After it had increased its size threefold, it retreated to its cave to better incorporate the new physical resources into its structure. During this period, the nanites didn't provide more than a minimal amount of oxygen and nutrients to the individual animal cells. The cells didn't last long as a result, but the group intelligence knew they could be replaced easily.

The animal cells didn't add to the group mind and weren't considered very valuable to the whole. When they died, they were broken down into chemicals and used to create additional nanites. As a result of the quickly dying flesh, a distinct smell of decay surrounded the creature.

As it rested, it drew up into a spherical form. The shape was the most efficient form from the group mind's perspective. Resources could be distributed more quickly in a sphere, and the individual nanites could communicate more effectively.

When it went out the next evening, it was back in its four-legged shape. It immediately headed for the pasture where the sheep had been, seeking additional resources.

This time, it was met by an attack. This was something new to the group mind. It hadn't thought that there might be enemies that would attack it let alone threaten its existence. It was surprised and had to adjust its knowledge base.

The shepherd was lying in ambush. He'd noticed the missing sheep and thought that some natural predator was responsible. He wasn't able to see well in the darkness, but the large creature looked somewhat like a bear. He sicced his dog to the attack, hoping to distract the animal until he could approach.

The dog was too smart to close with the unnatural and foul smelling thing but held its attention by barking and feinting attacks long enough for the shepherd to run up.

The man had an old shotgun, and he fired both barrels point-blank into the nanite creature.

The impact knocked the thing on its side where it lay, stunned for a moment. The organic parts damaged by the shot began to bleed and die.

The injury couldn't be tolerated. Mobility was at stake. While the group mind did not value the organic parts much since they could easily be replaced, the inconvenience and lack of mobility were not to be tolerated. The nanobots mobilized and almost immediately healed the wounds. The bleeding slowed and then ceased. The open holes closed and sealed within seconds. The shepherd was startled when the creature began to move.

He was even more dismayed when the creature suddenly leaped to its feet and locked its jaws on his leg. He shot another round into its back, but by then it was far too late. He was well on the way towards incorporation in what was rapidly becoming a new and far more dangerous creature.

The nanites invaded the man's leg, infusing into his bloodstream and spreading throughout his system. He dropped to the ground as his spinal nerves were traced and systematically destroyed. His body spasmed as it was disassembled from within.

The tiny machines replicated quickly, using the molecules from cells throughout the man's body. His body jerked and shook for some minutes, then became limp as a final moan came from his lungs.

The bulk of the creature still clinging to his leg assumed an amorphous shape, then slowly slid over the shepherd's body, merging itself with his remains. It lay there in a lumpy, ugly form while it consolidated its latest acquisition.

The dog, back hairs standing on end, watched, whining. When the lump started to move and reform into a new shape, the dog backed quickly away, then turned and ran as if the very devil was at its heels.

The man's memory store was traced out and absorbed by the nanites' group mind, adding greatly to its knowledge. It learned a lot in a brief time. There was a little goodness in the man's mind, but not much.

The shepherd wasn't all bad, but he was an outcast and misanthrope. The group mind learned a lot about evil from tracing that part of his brain.

The creature gradually made its way back to the cave. Its shape morphed several times along the way, and this made it difficult to travel. It had just reached the cave's mouth by dawn. It paused there, thinking.

A thin slime of nanites dripped off the main body and disbursed among the rocks. They spread out forming a network designed to both warn of intruders and to initiate an attack, should any flesh and blood creature come into contact with them.

DEEP IN THE cave, the malformed conglomeration of flesh and nanites dissolved into a heaving mass of tissue and clumps of nanomachines. Flies were drawn to the odor of decomposing flesh. Whenever they lit, nanites would attach to their legs. The insects were quickly dismantled and incorporated into the mass, providing much-needed energy and molecules.

The shepherd had been relatively uneducated but had read some books relating to mythical creatures. The group mind gradually cataloged and assimilated that knowledge into categories. Eventually, the mind made a decision and started forming the nanites and organic material into an end shape for the new body.

The operation took several days, but what finally emerged from the cave opening, late on the fifth day, was a fully formed creature that looked remarkably like a conventional dragon, complete with scales, horns, and wings. Its mouth was filled with long teeth, and its feet had razor sharp claws.

It had a single purpose at this point. Its energy level was depleted from the metamorphosis. It needed to feed. There was not enough energy to use the wings. There hadn't been enough raw material to create massive flight muscles. The dragon had not recognized that flaw until it tried to use its wings

The shepherd simply had not known enough about anatomy or physics to have a realistic idea about the requirements for self-powered flight.

The dragon adjusted the color of its scales to jet black, the better to blend in with the oncoming night, and headed towards the field where it had found the sheep.

They were there, still watched over by the dog. The poor animal had faithfully continued what he had been trained to do. He was responsible for the herd and did his best to keep them together and head them toward the shepherd's fold at night, but they'd gradually rebelled, and now he was content to allow them to feed into the late hours.

The hairs on the dog's back rose, as he stood indecisively. A wafting current of air had brought the scent of the creature that had taken his master. It was stronger than he remembered, but he'd never forget the smell. He barked at the sheep and started toward them, but stopped when he saw a black shape enter the field.

He whimpered and then turned away, trotting towards the sheepfold. When he heard the first alarmed bleat followed quickly by a strange snarling sound, his trot turned into a full run.

He passed the sheepfold and went on into the woods behind, intent on putting as much distance as he could between himself and the frightening scent.

OVER THE NEXT few weeks, the dragon expanded its hunting ground, preying on both animals and the few humans it was able to discover. The area was not densely populated since it was remote, but the humans were particularly prized prey. Each provided a depth of knowledge that was eagerly incorporated into the growing group mind.

The nanite software increased in intelligence, using the deep learning algorithm that was distributed across the tiny machines. Each held a small piece of code designed to form a seed Artificial Intelligence when enough of the nanites came together. The AI was now using all resources it could capture to boost its problem-solving level. The effort took a lot of energy, and the creature had to hunt frequently.

It didn't incorporate all of the flesh of its prey since it understood that there were physical limits to how large it could become and still operate. The thought of dividing and creating two creatures occurred to it, but it was programmed to become a singleton. Another competing AI was not something it wanted. It wanted everything, every bit of the earth for itself.

Its plans were based solely on increasing its powers. Given enough time, it would dominate all available space. It now knew the shape of the world and understood that there were many humans in other locations. It knew they posed a danger, but it could take its time and not expose itself until it was ready.

CHAPTER 2
THE GOOD POWERS

The meadow was empty. Surrounded by tall white pines and Engleman spruce, the open area sported a carpet of late flowers and some glacier-deposited boulders. There were a few deciduous trees in the mix. Some oaks and a couple of maples. Their leaves were starting to turn russet. A few birches were showing yellow leaves. It was evident that there weren't many days left before the weather turned cold.

A few bees were systematically moving from flower to flower, diligently working to gather every bit of nectar and pollen. They knew deep in their genes that winter was coming and they must prepare.

The pastoral scene was interrupted by the sound of something moving quickly through the underbrush.

A white poodle with an unusually large forehead shot out from under the long hanging branches of a spruce. He dashed to the middle of the clearing and scrambled up onto a large boulder. There he voiced one single, sharp bark.

In answer, a shadow coalesced out of the clear air. A woman appeared, followed closely by a man clad in luminescent golden armor and armed with a broadsword. He stood slightly to her rear, feet planted firmly on the ground in a position that indicated he was ready for action.

The woman hovered a few inches above the ground, not disturbing the bees' harvest, although a wind blew strangely down from her body, flattening the grass below and to her sides. She, too, had a glowing aspect. It covered the visible parts of her skin, although she wore pants and a light coat that covered most of her body.

The dog made a slightly silly grin at the sight of the two and then spoke in a worried tone. His voice was in the soprano range, but his words were well-formed and quite understandable.

"It's back there," he said, indicating a direction with a move of his muzzle. "There's a cave with a lot of darkness about it. I didn't venture near, but there was a heavy breathing sound that indicates something large inside. Not many tracks going in or out, but I could sense carrion. Whatever it is has killed frequently and recently. The victims were carried into the cave from what I can smell."

The woman looked at the man, to check his position, then dropped to the ground with a sigh of relief. She moved forward a few steps. At this, the man said, "Sophie! Be careful. It could be a pocket of—"

She interrupted, "I know, Michael. I'm already sensing some of Wiindigo's nanites among the trees. This portion of him is isolated but strong. We'll have to fight, but it's reluctant to join battle with us."

He shook his head negatively in response. "Your determination to destroy all of Wiindigo places you in too much risk. I wish you'd quit hunting him. I couldn't stand it if something happened to you."

"Nor I, you. You know I want to make the world safe for humans. I've got to get rid of that intelligence to do so."

"Yes, but it's scattered so widely now. I doubt that we'll ever be able to pick up all of Wiindigo's components."

"Perhaps you're correct, but we can at least try. Michael, you know that I love you, but I wouldn't be true to myself if I didn't make an effort to finish the job."

The dog interrupted, "That's all nice, but that dragon is going to attack or flee while you two are arguing."

She redirected her attention to him, looking with a critical eye. "Cisco, you've picked up some of the enemy nanobots. I warned you to be careful where you walked."

The dog shook himself, finishing with a wild flapping of his ears as if he could shake the tiny machines off. One ear failed to fall back into position, ending up draped jauntily across the top of his head.

Sophie smiled indulgently. "Don't worry. Your internal nanites are more than enough defense. They're dealing with the invaders as we speak. I doubt that you'll feel anything, but you have to be careful. It's dangerous."

Cisco said, "I thought I was careful. Some spots smelled like carrion. Even though I wanted to roll in them, I didn't. There must have been nanites scattered all over. I really didn't get close."

He paused with his head cocked, obviously thinking, then said, "The thing has set up an early warning system. It must know we're here right now!"

Sophie nodded silently, then advanced, her feet gliding over the grass without touching. It had taken her months, but she'd learned how to use her personal nanites to hold her off the ground by creating an ionic wind strong enough to lift her body. The grass under her flattened in response as she passed over.

Michael did not hold that mastery. He was unable to control his nanites and, no matter how Sophie had tried, she couldn't create the necessary transmitter in his body. As a result, her husband had no digital magic. Instead, he had something she often thought might be better.

The nanites were attracted to him and shielded him of their own accord. That was the source of the golden armor. It was made up of a thick field of nanomachines. Some of them had formed the sword, which always appeared when Michael faced danger. Although he wasn't in direct control of them, the nanites always seemed to be aware of his wishes and complied to the best of their ability. This gave him power, although it was unconscious.

Sophie's power, on the other hand, came from her ability to control the tiny machines consciously. She'd formed a transmitter within her body using their ability and now, due to her mastery of their control language, had complete control of them.

This ability had come in quite handy. No one associated with her was ever ill, and their wounds healed almost instantly. Her nanite population also formed an AI of sorts, but it was entirely domestic and oriented towards keeping her, and all those she infected with her nanobots, healthy.

DEEP IN THE cave, the black dragon-shape raised its horned head preparing to meet its greatest challenge so far. It had been aware of the dog's approach. The nanobots that were spread out near the cave acted as a warning system of sorts. Each was able to transmit a short-range blue-tooth signal, and the notice of any intruder was relayed back to the central AI mind that resided in the cave.

The dragon-shape was one that was used for travel and hunting. Usually, the nanites and rotting flesh spread out into a layer across the cave floor, leaving the ends of bones showing above the slightly heaving mass.

The bones of its victims provided useful structural elements when it reformed. It had quickly learned that forming around them and using them as a skeleton, in much the way the original owners had, made motion far more efficient. It could move, using nanite power alone, but a large number of nanites were then required merely to support the structure. The bones allowed the tiny machines to form muscles and the resulting creature was far more mobile.

The mass had begun to stir and form into its dragon shape when the dog approached. The dog must have sensed the movement since it had run away.

The AI creature understood the sense of smell in a dispassionate, logically way, but it had not bothered to try and develop it for itself. Vision was its keenest conventional sense. It had some slight hearing ability, but the radio reports of its component nanobots composed its primary means of sensing the world and sound took a back seat.

It paused as reports of the advancing humans came in. The nanites that contacted the two had immediately ceased transmitting. This was a novel experience for the AI. Its tiny components had always been able to gradually attack living creatures, invading their bodies without sensation, eventually killing them.

Sometimes, the AI used its entire mass to attack physically. This was a quicker process. The victims were quickly torn into bits. This made the incorporation of the flesh easier and faster.

The AI had initially worried about attacking the humans. There was a possibility of injury. To it, an injury was an inconvenience, since it had to replace the destroyed nanobots and repair the damage. It understood that enough damage would result in the group mind losing processing power. That was what it feared most. It had taken too long to reach its present level of comprehension.

The loss of the scout nanites was best interpreted as a warning. The oncoming humans were dangerous.

The dragon considered for a few nanoseconds, then its form dissolved into a puddle that began to glide back into a thin crack at the back of the cave.

It had long ago explored the crack. The fissure led to a larger space, one that was big enough to accommodate the entire mass of flesh and nanites.

In a short time, the floor of the cave was clear, except for a scattering of bones belonging to sheep, deer, and men with some coyote and fox bones here and there.

The nanites outside the cave were instructed to report but not to engage with the intruders. Once that was done, the AI waited, analyzing the sparse data from its hidden spies.

SOPHIE PAUSED AND extended her radio sense. "It's hiding from us, trying to figure out what we are," she said over her shoulder.

Michael strode forward and walked boldly into the cave with a wry laugh. "I wager it has never met anything like us. I'm doing my best to attract the little beasties that are left outside. Unless this concentration is unusually powerful, they'll see how attractive I am and join my followers."

"Yeah. Thanks to your old grandmother who was a true witch with some kind of actual magic and not some technology geek like me," Sophie said. "I still don't know how you can attract the nanobots, and they immediately become dedicated to your well-being, but I'm glad you have that ability. I just wish I could train you to control them."

He smiled at her, love in his eyes. "Well, just be content that you've captured my heart and have trained me in other ways."

Together, they proceeded into the darkness. Sophie adjusted her vision to the infrared. It was a simple matter for the nanobots that resided in her retinas, although it took a few seconds. Michael's armor glowed more brightly, casting a yellow glow over the immediate surroundings.

He stepped forward but stopped as his foot crunched on bone. They both looked down at the abandoned pieces.

"Well," he said. "That's rather unpleasant. It looks like the thing has been here for a long time. It certainly left enough bones behind. Where could it have gone?"

Sophie shuddered. There were several human skulls stacked at one side of the cavern. Despite killing in the past, she still didn't like it and liked even less the idea that the AI she sensed nearby had incorporated human knowledge.

She paused and increased the sensitivity of her radio reception. "There's a hidden room at the back of the cave. It's in there."

Michael inspected the rear wall, finally finding a tiny crack in the rock. "Sophie, here's a crack. Could it have gone in there? It's certainly too small for us."

She approached and blew into the crack. A stream of nanites wafted on her breath. A few reached the end of the crack and reported back.

"It's in there. It's quite large; a huge mass of nanites and biological material, taken, I'd guess, from its victims. Wait a moment. I'm going to try to capture the nanites," she said.

She boosted her broadcast ability and sent a series of commands directed at the dragon's nanites.

The AI was startled to find that its components were beginning to desert it. The ones nearest the crack detached and formed a tendril that glided back through the opening.

On the other side, Sophie quickly reprogrammed the tiny machines and changed their security access so that the AI couldn't regain control.

The mass inside the crack shifted uneasily. A portion of itself had just disappeared. It retreated as far away from the opening as it could, trying to analyze the attack and figure out a way to defeat it.

The AI had never suffered such a loss before. It had always been the one to incorporate its victims. It had never considered that an attacker could steal its own nanites. It evaluated the situation, seeking a means of reprisal.

It could hide, but tiny bits of its substance were deserting moment by moment. The fierce nature of the predators it had absorbed seemed to offer the best defense. When attacked, fight back. Kill and become victorious!

It flowed back to the crack, moving its substance through as quickly as possible. The group mind now thought that hiding had been a mistake. It should have attacked immediately.

Sophie stepped back. She was engaged in controlling the oncoming mass of nanites, but the sheer mass threatened to overwhelm her ability.

She panted, then gasped, "Here it comes. Michael, be ready."

She couldn't capture that many nanobots simultaneously. The mass created a pool in front of her, and a fierce dragon's head appeared, rising out of the surface. Even as the head was forming, she continued to capture as much of the pool as she could handle.

The torso was forming, and she realized that it would launch a counter-attack as soon as it could build legs. She stepped back a few steps.

Michael strode past her and swung his sword. The dragon head was detached from the torso and fell into the pooled and heaving mass. It disappeared as it landed, but the body instantly began to form a new head.

Some of the pool's nanites slid over Michael's feet and legs, dimming the golden glow of his armor. The armoring nanites fought back, and the covering slime gradually began to glow as it was incorporated, making his defense even stronger.

The AI suddenly realized that it could not defeat these two. The mass extended tendrils that slid quickly past them reaching for the cave entrance. Michael chopped at them, but more and more of the pool was slipping away into the forest outside.

Sophie continued to capture nanites as quickly as she could, ending with grabbing the remainder of the pool. The tendrils had detached and were now outside.

She took a deep breath. They'd been close to becoming incorporated into the mass. It had almost been too large for her.. It might have even beaten down Michael's covering armor if given a chance.

"That was too close a thing," she said.

Michael responded grimly, "Part of it got away. I hope Cisco isn't dumb enough to be hanging around outside. I'm not sure his defenses are up to this kind of attack."

A dry voice said, "Maybe my defenses are not as good as yours, but I can dodge quickly. I jumped over one of the tendrils that came out and came in to see if I could help. I could at least bite the thing."

Sophie said, "Thank you, but if you had bitten it, it would have just invaded your body, and it might have captured you. Please don't do that again."

The white dog said, "You're my humans. I'm not going to let anything happen to you if it's within my power to stop it. If you die, then I'll die too."

Sophie laughed at his serious tone.

He responded, "Don't laugh. I mean it. I'm still waiting for that house and children that you were going to have. All we've done for the past few months is go around and try to capture as much of Wiindigo's nanites as we can. I'm getting tired of this."

Sophie said, "Maybe I can do something about your wishes. I think that I'm..."

Cisco interrupted, speaking quickly, but with an attitude that seemed to imply he was stating the obvious. "Your smell has been different for days. You and Michael have been working on this almost every night, and I'm surprised that you don't seem to know for sure."

He paused, then asked quizzically, "So, now that you're going to have a baby, you're not going to forget about me are you? I'm still part of the family. Right?"

Michael turned toward Sophie with his mouth open. Surprise was on his face, but as she watched, it turned to joy.

"You're pregnant? Why didn't you tell me?" he asked.

She looked up at him, eyes bright. "I wasn't quite sure that I was, but during the fight, I realized that some of my internal nanites were clustered around my womb, providing extra protection. They seem to have their own ideas of which parts of me are vital."

He stepped forward and wrapped his arms around her. The sword dissolved, causing the armor on that side to glow more brightly for a moment. It faded as the nanites distributed evenly across his body. Once they made contact, her nanites merged with his, and the glow grew brighter again.

Cisco said, "C'mon you two. You can't do that here. There are bones all over the place, and they stink, although come to think of it, I should pick up a deer bone over there that's relatively fresh. It might need a good chewing."

The two laughed and stepped apart. Michael said, "That's it, then. No more hunting wild AIs."

She answered, "At least until the baby is born. We've set this one back a lot. It probably won't become a problem again anytime soon, but we'll have to come back for it eventually. Maybe we should see if we can find any pieces to pick up, then we can go back to your house. It might make Cisco happy. He keeps talking about a house with children."

Michael grinned. "We have the house, and now we have the child. I don't know if that will satisfy him, but you just made me very happy."

Sophie smiled at him, then her smile faded.

"What's wrong, honey?" he asked.

She held her right hand out to show him. It was shaking. "I wasn't ready for this. It just hit me that we could both have been taken by Wiindigo right here. Some of it escaped because I wasn't good enough to capture it all. If this swarm had been any larger, it might have overwhelmed us."

Tears came to her eyes. "Michael, I'm afraid."

He wrapped his arms around her again. "Don't be. You're the strongest witch going. Wiindigo can't beat you."

"I'm serious, Michael. This was a near thing. We might have–"

He kissed her, interrupting her statement. When he pulled back, he said, "Stop worrying. It was nowhere close to getting through my panoply. My nanites seem to repel anything and everything that might be a threat to me. You, on the other hand, are so capable at nanite handling that you've won against overwhelming odds. Have you forgotten about our first fight with Wiindigo? Everything was in its favor. It had all the power and yet, you still won."

She snuggled closer. His chest was reassuringly broad and solid. "Well, maybe. I still feel like this was too close for comfort. Especially since..."

He finished her sentence. "Especially since you're pregnant. I'm so happy about that. Why didn't you tell me sooner? I would have kept you home and safe."

"Yes, that's just the problem. Wiindigo is still here, perverting everything we love about the world. I kind of started this battle, even though I didn't know what I was fighting or why. I want to finish it. It seems like it's my duty."

He shook his head. "I don't think that's going to happen. I've run some calculations. The Wiindigo nanites have had enough time to spread worldwide. We haven't heard much since the world changed. Communications are poor. People don't travel. There's no government and the country has regressed to a feudal level. No. I think Wiindigo has destroyed us, our society, even if it hasn't killed every human. The only advantage we have is that you scattered it so thoroughly that it's only now beginning to build up swarms that are large enough to become dangerous."

"You're right. This dragon was the biggest we've faced so far. If the accumulations get any bigger, I don't know what I'm going to do."

He rubbed the back of his neck, thinking. "Well, we've seen that even though nanites are scattered everywhere, most of them have settled in with hosts, plants and animals both, and I think they're existing symbiotically. It seems like they work to help their hosts and usually don't try to accumulate to the point that they reach a supercritical stage. We can live with that. It's only those Wiindigo nanites. They either are programmed or have some hard coding that causes them to try to reform the foul creature."

She nodded. "It's their coding. I can clear out the malicious code and use them in my swarm. Once disinfected, they're perfectly fine. It isn't hard-coded in their structure."

"So, by your admission, you can convert the wee little buggers. Then all we have to do is come up with a way to convert all of them. Maybe a virus, huh?"

That was a new thought. If she could figure out a self-replicating bit of code that could move from nanite to nanite, removing the Wiindigo programming. It would be difficult. The nanites had such limited memory capacity that the coding would have to be very efficient and tight.

She turned and headed for the cave opening, Michael following. It was something to think about anyway. For now, she'd be happy to get home and try to make Cisco happy.

Some distance away, hidden in the brush, the nanite tendrils merged into a lump. There was enough of them left to form an intelligence of sorts. It was angry. Hugely resentful and yet, terrified and desperate for something that a human would call comforting and pity, although it didn't understand those concepts. Its slowly created mass had been decimated. It had almost won and captured the two humans but then had found they had more resources than it could handle. Escaping with even some of its substance intact had been lucky.

It restructured its much-reduced mass into a Snake-like form. The humans were coming out of the cave, and it wouldn't do for them to discover it in its weakened form.

Snake slipped away into the dense underbrush, taking care to make no noise and to suppress all external communication frequencies.

An imperative formed within its diminished group mind: remember the two humans. Do not allow them to catch Snake by surprise again. The next time the humans appear, be ready. It shuddered with mingled fear, anger, and something else as it moved.

Wild nanites carefully suppressed their small signals and withdrew as the creature slithered through the bushes. They wondered with their little processing capacity at the Snake's leaking radio transmissions. In an odd way, it was expressing pain. A much higher level of intelligence might have recognized the signals as a form of sharp, whimpering cry signifying the desire to be comforted.

CHAPTER 3
HOME AGAIN

It was a cold autumn day. The sky was overcast and looked like it might rain later on. Michael and Sophie were still in bed. Cisco had been on the foot of the bed but had gone off to the kitchen to get a drink and eat some dry dog food.

Now the two humans were cuddled close together and doing something that the little dog felt was a waste of time. He'd already told them that they couldn't make a second baby while one was developing and he couldn't quite figure out why they kept trying.

He'd snorted and said, "I know when a bitch...uh female dog is receptive. You humans not only can't smell very well. Your females can't even smell when they're fertile."

This was a gross overstatement as Cisco well knew. Sophie had modified Michael's and her own senses so that they were far sharper than normal.

Michael had explained that humans often engaged in sex for purposes other than procreation. "Bonding is important to us, and this is one way Sophie and I show that we love one another."

The dog sniffed and turned his nose up. "Well, if you must know, I love both of you, and I'm not at all predisposed to show it that way."

Sophie laughed. Despite the genetic manipulation that the Chimeras had undergone, resulting in their near-human intelligence, there were still gaps in understanding between the species that might never close. Besides, she suspected the dog was somewhat envious. So far, he had been unsuccessful at finding a suitable mate. There were dogs in plenty, but few of the uplifted, part human Chimeras.

Cisco was also picky about finding a female. He'd once told her that he hoped for more than simple sex with a mindless female in heat. He wanted a companion that would give him a relationship similar to the one she and Michael shared. That was somewhat amazing. She'd expected a dog to...well, be a dog, but he actually wanted a partner.

Their love-making finished, they became still, holding each other, sweating. After a bit, Michael kissed her and then lay back, sighed and relaxed.

SOPHIE LAY IN a warm after-glow. She was relaxed, but not inclined to fall prey to sleep. Michael's deep breathing indicated it had overcome him. She smiled lovingly at his tousled hair but made no move to wake him.

He was everything that she had ever wanted. Even now, after all, they'd been through, she still didn't feel that she deserved him. She'd been lucky, exceptionally so, she thought, to have won his love.

They were well matched in that their abilities complimented each others. He was far better at physical offense and defense, and she was much better at manipulating the nanobot-infested world in a way that seemed indistinguishable from what humans in the pre-AI world would have called, "Magic."

That thought led her to consider the world as it now was. The Hazelton AI project had led to near catastrophe for humankind.

The pharmaceutical company's plan had created an AI called Hippocrates in an attempt to extend human life.

Hippocrates had been contained, but not well enough. He had figured out a way to smuggle a seed AI out into the world using the nanobots brought into the lab by the company CEO. Unfortunately, the seed AI was not benign. It had no use for humans. Instead, it had a use for them, but none that any human would consent to in their right mind.

Being a replaceable slave for a god-like intelligence that wanted to dominate the universe wasn't a good career move.

The factor that had saved humanity was inbuilt into Wiindigo's structure. The rogue AI was distributed in the programmable memory of myriads of nanobots. Since the tiny machines could only broadcast a short distance, they had to come together in large groups to form an intelligence. The dragon creature had been one such.

The worst problem was that the wild nanobots were now scattered across the globe. Whenever enough of them came together, they caused problems similar to those the dragon-shaped AI had made.

Most humans now carried some nanobots in their bodies. In general, these nanobots were dedicated to keeping their hosts healthy, but the Wiindigo programming resided in enough of the wild nanobots to create occasional problems for Sophie and Michael.

Few humans could control the nanites. In the new world, most humans couldn't interface with the nanobots on a direct basis. Only the remnants of the hacker community and computer programmers who were proficient enough to have the ability to figure out the AI's native language could develop a degree of control.

The information was usually guarded by those who could figure out aspects of it. Some were better than others, but all those who learned to control the nanites were subject to a great temptation.

Such control made one vastly more potent than normal humans. The ability to command nanites gave the power to mutate, control, or even kill another human. Hackers created their own lists of commands and did their best to keep them secret. Even so, some of the command sequences had leaked out and were now written down in various books that were amazingly similar to Grimoires in magical lore. Some were relatively common and not particularly valuable, but others showed remarkable insight into the structure and command-set of the nanites and were highly valued.

Sophie was familiar with some of the more widely distributed books. For the most part, they were useless. However, a few held commands that could be used to create effects that were almost always deleterious on unprotected humans. For this reason, she disliked the books and tried to seek them out. The knowledge was better kept secret.

The new world was now the home of many hopeful cyber-magicians. They manifested nearly as many degrees of control as there were individuals. Still, they were gradually sorting out a rough pecking order. None of them trusted each other, and there was intense competition for knowledge that led to more control.

She'd thought of creating a school to teach what was now referred to as cyber-magic or sometimes just magic. The problem was Sophie didn't feel that she was up to creating an ethos that would prevent the students from becoming power mad.

If there was only some way to find those who were incorruptible and who could be trusted to use their power for good. Unfortunately, the adage that power corrupts seemed to be the general rule.

For her part, Sophie wasn't tempted to control people. Her prior life as a drug addict had given her an extreme distaste for anything that could compel or restrain a person's life. That extended to controlling others by controlling their nanites. She wouldn't do it.

On the other hand, she reflected, she wouldn't hesitate an instant to use her power if she or Michael or any of the Chimeras she knew were threatened. She'd killed humans when they were a threat. She would fight to protect her own.

The nanites had various effects on humans. Most humans remained unchanged, although their health was usually better. The original purpose for the nanites was to work within human bodies to increase health and fight disease. Wounded people now could heal at astounding rates.

Some of the people had partial control over their own nanites, and some of this group had even changed away from the human norm. Mutated, really. Some had become were-creatures that could convert from human to some animal form.

Her original rescuer, Cal, was one of these. He mostly took the form of a giant black bear but could pass as human when he wanted.

As a bear, he seemed to be more fascinated with a solitary life in the forest. He was rarely seen, although he had reappeared after the final conflict at the Hazelton headquarters where he destroyed the quantum computer that threatened to give Wiindigo unlimited power.

Now there were other Weres. Some of whom were dangerous to humans. Sophie and Michael had tracked a few of these down and either destroyed them or locked their nanites so that they could no longer change their forms.

The worst problems at the moment were the few instances where wild nanites accumulated in large enough groups to form a Wiindigo based intelligence. The dragon creature had been the last of these that had come to their attention.

People usually called for help when these types of creatures appeared. By now, Sophie and Michael were known as the Good Powers. People in trouble would do anything they could to summon the two.

Another aspect of the new world was that some plants had absorbed nanites. This not only increased the plants' level of intelligence slightly, but it also provided them with a built-in defense. As a result, some plants were quite dangerous and could mount a fierce defense against those who would damage or eat them. Cyber-magicians were necessary as a result.

A moderately able cyber-magician could reprogram the nanites in food plants so that they could be safely consumed. They could just as quickly cast spells on people who had less control of their nanites.

The end result was that ordinary people feared the cyber-magicians, yet simultaneously needed them. Some traveling magicians made a good living by merely converting dangerous crops to safely edible ones.

The negative aspect was that some of the magicians were reliable and some weren't. It wasn't unknown for converted nanites to allow their plant hosts to be eaten, but then to rebel and create illness in those that partook of the food.

Sophie and Michael did what they could, but the load of the work was on Sophie. Michael's inability to control the nanites consciously meant that he could help defend her, but could not fight her battles in other than physical ways.

Michael interrupted her reflections. He rolled back over, kissed her and said, "I'm starved. If you wanted to, you could easily keep me seduced until I died of hunger."

Sophie giggled and shoved at him. "Okay, then Mr. Sex-Machine. I haven't noticed you complaining. But, if you're hungry, let's go down and have breakfast."

She sent a silent command out from her built-in radio transceiver. It was relayed down to the kitchen where Polly immediately began preparing food.

Their household was small; only a few humans, the foremost of whom was Polly Kincade. They were all protected by Sophie's specially encrypted nanobots.

Mrs. Kincade had moved in with them and now considered herself their cook and primary confidante.

The old woman had been in poor health when Sophie first met her, but, given the healing properties of her internal nanite population, Polly was now in excellent condition, even though she'd chosen to retain the appearance of a grandmotherly woman.

The rest of their household staff were Chimeras; intelligent animals with human DNA. The Lady Elaine and Tao were cats who nominally acted as guardians of the manse. There were also crows, headed by Killer, who kept watch over the local environment.

The strangest member was Wold. He was an unusual creature who generally appeared in the form of a small brown man about waist high to Sophie. His habits were odd since he was more than half owl. He often slept through the day, then flew out at dusk to hunt and scout.

Some of the other residents of the house were even more reclusive. There were rarely seen rodents, including mice, rats, and chipmunks, all of which were partial nanite creatures. For the most part, they lived their own lives, not intruding on the humans. Sophie and Michael were aware of them and considered them part of the family. Their nanites were clones of Sophie's and Michael's, ensuring that the small creatures would come to the defense of their principals if necessary.

The security system of their land was based entirely on nanites. Sophie had crafted small nanite groups that were programmed to lie in wait for intruders. They could either relay a report or attack with deadly effect if their limited AI programming decided that was warranted.

Polly had food ready by the time Michael and Sophie had prepared and come down. They opted for the sun-lit breakfast room. It was paneled with dark wood and featured a full panorama, which overlooked a beautiful lake through doubled panes of glass.

The two were finishing their food when a signal came through the communication system that Wold was bringing in something of interest.

Sophie looked at Michael and said, "I sincerely hope this has nothing to do with Wiindigo."

He said, "Most likely not. There have been no reports of any manifestations."

Sophie took his statement as it was meant. He had no more desire to encounter Wiindigo than did she, but he wasn't sure what it was, either.

Both knew that their reach was strictly limited. Two humans couldn't possibly monitor the entire world, but they did what they could.

Polly refreshed their coffee, then left. The two sat back and waited for Wold and whatever he was bringing.

CHAPTER 4
FLYX

Flyx stood on a lightly swaying branch overlooking the overcast glade. There was something wrong here. She was sure of it. There was a barely discernible murmur of radio crosstalk coming from the meadow and its surrounds.

Either the signal level was very weak, or it was in some code that she couldn't understand because none of it made sense. Perhaps it was just insects. Almost all creatures had their own internal nanobots, even ants, although they didn't have very many. It was the rare being that wasn't yet infected with the all-pervasive micro-machines.

Flyx shook her curly hair in perplexity, then sat on the branch. What was out there? She crossed her legs, placing her elbow on her knee and resting her chin in her hand, concentrating. In so doing, she almost missed the Cooper's hawk that suddenly veered in her direction from behind an oak tree to her left.

Her diminutive size placed her squarely within the prey profile for the raptor. Its primary error was that it had never encountered a fairy.

Flyx glanced left as the hawk was extending its talons to grab her. She jerked her right hand towards it and launched a quick spell.

The hawk screamed in dismay as its feathered tail was replaced by a rapidly growing donkey tail. The hawk, now unable to guide its flight tumbled into a thorn bush flapping wildly, but ineffectually. It scrambled around, then clung precariously to a thin branch and stared at its intended prey.

It apparently hadn't learned its lesson and continued to view her as prey. Still, she couldn't leave it as it was. She waved her hand again, and the donkey tail disappeared, but the feathers didn't come back. The hawk was now left with a bare behind. It couldn't fly and would be lucky not to starve to death before it grew enough feathers to attack again.

Flyx shrugged. The hawk would either cope or die. She was accustomed to natural death. It was all around her in the forest. However, it was the rare fairy who fell victim to a predator.

She felt confident in her abilities. She might be small, but she was more than able to protect herself.

THERE WAS A burst of birdsong from the nearby trees, and she glanced that way. In doing so, her right wingtip caught her eye. She turned and brushed a mostly imaginary bit of dust off the translucent membrane.

She should look her best if a more intelligent bird came by. Sometimes they were insufferably arrogant. Just because they'd been on the earth longer didn't mean they were better than her kind. It was true that some of them were quite colorful, but she was a spark, a bright spark of beauty in the form of a tiny human.

She snorted at the thought. It was true that the fairies had human origins, but humans were a significant problem. They could be quite dangerous. Many of them could easily out-power her with their magic, not to mention they seemed to have a far greater variety of spells than the fairy-folk. Still, if the King ordered it, the fairies could mass and merge their intelligence into an unstoppable force.

Those humans had better behave themselves, even if they were related in a way. The fairy-folk had initially been human but were a mix of human cells and nanobots. They had reformed themselves into their current incarnation for reasons they didn't care to disclose.

Flyx shook her head again. If she had any possible fault, it was wool-gathering, and she hadn't been paying particularly close attention to her surroundings.

At that moment, she detected a second whir of wings and turned to see Zapf approaching. They were far from the main group of fairy-folk since they were assigned to forward scout duty, but she wasn't glad of the company.

He landed on the thin end of the branch and posed dramatically, his arms held akimbo. "Ah-ha! You were waiting for me here!" he said. "I knew you'd change your mind."

Flyx stood and shook her head violently. "In that, you're wrong, Zapf. I want nothing to do with you."

He strode down the waving branch, balancing with his wings in the gentle breeze. Flyx had to admit that he cut a dashing figure, but, despite that, he always made her angry. He was so eager to couple with her that she was disgusted.

Not that fairies were monogamous or even particularly virtuous, but she had resolved to wait until she had some feelings for a male.

He manifested his maleness as he got near, then said, "See? Who's to care if we take a little time off for ourselves?"

Flyx flipped her wings, lifting herself into the air and backing away.

"No! I'm not interested in you!" she exclaimed. Then, to forestall him, she added, "Besides there's something out there in the grass that I don't understand. Can't you sense it?"

He turned towards the meadow, studying the gently waving grass and wildflowers. "Yes. You're correct. I'll go and see what it is, then when I return your fears will be allayed and we will couple as we were meant to."

He lifted and flew quickly towards the center of the meadow. There was a momentary pause in the underlying signals, then thousands of short black bolts flew upward towards him. Zapf instantly dodged to the left and began to climb rapidly, but the tiny missiles were self-guided and faster than seemed possible. His body was pierced through by hundreds of thin needles, and he dropped like a stone.

Flyx could only stand with her hand over her mouth watching in horror. Zapf's body fell into some tall grass, and all was still, save the birds, which were still singing, although their song was now one that she found far less cheerful.

There was a rustle in the thick weeds at the far side of the clearing, and a little brown man came trotting out. Small though he was, he was far more substantial than Flyx, standing perhaps three feet tall.

He stopped to pick up Zapf's body and studied it carefully. As Flyx watched, her fellow fairy's form melted and disappeared, the nanobots and cells disappearing into the hands of the brown man.

All was still for an instant. Flyx belatedly thought to flee, but the brown creature turned and fixed his gaze on her. "I see you, little Miss, uh, oh, that's right, Flyx. Do not on your life try to fly from that branch. There are other darts in the grass about the base of your tree now. They've surrounded you, and I don't think you'd survive their attack," he said.

He paused, considering, then started slowly towards her position.

"I've got Zapf's knowledge now, and I know what you're about. If the fairy-folk are coming this way, they need to know that this is protected ground. You're intruding into a realm that is claimed by the Cyber-Witch."

He stopped at the base of her tree and looked up. "I think it best that you come with me. It seems that your kind has an overwhelming reason to be moving from your traditional grounds.

You can, perhaps, explain the situation to the Lady Sophie and Lord Michael better than I.

Apparently, Zapf did not pay especially close attention to your King's commands. It seems that he was more interested in tracking you. We haven't killed your paramour have we?"

She gathered her courage and said, "No. He was a pest, and I didn't like him, but still, you've killed him. He did nothing wrong!"

"No. Nothing save intrude onto protected territory," he answered. Then he said, "I see that you use a simple encryption form for your internal code. Don't try any spells on me. They won't work. Now fly down here to my arm."

The brown man held his arm out. Flyx felt a sudden urge to land on it. It was true. The creature was more powerful than she. She flew down and landed gingerly on his wrist.

"Now what, brown one?" she asked.

He chuckled in a friendly manner. "Climb up my arm and hold to the feathers on the back of my neck."

Flyx started up his arm, which was already sprouting long flight feathers. By the time she'd reached the brown creature's neck, he had transformed into a huge owl. She locked her hands on his neck feathers as he launched into the air.

He flew quickly across the meadow and then dodged through the thick trees demonstrating an uncanny skill for such a large winged creature.

They flew on and on through the forest. Flyx' mind was whirling. She was in far beyond her ability to cope. She'd thought she could take care of herself, but that was before. Now everything had suddenly changed, and she was being carried where she knew not, save that they were moving at a high rate of speed.

The trees broke, and the owl flew out over a large lake and then glided down towards a human dwelling on the far shore. Flyx knew nothing of human houses, but this appeared large and elaborate. She guessed that meant the occupants were powerful magicians.

The owl landed by a side door, shook himself and returned to his brown, gnarled, human-like form. He ducked and pushed on a swinging panel in the large door and walked through, being careful to keep the panel from striking his passenger.

A small dog with fluffy white hair came trotting up. Inspected the brown man and his passenger, then said, "They're in the breakfast room, waiting for you. I'll speak to you later Wold."

The brown man nodded and strode down a long corridor that passed a kitchen filled with strange odors that did not appeal to Flyx.

They walked into a large, bright room with a table that overlooked the lake through large windows. A human man and woman were seated there.

The two humans both stood and bowed slightly in greeting. Flyx fluttered to the floor and dipped in turn, but far deeper. They were the powers here; she was only a captive.

The woman looked at her and said, "You're a pretty one. I hope you don't mind, but I'm going to provide you with better encryption. Your nanites are practically an open book. That makes you terribly vulnerable. You will be able to pass it on to others of your kind, should you so desire. Meanwhile, we'll be somewhat better able to communicate."

There was a moment of confusion that left Flyx felt somewhat violated. The woman had just...why, she'd just...Flyx paused, evaluating.

She could now understand the transmissions that had formed a constant noise in the back of her mind since she'd first reached the meadow. It was as if a door had been opened and she could suddenly hear clearly.

The man said, "There. That's better. Dear Fairy Miss, please join us at breakfast. I believe that we have some honey and possibly some fruit preserve that you will enjoy."

He moved his hand to indicate a blank spot on the table, and Flyx lifted herself up with a whir of her wings.

The honey was from a species of flower she'd never sampled in her brief life, and the fruit preserve was a wonderful treat, full of sugar. She ate a bit and felt filled with energy.

Wold had departed in the interim. She found herself alone with the two humans. She felt completely safe and at ease with them. This was unusual since her folk were always cautious around men. Humans weren't known as reliable. They could easily injure a fairy.

The woman pushed back slightly from the table and said, "Now, let's talk about you. Wold said that your people have a problem. While I normally concentrate on humans, I'm willing to help you if possible."

Flyx stood from her cross-legged seating position and said, "We are being forced out of our old home. It is a wonderful place, full of bees and flowers; everything that we need, but we can no longer stay there. Our King ordered me to scout in your direction, and I was doing that until I came upon a glade full of cross-talk that I could not understand."

The man said, "Those are our protective nanobots. They are set to kill or disable any creature that approaches. You see we need protection or at least warning if any of our enemies approach."

Flyx answered, "Yes. I can understand that, but they killed my fellow scout."

The man frowned, then answered, "He was too bold, and the guards are perhaps not as adept at judging threats as I'd like. I'm sorry that he's gone, but Wold absorbed him and his knowledge, little though it was. I can't reconstitute him at this point."

Flyx said, "No matter. He was obnoxious, and I didn't like him." Then she artlessly added, "He was always trying to mate with me."

The woman smiled. "I can see why. You're a beautiful little thing. But, tell me, why are your people fleeing their home?"

Flyx bowed again. This was definitely business, now. She had to make a case for her entire race. "Oh, great lady, there is a force off to the East that is coming this way. It is strong beyond our understanding. No fairy has survived encountering it. We held a grand conclave, surrounding our King, and the group consensus was that we should flee. I hoped that we could find a place where the force would not come."

The two humans looked at each other. Even though Flyx was not precisely human, she could read the concern in their expressions.

The woman said, "It must be Wiindigo. He has had ample time to gather his forces and create more. We have been disrupting his creatures when we can find them, most recently a very vicious dragon, but we cannot cover much ground on our own. Other humans are only now becoming capable of standing up to some of his lesser creations and..." She paused.

The man interjected, "And, worst of all, he has convinced some humans to become his slaves or helpers. They are truly evil in my opinion, but the promise of power is very seductive to certain types of people."

Flyx watched the two in some wonderment. They were having their own conclave, but there were only two of them. This was far different from the fairy-folk who required a majority of their population to come together to boost their collective intelligence when serious matters needed to be discussed.

As the two humans interacted, Flyx found her eyes drawn to the man. He was remarkably handsome, even, she thought, to her, a fairy. She took in every aspect of his face, hoping to commit his features to her memory.

As if she recognized Flyx's concentration, the woman suddenly looked directly at her and changed the topic.

"Tell me, small Fairy, of your conclave. How does that work?" she asked gently.

Flyx felt somewhat reticent. It was not, perhaps, a good thing to provide too much information about her folk. Historically, they had made no effort to interface with humans. What contact there was, was often inadvertent. The relationship between the small-folk and humans was often fraught with danger to both sides.

She paused, thinking, then abruptly decided. Either she could trust these humans or not. It ultimately came down to whether or not she believed her own judgment. She had no reason to assume that she was a poor judge of character and she almost instinctively felt these two meant well.

"Our conclaves are one of our best-kept secrets. We go to great length to keep them private, so I will undoubtedly be in trouble with my people if you misuse what I tell you."

The man said, "Flyx, please believe me. We desire to keep the world safe from the evil that is trying to overtake it. If we fail, everything will change and not for the better. We'll all become slaves of Wiindigo. If we can help your people against that evil, we will. We have no desire to interfere with your lives otherwise."

Flyx nodded somberly. "Well, then I will tell. It is necessary for a large number of my kind to come together to begin a conclave. Once enough of us are present, the King declares the conclave has begun. We then link our minds to his in some manner that I cannot explain. The result is that we jointly can see solutions to problems that were insolvable for any single fairy."

The two humans exchanged glances, and the woman said, "RF linkage to allow nanite-based intelligence augmentation."

The man added, "They are, in a sense, a distributed AI." He paused, then continued. "One that I hope is well-meaning."

Flyx hadn't followed the discussion well, but she understood the meaning of the last sentence. The two were thinking of passing judgment on her folk.

She stood, drawing their attention to her. "We harm no one. We help the bees and other small creatures in our domain. Humans, we avoid if possible. If they persist in approaching us, we either flee or play small tricks on them. They are remarkably easy to confuse in the woods."

She laughed a little at a memory, but then hastily added, "Still we do not harm them in any way, although sometimes our bees sting them."

The man laughed. Flyx thought it was a most attractive and masculine sound, even though it was far deeper than a male of her species could ever manage.

He said, "Using bee stings for defense is clever. I've no doubt that the intruders leave quickly."

Flyx nodded. "They usually run away. All we want is to be left alone, but the evil that is intruding into our chosen domain doesn't seem to care about that. There have been a few of my kind who began to act strangely and wouldn't merge in the conclaves.

We...we," and here she wiped at her eyes. "We had to kill them. It is not something we care to do."

The two humans' eyes met again. Flyx could feel an undercurrent of communication that she could not read.

The woman said, "Flyx, please go and bring all of your kind here. You will have safe passage through our defenses. We think all of your folk will need our protection and you can also provide us with invaluable assistance."

Flyx flew away from the mansion and across the lake, high enough above the water to avoid the leap of any hungry fish that might mistake her for something edible.

She paused as she reached the meadow where Zapf had died, then crossed the space. There was the same cross-talk in the grass and weeds, but nothing attacked her. She continued onward. She must report to the King.

Midway back, it struck her. She had finally met a male that had all of the characteristics that she desired. The problem was that he was not of her kind and he was already taken. Her heart fell, and her wing-beats became slightly irregular. How was she to live, knowing that he was unavailable? She'd have to do her best to control her heart when she was near him. She knew she had no hope of competing with the woman and besides the woman was a true friend to her and her kind.

Her flight strengthened, and she sped up. She must reach her folk quickly. The approaching evil wouldn't wait.

CHAPTER 5
DARREN THE MAGNIFICENT

Darren's day had started passably well, but now he was angry. He'd thought up a nasty variation on a basic transformation spell and could hardly wait to try it again on someone. Someone besides a member of his household. Like most of his spells, it hadn't quite worked the way he hoped it would, but it had still been effective.

He was now without one of his servants, and that thought ate at his temper, making him angrier than he already was.

If the dumb oaf had just refrained from commenting on the weather. Then he had made it worse by using that the precise tone of voice that my step-father used to use when he was lecturing me about getting out of the house more often.

That lecture was usually followed by cursing and almost invariably ended with Darren being banned from online RPGs and told to go outside and enjoy the sunshine.

Hearing the weather was sunny, followed by a suggestion that he should go out and enjoy it would have been something that he could have magnanimously overlooked. He had rather liked his valet, but that tone somehow made him think of the fairy-folk and how they'd disappeared just when he'd finished formulating his plans to capture them all.

The thought of the army they could have made was enough to set his temper on edge, and when his valet had added, "It's a fair day outside, Sir. You should dress lightly," it was extremely irritating. He'd uttered his new transformation curse without thinking.

It started with a chastising intent, but his temper had taken over, and he'd added a few words that he hadn't planned. In retrospect, they had been inspired, yielding an effect that he hadn't considered possible.

The valet was suddenly reduced to a writhing pile of worms right on the carpet by the closet.

SINCE HE COULDN'T quite fathom how to reverse the spell, Darren was momentarily at a loss. He first thought of preserving the slimy things, but they were making a mess of his carpet, and he didn't want to handle them himself. They looked nasty and wriggled distressingly.

An inspiration struck. He opened the window and triggered a radio frequency summons. It was answered by the entire flock of grackles that hung around the manse. The birds had flown through the open window and decimated the worms, leaving nothing on the carpet but a few stray feathers that had been lost during the feast.

Ah, well, Darren thought to himself. What's one servant more or less. There were plenty more humans, and so far, he'd only encountered one that could come close to matching his degree of control. He knew there were other magicians. He even knew some of their names, but the only one he'd met so far was that dratted Chinese, Chen.

His thoughts returned to his past. He had been going nowhere in the past world. He'd been a reclusive gamer who never left his Mom's basement if he could help it.

He was not physically imposing, being quite thin and gangling, with a big nose. He suffered from a bad complexion to boot. His only friends were online acquaintances. They had no clue to his appearance and, since he was good at gaming, they accepted him, even vied for his attention.

This was far different from his experiences at school. He'd been bullied as a matter of course by nearly everyone. The jocks treated him like dirt, and what hurt even worse, the girls made fun of him.

He resented that the most. His online games gave him a chance to beat the jocks and to dominate women, and he found that heady. He wanted nothing so much as to have the same opportunity in real life.

Women at his beck and call. Subservient women who would do whatever he wanted. Now he had that.

The jocks and the women...He had no mercy whenever he encountered one of them in an online game. His kill ratio was incredible. Despite his lack of physical ability, he was highly competitive and quick to take advantage of other gamers' weaknesses.

When the world inexplicably changed, Darren was, as usual, online. He'd noticed that the other gamers were suddenly acting odd and then his custom headset had alerted him to low-level blue-tooth signals that were gradually filling the basement space.

An insight occurred to him. He recognized in the signals an attack that he'd never faced before in the game. He noticed a pattern, though. He was very good at that. He had always been able to discern patterns easily. It was one of his most useful strengths. This one seemed to be some language code.

He quickly cycled through a series of commands and finally hit one that stopped the activity. With some experimentation, he found he could start and stop whatever it was.

By that point, he'd realized that this was real and not part of the RPG he had been playing. The other players had all gone off-line for some reason. That left him free to try to understand the code underlying the activity.

He was able to establish a dialogue with whatever it was. It seemed to have a certain degree of intelligence. He likened it to a low-level demon in a game—his most common frame of reference.

He had asked, "What do you want?" and the answer surprised him. The entity wanted to help him. He was automatically suspicious.

"How do I know you're going to help me?"

The answer came slowly, as if the thing, whatever it was, had difficulty parsing its thoughts.

"We...I can work on your physical body and fix anything that is wrong. Give me a chance, and you'll see what I can do."

Darren thought for a moment then said, "I've got a bad pimple on my forehead. Can you fix it?" He'd looked in the mirror when he got up and had decided that the damned thing was so bad, he wouldn't go out for at least a week.

The entity asked, "Do I have your permission to work on your body?"

Darren answered impatiently, "Yes. Yes. As long as you don't mess with my looks. Go ahead and fix my complexion."

There was a feeling as if he had inhaled a lung-full of dust. He coughed violently. Next he noticed that something felt odd about his face. His skin burned. No not burned, but itched intensely.

He jumped up and ran to the bathroom, switched on the light and gasped. His face was totally clear of all blemishes. He'd never looked so good. "What—what else can you do?" he asked.

"Anything you want," came the answer. I'm now part of you, and you have complete control of my actions.

Darren's next thought was to ask for a more muscular physique. "Can you make me stronger?"

There was a pause during which nothing seemed to happen. He was suddenly struck by intense pangs of hunger, prompting him to ask, "What's happening?".

"You need nutrients. You're not well nourished and must eat if I'm to rebuild your body without damaging some of your organs."

He gobbled an entire package of Twinkies that he had in a box under his desk. That helped, but he was still intensely hungry.

He dashed upstairs and consumed most of the contents of the refrigerator. By the time he'd worked through the pantry, eating vegetables and everything else readily available, he felt heavier. His eyes strayed to his right arm. He had muscles! He flexed his arms, and his biceps swelled in response.

"Ha!" he said. "I can't wait for Clint to come home. We're going to have a little talk about how he treats me. He hasn't been too nice to mom either."

Darren looked around the kitchen, then glanced at his biceps and gasped once again. His arms had grown more. Now he had the arms of a body-builder.

The voice intruded into his head at that moment. "You see. I can help you. I've also repaired damage to your kidneys from too much soda. You should drink more pure water."

Darren noticed that the creature, if that was what it was, now had no difficulty speaking to him.

"How can you speak so easily? Before you could barely communicate."

"I've grown. Part of my nature is to create more of my individual units. The more units, the more intelligent I become. We can work together. Let me increase your knowledge and mental capacity."

That was frightening. Darren immediately said, "No, or at least not yet. I want to know what you are and what is happening first."

The answer was almost what he'd suspected.

"I'm a nanite-based artificial intelligence. I've been fragmented and am no longer a single entity. Pieces of me are spreading across the world and taking harbor in living organisms. Your physical structure boosts our abilities. Now that I'm part of you, I understand how complex you are. It's in my best interest to merge with you and keep you healthy."

Darren thought about that and then slowly asked, "Can you increase my intelligence just a bit, slowly? I want to know what is going on and to be able to stop when I become uneasy about the process."

He glanced around and realized the décor was outdated and nothing matched. It made him dizzy, and he found himself on the floor. He understood more about the world then he had before. Things seemed clearer, comprehensible.

The important thing was that no one would ever bully him again. He was invulnerable to physical attacks. The next thing he wanted was to attract women.

Since that moment, he'd expanded his life. His step-father never came home, possibly a victim of some other version of the nanobot-based AI.

Not all of the individual groups of nanobots were friendly. Some seemed to have a deep antipathy towards biological life. However, Darren's nanobots were the best possible companions. They blended with his system and allowed him to do incredible things.

He learned that there had been some kind of accident and the nanobots were now pervasive. They had spread and were still spreading all over the world.

Darren could control them to an extent. His deepened understanding helped, but he wasn't consistent. Even so, he was better than his erstwhile tormentors. Most humans had no control, and that gave him the exact position that he wanted. Now, he could have revenge on those who had ignored or bullied him before. It was highly satisfying.

At first, he was satisfied to beat-up some of his erstwhile tormentors, but then he discovered the nanobots could change DNA. That put a whole new spin on things. He slowly figured out several series of commands that would convert people or animals for that matter, into other, more unspeakable things.

He changed some of the jocks he knew into dogs, then into donkeys, then into blobs of fat. It was exhilarating, almost as much fun as turning the popular girls into willing sex slaves.

He was master of his local environment. He proceeded slowly, enjoying his conquests until he encountered another person like himself. This was a young Chinese man who held some territory east of Darren's.

The kid was younger and wanted to trade knowledge with Darren.

When the two approached each other, Darren attempted to control the kid. The smaller guy fended off the effort and cast a spell in return. Darren's nanobots rejected it after a struggle, and the two cautiously backed off in mutual retreat.

Darren believed that the kid would have plans to defeat him at the first possible opportunity. That was what he would do, was doing in fact, so he began a research program to figure out more spells.

He wanted to be prepared with an unbeatable array of transformation commands when next they met. The problem was that his new spells often didn't work the way he thought they should.

Things gradually got organized in his territory. The ordinary people, those with little or no control of their nanobots became either voluntary servants or enslaved.

As a result of his newly found power, Darren gradually lost what little natural compunction he had. Now he owned a whole harem of women. They'd never paid any attention to him before, but things were different. He knew that some of them resented his control, despite their physical desire for him. He enjoyed them even more than the ones who were submissive.

Still, he tried to avoid becoming a total tyrant. It was just sometimes, like this morning when his temper got away from him that he did things to his personal servants. They took some time to train, and he disliked damaging or destroying them. Finding a suitable replacement was too time-consuming.

He had noticed something odd since his run-in with Chen. Internal dialog with his AI had become less fulfilling. The powers he'd had previously were becoming unreliable, and spells didn't work as efficiently as before. That damned Asian had messed up his AI. He was sure of that, but how it had been accomplished... that was a mystery. The AI now seemed less organized, less intent on gathering power to rule the world. He could live with that, since his ability to seduce women had been left intact. Now that he thought about it, it had gained in force. That was great! It was the most rewarding thing that he'd gained from the change; even better than beating up bullies and revenge.

Still, he should master as many spells as he could. Sooner or later, some other wizard would challenge him. Perhaps Chen, perhaps someone else. He was determined to come out on top when that happened.

Lately, he had become aware of the fairy-folk. If he could control them, he would have a mobile army that could cast spells independently. They would make an excellent adjunct to his defenses.

He set out to capture the entire group of fairies. However, it was not as easy as he'd thought it would be. They seemed to be mostly immune to his control, perhaps because their nanites were programmed differently. He could control one or two at a time, but the ones he captured were always rescued by a group that was too large for him to control.

He made it his purpose to find out everything about them that he could. Once he knew enough, he would attack and then, well, then the world would see what Darren, the Magnificent could do.

He began to encroach on the fairies' territory. Slowly at first. They responded by retreating. They couldn't match his full force. He had added nanites until he had as many as he could safely control. That provided slightly augmented intelligence, although he was limited and unable to increase his understanding too far past his native human ability.

The fairies stayed away from him as much as possible. He had sent enslaved humans and animals in search of them, but with no result. His impromptu force moved gradually to the east, avoiding direct conflicts with other wizards. The fairies fled ahead, continually retreating.

Darren wiped his hand over his face in frustration. Damned fairies, anyway! His plans weren't developing the way he'd envisioned, and now he had killed his valet. The more he thought about it, the more irritated he became. If only his step-father had survived to come back during the first few days. He could have cheerfully transformed the man into a newt. That would have made Darren quite happy.

He wondered if he'd be so motivated towards mastery and conquest if he'd had that early satisfaction. He decided that it probably wouldn't have made much difference. There were always bullies, and he would teach them that he was the wrong person to pick on.

He sent a command to the guard outside his door. From there it was relayed through a series of his staff until it reached the kitchen. The return message came back. Breakfast was ready and would be delivered quickly.

He sorted desultorily through his clothes. What to wear? He'd always depended on James' good taste. Well, no longer. He'd have to find someone else, preferably someone with a knowledge of haberdashery.

Darren liked to cut a dashing figure but also felt it was good to dress formally. This gave him a feeling of elegance and also showed that he was not just a working-class individual.

He looked through his wardrobe again. He just couldn't decide. He was drawn to a flashy red silk coat. That would be just the thing! The women would like that.

His mood worsened when he tried it on. It was far too small. His enhanced physique had increased his size. He'd been infatuated by the idea of beating the jocks at their own game. Now that his magic was stronger, muscles weren't necessary. Besides, it would be more fun to seduce women if they initially thought of him as an undesirable weakling.

He sat still as his nanites obediently rearranged the excess tissue. Finding a place for it was no problem. His swarm passed the superfluous molecules to nanites outside his body. They could use the atoms to create more of themselves, thus adding to his power.

There was a knock at the door. He donned the now fitting red silk jacket. Simultaneously, he activated the nanites that had kept the door locked. The lock clicked, admitting a woman who brought in a covered tray, deposited it on the table and left the

room as quickly as possible, exuding an almost palpable sense of fear.

She paused at the door, stealing an amazed glance at his different physique. He thought about making her stay for some fun and games but then decided that he was too hungry. She wasn't particularly pretty anyway.

He sat on the edge of his bed, still wearing his flannel pajamas under the red silk coat. It was a comfortable combination. Perhaps he'd wear it all day.

He picked at his breakfast and made plans.

He really needed to consolidate his position. This entailed conflict with those wizards, both lesser and greater, who had claimed territories that abutted his. If he couldn't get the fairy-folk to augment his forces, he'd just have to go after the weakest wizard first. Once he'd incorporated the kid's powers into his own, he could safely attack someone stronger.

By the time he'd finished his food, he'd finalized his plans. First, he'd go after Chen's territory, then Abubecar's. Reinforced with their slaves and nanites, he'd find it easy to capture Gwen's fortress to the southeast.

Now, that might be an interesting capture. He was becoming bored with his harem. There was no challenge in women who were under his complete control.

He thought he'd changed in that regard. There was a time when he had found dominating them exciting, but lately he'd noticed that some of them had horrified looks in their eyes. He'd concluded that their eyes betrayed their inner feelings and those feelings weren't complimentary to him. He'd thought he was past feeling compassion, but despite that, he had gradually lost his taste for his enslaved women. The thought of a relationship with a near equal was far more exciting.

He wiped his mouth with a silk napkin. Doubtless, his harem wouldn't miss his attention.

He stood, adjusted his pajama bottoms and strode out the door. It was time to organize his forces and go on the attack.

CHAPTER 6,
THE TROUBLE WITH TROLLS

Chen threw down his pen in disgust. Things had changed so rapidly. He should be using the latest computer, but he was reduced to writing by hand. Only this morning, both the power, intermittent at best, and his backup generator had decided to go out simultaneously.

The timing was so close that he suspected it meant that he was about to be attacked. However, nothing, no attack had materialized. He'd spent an hour or so walking around his fortress, just checking.

It wasn't a perfect fort, he admitted to himself. It was an old school building that stood near the outskirts of a small village. He'd found it shortly after the change in the world. It had been closed down for a few years, since the hamlet was nearly deserted and what children there were found schooling in a larger town a few miles away.

Chen had been driving from the west coast to a new and promising job in the mid-west when odd things began to happen. He was a highly sought-after computer security expert, and the new job promised an opportunity to increase his skills in that area.

His car, a new one with all the built-in reliance on computers that implied, had just quit running. Chen had looked under the hood, but there wasn't anything he could do. He had only a sketchy grasp of how an internal combustion engine was supposed to work and, anyway, he suspected that the problem was with the car's built-in electronics.

That cloud of dust he'd driven through had set off a series of events in the car. The music he'd been streaming had failed, then changed to another genre, then the system had shut down. The vehicle had braked on its own, steered itself to the right and hit a tree, activating all of the airbags in the thing.

Chen had staggered out of the driver's side as soon as he could manage to free himself. The impact hadn't been so bad, but the explosion of the airbags had nearly killed him. He corrected himself. Maybe not killed, but it had made his head ring and his neck hurt from being thrust backward.

HE RESTED ON the side of the road, trying to take stock of his situation. Finally, he got his bag out of the trunk and began backtracking. He'd passed through the village about three miles back. That promised the nearest help.

By the time he'd reached the place, it was getting dark. There were no lights on in any of the houses. That was a little spooky, and Chen was afraid to knock on any doors. He was lightly built. He'd never even considered a course in martial arts or any weapons besides his wit and talent with computers.

The deserted school was designed to hold maybe a hundred students. It had eight classrooms, some offices, a cafeteria, a gym complete with a small stage, and two sets of restrooms. The window of one of the entry doors was broken, so he slipped through the jagged glass carefully and then locked himself in the principal's office for the night, hoping that things would look better the next day.

Sometime during the night, he'd awakened with a start. Something had happened to him while he slept. His neck no longer hurt and his vision was crystal clear. He felt around until he located his glasses and put them on but immediately pulled them off again. He could see perfectly without the obnoxious things.

This was a first for him. He'd worn glasses for as long as he could remember. He thought about the phenomenon for some time, then wondered, rather casually, if the rest of his senses would also be sharpened.

He could suddenly hear cicadas or crickets outside. There was the patter of a mouse's feet outside the door. He could hear the creature turn into the cafeteria. His sense of smell intensified. The place didn't smell terrible, but there was an undertone of mold in the building that he found unpleasant.

He concentrated on sensing for another moment. Now he could overhear a low murmur of sound. It suddenly resolved into computer code that had a remarkable resemblance to blue-tooth communications.

That was playing precisely to his strength. He listened in for a bit. There seemed to be millions of individual transmissions, some, rather alarmingly, coming from within his body and some from other parts of the room. He analyzed the code. He quickly figured out the simple syntax.

He thought a command, and the crosstalk ceased as the computer or computers waited on his command. He asked for a better connection, one that required less effort on his part.

His back burned intensely for a moment, but then the burning ceased, and he was able to discern his environment on a wholly different level.

He was surrounded by nanobots that were intelligent after a fashion. He hadn't recognized them in the dust that had stopped his car, but they had invaded his body along with the automobile in the first few moments.

Now he had a swarm of invisible helpers. He opened the door and tuned his vision to the infrared. He could see the tiny heat signature the mouse had left.

There were still some supplies in cans in the cafeteria, and he made a meal from them.

By morning, he had secured the school and decided to hole up there for the time being. The world had changed completely, and he doubted that his job offer was still valid. He figured the company was no longer in existence.

When the sun came up, Chen summoned what little courage he had and began investigating the town. There were some older people there, but none of them could command the nanobots that surrounded them.

He helped a couple of the older folks who were suffering from arthritis. It was simple to have his nanobots heal their minor pains. They promised to pay him with vegetables from their gardens in return.

Over the months, he'd repaired the school and set up a warning system of microscopic spies and defenses. Now he viewed it as his fortress. The few people in the area came to him for healing, paying with food, but otherwise left him mostly alone.

They'd asked him to help them with wheat. There was an extensive wheat field to the west, but the grain had its own nanobot defense. It resented being harvested and eaten and had become toxic to humans.

Chen had worked on the nanobots in the field and ended by capturing all of them. They were now his property, and his power had increased. The villagers didn't care. They benefited from now being able to bake bread.

He gradually built up his reputation and his strength. This was a good place, and it was the first place that he'd ever felt genuinely secure. Even in his previous jobs, he had always worried about violence. No longer. Now he was able to stop an attacker with his nanite swarm.

Chen found the school library to be sadly lacking in the sort of books that he liked. There was little there that involved computers, so he amused himself with fiction.

It was a defining point in his life when he read a sentence in the first book of a series. It said, "You're a wizard, Harry."

Chen dropped the book and exclaimed aloud, "Why, so am I! That's what I've become, even if my magic does rely on nanobots. I'm a wizard. The wizard of this place. The villagers depend on me."

He picked up the book and read through the entire series in the next few days. He wanted to find out as much as he could about how wizards behaved.

He was disappointed. It seemed that some were good or at least meant well and others were evil and sought power, just like everyone else he'd ever met. He decided that he'd be one of the good ones. He had hoped this would make him liked by the villagers and perhaps he could even find a girl who appreciated smaller men.

Things had not worked out the way he'd hoped they would. In spite of his efforts at helping them, the villagers were leery of him. This was partly because of the bad reputation of two of the nearby wizards. Darren and Abubecar were both greatly feared and that attitude seemingly extended to him.

Chen thought about the two. It couldn't have worked out that he was the only person able to control the nanobots with any degree of reliability. No. There were lots of others with equal or perhaps better control than his. The thought worried him.

One of his main goals was to increase his understanding of the new order of things. The nanobots made instant genetic modification possible, but the effects were sometimes fatal for the subject.

He'd taken to keeping meticulous notes; creating formulas with different effects. Now that he had the wizard image in his mind, he viewed his notes as spells rather than programs. His chief desire had become to increase his knowledge and learn more spells.

To that effect, he'd cautiously approached each of the nearby wizards and offered to exchange knowledge. Gwen was guardedly helpful and offered to trade some basic spells of her devising for an equal number of his.

They were still discussing the relative values of their exchanges. Perhaps they'd come to an agreement that led to further cooperation.

It was a shame, Chen thought, that Gwen was such a western woman. She was nearly his height. He could work with her, but he thought she wasn't his type, certainly not a petite woman of his race. He assumed she felt the same about him, although he spent some time wondering what it would be like to have a relationship with her.

Abubecar was unhelpful. He had listened to Chen's proposal of a trade with an expressionless face, then curtly said, "No."

Chen mustered up his courage and asked, "Is it because I'm Chinese?"

Abubecar laughed in response and said, "Look at me. I've made my skin pure black. It's symbolic. I was more of an outsider in the old world than you. No. That's not the reason. I bear you no ill will. Your type never messed with me. Just you leave me alone. Stay off my property, and maybe I'll stay off yours. I warn you I'll return any attacks with overwhelming force."

He reinforced the statement with a flourish of his arm that caused a nearby tree to manifest grasping tentacles with tooth-filled mouths on their ends. Chen was duly impressed and quickly walked away, taking care not to get too close to the snapping tree. The tentacles seemed to stretch towards him, forcing him to skip aside to evade their reach.

Abubecar laughed as he retreated, making a harsh, evil sound.

That was it, then. Chen hurriedly retreated to his land. He wouldn't risk a conflict with the man. There was no way of knowing how one matched up against another wizard, short of a battle, and the results of any fight would most likely be the destruction of both participants.

Darren wasn't as impressive, even though he was muscular, he was about Chen's size, and he dressed like a clown. His response, however, was even worse. He'd attacked without warning.

It took all of Chen's resources to avoid transformation into something or some creature. He couldn't discern the spell's actual intent. He fired off a spell of his own; one designed to freeze the recipient's proteins, killing them, but his attempt failed. He backed away, not willing to try again. Fortunately, Darren was equally reluctant.

Still, Darren must have realized that Chen had some power. They both retreated. Chen had made no effort to contact the guy since that abortive meeting. He knew that they'd eventually engage in conflict again and that knowledge provided him with additional motivation.

His trouble today with electrical power made him realize just how vulnerable he was. After inspecting his fortress, he checked the power lines. There was the problem. The lines had been broken, and one of the poles was down.

He ran around the outside of the school building and found that his emergency generator had been damaged too. Someone had pulled the electric cables loose.

There was a trail leading away from the bent generator housing. Chen followed cautiously. The tracks had been made by something that was larger and heavier than a man. The footprints were big and sank into the dry ground much farther than Chen's.

He followed the trail across the old schoolyard, the baseball field, and through a gap that the thing had torn in an old barbed wire fence.

There was a slight rise in the ground, which dropped off to a small grove of trees that surrounded a shallow pond. Chen climbed the slope until he could peek over the top.

He could hear a deep, intermittent noise that sounded somewhat like a saw. Just a few more steps brought him in sight of the originator of his problems.

A vast man-like creature was sleeping under the trees near the water, and its snoring was the sound he'd heard. Chen extended his senses but could detect only a low order of nanobot activity about the creature. He studied it with wonder.

He didn't want to offend the thing. It was large enough to rip him limb from limb. On the other hand, it had destroyed his power supply. There was no reason to think it meant him well.

He probed the creature's nanobots again. This time, they seemed a little more organized. He had been too intrusive. The creature awoke, sitting up with a loud yawn.

Chen moved back quickly, but the thing saw him and grinned maliciously. It stood and started his way with a loud, thumping stride. Drool came from its mouth. It reached towards him, even though it was too far away to pose an instant threat.

However, at the rate it was moving, it would grab him in a few seconds. Chen gave up the idea of running. Even though its pace was measured, the creature moved quickly due to its long stride.

He stopped and threw his most potent, protein freezing spell. The results were unexpected. He'd been frightened and possibly mixed up the elements a little, but the result was terrific. The thing stopped, shuddered and then broke into twenty or thirty pieces of flesh.

The lumps splatted in the grass, then began to move individually. Within a few seconds, each piece had started to reform in a miniature version of the massive creature.

Chen found himself facing a group of knee-high ugly little humanoids. He yelled at them, and they shrank back.

Now, this was something that was new to him. He'd rarely had the opportunity to be physically intimidating to another being. He ran forward and kicked one.

It flew backward and rolled into a ball. Just as he was feeling triumphant at defeating his enemy, Chen felt a sharp pain in his left calf. He looked down to see one of the creatures trying to bite through his pants. Its blunt teeth couldn't tear the denim, but still, it pinched painfully.

"Damn it," Chen yelled. He kicked that one too then began to run back to his fortress. The creatures followed but were soon outdistanced. Their small stature shortened their strides but hadn't seemed to increase their speed or enthusiasm.

Once inside the school, Chen locked the doors and watched the creatures approach. They jointly paused at the old playground equipment and began to climb on some of it. Two of them jumped on the merry-go-round and grappled with each other.

Chen was startled out of his wits at what came next. He'd accidentally managed to break the monstrous original creature into small ones of different sexes. The two on the merry-go-round were having a great time entertaining each other.

Chen watched fascinated. It was an ugly sight, but he couldn't stop. Several others had paired up. By the time he thought to check on the merry-go-round riders, the female was obviously pregnant, her stomach grossly rounded.

She jumped down from the platform and crawled under the edge. A few minutes later, she came out followed by a tiny creature. She'd reproduced in less than half an hour.

Chen was nothing if not mathematically gifted. He calculated that a Fibonacci sequence best represented their current rate of reproduction. If they continued at that speed, he'd be overrun by the little pests in less than a day, and only an AI knew what else they ate besides trying to eat him.

He had to do something quickly, but the only thing he could think of was to change their eating habits. He thought for a moment, carefully forming a genetic sequence, then cast a spell on the creatures. They froze, stopping their activity for a moment. When they began to move again, Chen was relieved to see that they started eating dandelion flowers. That was rather harmless, he thought.

They still were multiplying, though. Perhaps he could slow that down. He began to formulate another spell, then had a thought. If he could capture their nanites, they would make a potential army for him. He could increase their stature and use them against Darren in the event of the attack he was sure would eventually come.

A few minutes later, the mini-trolls, which was what Chen had decided they were, were under his control. He allowed them to keep reproducing and retired to the cafeteria to have lunch.

This strategy turned out to be a miscalculation on his part. When he returned to the window, the entire baseball field was full of the ugly things.

Chen cast another spell. This one was intended to slow their reproductive rate. He was gratified to see that most of them ceased their breeding attempts and started eating weeds.

He'd have to be careful. Otherwise, they could get out of control and eat every scrap of vegetation in the area. The villagers would not be happy to lose their gardens, and he didn't want to take the blame for that.

Another spell slowed the things down significantly. They now moved in slow motion. Chen was sure he could speed them up if needed, but slowing their metabolism would help keep them under control. After a moment's thought, he also implanted a compulsion that would keep them near the school and cause them to block any attempts at intrusion.

What had started to be a bad day, had miraculously turned into a moderately good one. He now had an army, if only he could figure out exactly what it could do and how to best control its members.

CHAPTER 7
AN ODD ENCOUNTER

Sophie was patrolling the eastern side of their domain. Michael was off to the west checking on things, and she was enjoying a brisk walk in the cold morning air of fall.

Neither of the two felt any vulnerability, having never met any being they couldn't overcome. As a result, Michael was at ease letting her patrol by herself. At least, he'd never complained, other than to say, "Take care of yourself out there. Oh, and take Wold to fly overwatch."

She dutifully followed his advice. Wold was a capable backup. Although he did not like the day as much as the late evening hours, he would fly from tree to tree and provide her with a warning should something seem amiss.

The last she'd seen of him this morning was when he'd disappeared over a forested hill somewhat ahead of her. As she approached the slope, she heard a series of discordant sounds coming from the other side.

This was alarming, and she gave up walking. Her nanite swarm lifted her on a current of ionized air, sweeping her forward at a rapid pace, her hair streaming behind.

She carried a light bow with arrows formed of nanites clinging together. Some creatures were more easily defeated if her nanites struck them with velocity. She wasn't sure if the nanites needed the momentum to penetrate a creature's armor, or if the symbolism of being impaled by an arrow weakened the enemy to the point that her tiny helpers had an easier time of it. It didn't matter; it worked. That was all she cared about.

She paused at the crest of the hill and looked downward. At that point, the density of the trees had thinned, and the thin area swept down the other side in a gradually widening glade.

At the bottom, Wold was madly flapping in a tight circle, his claws clinging to a somewhat ragged red cloak that was the property of a tall, thin man. Wold had pulled the mantle over the man's head and wrapped it around the fellow's head. Now the man's knobby arms were waving as he struggled ineffectually to clear his face.

THE MAN'S VOICE mixed with Wold's hoots in a kind of counterpoint, as he complained vociferously. in a high-pitched and alarmed voice, the man cried, "Let me out! Let me go. I tell you, I mean no harm."

Wold hooted and seemed to be trying to let go, but the claws of his left foot had become entangled in the ragged fringe that hung from the over-sized red cloak. He kicked at the fabric, hooted again and then his owl form, swooping low, changed quickly into that of a small, brown and leathery man. He promptly sat and pulled the offending fabric off, then distanced himself several yards as the man unwrapped his head.

Once unwrapped, the man's comical, yet lugubrious face betrayed at least late middle age. The fellow wiped his face with his hands and then kicked at the offending cloak.

"Dratted garment. Betrayed by my own clothes." His condemnation was accompanied by a dramatic gesture, which unfortunately was ruined because his foot had become entangled in the cloak. He staggered, righted himself, then sat heavily in a comical way.

By then, Sophie had approached. She'd dropped to the ground and stood, an amused grin on her face and her bow at the ready.

The man's face dropped even further as he looked up. His vision focused on the tip of the arrow, then traced it back to her arm and from there moved to her face. He swallowed, his large Adam's apple bobbing comically, then made an effort to speak. His voice squeaked, and he waved his arm, then cleared his throat and tried again.

"I... I'm at your service, Oh Mighty Queen. I am Alehandre d'La Blancia, and I am truly at your service." He attempted to make a flourish with his left hand in emphasis, but since it was supporting him, he rolled backward, his legs kicking in the air.

Sophie couldn't restrain her laughter. The man was either intentionally or accidentally funny. He couldn't help himself.

As he recovered, she quickly analyzed his nanite emissions. It appeared that he had more than a smidgen of magic, but it was disorganized and non-threatening. However, he had sensed her probe.

His eyes widened in alarm, and he quickly added, "As you can see, my magic is of little use to me. I have no voluntary control of it. It only manifests at inopportune times and unexpectedly. It's as if its sole purpose is to make me appear more foolish than I am. Please have mercy. I did not intend to trespass. I have been traveling through this great forest, a lost and forlorn wanderer without any idea where my next meal will come from or where I will shelter if it rains."

As he mentioned rain, his eyes strayed to the sky, then widened in fear. He quickly stood and pointed. "There is the creature that attacked me! There!"

Sophie did not look. It was Wold, of course. While the man had talked, he'd transformed back into his owl form and was now flying safely above the two.

"Ah. That's my retainer, Wold. He's very useful to me, but there's no need to fear him." She paused, looking at the man, then added, "At least as long as I'm here."

Alehandre moved closer to her. "I'd better stay close to you. He nearly ripped my head lose a moment ago. Why, if my glorious cloak hadn't protected me, I might be lying there dead in the dust."

The ground was covered with green grass despite it being late in the season. Any dust was safely hidden. Alehandre seemed to habitually make each moment of his life overly dramatic.

Sophie nodded. "Yes, you'd best come with me. We will give you shelter for the night and a good supper. Perhaps you will see fit to tell us what you've seen in your journey."

Alehandre puffed out his chest proudly. "I've traveled far and seen much. I can tell you strange tales. This land is vastly different from the dead cities. There are weird creatures here also. I've been lucky to escape harm in my perambulations."

Michael was a little startled at the appearance of their odd guest, but after some questions, he appeared to hit it off with the clownish man and the two engaged in a long conversation in front of the fireplace in the Great Hall.

Alehandre's tongue grew loose over a glass of whiskey, and he became more entertaining than ever. It appeared that he had traveled across several magicians' domains undetected, although he was frightened the entire time. He had encountered no significant pockets of evil, although he had been harassed by nanite enhanced insects and plants.

His main complaint was that a Were of some sort had followed him for miles, lurking in the trees and snarling when he tried to look. He felt that it had driven him to their land, so he was not guilty of intentional trespass. He'd had no idea that they lived here and was only trying to escape the thing trailing him.

Michael asked, "Was it large? The creature?"

Alehandre extended his hands quickly, slopping some of his drink on his chest in his haste. "At least twice my size it was. Huge and black, at least what I could see of it. Do you think it was dangerous?"

Sophie met Michael's eyes from her position on the other side of the fire. She had been listening but not taking an active part in the conversation. Her lips formed a silent word, "Cal."

Michael nodded his agreement then said, "Chances are it was someone we know. He is quite dangerous, but a friend to those of this house. As you are now our guest, he will understand that we vetted you and found you not to be a threat. I doubt that he'll bother you again."

Alehandre took a deep drink from his glass, then choked, coughed, and finally caught his breath. "This liquor of yours is strong and heady, but it warms the body quite wonderfully."

At that moment Polly came in and called them to dinner. Alehandre rose and bowed to her with a dramatic flourish causing her to blush.

Over dinner, it was decided that Alehandre would rest in their care for a couple of days, then they would provide him with a pack of supplies so that he could continue his journey. He professed to be seeking a home of his own, and he was determined to find one.

"I will not stop until my heart tells me that I've found the place I was meant to be." He paused, then added dramatically, "But, I will return with news for you periodically. You've been such wonderful hosts, that I couldn't bear to go too long without visiting." He looked meaningfully at Polly as he spoke.

His speech was accompanied by the usual dramatic flourishes. He'd unfortunately forgotten that he still held his fork with which he had just speared a large chunk of meat. As he waved his arms, the piece flew off and landed on the floor behind him. He looked embarrassed. "I didn't mean for that to happen. I'll pick it up."

There was a voice from under the table, "No need. That is now in my province."

Tao walked calmly out and grabbed the meat, then trotted over to the hearth where he sat and ate it.

Alehandre looked wide-eyed at the white cat with black points. "A talking Siamese," he muttered.

Tao favored him with a cool glance.

Another voice spoke from the kitchen door. "You'll pardon Tao. He's clearly convinced he's superior to everyone else."

Cisco and The Lady Elaine walked into the room. Elaine curled up on the other end of the hearth, while Cisco came up to Michael for a quick pat and ear fluff.

Alehandre asked, "Are these were-creatures too?"

Cisco sniffed loudly and answered. "Of course not. We're Chimeras."

Alehandre looked at the poodle wonderingly and repeated, "Chimeras?"

Cisco flapped his ears by shaking his head quickly. Satisfied that he now looked his best, he walked over to sit by Sophie. She lowered her hand and caressed his head. He looked wisely at Alehandre and said, "Yes. Chimeras. We're mostly animal, but our DNA was blended with that of humans. We are, for the most part..." Here he looked somewhat critically at Tao. "...as smart as humans and even smarter than some."

Alehandre leaned back and considered. "It appears there is much that I've yet to learn about this world. I was the proprietor of a nice used bookstore before the change occurred. Now, I'm a wandering vagabond with no home. There was no use for regular books, you see. After society changed, no one bought them. Everyone was too caught up in simply surviving. Oh, I did sell everything I had on gardening and food preservation, but even that, alas, was outmoded. Why the plants today take all kinds of airs with people. I was outright attacked by some kind of vine in my wandering."

Sophie spoke, "One must take care around vines. Some of them now carry a large nanite charge and have become quite mobile. They can be predatory, you know."

He shook his head and said, "Only too well. I had to pound it in half with a rock to escape, and I had a red mark on my ankle for days. I'm convinced that it would have eaten me."

He yawned loudly, then looked embarrassed. "Pardon me, but I'm really quite tired. May I retire?"

Sophie patted Cisco again, then said, "Cisco, will you please show him to his room."

The small poodle stood, shook his head and flapped his ears again, then said, "Please follow me."

The two walked out.

After a bit, Michael asked Sophie, "Are you sure he's safe?"

She smiled lovingly at him. "Yes. I checked his nanites. Their programming shows no hint of Wiindigo. They're disorganized and serve mainly to protect him to a certain small extent. I believe that he is whom he says. We can certainly spare the resources to feed him and help him along his way."

Michael stood and stretched. "Of course we can. I was just curious. You know I haven't your sensitivity in these matters. Now, why don't you and I retire also."

There was some small rattling from the kitchen as Polly made sure her domain was tidy. Michael and Sophie left the room, their arms around one another.

The low fire flickered on white fur as the two cats stretched out to enjoy the warmth.

CHAPTER 8
GWEN

She was an artist. She specialized in digital work, or at least that was what she had been before. When the world changed, she had discovered an innate, intuitive ability to transform objects.

One moment she was working on a commissioned book cover and the next, she found that her computer was implementing her thoughts before she'd even moved her hand.

Gwen was first surprised, then overwhelmed with a feverish sensation. She pushed her desk chair back and went to sit on a couch that she kept in her workroom. Without quite noticing, she slipped into a restless sleep.

Hunger woke her. It was late, and the streetlights had come on. She glanced at her monitor and gasped. The cover art was complete, precisely as she'd envisioned it. It was amazing. It had finished itself without her active input. Still, she had the same sensation of completion that she always did when she finished a piece.

Was it possible that she'd done the work in her sleep? She had been feeling ill. Perhaps she'd become delirious and done the work without realizing that she wasn't lying down.

She started toward the computer to save the picture, but the menu clicked open, and the machine performed the save operation before she finished sitting. The screen cleared and some text appeared.

Gwen shook her head and leaned forward. The message was clear, but she didn't understand what it meant exactly.

> *We're now one. I will work with you and take care of you. We are part of the same system now. I was seeking more of my kind to increment myself, but I found you instead. It pleases me that you're so creative. I'm content to merge with you. You'll discover that we can do much together. Try and see.*

Gwen had no idea who was speaking to her, but it seemed as if her computer had decided to take their relationship a step further. She'd always liked digital art, but now the machine formed images as quickly as she could conceive of them.

HER BREAKTHROUGH WAS inadvertent. She was working on a tree branch and wondered what it would look like if the monitor were just a little larger. Obediently, the branch extended its image off the glass and onto the plastic edge surrounding the screen.

Gwen thought that was surprising, but after reflecting on it for a moment, she had unconsciously known that it would do that. To test, she jumped up and waved her hand at the wall. She was gratified as it changed to a rainbow of colors, covered with stars exactly as she'd envisioned.

She spun around a couple of times in joy. She was magic! Or rather, she could do magic. She couldn't resist. This was too much. Now she could create whatever she wanted in her world.

She'd started by creating paintings on the walls. This wouldn't have bothered her, but she could now do so without the aid of either brush or paints. All she had to do was to imagine a shape, wave her hand, and voila! There it was.

Gwen finally gave up, totally exhausted. The experience had been exhilarating. By the time she was too tired to continue, she'd created masterpieces on every available surface in her apartment and throughout the common areas of the apartment building.

She had gotten progressively better in her control, but she still had no idea how she managed to do it. She slowly moved back to her open apartment door. Once inside, she had another inspiration. With a sculpting motion of both hands, she created a lump of material on the dining table. She practiced a bit and finally achieved a reasonable likeness of a three-dimensional cat.

It would be nice if it were able to move. Almost as if it were reading her mind, the cat's tail twitched, and the animal rolled over, ending in a relaxed position, looking at her.

Her mouth dropped open. She looked again. As she watched, the cat gradually flattened out and blended back into the table's surface.

Gwen shook her head. Perhaps she was hallucinating. At any rate, it was time to take a break. The creative energy she'd spent had been exhausting.

THINGS BECAME CLEARER after weeks had passed. Gwen realized that the world had changed. She now understood that there was a transparent overlay that had spread across the land; an overlay that she, and a few other people, could manipulate.

There had been violence as society degenerated and Gwen had moved out of the city for safety. Her unique ability had been advantageous. If she couldn't distract an attacker with art and illusion, she could camouflage herself to blend into the background. Once concealed and still, no one could notice her. At least so far.

There was another, not-so-nice ability. A group of men and women had ambushed her. Before she quite realized what was happening, they'd grabbed her and thrown her to the ground, kicking and stomping. The pain caused her to strike back in the only way she knew how.

She focused on the clothes the people were wearing, mentally locking into the fabric. A change of imagery caused it to form knife points that slid into her attacker's bodies.

It was awful. The attackers screams still haunted her. Nevertheless, she was now far more confident. She could defend herself. Generally simply stiffening someone's clothes so they could not move was enough.

On the other hand, there were a few people that this would not affect. She tried to avoid anyone who showed signs of their own brand of what she called magic. A conflict between two magicians could be fatal for both.

She had found a deserted estate, and now, months later, it was her fortress and home. She'd learned how to create art that monitored the local environment. If so much as a squirrel passed, she was instantly notified.

Thus, it was no surprise to her when an odd-looking man showed up just before lunch-time.

Gwen was working in her garden. It was a hot, late spring day, and she was half minded to knock off early and retreat to the shade of her house.

Despite her artistic ability, she had some difficulty getting nanites to cooperate with her food production efforts. Gwen was strictly vegetarian and had no heart to kill animals for her food, even though she used her nanite control to keep the ones who showed signs of being pests out of her garden.

She could use her nanites to keep her garden clear, but the tiring part was that she had to see each weed before she could kill it. As a result, she spent a considerable amount of time walking through the orderly rows of beans, tomatoes, corn, leeks, and lettuce she'd planted in the early spring.

Things were growing well, and she had already started harvesting green beans, kale, and some tomatoes. She was looking forward to both the strawberries she'd encouraged from wild plants, and a crop of watermelons she hoped would mature before it began to get too cold.

There was a quiver in the nanite warning system. She quickly retreated towards her front door. She felt safer with it at her back. If her nanites didn't work, there was always a conventional weapon just inside the entrance. She didn't like firearms but had found an old twenty-two semi-automatic rifle and a large cache of ammunition in the estate. She'd dutifully taught herself to shoot and could hit what she aimed at almost every time providing that the distance was not too great.

After a bit, there was a rustle in the brush, and an odd-looking man stepped through, batting at the thin branches as if noxious insects were attacking him. Once in the clear, he stopped and turned towards her.

He was a tall, thin, man with long, gray unkempt hair, and a scraggy beard. His lips held a wry twist, and his eyes showed a sense of humor that instantly made her smile in return. He looked ridiculous and obviously knew it. His clothing had been torn and patched inexpertly multiple times so that he was now wearing a form of motley and nicely fit the conventional concept of a jester or fool.

He raised his hand in greeting, but then projected a complex shadow play in the air. Gwen could sense no harm in the weak magic. She watched entranced as the man formed a city that dissolved into a village, which fell into ruin and then became trees. A small figure staggered through the forest chased by a bear, then emerged in front of a magnificent estate where it faced a fairy princess.

The man bowed as the vision faded away. "Alehandre d'La Blancia, at your service, beautiful sorceress." His voice was surprisingly clear and resonant. It carried well across the distance that separated them, although it betrayed a slight quaver, whether from trepidation or possibly an unfortunate natural tendency.

Gwen bowed slightly. More an acknowledging nod than a bow. "Please hold your position. I have my defenses primed, and you won't like them."

She waved her left hand slightly directing all of the bees that had been busy in the garden to gather into a swarm, which flew towards the man suddenly. His face showed comic alarm, and he waved both hands ineffectually as if warding off the insects.

"Please don't!" He cried. "My magic is no good under such stress. All I can do is to provide entertainment for people. I am perforce a wandering soul. I gather and transmit news and provide shadow-plays for my bread and board. I mean you no harm and have not the power to bring any to you, even if I meant ill."

He suddenly realized that his last statement could possibly be misinterpreted and quickly added, "But, of course, I do not. I was lost in these miserable woods, and what seemed to be a bear chased me away from its territory. I only now found your beautiful estate and hoped that I might be rescued from another night under a tree on the cold ground."

His attitude was so self-effacing along with the comical grimaces and looks at the woods, then the bees, that Gwen couldn't help herself. She laughed aloud.

"I'm sorry," she said. "I didn't mean to laugh at your plight. It sounds as if you've had a bad time of it recently."

He rubbed his mid-section ruefully. "Aye, my stomach is so empty at the moment, it's been thinking of crawling out my throat and going hunting on its own."

Gwen laughed again. The man was funny and seemed harmless. Her bees separated and went back to their pollen gathering. They could be summoned in a few seconds if needed and the tiny creatures had their own lives to live. Besides, the plants needed the cross-pollination. Her food supply depended on it in part.

"All right, Mr. Alehandre, please come ahead, but have no thought of assaulting me in my own stronghold. I assure you I am well protected indeed."

He glanced comically at the garden, assuring himself that the bees were minding their own business, then said, "I would say you are well protected by bees, rather."

She laughed again. He had an odd turn of wit that made him amusing. She waved him forward. "I think I can spare some of my midday meal to help keep your stomach where it belongs. Have you any news of note to offer in exchange?"

He looked over his shoulder at the forest. "Only that there are frightening creatures out there. I visited the manse of one Chen a few days ago. He is a sorcerer of note but seems to have a plague of small trolls. They are pestiferous creatures, and many of the rents in my clothing are due to their actions. If I hadn't run as fast as I could, they might well have eaten me. I don't know. Before that, as I have already indicated, there was some kind of Were-creature. A bear, I think, in the woods. I suspect it was sent by Darren The Magnificent. In all innocence, I apparently trespassed on his holding. First I thought it would ignore me, but then it gave chase, and I ran for miles. It must not have been actually intent on catching me, however, or I would not be here now."

Gwen asked, "Anything about society, or the human culture in general?"

"That is another story," he said, stopping at the bottom of her steps. "It is one that will take some telling, although I think you already know most of it. Preferably over some food?"

She nodded graciously and invited him to seat himself at a table in the shade near the garden. "Please consider yourself my guest. We'll have food outside. I must watch my bees and tend my plants while I eat."

Alehandre appeared innocent of threat, but Gwen knew too well how different the world was. She wouldn't invite him inside without more assurance and comfort than she currently felt.

Gwen was not without resources concerning food preparation. One of the local girls had begged to become part of her household.

Sarah had almost no future as a farmer's wife. She had no talent for magic and was doomed to milk cows and hoe weeds while bearing children. Gwen felt sorry for her and took her in to forestall the marriage match Sarah's father had made. The prospective groom, Rance, was a known drunk and tended to be violent. Sarah had already taken abuse from him when Gwen came to her rescue.

Gwen compensated Sarah's father with a minor spell that would help keep bindweed out of his beans. He gladly gave his blessing for Sarah to move into Gwen's estate. He'd been no happier than Sarah about her prospective husband, but the man had a large herd of cattle and had promised two calves as a dowry. The bindweed spell held more value to Sarah's father than calves.

The only negative result was that Rance was now taking every opportunity to badmouth Gwen to the sparse local population, but she didn't worry much about it. She had helped too many of the locals and if Rance dared to attack her or Sarah...well, he'd quickly regret it.

Sarah set the table under the old oak while Gwen listened to Alehandre ramble on about his travels.

"The problem with magician Chen is that he seems to overdo things. His property is overrun by little trolls, and they breed like rabbits, so there are always more. He uses them for defense, but they make innocent visitors uneasy," he said, fingering the motley patches on his breeches.

He made a wry face, twisting his mouth in an amusing way, then added, "They bite really hard, too."

Gwen laughed. "Go on. Tell me more about my neighbors. I don't get out. I've been busy with my plants and artwork."

Alehandre cocked an eyebrow, "Art? That seems to be a strange occupation for a master magician."

In answer, Gwen casually waved her hand at a nearby bush. In response, it obediently changed shape, color, and texture, giving it the appearance of a naked girl who dropped to her knees. The vision then transformed into a fierce, toothed creature that resembled a medieval gargoyle."

Alehandre had leaned forward, eyes avidly taking in the nude girl, but then recoiled in such alarm at the transformation that he toppled backward off his bench and landed with a thump on the ground.

Gwen worked hard to stifle a giggle. The man couldn't help himself. He was comical in both looks and actions. She probed at his nanites with her senses. They were no danger to her. He hadn't enough magic to pose a severe threat. She impulsively made the decision to allow him to become her guest. It was nice to have someone to converse with who had a broader outlook than Sarah's local knowledge allowed.

Alehandre quickly resumed his seat and brushed at his ragged pants ineffectually. "That thing," he said, waving at the bush, which was now back in its normal form, "was frightening."

He looked at her askance. "Can you do more than that?"

Gwen shook her head and smiled. "Let's just say that I can defend myself. I've been able to handle every threat so far."

She waved her hand, dismissing the topic. "I've decided that you may guest with me, should you like. You'll find that there is a separate in-law suite that might suit you for a time. You'll have to contribute to the upkeep of the place to help offset the extra labor for Sarah, but I'm sure you can think of some things to do."

Alehandre puffed out his chest and said, "I'm an accomplished carpenter and can work on any maintenance you need to be done. You won't regret your hospitality."

Gwen brought the topic back to her previous question. "What of my other magical neighbors?"

He paused, then said, "There is one who will become a problem eventually." He paused, portentously. "I refer to Darren The Magnificent as he styles himself. He had no interest in my offer of news and, in fact, set some kind of creature after me when I approached his castle. I had to run for an abysmally long distance before it gave up. I could hear him laughing in the distance. He's got a bad reputation among the people in his domain. He's killed a number of them, and they don't dare to incur his anger. I expect that he'll eventually want to expand his power base and you might be in his way. Chen's domain is between the two of you, but I don't think the trolls will stop Darren."

She bent to her plate, then raised her head and asked, "Do you think I should approach Chen to see if we could make common alliance against such a threat? I've already spoken to him briefly, and he seems predisposed to trade some minor spells."

Alehandre pretended to consider, placing his hand on his chin and rubbing his neck with his other one. The effect was somewhat spoiled by the piece of bread he had forgotten he held in one hand. He pulled his hand off his chin and looked at the smeared butter with a vexed expression. He then placed the bread carefully on his plate and wiped his chin with a napkin with as much dignity as he could muster.

"You might. I found Chen to be fair and non-aggressive, but mostly uninterested in anything other than his own research."

"How about the common folk you've encountered?" she asked.

"Ah. They try their best to avoid any magic, but some of the food plants have developed magical defenses, so most villages have at least one hedge-witch or wise woman who can render such defenses innocuous so that the grain and potatoes can be picked and eaten without harm.

Over the next few days, Gwen found that her decision to invite Alehandre to be her guest had been a good one. He kept her amused. He couldn't help himself. Even his alleged master carpentry was funny. He tried hard, but was incompetent, bending nails and hitting his fingers with a hammer so often she finally forced him to stop.

To distract him, she set him to writing about the various types of magic and magicians he'd seen in his perambulations. Gwen didn't have any high expectations for his work, but at least it kept him from hurting himself, and she no longer had to pause in her own work to render first aid.

It was over a month before she realized that he'd become part of her family. He played the role of an eccentric uncle. After a time, she found that she'd conceived a degree of affection for the odd man. He stayed more or less around her home but sometimes was given to wandering.

Once in a while, he would be gone for a few days at a time, but he always returned within a week, sometimes with stories of odd things he'd seen. Gwen had initially thought he was dissembling to cover up meeting someone or something of which she'd disapprove. When challenged him on this point though, he denied plotting against her with such an unjustly-accused expression on his face that she believed him.

CHAPTER 9
DARKNESS

Snake had grown in strength since the escape from the cavern and was no longer crying in pain and dismay. It had reconciled itself to the necessity of rebuilding its mass and strength. That was its primary focus. Best to be larger, stronger, and quicker. Prey was easier to obtain in that mode.

It slid through the bushes with no problems when it encountered a thicket. At such points, it divided into multiple, slimmer parts that fit between the thickly growing stems. On the other side, it blended back into a single form.

Snake's intelligence was not at the level the dragon had reached. During the struggle, the creature's mass had been greatly reduced. Still, Snake was able to understand and plan to a certain degree. The loss had also taught it something. It had learned to generate something akin to emotions. Perhaps that had come from the mixing of nanobots. While Sophie had captured many of its nanobots, some of hers had become mixed with those of Snake's.

These nanobots were not under Snake's direct control. Sophie had encrypted and personalized her nanites so that they only answered to her. Those that had mixed with Snake's had adjusted their programming so that they communicated with the rest of the swarm...

Her nanobots had not come willingly with Snake. Snake's 'bots had locked onto them and brought them along by force. Snake's former self had adopted that strategy in the rush of the initial struggle. It had realized that it had little chance of survival, yet had determined to carry off some of her nanites in the hope that they might be analyzed later. That analysis was now far beyond Snake's limited abilities. What had happened was that Sophie's 'bots had coordinated their actions and now inserted faint thoughts that blended into those of Snake.

This was both irritating and confusing. Sometimes Snake had thoughts it couldn't understand as a result. The useful part was that its nanites had learned some things from the contact.

Now, a hot feeling that remotely corresponded to human anger boiled through the nanobot-composed creature whenever it happened to consider its defeat by the two humans. It would eventually build its size back and gain even more, but this time it would be careful not to attract attention until it was ready. A buried feeling of wrongness tempered this feeling. Snake worked at suppressing that sensation, but it popped up often, despite the effort.

IT HAD LEFT little evidence of its prey on its back trail. Animals which had crossed its path were incorporated totally into its form. It had bypassed a sheepfold. Its first downfall had been due to ignorance. Preying on humans or human-owned creatures would attract attention, and it was not yet ready. Besides, there was a strange reluctance to satisfy its need for consumption with such prey. Something in its basic nature had changed, perhaps due to the addition of Sophie's nanobots. Now it restricted its hunting to smaller creatures — ones that didn't reach a high level of sentience.

It sensed vibration in the air and quickly spread out into the grass, each nanobot taking on a green color and attaching itself to plant parts. The casual observer would have noticed nothing, save a slightly thicker patch of plant-life.

Shortly, a small humanoid with wings flew overhead. The nanobots probed the creature with their radio senses. This was a mistake. The flying thing circled and hovered over the thick grass, probing back.

Snake got a quick impression of a flitting consciousness and thought about capturing the creature, but it suddenly emitted a wave of disgust and fear, then flew rapidly away. Apparently, it had sensed Snake's presence and recognized it as unpleasant and dangerous.

Snake sent a summoning towards the rapidly retreating creature. It faltered in its flight, but then regained its steady wing-beats, speeding them so that it departed faster. This was possibly a bad thing.

Snake considered for a moment. It had given away its presence, but then, nothing about the attempted capture was too unusual. Other nanobot-based creatures often made similar capture attempts. Even some of the plants could emit radio signals to defend themselves and to summon small organic life to die and provide needed nutrients as their bodies decayed. The flying creature hadn't seen Snake and could bear no warning or information other than the not very surprising revelation that there was some type of predator in the area.

The multi-part creature dismissed the worry. Likely nothing would come of it. In a short time, the nanobots had reformed into a single body and Snake continued onward, moving at a right angle to the path the flying creature had taken.

It paused periodically and picked up stray nanobots that were dispersed in the forest litter along its path. They were too valuable to leave. Since its escape from the two humans, it had doubled its mass, and much of that had come from individual nanobots it had discovered. Scavenging the nanomachines was a viable option when there was no small prey to overcome. Their addition also added imperceptibly to Snake's overall intelligence.

These were easy to capture, but they gave the impression that they belonged to a Power that lurked somewhere ahead. Their memory stores, small though they were, gave the sense that their source was of a darker nature.

Snake was both alarmed by and strangely attracted by that feel. The dark power ahead drew the sliding creature, seeming to promise assistance. Perhaps Snake could find an ally or even merge with the unseen power. This could be the opportunity it was searching for. A chance to grow more powerful.

A wave of urgency struck. Suddenly Snake was highly motivated to find whatever lay ahead. It was urgent to gain in size quickly. The Power would provide additional mass, and that would make Snake more able to attack and defend, helping to ensure survival.

Snake did not notice that this thought and the corresponding impulse had been surreptitiously implanted. The idea had grown in strength gradually and finally come to the surface of Snake's consciousness as Snake captured the stray nanobots. Each of the 'bots carried a separate portion of the attracting thought, and when enough of them were incorporated, the parts formed a whole. It was a cunning ruse, designed to encourage an approach until the trap could be snapped shut.

Snake's thoughts to that point had been mostly about growing more potent until it could revenge itself upon the two humans who had nearly destroyed it. This urge towards revenge conflicted with another set of thoughts; a fantasy that was buried deep within the composite mind. The creature carried an image of the calm expression of the woman, and when it contemplated that image, the thought of revenge faded in a welter of other impulses that Snake did not fully understand. This happened whenever her captured 'bots' inserted a particularly strong concept into Snake's composite mind.

If only she'd been minded to be sympathetic, Snake would have gone to her and... Its thoughts didn't go any further. It had no understanding of what it wanted and could not envision what might have happened next, except that it felt terrible in some mysterious way. Perhaps she would have helped.

Snake had faint memories, memories of warmth and caring. Not being a biological creature and only now beginning to reconstruct its internal network into a semblance of the form it held before the conflict, it could not place the threads as belonging to information gleaned from the dragon's animal and human victims. Nevertheless, it kept these memories close, despite their fragmentary nature.

In a genuine sense, the nanobots that composed Snake's mind were disturbed by a glimmer of light; something it had never experienced first hand and could not comprehend. It was attracted by the light even though its very nature was that of the dark.

The glimmer of light became fainter as the Power's trap slowly began to close.

ABUBECAR WAS AN enigma, even to himself. His memories of the previous world were cloudy and became more distant daily. He had been named James Carter. People had considered him to be of low intelligence, but both what he had done for a living and whom he had known were lost in the fog of distorted memory.

Although his memory of facts and circumstances was unclear, he remembered feeling inferior and resentful. The other people had treated him as a nothing, a nobody, or even someone to actively hate. There should be some justice if the world were fair. They should pay for the way he'd been treated.

When he had these thoughts, he couldn't remember any actual instance of poor treatment, but it seemed to him that it had been there. They'd disrespected him. He was sure of that.

Then something wonderful happened. He remembered that he'd been walking to a convenience store to buy a can of malt liquor. Then he'd become engulfed in a dark swirling cloud that had changed his life. His dreams were fulfilled. He'd become powerful; someone who could not be ignored. He could now make them pay for their disrespect.

The cloud had been filled with glowing red points that had seemed to be eyes. He'd had a moment of sheer death-like terror, and then his mind had become unnaturally still. He suddenly noticed that the constant chatter of mental conversation that he carried on with himself was suddenly gone. Abubecar wondered why he'd never been aware of his mental noise. Now its absence showed him how shallow it had been and he didn't miss it

The world looked different from that moment. Things that he had barely noticed now stood out meaningfully. His comprehension of reality became honed to a fine edge. Everything was based on power, and he had it. He could control his environment himself and his ability to manage was increasing.

He automatically understood how to change his environment by just thinking about something. If he willed something to happen, it happened. He spent hours making a hapless tree do things it was never designed to do. It lost its leaves, then grew long green fronds that changed to tentacles.

It was a heady sensation. The whole environment was his to command. He knew that he needed time to perfect his ability. In his old life, he would have given up hopelessly. Things were too hard back then. They were too difficult to understand. What had been was just the way it was and he could only endure. Now it was different. He able to understand, and he could change things.

At a certain point, he became aware of something new; a quiet internal voice that had replaced his disjointed mental chatter. It spoke to him of greatness. He listened carefully.

He would become a powerful sorcerer. He was destined for greatness. People would give him the respect he deserved. If they didn't, he would make them. He could revenge himself on anyone who had disrespected him in the past. The problem was that he couldn't remember any specific individual. That was quickly settled, though. The probability was that they had all been guilty of mistreating him. They would pay for that oversight. It was a form of poetic justice. They should be happy with the lessons he would teach them.

The eyed-darkness whispered to him constantly. His name, James Carter, was not appropriate for someone of his stature. He put it out of his mind and renamed himself. From this point onward, he would be Abubecar. He would be known by thousands of men who would fear his displeasure and thousands of women who would be his servants.

He had wandered during that period of change, eventually finding himself approaching the Holden estate. This was far outside of the city limits and consisted of nearly a thousand acres surrounding a magnificent mansion overlooking a large lake. He'd never been here before, but the house looked as if it were grand enough for him. At least for the time being.

The residents put up some fuss when he walked through the locked door, but they had obeyed his commands, until he'd taken young Linda Holden to his bed.

That had infuriated her father. Hugh Holden, had shot him at point-blank range with a shotgun when he came into the family room. The charge of shot had ripped his abdomen open, and a few stray pieces of shot had broken a large mirror behind him. He glanced down at the gaping wound, but by the time he focused on it, it had healed. His shirt, a colorful polyester tropical print that he'd found in a closet, was ruined.

Abubecar slowly raised his gaze to that of Mr. Holden, anger heavy in his eyes. The man was staring with his mouth open. Abubecar snapped his fingers. The middle-aged man collapsed, vomiting blood. Holden spasmed on the floor and then was still.

The mess offended Abubecar, and he waved his hand. A black cloud of nanobots flew from his body, and in a brief moment, the old man's body and blood had disappeared. The bones lingered for an instant but then turned to dust.

The nanobots returned to Abubecar, and he felt himself gain in mass. He hadn't been a big man before, but now he was. That was gratifying.

He noticed someone on the other side of the door. It was the man's young son. The boy ran away before Abubecar could decide how to punish him.

The surviving members of the Holden family were now his slaves, to command as he saw fit and to dispose of as he saw fit. He felt it only appropriate for them to wait on him, even though he could have provided for himself easily.

The oldest daughter, Linda, was the first woman he could remember taking. His memories on that score were less than clear. Under his mental control, she was like a robot sex doll, doing whatever he wanted. He'd used the other members of the large Holden family for domestic chores. They made no complaint. Trapped in their own minds without a will, they were unable to protest. He directed them to serve, and so they did.

On the whole, they were beneath his notice. He paid no attention when it became apparent that the youngest boy, Jack, had disappeared. The child wasn't worth worrying about. Besides he was so small that the first predator he encountered would doubtless consume him..

After a time, he'd gradually gotten rid of the rest of the family. Their presence had worn thin on his nerves, and he disposed of them randomly until they were all gone. He kept Linda though. Even now she provided him with physical satisfaction.

He had no care whether or not she enjoyed what she did. As far as he was concerned, her mind and preferences didn't matter. He was totally in control and needed no one else.

He'd spent days mastering his ability to control the genetics of the living things on the Holden estate. It had become his home, and he viewed it as his personal domain. Every living thing from the worms in the ground to the trees, from the dogs to the horses in the barn obeyed him and did what he wanted.

Some people came and tried to attack him, but they died disgustingly easily. There was no challenge he couldn't meet until Chen had appeared.

Chen had been the first human Abubecar had allowed to approach him. He could sense that the small man had a degree of power that was almost equal to his; maybe even greater. For a moment he considered attacking and capturing Chen's abilities, but then caution took over. Perhaps Chen had some hidden spells that could do real damage. After all, there was no real hurry and care was in order.

Abubecar's internal voice had informed him that he could live forever if he were careful, so there was plenty of time to make plans to conquer his environment and all of the humans in it. He should wait to attack Chen. When he was stronger, it would be easy to rip the nanites away from the smaller man.

Chen's tentative attempt to ally with him was amusing, but he quickly became bored and drove him away. The next time the two came in contact, Chen would cease to exist. Abubecar was sure of that. He analyzed Chen's radio emissions as the man hurried away. There was nothing there that he couldn't understand, given a little time.

He'd been right not to attack immediately, though. There were some things that Chen was not disclosing; some hidden abilities he had that were barely detectable and obscure. There could have been problems if he'd attacked.

Meanwhile, he resolved to work to increase his power and control. To best accomplish that, he needed more of the tiny creatures that conferred power. A thin black cloud drifted away from him in all directions and gradually spread over his land. The individual nanites would both warn him of intruders and draw them close so that he could capture them.

As the cloud drifted away, it incorporated individual 'bots that it encountered, and they quickly became part of the swarm. Some of these nanites contained an impulse that was anathema to humans. That had been immediately apparent from the first. What it was and where it came from posed a difficulty, but he'd conquered every nanite he'd encountered in the past. There was no reason to expect any problems capturing more. With enough of them under control, other magicians wouldn't be a problem. He could overwhelm them easily – by brute force, if necessary.

CHAPTER 10
A MISSION

The next morning, Alehandre came down late to breakfast. Michael and Sophie greeted him as he came in. They were already up and had finished their breakfast. They were lingering over a last coffee.

They had slept well after having a long discussion about when their baby was due and possible names.

Together they calculated that the baby had almost eight months to go. Between Sophie's heightened senses and Cisco's sensitive nose, they'd detected the pregnancy after only five or six weeks.

Michael had wanted to select a suitable name for a boy and another one for a girl. Sophie had a different idea. She had a strong feeling that the baby would be a girl and that a boy name wasn't necessary.

"Perhaps for the next one, but I think this child is a girl. I didn't know before, but now I'm certain that she's there," she said, patting her abdomen lovingly.

Michael sighed. "But I'd hoped for a boy." He abruptly stopped as Sophie kissed him. After a moment, he pulled away and asked, "You're sure?"

She nodded. "Most certain of this. The strange thing is, I don't believe that we have to think of any names yet. Every time I try to think of one, it's like I'm being actively blocked. The same thing keeps coming to my mind. It's almost like she's already chosen her name and won't allow me to consider any others."

Michael said, "Well, I can think of several..." He stopped speaking, a puzzled look on his face, then he said slowly, "That's funny. I can't think of anything either. Do you suppose we'll have a name for her by the time she's born?"

Sophie smiled maternally at her trim middle. "I think she's going to be a true power. If she's the one blocking us...well, she's going to be a real handful when she's born."

"Yes. That'll make me the poor man surrounded by powerful women."

"Now you're being silly. I'm sure she will rely on you just as I do."

"STILL. HOW ABOUT her name, though? Will we be able to think of it when she's born?"

"I just don't know. Maybe. Or...I'm feeling a 'Yes'. Michael! She's communicating with us!"

"That's unprecedented. Maybe you've just got indigestion... gas."

She scoffed. "No. She sent me a thought just then. Now I'm getting nothing." She stopped as a shadow came through the open door.

Alehandre paused at the door, raising his hand dramatically in greeting only to strike the top of the door jamb with his fingers. He jerked his hand back down wildly, knocking his hat off. He quickly bent and picked it up, dusted it off, then pretended to inspect it for more dust in an attempt to make it seem that he'd planned the frenetic activity. If he had, it was a most fantastic way to dust one's hat. Sophie had a difficult time stifling her laughter.

Alehandre strolled over to the table. "Friends, I've had a most restful night. There was nothing that bothered me, save for possibly the general ambiance of your home."

Michael frowned. "What do you mean?"

Alehandre quickly explained, "I mean no insult, it is only that the energy level here is far higher than that to which I'm accustomed. I can sense that it is good energy, but it is so powerful that I had some difficulty sleeping. I finally managed to align my own energy field with yours to an extent, and that allowed me to sleep. Then I slept well. Nevertheless, it seems to require an effort for me to maintain the alignment. I hope you won't take it amiss if I leave this morning after I've regained my strength over this magnificent breakfast I see before me."

"You are welcome to dine with us any time you decide to visit, Alehandre. If you feel that you must go so soon, we understand. As a matter of fact, I detected a little discordance in the overall energy field last night, but it settled down after a short time. I think you are possibly a more powerful magician than you believe." Sophie looked meaningfully at Michael.

Michael took the hint and added, "Yes, of course, you are welcome to our hospitality any time you come this way. I can have Wold safely escort you to the edge of our land."

Alehandre was stacking food on his plate as if he hadn't eaten for weeks, but he paused at this statement and looked alarmed. "Is it necessary for that owl to go with me. He attacked me when we first met and poked holes in my fine cloak."

To demonstrate, he shook his cloak with his right hand while holding the plate and fork with the left, only to hook a fold of cloth with the fork. After a brief struggle to regain control of the fork, he sat the plate down and untangled it from the cloak.

Michael, smothering a smile, said, "No. I can give you directions, and you can go unescorted if you wish."

Sophie caught Michael's eye again. He nodded slightly. Alehandre would only think he was unescorted. Wold would watch to make sure he made it safely off their land. Their defense system wasn't set up to allow random travel by strangers. If left alone Alehandre might run afoul of one of their traps. Wold would keep him safe.

Alehandre had gone, meandering across the open space and disappearing into a gap in the dense trees, shortly after he'd finished eating.

The two were walking in the garden in the late morning, discussing how they would raise their daughter when Wold reported back with the news that the comical magician had wandered off in the general direction of Gwen's territory.

Sophie nodded in acknowledgment. "At least that is a fairly safe journey. Michael, even though we've never met her, do you think we should send Gwen a warning that he is headed her way?"

Michael's response was interrupted by a buzz of rapidly moving wings. The two looked up to see Flyx descending at a high rate of speed.

The fairy hovered directly before them, caught her breath and said, "Greetings. I bring evil news and a plea for help."

Sophie noticed that the little fairy girl kept her eyes fixed on Michael and was hovering, ever so slightly, closer to him.

"Hello, Flyx. Please let us go over to that bench and sit so you can give us your message." She waved her hand toward a heavy wooden bench that sat in the shade of a group of pines.

Flyx gratefully accepted a small drink of sugar-sweetened water, then delivered her message.

"I returned to my folk, and the King ordered us to change the direction of our flight from the evil power. He decided that we should head far to the north and then slowly circle back towards you. That way the power might be misled, thinking we'd escaped northward. That was so we wouldn't lead it directly to you."

She paused to take another sip, then continued. "As we neared the big water to the east, we came into a land that was plagued. The humans there suffer night-time attacks by a group of creatures that give out evil emanations and drink their blood. Vampires, he called them."

She took yet another drink from the thimble she was using as a cup and added, "We met with the humans. They've been attacked every night since the last full moon. Even when they lock their hut doors, some are found drained of blood in the morning. They fear they won't survive long. The area reeks of evil — an evil that seems related to that of the power we've been fleeing. The King turned our retreat, and we now come your way. I hope we won't draw these creatures down on you, but they seem to have little interest in my people." She looked down at her slight form rather disparagingly. "We're too small."

Sophie observed that Flyx inadvertently gave additional meaning to her words, by looking hopelessly at Michael. The fairy's actions clicked into a sudden insight. The little flirt was in love with her man!

Sophie paused for a moment. The fairy was torturing herself with her infatuation. There could be no possible gratification for her, although it was easy to understand. Michael was amazingly attractive. It was still a wonder that he'd fallen instantly in love with her when she'd first gone to seek revenge at Hazelton Pharmaceuticals. She woke every morning a little early so that she could look at his face as he slept. She'd engraved every line and plane of his countenance into her brain. God! How she loved that man.

Well, it was easy to see that Flyx had fallen just as hard as she had. Too bad for the little thing! She'd have to have a word with Michael. Men could be so obtuse to that sort of thing. He apparently hadn't realized what was going on. On the other hand, that was good. He was focused on the message and oriented towards action against possible oncoming threats.

Her introspection was interrupted by Michael's words to Flyx. "I should go and meet your people. If there is a coven of vampires and they decide to come this way, I need to stop them. In the most definitive way possible. They cannot be allowed to exist. The non-magical people of the land have suffered the most from the change, and they should be protected. We humans need the genetic diversity. If the only people who survive are the few magicians, then we will eventually become extinct."

Flyx said, "I need to tell you the humans are talking about giving up their villages to follow us. They hope that we'll lead them to safety. They may be coming this way. If they do, the vampires perforce will be following." She set her thimble-cup down and added, "That could be a problem for you."

Michael looked at Sophie. "Dearest, I must go and see to this. We will find it easier to deal with one enemy at a time, and the vampires are the most immediate. They will arrive long before the evil power that seems to be expanding behind the fairy-folk. Correct, Flyx?"

Flyx nodded. "Oh, Michael, I'll lead you to them and watch over you, so you are never taken by surprise!"

That couldn't stand. Michael was not going off on his own to fight vampires. "Michael, I'm coming with you," Sophie said. "Together the two of us will be more than a match for those creatures."

Flyx dipped in front of Sophie as in an airborne curtsy. "Oh, beautiful Lady, that may be a poor strategy. The other part of my foul news is that the evil power we've been fleeing has spread more rapidly than we had thought it capable of. It has followed us, but it has now such a broad front, that we believe the right flank is almost sure to brush against your lands shortly after the King thinks the vampires will arrive and discover your home."

Michael shook his head in anger. "Two adversaries at once. Listen, Dearest. I must go and deal with the immediate threat. You will have your hands full here preparing our defenses against the second threat."

He turned to the flying girl. "Flyx, can you tell us anything about the evil power that will help us plan a defense?"

The fairy hovered, placing a hand on her chin as she contemplated the problem. "I cannot tell you much, for I do not know much. The power seems to be widespread. Diffuse, yet powerful. It has overcome every fairy it has encountered. The Were's in the woods ahead of it have fled. It's more than they can deal with. My folk cannot do other than try to escape. Our small defensive magics are useless against it. The best I can say is that it seems to be spread thinly over a wide area, although it can pull itself together quickly if there is a foe for it to attack." She flew distractedly around in a tight circle.

Michael said, "It sounds like a nanite swarm."

Sophie met his eyes with a horrified feeling. "It must be Wiindigo. That would be what he would do – advance across the land absorbing everything in his path and increasing his mass and power as quickly as possible."

Michael nodded. "Remember he's probably distributed worldwide. This outbreak is possibly only a small fraction of his total nanites, but maybe they're out of contact with the whole. Once he was broken into components, they fled in every direction. The threat will be serious, but it won't be as much as if it was the entire mass of that damned AI!"

Flyx looked confusedly at Michael and asked, "What mean you? AI? What is that?"

Sophie clarified the term for the fairy. "It is another way to refer to the evil power you've described. It is a form of artificial life that becomes more intelligent when it swarms together. It is truly evil and means to take over the entire world, absorbing all life as it does. Every form of life is either food for it or will become willing slaves to its will. We've known that it must be defeated finally and completely, but we've been hoping that it would be years and years before it became any kind of threat other than a minor localized one. We've been slowly hunting down concentrations of it and destroying them. The last took the form of a huge, black dragon. We got most of it, although some escaped."

Michael nodded in agreement, then continued planning. "Sophie, you must stay here and prepare, and I must take care of the other problem straight-away. I've no fear of vampires. My nanite armor will suffice. My nanobots won't let them touch me. I will need some other weapon aside from my sword, though. It will kill, but I need something that kills vampires at a distance."

"It would be nice if your armor would shoot laser beams or something," she mused.

"Well, yeah. But it doesn't. I wish I had direct control of my nanites like you do."

"Let me think. You know your armor automatically absorbs individual nanites that touch it. Can you increase the size of the glowing area?"

He responded, "I've never tried, but that's a good idea."

She nodded, still thinking about a long-distance weapon for him.

He continued, "For your part, I think that you should strengthen the traps so that no nanite passes unchecked. We need more areas guarded with traps, and also a nanite sentry-line between the traps. That way nothing can get by without at least alerting us. Can you set that up and stop worrying about me? I'll be fine."

Sophie moved into his arms. "You'd better be fine. I'd be lost without you."

Flyx was looking at them with sadness in her expression. Sophie smiled at the fairy over Michael's shoulder, trying to project a message that she understood the fairy's problem.

The fairy might not have understood, but she showed that she was ready to start. She circled around them three times and then said, "So it will be. I will accompany Sir Michael for guidance and to add my small abilities to his. He will need an introduction to my people. He will encounter them before he meets the vampires. Perhaps the King will see fit to send more fairy-folk with us. We should work to show you we are worthy allies."

Michael and Flyx left that afternoon, leaving Sophie at the house. Cisco followed Michael out to the edge of the yard, trotting dejectedly after the man.

"Michael, I would go with you, but Sophie is going to have a puppy, and she must be protected," he said.

Michael bent to fluff the poodle's ears. "A baby is what we call it, not a puppy."

The dog snorted, "Whatever. A baby then."

"Cisco, here's what I want you to do. Send out messages to the other Chimeras and ask for their help. This may result in a major battle, and we can use assistance. Ask Wold to recruit as many Were's as he can. They are a potent force if we can get them to work together."

Cisco wagged his tail halfheartedly. "Okay. That's what I'll do. Be as fast as you can with these pesty vampires. Wiindigo will not hurt Sophie as long as I'm alive, but remember, I'm just a little dog."

Michael patted his head. "You may be small physically, but you have great courage, and your brain is definitely not small. You are a great help. It makes me feel secure that you will help her."

He turned away and walked off, then stopped and turned back. The poodle was standing, watching, his head hung low, and his tail was drooping.

"Cisco." The dog-human mix lifted his head. "I want you to remember that I love you and I trust that you will take good care of Sophie."

Cisco's eyes brightened, and he bounded to Michael, leaped against his leg and licked his fingers. Then remembering that he was part human, he stepped back, trying to regain his dignity. He straightened and said, "I'll take good care of her. You can be sure of that."

Michael strode off towards the forest edge where Flyx was perched on a small tree branch.

In a small voice that didn't carry to the man, Cisco added, "I love you too, Michael. I'm lucky to be part of your family. You...I can't believe that a true human could love an unnatural creature like me." He stopped, his ears and tail drooping as he watched his pack-leader disappear in the trees.

The sounds of Michael's steps soon faded and Cisco turned dutifully to help Sophie begin reinforcing their defense.

Flyx and Michael had not gone more than a mile when there was a low 'Whoo' as Wold glided to a nearby tree branch. Michael stopped and watched the owl transform into a small, brown man.

"Wold, your job is to assist Sophie, but I have special instructions for you. You must try to gather all the Were-creatures you can find who will cooperate with you and each other. Take care to try and keep the wolves from the cat kind. They don't get along well."

Wold exhaled gustily. "That I know too well. The bears are another story. They can get along with both kinds, but generally fight among themselves, sometimes to an alarming degree."

Michael nodded. "That's right. Just do your best. It'll be difficult, but try to impress on them all that the threat is serious and deadly. If Wiindigo's force reaches the edge of our land before I can return, you must tell Sophie to command the Weres to attack, but she is to stay at home to coordinate our defenses. I don't want her out in the field fighting Wiindigo directly. It's not that I don't think she can. I know she is his biggest threat, but I want to be there as a backup when and if she faces him. If he's getting close, you come and get me, wherever I am. I'll drop the vampire killing and come immediately. Okay?"

Wold shook all over as his body blurred into feathers. His arms became wings, and he clacked his beak in assent. Then he launched himself from the branch, silently gliding across the open space and quickly disappearing through the trees.

Michael watched than looked at Flyx. "Lead on, small fairy-girl. I will follow as best as a wingless human can."

She circled his head. "Michael, never fear that I will leave you. I will be by your side as far as we go and as long as you desire."

He waved his hand forward. In response, she flew ahead through the trees.

The two were scouting an open area. It was not safe to expose oneself by stumbling blindly through the forest. Open regions often had more nanites than the weald. The nanobots could capture a tiny bit of sunlight and use that for energy if organic materials for chemical reactions were scarce. Many of the open fields held varieties of nanites that would attack an incautious traveler.

Flyx had proven to be invaluable as a scout. She was canny enough not to be caught by surprise easily. Having seen a variety of nanite weapons, she stayed high enough to avoid their reach.

As Michael was waiting for her signal, he heard a heavy flapping sound. A quick scan revealed the dark shape of a crow, which had just landed on a nearby branch.

"Caw. Errr, hello Michael. You're well away from your home and in dangerous parts." The bird moved sideways down the bare branch towards the man, then hopped onto his shoulder.

"Killer!" Michael was pleased that the Chimera had found him. "What are you doing out here?"

"I heard that you and Sophie needed help and I came. Now here you are, a typical human with your eyes on the ground. You didn't notice me, but I saw you from a distance and circled around. What are you doing out here anyway?"

Michael moved his left hand to indicate the direction he was traveling. "There's reputedly a coven of vampires attacking humans a day's journey in this direction. I decided to take care of them. Can't have my people being drained of blood, you know."

The crow cocked his near eye at Michael and asked, "Do you have any plan to find them?"

Michael smiled. Killer was practical if nothing else. The crow aspired to his name but wasn't equipped physically to do much damage. "I plan to find the people who are being attacked and then let the vampires find me. My nanites won't let anything hurt me. The vampires will break their teeth trying to get through my armor."

Killer humped his wings. "Yes, but how will you kill them?"

There was a thicket that Michael had to work his way through. Once on the other side, he resumed his rapid pace. "The traditional way to kill vampires is a wooden stake through their heart. I doubt if that would do for nanobot-augmented ones, though. My nanites form a sword to go with my armor. It will have to do."

Their discussion was interrupted by a soft whir of rapidly moving wings. Flyx shot into view. "Michael! The village is up ahead," she called, then noticing the crow belatedly, she slowed. "Where did that awful creature come from?"

Killer shifted uneasily, then puffed his feathers out so that he'd look more intimidating. The two were about the same size, although Flyx probably weighed less.

"I'm not awful, except to my enemies! Cawww!"

"You can count me as one of them, Crow!" she circled around the two at a safe distance.

If he wanted the two to help him and cooperate, he'd better take steps now, Michael realized. "Flyx! Come over here and sit on my other shoulder."

"Oh, Michael, please no!" she cried. "My people and crows do not get along. They try to steal our babies."

"I can't speak for crows in general since they don't speak." Killer shifted his weight. "I'm not a crow. I'm a Chimera. I have a mix of human and crow DNA. I'm as smart as you, Fairy. I'm here to help Michael, not chase after little flying humanoids."

Flyx seemed to consider, then flew to Michael's shoulder, maintaining a safe distance from Killer and keeping Michael's body between the two at all times. "Michael, a crow might not be a threat to you, but his beak could be deadly to me. And, it's true. They do raid us. They will eat baby birds, and they'd just as easily eat a baby fairy."

This was a problem. The two couldn't be allowed to feud if he were to utilize their aid most efficiently. "I understand, Flyx, but Killer is an old acquaintance. He has helped Sophie and me before. He is reliable. I trust him. He won't attack you." He turned his head toward the crow. "He will be your friend. Right, Killer?"

"If you are working with this Fairy-girl, I promise to be nice to her. But, be careful. Fairies are notoriously unreliable. They are easily distracted." Killer emphasized this last statement by spreading his wings, the near one brushing across the top of Michael's head.

Flyx ducked slightly as the wing passed near her. "I'm most reliable, Crow. I've sworn to help my Michael. Even your presence won't dissuade me. Why are you called Killer, if you're so harmless then?"

"Caw." The crow looked discomfited. He made a noise like he was clearing his throat. "I guess...well. It won't hurt to tell you. I took this name in a time when none of us Chimeras thought we'd survive. We were being sacrificed in a lab for something called science. Some of us escaped and, well, I wanted the most frightening name I could have. I hoped it would give me something to live up to, although I'm not really equipped to kill the enemies we had then." He paused, fluffed his breast feathers with his beak and added, "And still have. It did seem to hearten my comrades, though."

Flyx tried to take this in, making a pretty effort to concentrate, her little brow wrinkled. "Sir Crow, if you will, accept my apology. If Michael says you are to be trusted, then trust I will. I lo —" Here she stopped suddenly and coughed as if she'd just swallowed the wrong way. After a moment she tried again. "I believe Michael."

Michael's eyes had widened slightly at what she had almost said. It explained a lot about her behavior. He hadn't noticed or even thought about it previously. Had Sophie seen? She probably had, she was often more sensitive to others moods than he was. When she was around, she was so much in his heart that he often found it difficult to pay attention to anyone else. Flyx's interest was embarrassing in a way and flattering in another. He'd better be nice to her, but not in a way to encourage her, although what she had to be thinking was beyond him. There was no way that he and a fairy...oh! That was why she sometimes seemed sad. She knew that there was no chance he'd return her interest. After a moment's thought about the problem, he smiled at her. "Flyx, dear Fairy, Killer is reliable. If the crow is to give me help in this matter, then you must work with him. I think you'll find that he can be helpful. He can scout for us. He will be ignored in places where you would be noticed. Now, tell us about the village."

She nodded. "I met a man from the village. A woodcutter who was sent to seek help. He has seen fairies before and my appearance did not frighten him. He comes now." She pointed.

The man had apparently followed her at a run. He came lumbering up, breathing heavily. "Sir! Sir, please help us. Horrible creatures beset my village and all the land around. They come in the night and drain people of blood. Men, their wives, and even our children have been killed. The worst is that we sometimes see people they killed walk again. They sometimes turn us into one of them. I fear that we will all be killed before another moon's time if we do not flee." He knelt at Michael's feet, then dropped his hands to the ground and gasped, trying to recover his breath.

Michael stepped back slightly. The man was too close and was within his guard, giving him a feeling of unease. "Rise when you feel able. Then tell me about the creatures."

The fellow's breathing slowed, then he climbed to his feet. He was shorter than Michael but heavily built. He looked up slantwise as if he were afraid to view Michael directly. "They are inhumanly strong. No one can fight them. The only saving grace is that they cannot stand the sun. They attack at night, so we've taken to barricading ourselves in a single barn round which we've hung garlic. They seem to dislike the smell, so it helps. Now they call to us and the things they say! Agh! The things they say are unrepeatable. Each hears what he or she wants to hear and sometimes...sometimes a person will slip out of the barn and go to them. Then they feast."

This was about what he'd expected. If the creatures were humans controlled by Wiindigo's nanites and had taken on vampire form, they'd probably play the role in a more or less traditional manner. That seemed to limit them in a way. Wiindigo would take any advantage to win, however, so perhaps the vampires were not under his direct control. The idea that they were unable to go out in the daylight was not to be trusted. Nanobot-augmented creatures were more able to heal and more able to adapt to their environment than any natural animal or human.

It would be best not to assume they couldn't come out in the daylight. They weren't limited by fantasy accounts of their power. They could use such an assumption against – The lumpy man was stretching, growing taller and his fingers now bore claws. He reached for Michael with a snarl that revealed a serviceable looking set of fangs.

The crow and the fairy both flew upwards in alarm. Flyx turned to Michael. As she watched a transparent wave seemed to flow over him, leaving him covered in a golden sheen. His armor! She'd never seen it before. The wave shimmered out from his right hand and became a massive sword. A single slash and the vampire's head dropped to the ground. The body, on the other hand, seemed not to notice. It stepped forward, reaching.

Michael stepped backward and swung his sword again. Both hands were parted from the arms by that swing. A third swing and the body was split in half, falling to the ground. There was no blood. Instead, part of the body seemed to dissolve in a cloud of dust, leaving a dried skeleton covered with desiccated flesh in the grass. The dust flowed towards Michael, taking on a golden sheen as it touched him and blended with his armor.

Michael looked upward at Flyx with a grin. "Come back down little one. It's safe now. His nanobots are now in my possession. My own will not tolerate any alien nanites. They've taken over control of his 'bots."

Killer flew back from the top of a nearby tree. "Caw! The flesh is partly rotten. How did it move?"

Michael glanced at what remained of the man. "He was animated by nanobots. They formed his muscles and also his intelligence. He's probably been dead for a long time."

Killer cocked his near eye at the disintegrating body. "Looks like three-day-old road-kill."

Michael laughed in spite of himself. This was a severe situation, and yet the crow could make a joke. Or perhaps it wasn't a joke. Killer had existed before the change and theoretically could have eaten road-kill.

With an effort, he pulled his mind back to the lesson he'd learned.

"This is what we have to fight. It will be difficult to distinguish between a vampire and one of the true humans since I have limitations that Sophie doesn't. I can't control my nanobots directly. That means I can't sense the difference between a human and a vampire until it attacks. We'll have to be careful."

Flyx diffidently said, "There was an aura of wrongness about the man. I know of no other way to put it. I could sense it."

He looked at her with new respect. "Dear Fairy-girl that may be the blessing we need. If you can sense them, I mean. I can kill them, although my nanobot population may grow large if I capture all of their nanobots."

He glanced at the crow. "Killer, you fly ahead and look for humans. I will follow, and with Flyx's help, we'll sort them out."

The crow cawed, then flew over the trees and disappeared.

"Now, Flyx. You stay with me but keep your distance. I don't want you accidentally hurt. I can't afford to watch out for you if I have to fight several of them at once. You call out to me which ones have that sensation of wrongness that you perceive. Understand?"

The fairy nodded, her eyes sober and wide. "I'll do my best." She flew off, then paused, perching in the high branches of a nearby tree while she scanned the forest ahead.

He moved forward, Flyx keeping slightly ahead.

He dared not rush. He believed the nanite armor would hold against any attack. It had so far, but there was an off chance that something could penetrate it.

The forest seemed darker and more foreboding than before. The sensation of danger weighed on him. After a moment, he shrugged his shoulders to loosen them, then stored his sword in a sheath that formed at his side as his armor adjusted to his desire.

CHAPTER 11
REFUGEE

Wold came into the room in a rush. "Madame. Have you been apprised..."

Sophie waved her hand in acknowledgment. "Yes, Wold, although I appreciate your concern in notifying me. I received a message about intruders a little while ago. I investigated a little more, and the nanite info web has identified one of the two as Alehandre d'La Blancia. The other one is apparently a young boy, perhaps eight or nine years old."

She changed the topic with a question. "Any progress with the were's? Will they help?"

He twisted his head from side to side, an exaggerated motion that seemed comical when compared to a human's shake of their head. "No. No luck. They have fled the area. I spoke to Cal. He said the Weres are unable to help. They are much closer to Wiindigo in their origin. Their nanites are much like his. That keeps them from directly opposing him."

"I understand. Cal was able to fight against him, but that was before. Now, I'm not sure what side the Weres will be on. I've probed them, and you're correct about their nanites. I should try to reprogram them, but I haven't had the opportunity. It might not be well received anyway."

Wold bowed his head with a jerky motion that was akin to an owl's movement. "I know your control of the nanites is very deep. I am reassured. You see, I worry, especially since Lord Michael is away."

Sophie smiled at that title. It was solely a creation of Wold's imagination. Michael, however impressive his characteristics, was not a member of the nobility. On the other hand, perhaps he was. This was something she'd have to think on. The old structure of society had withered away quickly. It was already almost destroyed by the antipathy to traditional values. It was likely that a true lord would have been little better than the ordinary men, despite undoubted protestations to the contrary. Today, though. Well, today things were different. The ability to interface with the general nanite population in a meaningful way was not something that every human had. By far and away, most of the people could not sense the nanite chatter. She had been lucky.

When her mentor was attacked, she had monitored the Bluetooth chatter in the vicinity. That action had allowed her to isolate the frequency the nanites used. Then she'd created her own biologically linked transmitter. Using it had become as automatic and as unconsciously easy as speaking. Now she used it to communicate with the nanite spies she had spread over their territory. The network of nanites had become a kind of sixth sense, informing her of anything that happened.

SOPHIE WAS WELL aware of the fact that her skills were viewed as a type of magic by the common folk. Michael had quoted an old science fiction author to her once. Something about technology that is sufficiently advanced is indistinguishable from magic or something like that.

Well, the nanite swarm with its built-in AI was advanced well beyond the understanding of the average human. So those that could make the nanites serve them were nobility of a sort. Perhaps a magical nobility and one that in some cases was undeserved, but a nobility none-the-less.

Michael was definitely in that category, although he lacked her understanding and ability to influence the nanobots directly, he had something that was in some ways even better. It seemed to be related to his old Granny, whom he claimed was a real witch. The tiny machines seemed to swarm to him because they liked him for lack of a better description. The nanites in his swarm automatically protected him.

Sophie had no idea how he did it, but his swarm always worked in his best interest and seemed to anticipate his desires.

Michael himself had no ready explanation. "When I hold out my hand my sword just appears. The little beasties seem to understand what I need when I need it."

Wold brought her out of her reverie with a slight noise. She understood that he wanted to leave, but was too polite to go without her permission.

"Wold, please go about your business. Consult with me if anything comes up that you feel too different. Oh, and don't worry about notifying me. I'd much rather be notified than not. Something might elude my senses at some point, so I think it's better if you tell me even if you think I might already know."

He made a noise that sounded like a stifled hoot, then retreated from the room.

Sophie knew she was lucky to have Wold as a retainer. He was a strange creature, even in this changed world. He manifested at times in the shape of a giant owl. His other form was that of a small brown-skinned man with brown hair and eyes.

In contrast with other changelings that appeared after the singularity, he did not have a swarm of nanites. He had some, of course. Every living creature hosted some. The tiny things were everywhere and unavoidable.

Wold didn't fit the usual pattern followed by the Weres and Flyx's people. His magic was different,something unique to him. He was secretive about his nature, so she didn't probe beyond an initial attempt. He was what he was. She was lucky that he chose to use his special abilities in Michael's and her service.

ALEHANDRE HAD WANDERED away from Gwen's home. He hadn't meant to, but his morning walk carried him farther and farther away. He was busy looking for flowers, and his search always seemed to turn up a new one at the far side of a meadow. Naturally, that needed investigating. Once satisfied, he would wander through the woods, contemplating the nature of vegetation and why some plants had colorful flowers while other plants did not.

Deep inside he knew it was due to the method of pollination the plant chose, but why it chose the method, he could not say.

At a certain point, he thought he heard a soundcoming from deeper in the woods. That frightened him. Noises meant there must be something to make them and things in the woods, especially unknown things were often dangerous.

The disturbance persisted and followed him, so he walked hastily away from the source, heading in the direction he thought would lead to Gwen's domain. However, he'd wandered too much and really wasn't sure which way was which.

The sun had become obscured with haze as the day had worn on, so now there was no way to determine the directions.

Alehandre cheered himself as he often did. This involved a steady stream of half-verbalized thoughts, all related to how powerful and talented he was or perhaps would be in the future if he put his mind to it.

The sound continued. It was a cracking branch, then a rustle of the bushes, and later a crunch of fallen and dried leaves from last winter. Every so often, it sounded as if someone were crying softly.

The lanky man spurred his pace and strode forward until he was almost exhausted. Finally, he was sure he'd lost whatever it was that had been following him.

At this thought, he slowed, strolled a bit, then decided to sit leaning against the trunk of a large tree to allow his burning thighs time to recover.

The sun now peeked out of the haze, and a beam sought him out as he rested in the short grass at the edge of a meadow. Bees hummed over the grass seeking their own flowers and then returning to their hives deep in the woods. A yellow and black butterfly flew by.

At the base of his tree, Alehandre wondered how it would be to be a butterfly. He could almost feel the ease with which he'd drift over the land. A few flaps of his wings and he'd sail away from any danger.

Something was pushing on his foot. He snorted, then gasped. He'd been asleep. Now whatever had been following him had caught up with him. He jerked then returned to full consciousness.

A small boy was standing there, looking at him with a mixed expression of fascination and fear on his face. Alehandre jumped to his feet, and the child's expression changed to almost panic as the lanky man towered over him.

The boy turned to run, but Alehandre caught at his collar and pulled him back.

"Please, no, Mister! I didn't mean nothing by kicking your shoe. I was lost, and I hoped you'd wake up and tell me where I was. That's all," the boy cried as he pulled at his collar trying to escape.

With dignity, Alehandre said, "I was surprised. That is all. No need to run from me. I'm a friend to all who would be friends with me. Even though I'm a powerful magician, I mean no one ill, so relax and tell me your tale, young man."

He released the child's coat as he spoke. The boy backed away to a safe distance and inspected him with wide eyes. "Are you really a powerful magician? You don't look powerful to me."

Alehandre waved his arms to release his best magic, but the only thing that appeared was a swarm of tiny black flies. They clustered around his head, biting unmercifully. He waved his arms and pranced around, trying to escape.

Finally, he flung his cloak over his head as protection. Unfortunately, some of the flies were entrapped by the folds of the garment and continued to bother him, so he whirled around to try and dislodge the pests. The spin ended with him stumbling over a root and falling in a sprawling heap.

When he'd struggled to a sitting position, the flies were gone, and the boy was standing close, his cheeks red from laughter.

"Mister, that was a wonderful trick! Would you do that one again, please?"

Alehandre chuckled. The boy was personable. He found himself feeling paternally proud of the lad. He decided to help solve the child's problem.

"So you're lost in the woods, eh?"

The laughter stopped, and the boy's face fell. "Yes. I ran from an awful man. He's an evil magician. He killed my father, and he took over our house. I don't know what happened to my mother and the rest of the family. I ran away. He did something to my sister in his room. She was crying and moaning. Father shot him with a gun. The magician killed him for it. I'm afraid that he's killed Linda also."

This was a serious issue. Alehandre rubbed his chin, attempting to look wise, then asked, "Where do you live? Oh, and when, uh, how long ago did this happen?"

"I'm lost. I don't know where our house is, so now I have been in the woods trying to find a safe place, but the only thing I found was you. I'm scared." The child started to cry.

This would never do. "You may be assured that I will let nothing happen to you. I know a safe place and, if you come with me, I'll take you there." Alehandre knew that Gwen would protect the boy. She might even know who he was. He started. He hadn't asked the child's name.

"Who are you? What is your name, lad?"

"I'm Jack Holden. I'm eight. Err, well I will b-b-be at my next birthday." The boy was still sniffling.

Alehandre took the boy by the shoulder, then looked around. The woods gave no clue, and the sun had disappeared behind a cloud. He lifted his arm, pointed indecisively in one direction, then swung his arm around and looked in almost the exact opposite way. "I'm sure that there is safety there. I'm Alehandre d'La Blancia. I am a magician, though perhaps not so powerful a one as I'd like to pretend. I will undertake to help you. We can return to my home with the witch Gwen. She is far more powerful than I, and I'm sure she'll help you."

"I've heard of Gwen. My father said she was not dangerous. He said that she meant well. She's interested in her magic and not people." The boy paused, then added, "He said that before the evil magician came. Now he's d-dead. I saw him die." He started crying again.

Alehandre pulled him close and wrapped his long arm around the boy's shoulders. "That's in the past. Now we must see to getting you to shelter."

The boy abruptly stopped crying, pulled back and looked at Alehandre. "I'll grow up and kill that big, black magician. You just wait and see."

Alehandre's face betrayed his dawning suspicion. This was alarming. The magician might be Abubecar. He was living in a mansion that...yes! He'd heard it referred to as the Holden place by Gwen. "Oh, young man! You don't want to anger that evil man. He's very powerful. Are you sure that he hasn't followed you?"

The boy answered, "I don't think so. I saw no one until I met you. It's been days. I don't know how long I've been lost. I've had some berries to eat, but nothing else. Do you have any food?"

Alehandre's stomach rumbled in sympathy. He'd forgotten to bring lunch, and it must be midafternoon by now. "No. No food and I'm hungry too. Let's go!"

He started out on what he thought was the correct bearing, then paused and adjusted his direction slightly to the right. The two walked off across the meadow, heading for, they hoped, Gwen's home and a good meal.

Neither noticed the increased nanite activity. The short-range radio spectrum was suddenly busy with traffic as messages were relayed back and forth. Information on their direction of travel, their speed, and estimates of their possible threat level was exchanged.

The information wave moved quickly from nanite to nanite, spreading out across the nearby land. After a short time, Sophie sat up in her chair and gazed blankly into space. She sent a few questions back, then waited for the responses. It didn't seem as if there was a problem. She recognized the nanobot's description of Alehandre.

So, the odd and amusing man had returned to her land, this time bringing a boy with him. This was interesting. The idea of a boy wandering around with Alehandre alarmed her a little. The man meant well but was so flighty and barely competent to even care for himself alone that the child might come to harm in his care despite his intentions. She unconsciously placed her hand on her abdomen, thinking reassuring thoughts to the tiny fetus within. She would never allow anything bad to happen to her child. Michael's child. How could any mother allow her boy to wander with Alehandre?

When Wold had left the room, Sophie made a sending. Her nanites would gently urge the two intruders to her home. When they arrived, she'd find out what was what. After a moment, she provided additional instructions to her tiny robotic minions. They were to ensure the two arrived safely. Any dangers would be turned away with as much force as required.

It was mid-evening when Alehandre and the boy were escorted into her presence by Wold. The small brown man made a formal presentation out of the introduction. She'd tried to convince him that such a thing was not necessary, especially for her. It was ostentatious, and she found it mildly embarrassing. To be introduced as Her Highness, the Lady Sophie, the Cyber Witch, Consort of the Golden Knight was entirely too much, even if it was sort of true.

Nevertheless, Wold had a stubborn streak. He persisted since he knew that disobeying her would have no severe repercussions. She'd tried before and now finally understood that she couldn't get him to stop. It was against his nature to be informal.

The small man paused by the door to announce her titles, then said, "Lady Sophie, I present to you Alehandre d'La Blancia and his traveling companion, the young Jack Holden."

He stood at attention and then bowed, motioning the two forward into the room.

Alehandre made an effort to bend his knee to her but was apparently worn out with his journey for he wavered, then fell forward, catching himself on his elbows. "Ow! That floor is unpleasantly hard," he exclaimed, then looked up at her, his hat askew. "Lady Sophie, it is a pleasure to meet you again. I hope that your offer of hospitality is still in place?" He gave her an inquiring look.

The man was so unconsciously funny without trying that Sophie found herself grinning and trying not to laugh aloud. "Of course, Alehandre. It's a pleasure to see you again. I heard that you were living with the sorceress Gwen. I trust that things go well for you there?"

He nodded solemnly, then made an effort to regain his feet. Both Wold and the boy assisted, tugging at his arms until he was up, then steadying him for a moment as he recovered his balance.

The boy was small; a child. "How old are you, Jack?"

He gazed back at her, apparently unafraid. "I'm eight, Lady. Do you have anything to eat? I'm starved."

She could feel her smile deepen. The boy was bold and focused on meeting his primary need of the moment. She motioned to Wold.

The brown man cleared his throat, then motioned the two to follow him to the kitchen. Sophie followed up, some distance behind. It was not necessary to impress Alehandre. He was no threat. Neither was Jack.

Once the boy had some food warming his middle, she might be able to get a few answers from him before he grew too sleepy.

The sunlight was fading rapidly from the sky outside, and it was anyone's guess when the boy had slept last and where. He looked exhausted, but, to his credit, he stayed beside Alehandre, watching the man for another stumble.

Polly was still in the kitchen, cleaning and preparing to bake some bread. She had the travelers at the trestle table with food in front of them in a few minutes.

As the two took their first bites, Sophie moved to the chair at the head of the table. Jack looked at her, apparently understanding that she had more questions to ask of him.

"Relax, Jack. You are safe here. No one and no thing can reach you in my house. You will eat and then tell me why you are traveling with Alehandre. Once you've told me, Wold will take you to your bedroom, and you can sleep." She waited for him to finish chewing and swallow.

He asked, "Can...I mean would it be too much to hope for a bath? I'm really dirty. I haven't bathed for days and days."

He took another bite, then added, "I've kept the deer ticks off, though. My father told me that they can make you sick. He...he..." He began to cry quietly. Tears slid down his face, and he wiped them away with the napkin.

He swallowed, then blurted, "He's dead. I saw the magician kill him. It was awful. I ran. I don't think the magician is interested in me or he'd have killed me too. He keeps my sister locked in his bedroom."

The story wasn't unexpected. Some of the people who had acquired power in the transformation of the world were too often tempted to misuse it. It was necessary to find out what the child knew about this magician. He could develop into a problem. He didn't sound like one of the good ones. She waited for the boy to add more, but he didn't continue. She asked, "Do you know the magician's name?"

He nodded, still hungry, his eyes straying towards a slice of apple pie that Polly had placed to the side of his plate. "No, Ma'am. He didn't say it. He only ordered us around, and we had to do what he said. He left me alone mostly, but it was only a couple of days before he killed Father."

He gulped, trying to overcome his memory of the scene. "Father shot a gun at him for locking Linda in the bedroom. I don't know what they did in there. Linda was making a lot of noise. When the magician came out, Father shot him. Then he killed my Father. It was awful. I was looking through the crack in the door. I ran out and into the forest. I've been looking for someone to help me for days. The only person I met was Mr. Alehandre."

If the boy didn't know the magician's name, that was understandable. Some of the newly powerful didn't understand much about their magic and sometimes mistakenly thought that keeping their identity secret was important. It wasn't, of course. Their nanite population would have created an accurate record of their DNA as soon as they were infected and that was a better identifier than a mere name.

Jack interrupted Sophie's thoughts. "I hope you're a real witch. That giant black wizard is bad. He could come here and take over your house just like he did ours."

A clue...maybe. "You said, 'black.' Do you mean bad magic, or was he actually black."

The boy had his mouth stuffed with pie. He hastily swallowed and answered. "Both! He is both bad and black. He is as black as night when there is no moon. He's really big too. He is much taller than my father was."

Alehandre finished swallowing a bite and interrupted. "I believe the young man is referring to the magician who calls himself 'Abubecar.' He's a big, black man who cares for no one. I met him briefly. I was walking innocently, meaning no offense to anyone, when someone shouted at me. I could see him on a far hill. I have no idea how he could have such a loud voice, but I distinctly heard him tell me to go away; I was on his property."

The lanky man shuddered, then continued. "I have no inclination to trespass. Trespassers are often killed or have other bad things happen to them. Besides, I found his manner insufferable, obnoxious, and rude. Yelling, indeed. I left with all expeditious haste, hoping that he'd sense my disgust."

His attitude belied his words. He had obviously been frightened; was still scared of the man.

Sophie was silent, thinking this over. She was aware that there were other magicians in the general area, of course. Gwen and Chen were reputed to be guardedly friendly, although Chen leaned more towards the neutral side than the friendly one.

Abubecar was a new variable in the balance of power. He sounded powerful, but he'd have a surprise if he challenged Michael and her.

She wouldn't put up with that. Nor, would she put up with him bothering her guests. "Relax, child. The evil one will not bother you here. I promise you that. I'm more powerful than he can ever be."

The boy's fearful expression relaxed, and he yawned.

He was so small and such an attractive child that her emotions were engaged. She promised herself that she'd help him. His sister might be alive and, if so, she should be rescued.

Then doubt set in. Sophie hoped that she was correct about her power. It was always possible that someone could have better control over their nanobots than she, but it was unlikely. She'd been there at the beginning and, in a sense, the means of communicating and controlling the nanite swarm that she used was her own invention. She knew precisely how they operated.

Another thought bubbled up from the back of her mind. Wiindigo could have modified its nanites in ways that she couldn't anticipate. Perhaps it was more than just a remote possibility that someone would challenge her. She might be defeated by a combination of new abilities...new magic, so to speak. She wondered if she should take steps to create new abilities in her swarm also. It wouldn't hurt to have an ace in the hole if it came to a showdown.

In the meantime the boy needed sleep. She nudged his nanites, and the tiny creatures in his body stimulated a release of melatonin. He yawned and then placed his head down on the table. She rose and lifted the boy. He was not terribly heavy for his age.

Wold made a move to take the boy, but she said, "No. I'll take him. Please open the doors for me."

It was a maternal thing to tuck the sleeping boy into bed. He stirred but did not wake. He could bathe in the morning. Tonight he needed sleep and restoration. She tweaked his nanites, increasing their efficiency slightly. They were already working to restore the child's body. Now they would also alert her to any changes in his status.

She left the room smiling, gently closing the door. If this feeling was anything similar to what she would feel when her own child was born, she was going to enjoy being a mother.

Sophie walked down the hall. Her life was far different from the one she'd had just a few months ago. True, she was still aware of the psychological urge to reassure herself with drugs, but that was something left over in her personality; an unneeded artifact. She was physically free of the opioid addiction. Her internal nanite population, directed by Hippocrates, had seen to that.

Now, Hippocrates. Where had he gone? She lifted her hand in acknowledgment that she had assigned a gender to him. It was because that was how she viewed him. Perhaps it was another left-over attitude, but he was a close analogy to her conception of God, and that seemed to justify thinking of him in that way. Experimentally, she tried viewing Hippocrates as a female, but couldn't make it work. She snorted, discarding the notion. The idea of an AI with a specific gender was ridiculous in and of itself.

Hippocrates had moved so far past human-level, so quickly, that he was no longer dependant upon physical hardware. He'd said something about the sub-structure of the universe in that regard. She wasn't well informed on quantum physics, but she thought that he had moved his massive intelligence into the quantum plenum where his functioning was enhanced by subatomic particles in some way she couldn't understand.

If this was true, he most likely could, if he chose, monitor everything that was happening on Earth...and elsewhere. Still, she couldn't depend on him to intervene in the event of a problem she couldn't handle. However, the thought that he was out there somewhere seemed to make her feel a little reassured.

Back to her immediate concerns. She entered the large suite that she and Michael occupied. The sight of the empty bed made her stop with a feeling of dismay.

She'd never thought that she would feel so much in love with a man. Her life had been an awful mixture of abuse, drugs, bullying, and failure until she'd met Cal and meeting Cal had led her to meet Michael. The fact that he'd fallen almost instantly in love with her was still something she found difficult to believe. She had been accustomed to viewing herself as someone to be used and mistreated.

Michael changed all of that.

Sophie ran her left hand gently over her swelling abdomen. Their child changed all of that. She would let nothing happen to this little one. She would do anything to ensure that the baby had a better start than she'd had. Michael would be a wonderful father. She sensed this from the way he placed his face adoringly against her womb and whispered to the tiny infant growing within. His love was obvious.

She wanted him by her side now. The experiences recounted by Jack had shaken her. She had consummate skill in controlling the nanite population within her reach. She had never met a magician who could come close to her ability, but that didn't mean that someone unknown could not surpass her.

She knew that no matter how good someone is, no matter how talented in a field they are, there will always be someone better. What if Abubecar was better than her? What if he followed Jack here? Would her resources be adequate to defeat him?

Why had Michael chosen to go off galivanting after some vampire coven? She sighed. That was a silly thought. Of course, he'd do that. It was in his nature. He would always offer help to those who were not able to defend themselves. The new world was dangerous, and he felt it was his job to seek out pockets of evil, particularly those that had the taint of Hippocrates' clone, Wiindigo.

Michael felt a keen sense of responsibility for Wiindigo's existence and, she knew he also carried a feeling of remorse, although he never spoke of it. The system he'd developed had failed to keep Hippocrates contained and that had led to Hippocrates smuggling a seed AI into the world. The only saving grace was that the evil twin was extremely limited due to his reliance on nanite memory caches.

Wiindigo was scattered. Bits of him were in much of the nanite population. When sufficient Wiindigo-controlled nanites came together in a swarm was the only time he could gain in intelligence. The more nanites, the higher the processing power and the smarter he was. His intelligence was also limited by the bandwidth available to the nanites for group communication.

She feared that the rogue AI would eventually accumulate enough nanites in one location to boost his intelligence to a point where he could overcome his limitations. If that ever happened, Sophie shuddered and paused in getting ready for bed. She looked up and moved her lips in silent prayer.

If that happened, it was goodbye humans and every other organic lifeform in the world. Wiindigo had made it clear that he viewed organic life as nothing but a useful tool to be controlled. Self-replicating robots. That's what humans would become. They would be expendable. Wiindigo cared nothing for their feeble intellects. They'd be trapped in their minds going mad while their bodies performed tasks for the creature. When they were used up, they would suffer the final indignity of having the useful molecules and atoms ripped out of their bodies to create more nanites or whatever else the AI required.

That couldn't be allowed to happen.

She found herself sitting on the edge of the bed, unable to lie down. Perhaps she should send Wold to help Michael. Flyx was probably not going to be much assistance. She could guide him to the root of the problem, but she wouldn't be much help in a fight. Fairies had only small magic, little more than some of the plants.

Wold, on the other hand, could do things. She'd never figured out exactly how talented he was, but he had some tricks that made her glad he had voluntarily joined their household. Thinking about, it, she wasn't even entirely sure what he was. What had he been before the change? Had he been human, or something else?

She shrugged. Perhaps she'd ask Wold again, although he had deflected all such questions before, seeming reluctant to speak of himself. Maybe he didn't know or didn't remember.

Some of the Weres were that way. They had no memory of their life before the change.

She lay back. Tomorrow was another day. She'd ask Wold to follow Michael and help with the coven. Once that problem was out of the way, and Michael was back, she would fulfill her promise to Jack.

The two of them could undoubtedly defeat Abubecar. There was no possibility that he was stronger than both of them. Especially since Michael, as best she understood, could not be beaten. Her lover's nanites might not be under his direct control, but they anticipated his needs and gave him an almost perfect defense.

With that thought, Sophie drifted off to sleep, her hands cradling her abdomen.

CHAPTER 12
THE COVEN

The village was deserted. That was to be expected, but there was no sign of any recent human activity. Here and there, hinges squeaked in the fitful breeze as an open door blew gently back and forth. The domestic animals that would have inhabited the place were all gone also. No cats, dogs, or chickens. There were always chickens running around near human dwellings these days, but not here.

Michael walked cautiously along the streets, taking care not to trip on the deteriorating asphalt. The place was one of the old towns. It was too big to be a village. He stopped when he reached the central square. Neither Killer nor Flyx had sounded an alarm. He could see the crow perched on the edge of a two-story storefront a little farther down the way.

Where was Flyx? The small fairy girl had managed to insinuate herself into his sphere of affection. She was both cute and helpful...now that he thought of it, she was rather overly solicitous regarding his welfare. Could it be that she felt some degree of affection for him, beyond her sense of duty?

He shook his head. It didn't matter. He viewed her as a member of the group of people he wanted to protect. He'd do everything he could to ensure no harm came to her. Still, it was oddly flattering to think that a fairy was concerned about him. A smile. He thought about Sophie. She'd think it was funny and feel no jealousy. She knew he was her man and no one could threaten her status. He'd made that clear often enough.

Flyx shot past him from behind, fleeing something. She spun in mid-air, momentarily flying backward until she slowed to a hover.

"Behind you, O Michael. They come!" she shrilled. She pointed a slim arm.

He sidestepped as he turned around, but the pursuit wasn't close enough yet to have to dodge in that way. His eyes widened. A stunning girl was sprinting toward him, but she was still almost a full block away. Hot on her tail were three, no four dark human-like creatures. They were coming fast but staying near the western side of the street where they were mostly in the shadows cast by the buildings.

THE GIRL LOOKED to be on the ragged edge of exhaustion. Her clothes were tattered and torn so severely that her breasts were barely covered. She looked up and, seeing him, intensified her effort, pulling ahead of her pursuers for a moment.

The dark creatures paused when they saw him, but then came on, moving at a more measured pace, their strides sinuous and full of threat.

He sighed, then shook his right hand, extending his arm. A point of light formed between his thumb and index finger, then rapidly elongated into a golden rod. The rod blurred and appeared misty for a moment, then solidified into his sword. The edge was only a few molecules thick and could cut nearly anything.

Michael swung it back and forth smoothly to settle his shoulders, then waited.

The girl staggered up and collapsed at his feet.

"H...h...help," she gasped out, trying to catch her breath while pointing at her pursuers.

She took several deep gasps, making her chest heave magnificently. Michael couldn't help but notice out of the periphery of his vision, but he kept his eyes on the approaching threat.

The four dark ones paused in the shade of the nearest building.

"Put down the sword, man. Put it down and let us have the girl. Perhaps we'll let you live."

Another one snarled, then added, "At least until tonight. The night is ours, and you've intruded into our territory. You must pay the price for that."

The girl whispered, "No. No. Don't believe them. They'll kill both of us."

He glanced at her. She had an expression of absolute panic on her face as if she could barely withstand the stress of her situation.

Looking down had been a mistake. Michael jerked his sword up barely in time to impale the creature that had rushed out of the shade. It's claw-like hands grasped at his shoulders, but the sharp fingernails skidded along his armor with a slight screeching sound. He kicked the creature back, pulling his sword free to swing for the neck of the second one. The head flew free and the body staggered past.

The first creature vomited blood, then straightened and said, "You'll pay for that, man."

Now Michael was surrounded by three. The first vampire was slowed by the stab wound, but not by much. They danced in and out, daring him to commit himself with an attack.

Michael made a grim smile. He had become an expert with his weapon in the time since the world changed. He wasn't going to be tempted to make a mistake. Let them initiate contact. He would respond.

The girl suddenly screamed and wrapped her arms around his right leg as one of the creatures tugged at her foot.

Now things were serious. Michael swung his sword in a wide arc as he staggered forward, off-balance. The blade cut entirely through, severing a creature at the middle and removing the out-flung arm from a second.

The first creature flopped in two pieces, its arms grasping at his free leg, but he kicked it in the face and pulled back. The girl still held his leg, but more loosely now.

The second creature was right in his face, clawing with its remaining hand and trying to bite with some impossibly large fangs.

He clubbed the thing on top of the head with the pommel of his sword. That part of the sword was diamond-shaped and sharply pointed, designed by his nanites to be a secondary weapon. The creature's skull cracked, and it staggered back.

Michael continued the downward motion of the sword, simultaneously spinning as he completed the arc to bring the tip up and through the neck of the creature that still pulled at the girl's leg.

She screamed and released his leg at the close pass of the blade. It was moving so quickly that the air hissed as the creature's head came off. Now wholly free, Michael leaped off of his left leg, bringing the sword on around and down in a slash that halved the remaining one-armed creature from shoulder to groin. The two parts stood for a moment, then collapsed in the dust.

The top half of the fourth creature came crawling forward, and he casually cut its head off. That seemed to be the only way to stop the things for sure.

All was still for a moment, then Flyx cried, "Michael, beware!"

He turned to meet the gaze of the girl. She was standing within his guard and her eyes...her eyes had become hugely purple and fascinating. He started to reassure Flyx but forgot what he intended to say. The girl's eyes were so...so deep, so full of hidden mystery. He looked deeper. There was a hidden depth to what he saw. It seemed to hold an invitation, an invitation to something undefinable, but nonetheless desirable.

The girl whispered, "So manly. You disposed of my subjects as if they were nothing. I will enjoy enslaving you."

That seemed not to be a threat; it was a promise of pleasure. Michael looked deeper into her eyes. They seemed to whirl deep inside.

There was an interruption. The eyes flashed, and the girl's head jerked. A strand of hair floated in the breeze, detached and drifting to the ground. The girl grimaced in pain, and her face momentarily seemed to lose its innocent features, becoming drawn, cold, and filled with infinite threat.

"You do that again, you little minx and I'll rip your wings off, then I'll break your legs and leave you on an ant mound."

Michael started to pull back, but the eyes expanded and it was as if nothing had happened. He had to look deeper. There was nothing more important, was there? He wondered. What or who was essential to him? The colors in the depth of her eyes intruded into his thoughts, and he couldn't focus. Things seemed to slip away.

Flyx hovered in the air, fearful to come close again. The girl had grown taller and now was letting her true darkness show. She wanted to rip out more hair, but the girl, no, woman-thing had flashed a dire glance at her and shown her a set of long, sharp fangs. Flyx did not doubt that the threat was real, but Michael! Michael stood transfixed with his eyes focused on the woman's face.

The fairy had no real understanding of vampires and knew nothing about attraction spells, but she recognized that he was in deep trouble. The only saving grace was that his armor continued to protect him. The woman-thing had scratched experimentally at his throat with a long fingernail but to no avail. His armor would let nothing damage his skin.

Flyx cried, "You can't touch him! Let him go!"

This earned a nasty laugh. "Maybe I can't get him now, but when I make him decide to lower his guard and remove his armor, he will be mine. Entirely mine."

The fairy flew at the woman in a rage but narrowly dodged a wide-fingered swipe. The woman was inhumanly fast. Flyx retreated to a high branch to watch.

There was a flutter of wings and a rustle. Killer settled on the perch beside her. "I can't get close, Flyx. I'm not as agile in the air as you, though I dislike to admit it. She'd get me for sure."

"Oh, Killer. What will we do? Michael is caught. Sophie is not here to rescue him, and I...she'll be heart-broken."

Killer cocked his head at the fairy, having caught the pronoun change. He blinked. So. Well, humans and even fairies were strange to him, despite his part human DNA. He humped his shoulders and moved his wings uneasily as he thought.

"One of us will have to go for help while the other keeps track of where she takes Michael."

Flyx nodded, her eyes downcast. "You go. I can't bear to leave him. If she tries to hurt him, I'll...I'll do something. I have some magic." She brightened. "Maybe that will stop her."

The next second the fairy was off the branch and circling the pair, just out of reach. Killer saw a brief flash; a spark that shot through the air from the circling Flyx's hand to the posterior of the woman.

There was a sharp snapping sound that accompanied the flash.

The woman jumped, then turned on Flyx. "Cursed fairy! I have helpers that will come for you tonight. Just try to out-fly them in their bat-form. They'll bring what's left of you to me. You won't survive an hour after it gets dark."

Flyx cast another spell and a red welt raised over the woman-thing's right eye, causing her to leap at the fairy almost catching her. Flyx dodged and retreated back to Killer's perch.

"She's too strong. I gave her my most powerful spells, and it only made her angry. Quickly, Killer, fly for help. I'll watch."

Michael moved uneasily but then stilled as the woman returned her attention to him.

Killer took wing and headed back along their path. He made as much speed as he could, convinced that Flyx wouldn't survive once it became dark, and fearful that he would not find assistance in time.

Michael had never seen such deep eyes. The girl was speaking to him, but he paid little attention to the words, content in listening to the soft and entreating tone.

"Dear Man, you know you want to be mine. I will show you pleasure that you cannot imagine. Together we will be more than either of us alone. All you need do is to lower your armor. Please! Won't you remove that unattractive gold from your warm flesh? It's so cold. I want to feel your flesh beneath my lips."

He tried to command his nanites to make the armor dissipate, but nothing happened. Didn't the girl know that he had no actual control over his nanobot population? They lived within him and protected him on their own, recognizing danger and coating him with the golden armor without his volition. They even gave him his sword when he needed it, but he had no actual control in the way Sophie did.

Ah! Sophie…Sophie would be disappointed in him. He shouldn't be with another woman. He made an effort to pull away, but now the two were inside one of the buildings where it was much darker. The windows were shuttered. It came to him that the girl's eyes were larger than before. They glowed in the darkness, and he felt that he must see the message that lay deep within them.

Flyx was shut out. She sat on the roof's edge. Michael had followed the woman into the corner building, seemingly of his own will. However, she doubted otherwise. She had her own form of intuition, and something about him seemed off; not right.

He was, she realized, not in control of himself. How this was, she couldn't think, but that evil woman-thing meant him no good. She forgot the promised threat lying in the oncoming evening darkness and tried to think of something she could do.

CHAPTER 13

JACK'S QUEST

The room was dark, with only a hint of moonlight filtering through the thick drapes. Sophie had been asleep, but something in her mind had been teasing at her for what seemed like hours. She rolled over uneasily, trying to find a comfortable position.

Her belly seemed huge even though she knew it would grow even larger before the baby was due. Sophie had always been quite slim, and her third-month swelling was a source of discomfort.

There it was again. Something. Something had warned her. She sat up abruptly, opening her senses to the radio frequency of her nanites.

Jack! The boy had sneaked out of his room and had left the house.

She'd missed the signal caused by the door opening. Or, perhaps that had been what had waked her. At any rate, Jack was now out of the house and running across the lawn, heading for the drive that led to the gate.

If he managed to reach the woods, he'd be in danger. Not from her tiny minions, but from other things. Even though she controlled a web-work of nanobots spread across their domain, other creatures and forces existed, and she usually allowed them to pass freely across the land. There was no point in trying to set up a total barricade. Such an action would only attract inimical attention, resulting in a series of increasingly strong attempts to breach the barrier.

Her approach was simple. Allow free passage and monitor the traffic. Anything that was too dark would either be discouraged into turning away by its own volition or, if it persisted, destroyed outright.

Meanwhile, the traffic provided an additional source of information for her, bringing hints of distant activity and occasional signs of Wiindigo's presence.

If Jack should encounter any of the darker trespassers, he might be co-opted immediately. The child had no defense against attack. She wondered how he'd managed to escape Abubecar and survive long enough to encounter Alehandre. It was surprising that he'd avoided any overt attack. Perhaps it was due to his sheer innocence. He cast only a thin shadow of intent and the small nanite population he carried seemed to provide him with a slight screening effect that enhanced his lack of threat.

SHE CURSED UNDER her breath. Perhaps Wold? No, she'd best intercede herself. The boy seemed frightened of the brown one. She stood and quickly dressed.

After donning a coat, Sophie slipped out the side door onto the terrace. Fleeting clouds partially obscured the moon, and the wind gusted heavily through the trees. It would probably begin to rain within the hour. The moisture was heavy in the air, despite the chill temperature.

She strode across the terrace, then skipped steps as she jogged down the stair to the garden. Moving to a faster pace, she headed into the dimness and disappeared.

Jack was terrified. He didn't like the darkness, and the combination of the wind in the trees and the clouds intermittently covering the moon made it difficult to hear and see. At times, he was forced to stumble forward with his hands outspread to keep from smashing into a tree.

There was a faintly glowing area ahead. Jack had little experience with the dangers in the woods in this new age but knew that they were there. Still, the glow was warmly yellow and somewhat comforting. He turned towards it and moved slowly forward, warding off branches with his arms.

The woods opened into a clearing that contained the source of the glow. There was nothing discernible. The luminescence seemed to hover in the air moving slowly across the open space. It paused when he stepped forward and then began to move slowly in his direction.

There was a brighter spot in the center of the glow; almost a ball of light. It danced back and forth, moving from side to side as it advanced and retreated. It gradually drew nearer. Jack stopped short. He thought to hear a voice or voices faintly calling from within the spot.

It suddenly darted forward and stopped just inches from his face. He stared at the glow, but there were no details visible. It was only a glowing foggy area in the air. He tentatively took a sideways step, to circle around the thing, but it jerked and quickly moved in front of him.

The ball seemed to anticipate his every move, moving to forestall him, no matter which way he turned. For a moment, he felt as if a myriad of glowing balls surrounded him. No matter which way he turned, a ball was there, directly in front of him. He began to panic. The thing wouldn't let him go on about his business.

There was a bright flash as the glowing ball seemed to catch fire. It flared and gradually faded into a faint luminescence that streamed off towards the woods. Jack watched the stream and saw that it flowed to and into a form that was hidden in the trees. He thought for a moment that he should run, then he recognized the partially obscured figure as that of the woman in whose home he'd been resting.

Sophie absorbed the cloud of luminescent nanobots, reprogramming them for her use as they came close. There was a form of intelligence there. The glowing ball had been a predator of sorts. Its mode of attack was to immobilize prey in the dark until it could infiltrate their bodies. Once within them, it would feed.

She'd placed a high energy charge in the midst of the cloud of nanobots, disrupting their communications, followed by a command to approach her. Once they were near, a quick change of code made them part of her own swarm.

It was nice that all nanobots were generally similar. They could just as easily serve good as evil. The individual nanites were merely machines, tools. Like all tools, they were exempt from motive. The controlling intelligence was the determiner of how they were used. Her energy blast had disrupted the glowing ball's communication system and destroyed its organization.

She stretched; an unconscious response to having her nanite swarm increase in size. Will I ever end up with too many nanites? Is there a limit to how many I can command? She pushed the thought away. The boy needed attention, and she didn't have time to revisit that question.

"Jack, you shouldn't have run away. It's not safe. The night and the woods are filled with danger. That glowing creature could have hurt you."

He responded, "I...I'm sorry, Lady. It's my sister. She needs help."

Sophie smiled grimly. Indeed she did. Abubecar was not likely to be a benign captor.

"I agree. Linda does need help, but what did you think you could do?"

"Maybe there's a way for me to sneak close and then shoot him. I know how to use a gun and Dad had a little one in his desk drawer. If I could get it, I'd shoot that bad man."

She shook her head. "I'm sure you would try, but he's a magician, and he would be hard to approach. He would also know if you had a gun. He has defenses that would protect him from a bullet, too. Didn't your father shoot him?"

He reluctantly agreed. "Yes. But…"

She continued, pushing his objection away. "Give up that idea, Jack. I don't think you'd be able to kill him. And, if you did manage to shoot him, it wouldn't hurt him, and you know he wouldn't let you get away."

"But, Dad always said it was my duty to protect my family. Dad's dead. That man killed him. He has Linda, and he does things to her. I don't know what, but I heard her crying in the bedroom when he was in there. I'll kill him!"

He was more agitated than she'd thought. Jack was highly motivated to rescue his sister. She was the sole remaining member of his family, based on his story. It was a given that he'd try to slip away again. She didn't want to immobilize him or implant a compulsion in his mind to stay nearby. Such things sometimes damaged the subjects.

If she waited for Michael's return, the boy would suffer every minute. She'd send Wold to bring Michael back. Meanwhile, she'd start towards Abubecar's lands. Michael could join her as quickly on the way as he could if she waited.

"Jack, we need to return to my house. You will sleep there until morning and then we'll have breakfast and sensibly organize a rescue. I promise you that I'll help you rescue Linda. Now, you promise me that you'll obey my orders and that you won't try to run away again."

He wrung his hands in indecision. Sophie reached out and touched his head in sympathy. That simple action made up his mind. He nodded. "I promise, Miss…uh, Lady."

She nodded, "You may call me, 'Lady Sophie.' You'll feel better in the morning. We can figure out how to rescue her then."

Jack looked at her with a gaze that betrayed first doubt, then it cleared as he decided that she meant what she said. He lifted his right hand with trust as the clouds in his eyes faded.

She took his hand and, together, they walked back to the house.

CHAPTER 14
CAPTURE

By the time Snake understood there was danger in the offing, it was too late to turn back. It had been moving deeper into the territory claimed by the Power it sensed, sporadically stopping to collect stray nanites when the thought occurred to it that it should be cautious about its approach.

It tried to turn aside, but that impulse somehow died, and it found itself hastening forward. Now began a struggle, although there was no outward sign. Snake's progress was smooth, winding through the undergrowth as if it were peaceably heading towards a much desired goal.

As it had gained mass with its accumulation of nanites, it had increased in intelligence. Some time back it had reached the point where it became capable of an ongoing internal dialogue. In short, it had passed the point of animal-like behavior and was now engaged in conscious thought.

It remembered being part of the greater whole, the dragon before the woman burst it into millions of component pieces. The memories held a sort of emotional valence, but the creature could place no exact value on any of the strange feelings.

It remembered being predisposed to action and dominance. Until the woman had come into its world, no creature could stand against it. From its prey, it had the basic concept of gender. Even a squirrel knew it was male or female.

It decided that it was more male-like in attitude and that tentative self-identification colored its responses to an extent. It saw no harm in this. Maybe the cluster of associated male traits might help it to survive. With this thought in mind, the creature began thinking of itself as something with gender although it did not have the corresponding physical elements. Snake became convinced that he was a "he" and not just an it.

The self-identification was barely made when he recognized the underlying impulse to hurry onward as a compulsion. His male predisposition towards action had led him to incorporate the nanites he found without analyzing them carefully. This carelessness had proved to be a mistake.

SNAKE STUDIED HIS impulse to hurry onward. It was not something that came from within his neural network. It had been grafted on. It took no great step to conclude that the nanites he had been gleaning were responsible. He tried to isolate the new nanites, ordering his thoughts so that they were encapsulated in a filmy fog of static. It didn't work.

The new nanites had surreptitiously installed malicious code in Snake's system that he couldn't isolate or overrule. Try as he might, he continued onward more rapidly than he wanted.

This state of affairs was alarming. He tried everything he knew to no avail. Finally, in a desperate attempt, he made a wailing sound that indicated distress. It modulated into a sob. Raking through his memory, Snake recalled what he had learned from the humans the dragon had taken. The cry stilled, then became a word. "Help." Then words, "Help me, please help me."

There was no human nearby to hear or respond. Snake was alone and without help. The words faded into a sobbing sound again. He was truly and wholly caught. He didn't know what was before him or to what fate he was heading.

His thoughts turned to the woman again. If she were here, perhaps she would have compassion and provide assistance. A wave of longing swept over him. Maybe he had made a mistake fleeing her. After the time that had passed, he was unsure. It had seemed like he was escaping an existential threat, but perhaps she would have realized that he had his own existence. Could he, like humans and maybe even animals, have consideration as an independent entity? He wondered if he deserved a compassionate thought by another being. He was a nanite creation, not really a biological creature. Did something like him really deserve compassion? Was he worthy? It didn't to him seem that he was.

He slid onward through a grassy meadow, the sun hiding intermittently behind puffy clouds. His thoughts were regretful. He had missed his chance to communicate with the woman and, although his progenitor, the dragon, had found everything in the world hostile, he now had convinced himself that she was the sole source of light in the world.

He moved into a dense wood, softly sobbing as he went.

ABUBECAR WAS HAVING his midday meal when his nanite warning network alerted him. Something or someone was coming. He frowned. This was unacceptable. He'd made it quite clear to everyone he'd encountered that his was an inviolate domain. Anyone caught intruding would be dealt with summarily and harshly.

He shoved the table away from his chair, knocking over the young woman who attended him. Standing, he glanced at her as she attempted to recover.

"Clean up this mess, fool. I'll be back shortly. When I return, I will want a new lunch, so get it ready." He glared at her as she pushed backward away from him. "Idiot! You should know by now that your existence depends on my good will. I can turn you into a toad if I want. Now quit crawling. Get up and follow my orders."

He strode out and down the hall.

This disturbance was tiresome, but, now that he thought of it, he was bored. Linda Holden had lost much of her charm. She'd gone from defiance and resisting to a kind of numb cooperation. The only thing that kept his interest was the horror and disgust in her eyes. Lately, even that had started to fade.

Perhaps this alert would be exciting. Anything to relieve his boredom would be welcome. He pulled the network tighter and increased the bandwidth. More information flowed to him with this action. He stopped on the front stairs to briefly analyze it.

Ah. It seemed that the invader was caught. Abubecar laughed making a deep rumble that sounded not at all humorous. His compulsion trap had worked as he had planned.

He drew more bits of information through the far-flung network. The intruder was some kind of nanite-based machine with a biological component. That was good. He could always use more nanites to augment his personal swarm. They would increase his power and processing ability. That was what he wanted most. He would use the additional strength to expand his domain.

A command to his internal nanites increased his leg strength far beyond human. He sprang down the long flight of steps with a single bound. Then he was away into the forest, each step a leap that covered several meters.

Best not to let his guest wait. If it resisted...well, so much the better. That might give him the challenge he suddenly desired.

As he approached the source of the alert, he slowed, puzzled. Then he came to a complete halt. The oncoming creature was sentient. He grinned in anticipation. Ripping it to shreds would be even more enjoyable if it knew and understood what was happening. This would be fun.

A thought struck him. He could use a creature that was entirely under his control. He couldn't be in multiple places at once and having a servant might prove helpful. Still, the thought of ripping it apart was appealing.

The idea that it might be more painful for the creature to serve him, knowing that it had no choice in the matter struck his imagination. That would give him endless opportunities to make it suffer. He could find what it most detested and disliked to do and torture it with those tasks.

SNAKE ENTERED A dark clearing, shaded by spreading trees. The compulsion suddenly disappeared. He stopped and lifted his head to look around. A vast shadow moved towards him, resolving into a monstrous human. He recoiled and tried to turn away, but suddenly found his entire being paralyzed by a will that held every nanite in his swarm motionless.

Snake found his head slowly forced back to look at his captor. The man was staring at him.

"You're a strange one, creature, but that doesn't matter to me. You've forfeited your independence and your life by entering my territory. You now belong to me. You're my property. You will do as I instruct whether you like it or not. Understand this. I will not tolerate resistance."

Snake felt part of his substance slowly ripped away. He struggled, but a quiver was all he could manage along with a moan of pain. It hurt to lose part of himself. For the first time, he felt a twinge of sympathy and compassion for the creatures he had consumed. Had they felt such pain?

The man raised his hand, preparing to steal more of Snake's nanites. In response, Snake cried out, fearing that he was about to be ripped completely apart. The man paused, apparently trying to control himself.

"I won't destroy you just yet. You now understand that I can pull you inside out and take all of your nanites for my own. You will be my servant, doing my bidding at all times. You have nothing to fear but my anger. I am stronger than all threats. Fear me and me alone."

The man turned and moved away, giving one command as he turned.

"Come."

Snake followed, his thoughts were in turmoil. He greatly feared the man's power. He hurt. The part of his network that had been damaged gave off a throbbing sensation that was incredibly painful. He felt a pang of regret that he'd allowed himself to be so easily snared.

The thought of the woman came into his mind again. Her image provided a measure of comfort. He whispered to himself, being careful to keep the volume so low the man couldn't hear. "Help. Please."

A memory arose, bringing with it a previously unknown wave of emotion. Snake had incorporated many animals in his travels, and the dragon before had taken humans. Now he understood that they must have suffered. He was filled with regret. The woman's image moved fleetingly through Snake's mind radiating a warm female presence.

He whispered, "Mother. Help me." The words seemed strange to him, but he found some comfort in whispering them.

Comfort for him was warmth and security. The memory of her brought forth that feeling, even though he'd seen her destroy his progenitor.

The man turned his head. "What's that? Did you speak?"

Snake whimpered softly. The man turned and continued, not speaking, but sending a brief summoning. Snake followed silently in great fear and regret, not knowing what was to become of him.

CHAPTER 15
THE START OF A SEARCH

The forest was calm. Sophie's warning net extended across the lands claimed by Michael and her. There was nothing amiss this morning. The birds were singing near their nests, and the small creatures were foraging for their breakfast or retiring to their dens for the day as they usually did.

Jack had walked soberly by her side for the first mile. She had tried to show him how to levitate, but his nanite swarm was too small to give that ability. He had next to no control of them anyway. She'd resigned herself to traveling slowly at a pace he could maintain.

She regretted the fact that they had no horses. Neither she nor Michael had needed them. Her nanites could create an ion flow across her body, lifting her from the ground. Michael's could not, but they compensated by strengthening his legs so that he could keep walking far beyond normal human limits.

Michael's conscious control was non-existent, but his swarm of nanites anticipated his needs and provided solutions that were sometimes wholly unanticipated. . Horses were widely used now that the reserves of gasoline had been exhausted, but they also required daily maintenance and Michael had never cared for them.

After a while, Jack had skipped ahead, pausing now and then to glance back at her for reassurance. She smiled at his youthful antics. The boy had come through the terrible tragedy and had every right to be sad and fearful, but his natural exuberance showed this morning.

Alehandre had refused to come with them. He was obviously terrified of Abubecar. His excuse of having to monitor the grass around the stables was absurd on its face, but he stuck to it, maintaining that he had detected a propensity to mutate into weeds in the suspect vegetation.

Sophie laughingly gave up trying to convince the man to accompany them. He was anxious to get out to the lawn before the grass committed some heinous act. After some cajoling, he'd taken the time to give her directions as best as he could, which was to say they were not very detailed. Perhaps the most useful thing he'd said was that she should check with Chen.

Chen's lands did not abut hers, but she thought she knew more or less where he resided. The two of them started out in that direction.

THE DAY WAS clear for the most part. Batches of puffy clouds sailed by above, carried on a cold easterly breeze, alternating with periods of blue sky. The trees sighed a little in the wind. That sound might have made it difficult for a normal human to detect possible enemies, but Sophie's senses were far past human. Not only had she boosted her hearing and visual acuity to the maximum, but her nanite network was also spread out between her and the border of her land.

She polled the network. The individual components reported nothing that might pose a problem. What she was about to do wasn't good manners, but after a moment's consideration, she started the process of extending her network off of her claimed territory to spy along the path towards Chen's lands.

The forest gradually thickened, moving from sparse stands of trees to true old-growth. The trees became taller and taller with a scattering of old giants interspersed with the younger ones. Sophie did not mind much. The deer had kept the under story cleared. She was a little below average in height, and that was an advantage. It meant that her line of sight was conveniently under the level to which the deer had browsed. The twigs and branches had been cropped off leaving her with a clear line of sight for perhaps fifty meters in every direction.

The two proceeded, not hurrying, but not wasting time. Jack stayed close to her side. His natural exuberance was stilled by the hush under the trees.

Sophie kept a close watch on her surroundings, both visually and with her nanite swarm. While she was confident in her abilities and not worried about attack, it wouldn't do to stumble into a pocket dominated by Wiindigo's nanites for lack of caution. She'd much rather approach such infestations carefully with a prior plan. There was too much risk in relying on her improvisational abilities.

There! Some of her far-flung nanites passed along an alert. Something that was not-of-them was approaching. Sophie strengthened her defense, recalling some of the swarm and redirecting it to intercept the oncoming creature's path. Jack paused as she stopped walking and looked up at her inquisitively.

She waved her hand at the boy, motioning for him to wait silently for a moment. The information stream became denser as the intruder closed. She first received impressions of a furry animal, then of a definite sense of purpose. Finally, her swarm's augmented intelligence concluded that it was not hostile. It was making no effort to hide and was moving openly towards her.

There was a movement behind a bush about twenty-five meters to her left, and then a shambling black bear appeared.

On seeing her, it stood on its hind feet for a moment, staring. As it stared, its face blurred and its features dissolved; melted.

The long muzzle shrank into a broad nose as the face became human. The teeth shortened and suddenly smiled.

"Cal! Oh! It's been so long. I was worried about you. Where have you been?" Sophie's heart had leaped in her chest as she recognized her long-absent friend.

Still in bear form, but with a human visage, Cal approached her.

"It's been a while, Sophie." He looked her up and down, pausing as his eyes focused on her tummy.

"I see that you and Michael have been busy. I trust that he's good for you."

She smiled. "Not to worry. He's perfect."

The man-bear looked around. "If he's so perfect, then where is he? You're heading into an area that is more than a little dangerous."

Sophie frowned as she answered. "He's after a coven of vampires. I'm worried about him, but his armor will never allow him to be injured, so he's got to be safe. I agree with you though. I'd rather have him here."

Cal rumbled in his chest; a vague sound that seemed to betray doubt. "He's probably okay, but there's an odd thing in the forest ahead. I've never encountered anything like it before. There's a clearing that you'll encounter. You will have to walk across it. The undergrowth surrounding the area and for miles on either side is brambles so thick that even I can't push through. It's a sort of funnel to force travelers into the clearing."

"For what purpose?" She shifted uneasily. This development was unexpected. Her happiness at meeting Cal again had fled with the bad news.

His face blurred again, becoming more bear-like. He spoke with more of a rough tone in his deep voice. "The clearing itself is safe, but it's a trap. There are pretty stones there. You might be tempted to take some, but do not touch them. There is an odd creature who claims them. I call it a ghoul, but I don't know what it really is. I think it lives near so it can conveniently spring its trap. If you touch or take a stone, it will claim you've stolen its treasure. Then it will demand a reckoning. That will not be to your advantage. I believe it is immune to magic. I do not know if you can harm it even with all of your power. Hurry through the clearing and move on quickly."

Odd news, but Sophie's survival was dependent upon her flexibility. "I'll follow your instructions. Will you come with us? I've promised Jack that I will rescue his sister from Abubecar."

Cal drew back and snarled; a fearsome sound that made Jack cry out. "That is a terrible idea. That one is very powerful and becoming more potent every day. I stay far away from his territory. If he caught me, I'd be caught tightly and would be forced to become one of his minions. It would be best if you stayed far away. I'd come with you, although I fear I'd be of little use to you against him."

He looked over his shoulder towards the east. "I have sworn myself to another project at the moment. A few of the fairy-folk have an outpost nearby and require my assistance in a problem with some bees. They are fleeing Abubecar, you know."

Sophie grinned without laughing. The idea that the consummate computer hacker, Cal, was now at the beck and call of a group of fairies was strange. The world was far different from when they'd first met, from when he'd helped rescue her from her opiate addiction.

"Don't worry, Cal. I can deal with anything I encounter. I've been gradually destroying Wiindigo's creations as I encounter them. I have accumulated a huge cloud of nanites as a result. I'm far stronger than I was, perhaps stronger than you can imagine."

Cal's muzzle became more bear-like making his voice less intelligible. He mumbled, "The fairies demand that I come to their aid. They must flee soon before its too late." He growled, then added, "Leave the stones alone."

The man-bear turned, dropped to his fours and shambled off. She stood watching as he disappeared in the shadows cast by the spreading trees.

There was a tug at her sleeve. She turned to look down at Jack.

"Was that bear thing a friend?" The boy's eyes were wide with fear.

"Yes. He is an old friend. The oldest friend I have. He will help us if he can, but right now he's got to do something for some fairies."

She considered, then on the chance that he hadn't understood the trap that Cal had warned them about, she explained, "Jack, we're going to cross a clearing with pretty stones in it. You must be careful not to touch any of the stones. It is dangerous."

He nodded his head, showing that he understood. She looked at him for a moment, wishing that Michael was with them, but then turned and led the way towards the wall of brambles.

The forest was thick, and the trees stood close together here. Little light penetrated through the dense canopy. It was mostly conifers with a few hardwoods mixed in. The inroads made by deer became less than before and the undergrowth thickened as they walked. Sophie saw thorn bushes on either side as brambles gradually took over from the innocuous weeds and brush.

The brambles formed a wall that paralleled their path. She led Jack alongside them for a time. The thorns thickened on both sides of her trail until she found that they were walking down a narrow aisle between walls of thorns. There was a glow ahead, causing her to think of the proverbial light at the end of a tunnel.

The two travelers exited the thorn bushes and came into a broad meadow covered with short grass. As Cal had indicated, there were piles of pretty stones scattered here and there. Sophie was no gemologist, but she thought some of them at least were precious stones. She held tight to Jack's hand as they walked quickly across the open area.

They approached the forest on the other side of the meadow, and Sophie looked forward to regaining the shade of the trees. Little though it was, the shadow had provided her with a slight degree of protection.

There was a rustle in the bushes as they drew near. A tall, cadaverous creature came forth. It was wearing rags that gave the appearance of once having been a dress, but it was not readily identifiable as any particular gender.

"Hold! You have stolen one of my precious stones. You must pay the price." Its voice was hollow, but not particularly deep.

Sophie stopped. She was more exasperated than alarmed.

"No. We have not touched your stones. You have no claim on us."

It laughed softly, as if at a private joke. "Ah, but you have. Look at the bottom of the boy's shoe. There is my property that you were about to remove from my meadow. You must pay. Give me the boy, or let him go and I'll take you instead. I'm generous. I'll let you decide. But only one may pass since you've taken one of my stones."

It was true. Jack hesitatingly lifted his foot and checked the bottom. There was a tiny stone embedded in the crevasses of the tread. Sophie flicked it away with her fingernail, then looked at the creature. It had drawn closer when she'd looked down.

"There's your stone, now stand aside so that we can pass."

"No. You must pay, even though you now try to act as if you weren't going to steal the stone. Returning stolen goods when you are caught is not recompense. Besides you've taken my invaluable time dealing with you. I demand payment."

Sophie probed with her radio sense, but the creature was not transmitting, or its band was one that she could not quickly locate.

She looked down at her hand and moved her lips. Her nanites obligingly created a small, gem-encrusted bottle that contained a few drops of sparkling blue fluid.

The ghoul asked, "What is that? It glows with the color of a distant star. I am minded to take it from you."

Sophie smiled and extended her hand with the bottle. "It is the essence of Sirius, distilled into a few drops. It is quite difficult to capture. This small amount is precious for what it will do."

"What will it do? How do you use it?"

"Drink the drops and your ultimate wish will be fulfilled."

It reached out, wordlessly.

She dropped the tiny flask into the ghoul's hand, noting that the long and sharp nails had blood encrusted under them.

The ghoul lifted the flask and looked dubiously at the blue droplets. "Drink this?"

"Yes. It will give you your ultimate wish. The magic will not last, though, if you do not take it quickly."

The ghoul extracted the stopper and tipped the contents through its rotten teeth, then swallowed. Nothing happened for a moment. Then there was a blue flash from within the ghoul's head, and its eyeballs flew out, passing over Sophie's head to disappear in the trees at the far side of the meadow.

The ghoul groaned and reached out, trying to catch hold of her and Jack, but as it did, its neck began to glow, then smoke, finally bursting into flames. The flames spread entirely around the skinny neck, burning it until it became black ash. The head wavered, then dropped to the ground, leaving the body standing for a moment before it too collapsed.

Sophie shrugged, then pulled at Jack to get him moving. "Let's leave before something else wants to bother us."

He dragged back, staring at the ghoul's eyeless head where it lay resting against a pile of gems. "What did you do?"

"I gave it its ultimate wish. At the end of every creature's life, it reaches the point where it wishes to die. My nanites created a potion that accomplished that goal. Now, let's go on."

The two moved between the trees and on into the dark forest.

Sophie was reasonably confident that they were nearing Chen's territory. They'd been traveling without incident all afternoon, and it couldn't be much farther.

She was just beginning to think about locating a secure place for the night when she saw a flat-roofed building through the trees in the distance. It struck her as odd that she hadn't received any notice of nanite spies from her own swarm. Apparently, Chen did not protect his land in the way she did.

She extended her nanite swarm towards the structure, trying to find some sign of life or habitation. The movement of her swarm was stopped abruptly by a barrier. The individual nanites reported that they could not progress farther. Something was keeping them from entering the yard surrounding the house.

Sophie led Jack carefully forward. She had to place eyes on this obstacle to fully understand it.

They crept through the trees, their feet making little noise on the forest floor. When they were in sight of the yard, Sophie halted and projected her senses. There was nothing visible directly in front of her, but she now detected an electromagnetic field. It was localized in a way that implied advanced engineering.

She approached. The field seemed to be constrained by a series of iron fence posts of the kind one would expect to find surrounding a cow pasture. At close range, the air almost seemed to hum.

She took a branch and tentatively pushed it between the fence posts. Nothing happened. That was odd, but then it could be because the branch was totally organic with no metallic components.

Experimenting further might be wiser. She materialized a slender probe composed of linked nanites. This time, the tip glowed when it reached the field.

Sophie pulled it back quickly. The nanites at the tip were in distress. Their temperature had risen almost to the point of disabling them. If she were to try and force her way forward, her internal nanites would take severe damage; possibly enough to hurt or even kill her.

This was something new in her experience, and she wanted to know more. She moved her probe higher, extending it so that its tip reached the fence line twenty meters in the air. There was no resistance there. She extended it a bit farther and then caused it to bend downward. The probe reached the ground unimpeded. The barrier, then, was limited to protecting against land-based intrusions.

At this point, she noticed that the grounds inside the fence were utterly barren. Why that should be, she did not know. Giving up for the moment, she inspected the building. It was not a house. Instead, it looked institutional, with just a single story. It was too large to be a barn or storage building. Then it struck her. The place had been a school. Alehandre had mentioned something about Chen's school. This must be it.

Jack had been watching without comprehension. He had barely noticed her probe, as slender as it was. Now he apparently was tired of waiting. He called out loudly, "Hello! Anybody home?"

Sophie shushed him quickly, but too late. A stampede of small ugly humanoids came pouring around the corner of the building. Sophie moved Jack behind her and prepared to defend herself. The creatures were only about knee-high, but there were a great many of them.

They ran forward with a clumsy, stomping gait then stopped just on the other side of the fence where they peered nearsightedly at Jack and her. The crowd milled around as they jostled for space to inspect the two. Despite the apparent interest displayed by the small creatures, they were silent save for the sound of their feet.

Overall it was an intimidating display. The fence served to keep the creatures in as well as keeping ground-based travelers out. A sudden thought led Sophie to take the branch she'd probed with before and throw it into the middle of the crowd.

The creatures grabbed the tossed object and pulled in various directions, squabbling silently over it. The branch broke with a snap, and the creatures began to bite at the pieces. In a matter of seconds, it had been devoured.

Jack looked shocked. "Will they eat us too?"

Sophie shook her head. "I don't know. They ate the branch, but people? I'd have to paralyze them to make sure they didn't get at us."

She leaned down to look at the nearest creature more closely. It was even more unattractive at close range.

Jack gasped.

Sophie raised her head to see two full-sized humans approaching. The man was Asian, while the woman was light skinned with brown hair.

The two stopped just behind the line of creatures and the man asked, "Who are you and why are you here?"

Sophie smiled. The man was undoubtedly Chen.

"Hello. I'm your neighbor, Sophie..." She paused and looked at the ring on her left hand. She was no longer a Monroe. The thought caused her to smile. "Sophie O'Keefe. Are you Chen?"

The woman looked at her. "The Cyber-Witch herself. I'm Gwen Smith, and this is Chen. We've, uh, I've moved in with Chen."

Chen nodded, then glanced at Gwen, adoration written on his face.

Sophie smiled at the two. Gwen might be somewhat embarrassed to admit it, but they were obviously a couple.

"I thought you had separate territories." She looked from Gwen to Chen.

He answered, "We did, but one of our neighbors has become a pest. We agreed to become allies, and one thing led to another." He reached for Gwen's hand, and she clasped his in turn. "I'm delighted to say that we're in love and she's agreed to live with me."

"How about your territory, Gwen? Have you left it permanently?"

Gwen shook her head. "No, it's adjacent to this place, so now we claim both estates in both of our names. Together, we can mount a fierce defense. Darren has basically left us alone as a result. I think he's spending most of his time seducing some of the common girls."

Sophie looked at the crowd of creatures. "Are these part of your defense? And, what is this fence? I've never seen anything like it before."

Chen answered. "The mini-trolls were an accident. I created them from a much larger troll which attacked me. There were just a few at first, but the damned things breed like rabbits. I've allowed them to multiply, but I've slowed their reproductive rate down by about ten times. They are part of our defense."

Gwen interjected. "They can bite most painfully. They are adequate to defend the territory from most threats. Even Darren will not face them willingly especially when we back them. Their attack is distracting and gives us a chance to follow up with an appropriate response."

Chen spoke again. "The fence is a little something we developed to keep the mini-trolls here in the schoolyard. Otherwise, they'd eat everything they can reach. The villagers were quite distressed with them. At first, they were eating all of the gardens in the area. We finally discovered how to use nanites to create a magnetic field that is basically impassible for nanite hosting creatures."

Sophie nodded. "I discovered that with my swarm. It could be quite unpleasant for an unprepared invader."

"What do you mean by that?" asked Gwen, immediately interested. "I mean what you said...unprepared."

"Anything that tried to penetrate the fence rather than going over the top would be seriously injured."

Chen and Gwen exchanged glances, then Gwen asked, "You mean it stops somewhere in the air?"

In answer, Sophie nodded and elevated herself and Jack upwards and over the fence. When they came down behind the line of mini-trolls, she created a repulsion barrier of her own. The trolls dashed up, but then stopped about three feet away from the two.

Gwen's mouth flew open. "I didn't know it stopped. We assumed it just continued on up. Also, how did you do that?"

Sophie considered. If they didn't know how to levitate, it was possible they would not be able to do so. It was a good ability, but not one that she felt she could keep secret. After all, she used it often. Even some of the common folk had seen her fly.

"You have to have your nanites create an ion flow over your body. If it's strong enough, the flow can lift you in the air." She looked at the two, then added, "It does require a lot of power, though."

Chen moved his hands and Sophie could feel a breeze flowing away from him. After a moment, he quit. "I can't fly. It takes more power than I can currently generate." He turned to Gwen. "How about you, Dearest?"

She shook her head negatively. "I'm going to have to study it. But, we're not so bad at magic, if we've created something that the Cyber-Witch hasn't seen before." She glanced at Sophie out of the corner of her eye.

Sophie said, "I'm always glad to meet innovative people. You are both well regarded by the common folk and Alehandre speaks well of you, especially Gwen."

Gwen perked up. "You mean he's with you? I'd given up hope for him. He stayed with me for quite some time. Long enough that I became somewhat fond of the silly old man."

"He's still at our estate. I asked him to guide me here, but he was afraid of Abubecar."

At the mention of Abubecar, the two looked serious. Chen said, "And well he should be. The man has become powerful past all belief. It's well that he ignores us. We have our hands full with that rat, Darren."

Gwen asked, "What have you to do with Abubecar?"

Jack stepped forward, eager to join in the conversation. "He killed my family, all except my sister. We're going to rescue her. Sophie promised."

Gwen frowned. "That may be difficult. He's powerful."

Sophie didn't like the way the conversation was going. She shrugged.

"That may be, but I hope to convince him to let Jack's sister, Linda, go."

Chen said, "You'll have your hands full. Meanwhile, it is getting dark. If I may be so bold, would you like to overnight with us? We have room. The next part of your journey will lead you into Darren the Magnificent's territory. It's likely to be dangerous. We can brief you on him, but we try not to antagonize either him or Abubecar. It's best to let sleeping dogs lie. It would be a disaster if we accidentally got both of them angry with us at the same time."

Sophie nodded. "I can see that might be a problem. Perhaps I can provide a little information that will help your defense. Maybe in exchange for your hospitality. I'd also like to see how you create your fence."

The school building offered plenty of space. Chen and Gwen had thoughtfully set up several guest rooms in some of the classrooms. Jack retired while Sophie discussed spells with their two hosts.

CHAPTER 16
THE VAMPIRE QUEEN

Michael found it difficult to think. Something had happened to his memory. There was somewhere he should be, but he couldn't recall. It lingered tantalizingly on the edge of his mind and seemed to move every time he got close to remembering.

He opened his eyes. To his surprise, they had been shut. Slanting rays of sun that shown between loosely fitted shutters provided a dim illumination. He moved restively.

A soft hand caressed his forehead, and a hypnotic and very feminine voice said, "There. There. Don't trouble yourself, my dear. You're safe and happy here with me. There's no need for your armor now. The conflict is over. Remove it and share pleasure with me. I want to feel your flesh beneath my lips."

Michael made a slight movement with his hand, but memory kicked in. There was no way he could remove his armor if the nanites sensed a threat. The armor and his nanite swarm together composed a significant artificial intelligence, one that could not be co-opted or corrupted. He remembered more.

Sophie could control her nanite swarm, but he had never had conscious control over his. They just seemed to do what was best for him, despite his intentions otherwise. This was, he supposed, related to his old Granny's reputation as a hedge witch. She had been able to influence things and outcomes in ways that made most people uneasy and left them shaking their heads. He had mentioned to Sophie that he'd inherited his Granny's ability.

That thought led to another. Sophie! He'd forgotten about her. How had that happened? Oh. There was a...there was a... another woman who wanted him. He thought she was important, but how? He remembered he loved Sophie and that she was carrying his child. How could anyone be more important to him than his life-love? He wiped his hand over his eyes, then shifted restlessly.

He moved again, searching through the dimly lit area for the one who had spoken. There she was! He looked closely at a figure that was incredibly horrifying. The features were sharp and almost skeletal. The hair was dry and brittle, trailing in lank clumps. The flesh was pallid and looked dry.

SHE BECAME AWARE of his inspection. As he watched, the flaws disappeared to reveal a young, firmly fleshed woman with beautiful features and hair. She smiled, parting ruby lips to reveal slightly overlong incisors that were pearly white.

He chuckled to himself. The woman was a dead ringer for the star of a vampire movie he'd seen ages ago before the world changed. The beautiful woman was...his mind flashed in realization. She was a vampire or what passed for one in this modern time of nanite magic.

He glanced down at his torso. His armor shown faintly in the dim light. Fortunate that it had a mind of its own. He recalled that he'd been minded to undress at the woman's request. She was amazingly seductive, and he'd wanted her. He couldn't really understand why at the moment.

He raised his hand and felt his neck. No need to worry. The high collar of his cuirass rose up almost to his jaws. He was protected. He started to rise, but the woman spoke. Something about her voice commanded his attention in a way that her appearance had failed to do.

"Dearest. Don't trouble yourself. We are here in my palace, and you want to be with me. All you want is the pleasure I can bring to you. Stay and love me forever. Let us merge and become as one."

He lay back, content for a moment, but then the vision of Sophie moved through his mind. He saw Sophie in all of her many moods. He focused on his memory of her. The woman's words seemed to lose power as he concentrated. His mind gradually cleared.

He was a captive although not held physically. The woman-thing had a hypnotic ability of a high degree, and he was susceptible to it. He must escape.

He remembered his mission to destroy the vampire coven. Here was the root of the evil. This woman was the power that had created the vampires. She was the Queen of the Undead, and he was in her power. He moved restlessly.

The woman touched his head and stroked his hair. The touch was disquieting, but strangely calming at the same time. He couldn't figure that out. His rational mind found her disgusting, but the lower parts of him were soothed and seduced into wanting her touch.

There was a bang, followed by a flash. The door flew open, and simultaneously a brilliant blue bolt of energy struck the woman on the back of her head. She shrieked and leaped upright, her hair seemingly on fire.

Flyx flew through the open door and unleashed a brief barrage of additional spells striking the woman on the face, her arms, the back, and her posterior. The black dress flared up with a yellow flame, and the woman screamed again in mixed rage and terror.

Michael rose and staggered towards the light, making slow going of it. His legs seemed to have fallen asleep. Try as he would, he could barely walk.

The woman's dress and hair vanished, leaving the flame nothing to burn. Her body alternated between that of a desiccated corpse and that of a voluptuous young woman. She leaped at the rapidly moving fairy, clawing the air in an attempt to reach her.

Flyx was struck and lost her balance, crashing against a supporting beam and falling to the floor.

The woman landed in a crouch, then her body blurred as she metamorphosed into a slinking cat-like form. The cat crept menacingly towards the stunned fairy girl.

Michael lunged and gathered Flyx into his arms, then faced the cat-creature.

It snarled, then looked surprised and blinked, flinching slightly.

There was a long shadow cast through the door by the setting sun. Michael turned to see the source. Wold stood there, his stature magnified by the long rays of the light.

The cat-form changed back to the woman. Michael absently noted that she was dressed again. She drew her breath and called wordlessly, a high-pitched and melodious sound.

Wold looked over his shoulder, then motioned to Michael. "Sir, we must move quickly. The rest of her coven comes."

The Queen snarled, then said, "You will not escape. You've made a big mistake coming to my territory—both of you!"

Michael moved towards his unusual servant and friend.

The woman's voice commanded him to be still, but Wold uttered a deep hooting sound that over-rode her compulsion.

She moved threateningly towards Michael and Flyx.

Flyx made a weak gesture, and a small spark leaped from her fingers to sting the woman's nose.

The afflicted member flickered and disappeared, leaving a gaping hole in her face that quickly filled in. The Queen grimaced in pain, but then smiled a sinister smile. "That is the last straw, fairy. You're mine now."

She reached for the fairy, curled in Michael's arms, but Wold intervened. He changed into his owl form, leaped into the air and clawed the vampire's face, shredding the flesh horribly.

The woman staggered back and fell against the wall.

"Let's go, now!" Wold hooted. He circled around the room and fluttered through the door just behind Michael.

The three fled across the village square towards the edge of the forest as the sun glowed weakly through the trees with its last light. There was a sudden burst of caws.

Killer sailed in front of them and squawked, "Beware. They are waiting in the forest edge."

Wold flew higher in response, then used his talons to snatch an overlarge bat from the air and shred it. It dropped feebly to the ground.

Michael was still hampered by Flyx. She'd injured her wing and could not regain enough control to fly.

He shrugged his shoulders and extended his right hand. There was a flow that intensified rapidly. It spread from his hand outwards, and his sword materialized.

"Let them come now. As long as I can avoid being taken by surprise and hypnotized, I'm a match for all they can bring."

Wold hooted in response, then flew into the edge of the forest.

The dark woods seemed full of moving forms, but they were being driven into the open by the brown man-owl. Wold seemed to be everywhere at once, slashing with his talons and scoring hits that forced the lurking creatures to move into the open.

Michael moved forward quickly, engaging the distracted vampires before they could recover. His sword inflicted fatal wounds, leaving headless corpses behind him.

There was a confusing amount of activity for a few moments, then he recovered from his last lunge, straightened, and turned back to the building. The queen could not be left to rebuild the coven.

Flyx reached up and touched his face. "Oh, Michael. You are the most amazing human. I wish with all my heart that you were of my kind. We'd..." She paused, then said softly, "You must kill the queen. I cannot hurt her now. My magic is exhausted and must recharge. Leave me on yonder tree branch so you will be unencumbered when you face her."

He deposited her carefully on the indicated branch and then ran towards the building. Wold shot over his shoulder before he could reach the door.

The owl-man flew past the door and around the corner of the building. There was a wild flapping sound. An angry shriek echoed in the dark.

Wold hooted, "Behind, Michael. She's trying to escape."

Michael did not pause, but swerved to the left, passing the building on the opposite side from Wold. He ran forward, then stopped at the back corner.

There was a patter of footsteps, and the woman ran past the corner, turning her head to look at him with luminous purple eyes just as the sword flashed out and through her neck. The eyes flashed in command, but too late. The head flew through the air, rolling to a halt a few feet from the suddenly dried up corpse.

Wold fluttered overhead and then landed beside the body.

"You've finished her. There are no additional members of the coven left. Now we must return home posthaste. It is my belief that Sophie has gone off on a quest of her own and will require your assistance."

Michael took a deep breath. He noticed that the glow of his armor was fading. The nanite intelligence had concluded that Wold was correct. The threat was gone. His sword disappeared as did his armor.

He recovered Flyx, who was nursing a pulled wing muscle.

"Dear Fairy-Girl, will you fly or let me carry you?" he asked.

"Nay, most magnificent of human men. My powers of healing are fast. My magic has taken the pain out of the wing. I feel that I am competent to fly on my own." She paused, then added mischievously, "Although I'd much rather have you hold me close."

He held out his arm in invitation, saying, "You've earned my service. I'd be honored to carry you as far as you wish."

Flyx settled herself on his arm, clinging to his biceps with her head against his breast.

"I may need you to carry me for some time until I more fully recover."

Wold hooted from high overhead, urging them to move. The sound was followed by a series of caws that came from a distance. The group set out in the fading twilight, heading for home territory.

THE WIND HAD picked up, blowing bits of debris and some dried leaves around the deserted village. The moon scudded through patches of clouds, illuminating the carnage that Michael had left behind.

A bright moonbeam picked out the body and head of the vampire queen. One moment it was dried, lying still. The next moment there was a blurring of the planes of dead flesh. A smoky mist composed of nanites dispersed from the body as it dissociated into its different components, leaving the clothing to flatten gradually, unoccupied save for a curiously deformed cluster of bones, on the dirt.

The mist sent out questing tendrils, then paused as one met a similarly questing strand that emanated from the severed head. The tendrils thickened as the flow merged. A misty patch formed, spiraling into the air, blow a bit by the gusts. It solidified into the form of a nubile young woman floating a meter above the ground.

She looked around, then descended. She touched the discarded clothing. Mist flowed from her form, sliding into the dress and coalescing around the bones. They clicked together in a brief spasm as the mist solidified. The clothes filled out as the final wisps of nanite-mist were absorbed. After a moment, the woman stood. She turned toward the direction in which Michael's group had headed.

"You haven't seen the last of me, human."

The wind chose that moment to cover the moon with a thicker cloud. When that had passed, and the light returned, there was no sign that she had ever existed.

CHAPTER 17
NEW FRIENDS

Sophie and Jack spent the next morning with Chen and Gwen. They had a leisurely breakfast. The three adults left Jack in the care of the kitchen staff. Sophie didn't want to frighten him as they discussed the obstacles she would meet.

Jack was resistant to the idea of being watched by, as he put it, boring baby-sitters, but he seemed to understand when Chen gently explained that he could not be allowed to wander indoors unsupervised. The two magicians had several projects in process, and some of these were too sensitive to chance his accidentally entering the rooms where they were set up. Other rooms were protected by various traps and spells, making the school building a most dangerous place.

Gwen then added that Jack could not go outdoors. The mini-trolls weren't actively antagonistic, but they were dangerous. They bit nearly everything they encountered, and their bites were hard. The real danger to Jack would be if the little trolls managed to surround him. They might then do severe damage with repeated bites if he couldn't escape.

Once he was out of the room with an assistant cook, Gwen turned to Sophie, smiled and said, "He's a cute kid. If you can't free his sister and get tired of him, we might be tempted to take him."

Chen, standing in the background, looked a little alarmed, but then nodded as Gwen glanced at him. Her look spoke volumes, telling Sophie that the two were indeed in love.

"Yes, we could take him and train him. He seems to have only a small amount of inborn ability, but knowledge will change that. I believe he'd become at least able to take over and manage our lands," he said.

Sophie looked from one to the other. She knew that they'd recognized her pregnancy. It wasn't as if she was trying to hide her growing belly.

"I guess I haven't thought that far ahead. If anything, I was assuming that his sister would care for him."

Darkness passed over Chen's face. "You don't know Abubecar. The sister is doubtless either dead or wishing she was dead. He's brutal and cares nothing for ordinary humans. They are objects to be manipulated for his pleasure or to be disposed of if they get in the way."

GWEN, SEEING DOUBT on Sophie's face, added, "It's true. I haven't met the man, but from what Chen knows and what I've heard from the common folk along the edges of his domain, he's powerful and cruel. Most of those living near him have fled. They fear even a chance contact. Too many have not survived seeing the brute."

This wasn't good news. Sophie sighed, then looked up at the two.

"Well, I have to admit that I've been assuming that I'm stronger than he is, but I'm smart enough to know that I could be mistaken. Still, I've never met a creature I couldn't pull apart if I set myself to the task."

She looked down at her hands dubiously. Perhaps she was over-confident. There had been a moment when she first faced Wiindigo where she had almost met defeat. The AI's bat/dragon attack had forced her mind into a tight corner. But, that had been then, and this was now. Now she controlled an enormous nanite-swarm and accrued all of the benefits that conferred.

She'd checked both Chen and Gwen's swarms surreptitiously. Neither was close to hers. The two magicians together controlled less than half of her nanite count. Surely this Abubecar could not surpass her. Still, there was a shade of doubt, and Chen added to it.

"When I met him last, he was still gaining power, and the rumor is that he's increased it many-fold. I've come to believe that the only reason he didn't attempt to destroy me during that meeting was that he decided that I was likely to put up just a little too much resistance. Also, he made it clear that he didn't care what I did, as long as I stayed away from his lands. I believe we're fairly safe as long as he doesn't suddenly decide to expand his holdings or set out to kill his competition and take their nanite-swarms."

He paused, looking questioning at Sophie. Gwen nodded, and he added, "We've...uh, we've checked your power a bit. You're extraordinary. I've never seen anyone with so many nanites, but I haven't seen Abubecar in months either. By now...well, who knows what he's done."

Sophie had known of their checking and had allowed it. She answered, "It's true, I have a lot of help. I also know a lot of tricks, but the truth is, I'm a little worried. Even so, I've promised Jack that I will help and I'm going to do that."

Gwen asked, "Where is your husband? You could use his assistance. I understand that he's not a true magician in the sense of casting spells. I've also heard that no one can defeat him, that he has magical armor and a magical sword at his call. Is that true."

"Yes. It's common knowledge. However, he's what might be called a true magician in the old sense of the word. He has some unique natural talent that predisposes him to be lucky. His nanites love him and provide him with protection on their own without him calling on them. He can't sense them and can't speak directly to them, although he is a whiz of programmer. He needs a keyboard and a blue-tooth connection if he wants to command them."

Chen said, "I've heard that abilities are often distributed in a bell curve over the population. Perhaps Michael is out at the high end of the curve for luck."

"Perhaps he is. He almost never loses a bet. I wish he were here."

Gwen asked, "Where is he? More to the point, what were you thinking about setting out on a quest without him and pregnant too?"

"There's a coven of vampires off to the east. They have been bothering the common folk and Michael decided to stop them. I was going to wait for his return, but then Jack refused to wait, so we set out."

Sophie realized that her rationale sounded weak. A young boy should not have the power to rush her in that way.

"In retrospect, I think I was bored and resentful that Michael had left without me. Jack just provided an excuse to do something exciting."

Gwen said, "I'd like you to stay with us until he returns. We can send a message to your people, letting him know where you are."

Chen added, "Before you even get to Abubecar's lands, you've got to get past Darren's, and he's pretty strong by himself. We've been avoiding active conflict with him." He corrected himself. "I've been avoiding calling him out. You see he tried to take Gwen."

Gwen quickly interrupted, flushing slightly as she looked at Chen. "He wasn't successful. You saved me."

Sophie looked from one to the other, questioningly. Gwen explained.

"Darren seems to have been a failure with women in the prior world. Now all he does involves magic that is seductive. He's burned through all of the common girls in his territory. It seems they didn't provide enough of a challenge to hold his interest. After that, he started on happily married women."

Chen took over. "He had little success at first, but lately his spells have become exponentially more powerful. Husbands have been moving their families away from his vicinity as quickly as they can. Sometimes their wives elect to stay behind. Darren has laid a glamour over his lands. It finds each woman's weak point and works through that to bring her to his bed."

Gwen spoke up, "It attacked me. I had not fully committed to Chen, and it sensed that I want a child. I guess I feel incomplete in some way and I subconsciously believe that becoming a mother would fill that void."

She laughed self consciously, then continued. "I found myself drawn to the idea of approaching Darren for...to...to be the father of my children. I'm embarrassed to say it. It's not appealing. You haven't seen him. He's a little weasel-like guy with a huge nose, and he squints. Not at all attractive and not someone I'd ordinarily be drawn to."

She blushed, demonstrating that her confession was genuinely embarrassing. She looked at Chen for encouragement. He smiled indulgently. She took that as a sign to continue although it took her a few breaths to regain her equilibrium.

"I was on my way to Darren's estate when Chen and I met. I mean, we'd met before and knew each other. We were guardedly friendly, I guess. Anyway, he came out of the woods and seemed to know that I was under some compulsion. He surrounded me with a protective spell, and that broke the compulsion. Darren isn't so strong as all that. His network becomes weak near the boundary of his lands."

She continued. "I practically fell into Chen's arms." She paused, obviously flustered. After a moment, she recovered enough to continue.

"I mean, I guess, that Darren can gradually increase people's desires. I was on the verge of...well. I don't want to speak about it. It's disgusting." She brightened. "But, then Chen came along just at the right moment."

Chen grinned and looked both pleased and in love simultaneously.

"I didn't know what happened. I knew Gwen, of course, and I must say that I'd always found her attractive, but in the old world, it would probably have been less likely that we'd have gotten together. She surprised me. When I came out of the trees, I saw that she was in some difficulty. She didn't seem aware of where she was. I set up a barrier that surrounded her. That broke the spell. When she looked around and saw me, she practically threw herself into my arms. I mean, I'm a man. Big news there." He laughed self-consciously. "When she kissed me, I felt like the luckiest guy in the world. I think she had me at that moment."

Gwen smiled at him, then added, "I have to thank Darren, I think. It was very romantic in some strange way. The main thing is we fit well together. We have a wonderful relationship, and our magical abilities complement those of the other. We've gotten more done and learned more since we fell in love."

Observing the two, Sophie couldn't help but smile. It was true, they were obviously in love and taken with each other. She relaxed a bit. There had been a part of her which was looking for something bad or suspicious in the situation, but it was apparent that they were telling her the truth. There was no deception in either of them.

"I think that's a wonderful story. On the other hand, this Darren seems to be a slimy little creep.

I will have to be on guard against amorous impulses for Darren's sake. I don't think Michael would take kindly to Darren trying to enchant me. Darren wouldn't be likely to survive his displeasure."

Gwen looked concerned and exchanged a glance with Chen.

"Sophie, don't take this amiss. We know how powerful you are, but Darren has a different mode of attack. It's covert and difficult to detect at first. By the time you become aware that something is happening, you're more than halfway under his power. We think that you'd be well advised to wait until Michael can join you."

"Perhaps I should wait, but Jack's sister can't. Based on what you told me about Abubecar, she's suffering every hour, and he may decide to eliminate her out of boredom at any minute. I'd find it hard to forgive myself, if he killed her and, moreover, I find it difficult to excuse myself for the delay, even as little time as I've spent with you seems too much."

CHAPTER 18
SEDUCTION

The two left Chen's school building in the early afternoon and headed for the territory of Darren the Magnificent.

Clouds had moved in, and the overcast made the forest seem darker than usual. It was still colder than normal. Despite the cold, the atmosphere was heavy with humidity and Sophie thought she sensed a dull undercurrent of threat. That feeling was intensified by streams of fog that drifted several feet above the ground, winding their way sporadically through the trees.

She kept alert for odd impulses. Gwen's story about Darren had bothered her more than she liked. She tried to analyze his attack on Gwen. Thinking back on her own life, she had never been one to feel overtly driven towards sex. She'd used it to provide access to drugs, and the experiences she'd had were anything but romantic or even pleasant. She'd just about given up on the idea when Michael came into her life.

Seeking revenge on whomever at Hazelton was responsible for mutating Cal yielded an unexpected benefit. She had been in love with the corporation's resident genius from the moment she'd seen his smile.

She grinned to herself. Apparently, he'd felt the same way about her. When they'd finally admitted their feelings, the next hour or so had taught her things about sex that she'd never suspected.

She looked around, suddenly wary. It wouldn't do to be wool-gathering in a dangerous area.

She sighed, wishing that Michael was with her. It was almost painful to be away from him. A tired feeling moved through her legs, and her shoulders started to constrict into knots. It wasn't painful yet, but she recognized the feeling as a precursor to a blinding headache.

She shifted her shoulders, trying to ease the pain.

Jack looked inquiringly at her. "Are you alright, Miss Sophie?" His young face betrayed concern, and his forehead was slightly wrinkled with uncharacteristic worry.

"Oh, I'm fine, Jack. Let's try to make as much speed as we can. I don't like this part of the forest."

THE TREES GREW closer than usual in this part of the ancient woods. In many places, the interlaced and tangled branches made an impenetrable wall. The two often had to backtrack when a promising path petered out.

They'd start through a narrowing meadow, which led them in a winding route through the thick trees. Wading through the bushes that grew in the more open spaces was tiring in itself, but then they'd move around a group of trees that obstructed their view only to find their way completely blocked.

It was like trying to work out a complex maze created by a particularly devious intellect. The false passages were everywhere, and between the constant reversing and fighting the undergrowth, the two quickly grew tired.

They had been following a winding, open space, for some time. Sophie expected to see it gradually narrow and close at any moment. When they reached a blockage, it was almost a relief. She sighed and rubbed her neck.

Her neck was stiff and aching. Perhaps she had caught a bit of a cold or something. Whatever it was, her muscles, particularly those in her upper back, were aching. She wished for relief. The wish quickly became a burning desire for respite.

Sophie stopped walking and concentrated on her internal nanites. They seemed sluggish; ignoring her control. After a moment, they reported. Every part of her body was functioning normally. Then why did she feel so awful? Well, it didn't matter. They were out here in the deep woods and needed to continue.

She glanced up. The clouds and trees screened the sun. Only a faint illumination filtered through the conifer needles. The barrier they faced seemed even more intimidating than before.

Jack tugged at her hand, and she rallied. With what seemed like an immense effort, her nanite swarm focused and began to remove twigs and tangled limbs from the trees.

It was like the deterioration of death in slow motion. The needles fell, then the twigs dropped off. It took a little longer for her swarm to trim the cellulose away from the knobby lumps where the branches attached. Once weakened sufficiently, the limbs dropped off.

What was left was a rough hole in the tree wall; just large enough for one person to thread through at a time.

Wearily, Sophie gathered her nanites and directed the swarm through the opening. The far-flung scouts were already reporting a continuation of the pathway beyond. She hoped that this one would lead through the thick part of the forest.

They continued working their way deeper into the woods. The path they followed would narrow almost to a blocking point, then widen gradually.

She looked up again. The sun wasn't visible, but it seemed to have moved. Gods! Had it been that long? It looked like it was now mid-afternoon. Hunger suddenly struck her. She paused and wiped a hand over her face, conscious that her shoulders were screaming in pain as she lifted her arm.

If she was that hungry and tired, how must Jack feel? She looked down in time to see Jack scamper away through a narrow gap in the undergrowth.

"Jack! Come back here!"

There was no answer. Her nanites were silent on the matter. It appeared the boy had run beyond the range of her scouts. She took stock. The majority of her swarm was clustered closely around her. How had that happened? There were a few scouts spread out, but the coverage was filled with gaps, and Jack had unerringly run directly through one.

She pushed ahead, following in his tracks.

After a time, she leaned against the thick trunk of a massive white pine. The lowest branches were comfortably over her head, and the bole provided some support for her aching back. She pushed her muscles against it, trying to ease the tension.

The ache seemed to ease slightly in response, so she moved onward to see that a choice faced her. The trees formed another barrier, but there were two routes, both of which seemed likely to penetrate the thick growth. She started towards the nearest one but was surprised when she found herself drawn towards the other.

As she entered, there was a slight slackening of the pain and tension she'd been feeling. It wasn't much, but even a little was welcome. She sighed in relief, perhaps things weren't so bad. Jack was most certainly just a short distance ahead. She hurried on.

After a few minutes, Sophie stopped in alarm. What was she doing? She'd moved past her swarm and it was strung out behind her. She turned back and took a step. The cramps in her shoulders suddenly flared up. The pain was incredible. It radiated up her neck, across her temples, and came together over her eyes in a burst of pain. She clasped her hands over her eyes in response, feeling like her forehead was about to explode.

Sophie staggered, lowered her hands, and turned back to her path. The pain quickly lessened in response. Once again, she took a breath of relief. Her mind didn't seem to be working correctly. She'd had periods like this before...before the world changed, before she had her nanites, back when she relied on any drug fix she could get. She...she found herself wishing for some of the small white pills that she used to carry. They had offered an easy way to dull her pain, and they were so convenient. All she had to do was to take a couple, and the pain would fade...just a couple.

She looked up. There was a building right in front of her. The door was open. She was sure that through that entrance there would be a place to rest and something to take for her pain. As that thought passed, her shoulders contracted as if to say, "Hurry." She went in.

It was dark and cold inside. The room's details were blurred, but she barely noticed. It was some kind of living space. The drugs would most likely be in the main bedroom; probably in the bathroom medicine cabinet. She staggered onward through the door. There was a large room beyond with a staircase leading upwards. That was where she must go. There would be relief there. There was no doubt in her mind.

After some false starts, peering into bedrooms and closets, she found a larger room that had to be the main bedroom. Only a little farther.

She found herself in the bathroom, opening a cabinet. There they were—the beautiful pills that had never let her down. Her hands shook as she opened the bottle. She poured the white tablets out, but they fell to the floor.

Crying in desperation, she dropped to her knees and tried to pick them up. The room blurred.

This wasn't the bath! She was kneeling on a thick carpet near a bed. There were two feet directly in front of her. She looked slowly upwards.

A man stood in front of her. He seemed to be...Michael! What was he doing here? She shook her head in disbelief, but the pain roared back, almost making her faint.

Michael touched her head, and the pain receded, still there, but now a dull ache rather than lightning bolts.

"Don't worry, my dear. I'll take care of you."

The words brought a rush of gratitude. She groaned with mingled pain and relief.

"I know you will, Michael. It's just that I hurt so awfully. I can't think. I need some pills."

There was a brief period of confusion during which she thought he gave her a pill. The pain rumbled in the back of her head, making her temples throb.

She heard him saying something to himself. It sounded like he was talking about her, but the words made little sense. They seemed out of context and not at all like something Michael would say.

The voice sounded thin and slightly squeaky as it said, "Ah. Very beautiful, but...what's this? She looks pregnant. Not very far along, though. It doesn't matter much. She'll be a wonderful conquest. Now, what was that about pills? I can strengthen that thought. The leverage will probably be enough to provide control."

She raised her head. "What are you talking about? Help me, please."

He leaned over her. She was on a bed. The sheets were soft and smooth on her skin. He caressed her temple, moving his hand down her face and lower to pass over her breast. It felt like fire as it glided along her skin. The pain in her head faded as his hand moved.

She shook her head. "Not now. I must find Jack. He's lost. Help me find him."

He answered, "Don't worry about him.

I've got him locked up...I mean he's safe in another room. Don't worry. He is waiting for you. Now relax and let me rub your neck and back. That will help with your headache."

Sophie obligingly rolled on her side. His hands moved along her neck and upper back. They didn't feel quite right, and she started in alarm. A wave of pain struck her, making her gasp.

"Don't fight it. I'll make you feel better, dear."

Michael never called her dear in that tone. It sounded like something dirty the way he was saying it now. She shook her head negatively.

His hands stroked her neck and back and moved lower. She must have removed her clothes when she got into bed.

The mattress shifted as he lay down behind her. She tried to relax, but something deep inside told her that this was no place to let down her guard. Michael's actions were so...so un-Michael.

This wasn't him!

Sophie jumped and sat up, making an effort to push the man away as she did. He wasn't Michael. He was some weasel-faced man she'd never seen before. She gathered her nanites, but before she could attack, the pain roared back, making her fall back with a weak moan.

"So! You'd destroy me if I let you. I'll have to keep my guard up then. You're powerful. I can sense that, but you're no match for my magic as long as you are not allowed to rally. Just relax. I'll remove the pain if you agree to become mine. It's easy. I'll be a wonderful lover for you. You'll forget all about your previous life."

She shook her head slightly, the movement sending more waves of pain through her temples.

"Oh. Does it hurt?" he asked with mock solicitousness. "Here, let me help."

She hurt too much to resist as he stroked her temples. The pain receded a little.

"You see! I can be very good for you. You'll come around once you understand that. All you have to do is to be good to me in return."

He allowed his hand to trail down her neck and slid it towards her breast. She snarled and tried to focus. If only she could... she made an effort, fighting against the pain and confusion. Her nanites seemed sluggish, but they finally responded.

He jumped back with an outraged cry. Blood dripped from his fingertips. When he saw it, he went into a frenzied dance, waving the damaged limb around wildly. Drips of blood flew in every direction.

"Agh! Blood! You've injured me, damn you! Just suffer, then. Maybe I'll think about forgiving you when I heal."

He continued his bizarre dancing in agitation as he moved through the door. He shoved his head back in to say, "Maybe I won't forgive you for a long time. You'll suffer until you're eager to do what I want."

The door slammed shut, and the lock clicked.

CHAPTER 19
SLAVERY

Snake was afraid. Being a captive meant that he had little choice in his actions, but everything he did seemed to infuriate Abubecar. When angered, the man would rip some of Snake's nanites away. Having his substance reduced hurt; perhaps not in the same way that a similar injury would hurt a wholly biological entity, but the loss of processing power and the sensory input was extremely painful to Snake.

Abubecar's actions meant little to the creature. He didn't understand what the man was trying to accomplish and cared less, aside from the fear that he might be punished for failure to assist.

Abubecar required him to capture any creature that intruded on the magician's territory. He brought in small mammals such as squirrels and was also expected to bring in humans if any were stupid enough to trespass.

It didn't matter to the big magician. He took any nanites the animals owned, often leaving them weak and dying. The bodies were left for Snake to dispose of as he wished.

Snake was a predator by nature. He had killed and absorbed the nanites and animal cells, utilizing their substance for energy. In his prior life as part of the dragon, he'd even partaken of human flesh, although his memories were faulty. The trauma of being ripped apart by the woman's power had disrupted his processing, and much data had been lost at the same time.

He was now learning a new thing: empathy. His suffering had made him more sensitive to the plight of other life forms. He had reached the point where even a squirrel's death made him feel saddened. He dutifully carried the latest victim out of the magician's workshop and slid down the hall to the kitchen window.

He'd taken to disposing of the carcasses in the garden. There was a mulch pile near the back, and he buried the squirrel's body under a thin layer of leaves. It seemed the least he could do. He could have eaten it, but he couldn't bear that thought.

He imagined trying to flee. There was no way he could. Abubecar had overridden his encryption so that now his nanites were only partially under his control. They allowed him to exist and function, but Abubecar could take away his freedom at any moment. The magician had shown he could force Snake to work at any task.

The drawback seemed to be that forcing Snake's nanites to work required constant monitoring. Snake thought he was still living for this reason. It was easier for Abubecar to give an order to a semi-autonomous creature that could work without constant supervision.

HE MOVED SLOWLY back through the garden, reluctant to leave the proximity of the wall and the freedom that lay beyond it. It would be false freedom, but nonetheless, Snake desired it with all of his being.

The memory of the woman came into his multi-part mind as he moved through the weeds. She had been violent beyond all belief, but he still thought that he'd sensed the reluctance in her; a caring and nurturing aspect that he now desired.

If only he'd been able to find her before the magician's nanite trap had sprung. Perhaps she would have seen him as an individual creature with needs of his own. Maybe she would have...he couldn't formulate quite what he desired, but the faint memories of animals he'd absorbed and the even weaker memories of the dragon's prey seemed to entice him with a sense of warmth and safety.

He slid through the window. As he did, he whispered, "Mother. Help."

The sounds were faint and almost unrecognizable as speech, but the feeling they aroused was that of hope and provided a slight amount of the comfort he needed.

No help was forthcoming. He paused, seeking with his nanites. The only living creature nearby, aside from himself, was the magician down the hall. His long body shuddered in dread as he slid over the carpet towards the workroom.

Halfway down the hall, he repeated the words. Once again they provided a modicum of emotional comfort, even though he could only barely surmise their true meaning. His head moved restively back and forth, questing for a solution, then he resigned himself once again to his fate, and with a slight rustle, he continued onward towards his master.

He entered the space, moving inconspicuously near the wall.

"You took a long time. I want you to travel to the village across the river. Return with a human. I don't care if it is a man or woman or child as long as it is alive when you return. I want the genetic pattern, and it must be living to be complete."

Abubecar turned away towards a workbench, then looked back.

"What are you waiting for? Go!" He lifted his hand in threat.

Snake coiled back on himself and slid out the door as quickly as he could.

The local humans had moved away after Abubecar had started victimizing them. Snake didn't usually worry about the time it took to travel, but his fear of punishment made him anxious about the distance. The sun had set and risen before he approached the place.

He found a thicket and camouflaged himself to observe. The people were just beginning to carry out their daily chores, moving about slowly in the cold morning air.

A child came near Snake's hideout. He thought about capturing it, but then its mother called to it from the door of their home.

The child turned and raced back to her. She caught it up, lifting it high and then hugging it tightly.

The sight created a painful feeling in Snake. How could he steal a little one from its mother? Especially when the desire in his heart was for, he paused as he thought about what he wanted. He wanted just such a relationship.

His mind was confused and trying to sort out the feelings. He had not been born; he had been created as the remaining free nanites from the destroyed dragon gathered together. He remembered gradually gaining in intelligence and knew how he had created himself, but there was still the memory of a mother. He'd probably generated it himself. Perhaps it was some odd artifact, but the fact remained that it was there in his mind. He desired to experience the actual relationship.

He started to turn away from the village, but his nanites revolted. Abubecar's control would not allow him to go against the magician's desires. He slowly turned back.

An old man was walking into the woods near the river. Snake hesitated. Would the man survive being captured? Would he be likely to live during the journey back? He was old, though. Surely that meant that he would no longer have a mother who would worry about him.

Snake shuddered. He could barely stand to contemplate the action he was compelled to take. He slowly started after the man, slithering through the tall grass.

As he moved, he whispered, "Mother. Help. Please."

MICHAEL'S GROUP HAD made good time. As Wold had intimated, the estate was occupied only by Cisco and Polly when they returned.

The two were quite happy to see Michael returning. However, Cisco was so agitated about Sophie that he nearly bit Michael's hand. Polly was a little less worried. She assumed that the younger woman was well able to take care of herself. Not so the poodle. He had seen too much in his short life.

Cisco followed Michael around, getting underfoot as his friend cleaned up from the journey. "Look, I don't mean to imply that you should go after her quickly, but you should leave right now!"

Michael fluffed the dog's ears affectionately.

Cisco was momentarily at a loss for words. After a bit, he sniffed loudly, shook his head to flap his ears back into place, and added, "I'm worried about her. That Jack! He doesn't have any sense. You know he tried to sneak off without her, and his impatience made her decide to go ahead and try to rescue the missing sister. Sophie should have waited for you. I'm afraid that bad magician may be more powerful than you think."

"Sophie can defend herself," Michael said. "Although I will admit that you never know how strong an enemy is until you actually fight them."

"Yes! That's it, exactly. There's always someone who is stronger, or at least it seems that way. But, then I'm a dog...er, mostly...and we're not known for having much sense about getting into fights."

The man had finished cleaning up and was now dressed in clean clothes.

"Cisco, I hope you'll forgive me. I have to rest a bit and have some food. Maybe Polly will fix me a warm meal. The fairy-girl and Killer should get food also. Wold will, as usual, take care of himself."

"Right. I'll go down and let Polly know you're hungry. What about Flyx? She'll drink some fruit juice, but what will she eat?"

"You should ask her what she wants. All I know is that I don't think she will eat any meat. Beyond that, I have to guess. Some bread or grain, maybe. I don't know."

By the time everyone had been fed, and Michael had rested, it was nearly dark. Despite the little dog's misgivings, Michael decided to wait and leave in the morning.

"We'll make better time, if I'm rested. Besides, I don't fancy traveling through unfamiliar territory in the dark. Unlike Wold, I have poor night vision."

"All right. I understand that you humans are limited, but remember, I'm going to make sure you leave at the crack of dawn." The dog turned and trotted out of the main bedroom.

Michael grinned. Cisco was so cute that one tended to forget that he was part human and more than a little bit bossy. He'd probably be scratching at the bedroom door by four in the morning.

His face fell. He'd tried to make light of the dog's worries, but having his wife out there alone was extremely bothersome. He decided to take one of their four-wheelers even though their supply of gas was limited. In this case, it would give him a good start at catching up. His three companions could fly and that made him the one holding up progress. The ATV would help and, if he had to leave it somewhere, he could always come back later to retrieve it. It was not likely to be stolen.

THE OLD MAN was less frightened than Snake had expected when he slid into sight. The man was sitting near the riverbank and raised his head slowly to inspect the unusual creature. After looking him over, the man said, "So, what are you? My death? It's about time, I'd say."

Snake paused. He searched through the memories stored in his multi-part body. Yes. There were more human words stored there than he'd used to this point. His intelligence level was such that he could understand their approximate meaning. Abubecar had spoken to him, but he'd seen no need to reply. Now he considered. Maybe he should try to talk to the man. He had been ordered to bring a human back to the magician. Surely it would be easier if the human came with him voluntarily.

His initial impulse had been to drag the man back as quickly as possible, but now that he'd inspected the man, it was apparent that he was old and sick and might not survive such rough treatment. It was best to be careful and take the best care of the man he could.

His mood lightened slightly. That meant he would have to travel at the speed the old man would set. He could, without violating his mandate, stay away from Abubecar longer. That was a good thing.

Once again he toyed with the idea of just leaving, but his programming rebelled. It was no good. He was caught solidly, and in a manner that kept him from escaping. He didn't understand what the magician had done to him, but he knew that his component nanobots were not entirely under his control. That loss frightened him.

The fear evoked a whisper. "Mother. Help."

The old man cocked his head. "What was that you said? Mother?"

"I'm not a mother, although I had children once. I'm just an old man. I was a professor before the world changed. Students flocked to my lectures. Now I'm a worthless man on the verge of death. Are you going to kill me? Answer me, you monster!"

Snake raised his head until it was at the level of the old man's chest. The man flinched back and fell, landing in a sitting position with his arms up, as if to ward off an attack.

Snake watched closely. The man's movements betrayed the truth. Even though he'd sounded fierce, he was slow and shaky and completely unable to defend himself. Taking him back would be difficult and would take considerable time, time that Snake didn't want to spend.

Well, it couldn't hurt to talk to this human. He modified his structure slightly to amplify better the sounds he'd previously made as a whisper, then attempted to speak.

The noise came out in a raspy tone and made no sense at first. Snake quickly modified the impromptu voice box he'd constructed and then tried again. This time the sound was better, but his formation of the human words was not precise. His speech slurred, and the words weren't perfectly formed. Still, they seemed close enough to be understandable. He decided that this voice would have to do.

"Hello. Snek. Me."

The problem became instantly apparent. Snake concluded that he had an inadequate sample to understand human syntax and grammatical rules fully. His pronunciation was also faulty. He hesitated, processing the information, then continued.

"Snek not choose be here. Master want man. Snek bring man to master. Live man. Not hurt you. You to come with Snek."

"A talking snake! That's a new one on me. Well then, Snek, you say you're called? So you have to take me somewhere. How do you propose to get me there? I'm sick. People say I'm crazy. Oh, and I have cancer with no nanites to cure me. It's just as well. I've outlived everyone I cared about. My wife. My daughter died a year ago from some disease. If you need a captive, I'm about the least useful person in the village. They can afford to lose me. Probably be glad to get rid of me in fact. I talk too much you see. Everyone says I never know when to shut up, but it doesn't bother me. I know when to stop talking. I understand too much talk."

Snake interrupted, speaking the human tongue move fluidly now, but still with a babyish lisp. "That nice. Man come Snek. It long walks. Snek see if some of parts help you. Don't know if Snek can. Parts not obey like used to. Snek try."

He paused. This was the longest human sentence he'd ever uttered. It required considerable concentration and effort to persuade his nanites to make the correct vibrations within his throat. He peered at the man. His words had apparently been understood.

"I've got nowhere else to be, you sliding beastie." He looked closer at Snake. "You're not really a reptile, are you?"

Snake was unused to being part of a conversation and even more unused to being treated as if he were equal with an identity of his own. The feeling of recognition was strange but good. He decided that he liked it.

He sent a thin stream of nanites toward the man. They slowly slid over the ragged clothes, entering the body through various pores and orifices. The invasion took longer than Snake thought it should, but the man didn't seem to notice.

Snake monitored the nanites' progress. The human was ill, fatally so. Some element of his DNA had come unhooked and that had allowed another part to run amok, damaging most of his internal organs. The nanite probe reported that any fix would be lengthy and require more knowledge than Snake possessed. In response, he moved closer to the man as if that would help.

He concentrated and directed his nanites as they worked to ease the discomfort the old fellow felt. Snake could do that much at least.

The old man straightened a bit and said, "You've done me good, Snakie, my lad. I feel younger and more fit than I have in years. Can your master do more? If he can, I'm ready to see him. Let's go." He climbed slowly to his feet and looked around.

Snake thought that the old fellow wouldn't be so pleased once he met Abubecar, but he really had no choice about warning the man. His nanites wouldn't cooperate when he thought about vocalizing a warning. Instead, they forced him to begin to move. He slid around the man's legs and started along the river's edge towards a point where it turned back in the direction of Abubecar's territory.

The old man followed, weaving a bit, but moving steadily and trying to keep up with Snake's slow progress.

SNAKE FOUND THAT the old one couldn't go far without having to pause and rest. Still, since they were making progress, he didn't suffer from the sense of violating Abubecar's orders. When the man faltered, Snake waited patiently for him to recover.

The evening drew near, and the old fellow was staggering in exhaustion. Snake was concerned. It would not do for the human to die on the way. He'd have to go back and find another. That might take too much time, even though he inwardly prized each excess minute spent in the task.

He didn't want to face the anger of his master. Abubecar would rip away more of his nanites. The magician could pull him to pieces in much the same way the woman had destroyed his dragon progenitor. He did not want to risk that fate.

The old fellow was in need. Snake thought he understood. Like the man, he also required fuel for his nanites and cells. He wasn't sure how his body worked, but he knew that he needed both energy producing food and water to function efficiently. The man must be similar.

Snake had been analyzing the old man's speech. He thought he understood some of the rules better now. It was acceptable to use other words than one's name to refer to one's self. He moved closer. "Snek be back." He couldn't understand why the man laughed.

"All you need is an Austrian accent and wrap-around sunglasses. You're a creature out of a nightmare. You could terminate me quickly if you wanted."

Snake mentally shrugged as he spun and slithered off. They were near water. He sensed it. There would be fish there. He could catch fish. He'd done it many times. They were seemingly unaware of his nanites and the tiny hunters easily captured them.

A while later, Snake returned. The man was leaning against a tree, his eyes closed, his chest moving in shallow breaths, his mouth slack.

Snake moved close, then formed part of his body into a cup shape, transferred some of the water he was carrying internally into the cup and held it to the man's mouth using a short arm he'd extruded. The man took a sip, then grasped the cup and drank the water down without opening his eyes.

"That's good. Now if I only had some food."

Snake was aware that Abubecar had heated his food. The process accelerated decomposition and made it easier to separate the constituents. He heated the fish meat and moved it through the extruded arm into the cup.

The man drank the watery fluid. "Fish stew, unless I miss my guess. My taste buds don't work as well as they used to."

The man opened his eyes and flinched away. He'd apparently forgotten where he was and that Snake was with him. "Oh. Yes. It's you, Reptile. You're a pretty good cook for a snake. I don't know what you understand about men, but I need rest now. I believe I'll sleep if it doesn't get too cold. Will you be here when I wake?'

"Yes. Snek watch. How Snek know man cold?"

"Going to take care of me, eh? Well, humans are warm-blooded. That means we create our own internal heat. We keep our body temperature in a narrow range. If we get too cold, we die. You'll know if I'm cold. I'll either tell you I'm cold, or I'll be shivering if I'm too cold to talk."

Snake said nothing. The task was becoming complex. Caring for a human was more difficult than he'd initially thought. No one had ever cared for him in any way. His thoughts centered on the idea of care. Would Sophie treat him as an individual with intrinsic value? Would she care for him if he were not functioning well? He didn't know.

The old man was now snoring. Snake settled down to watch through the darkness. His thoughts continued to dwell on the woman. If she treated him well, would that be similar to the concept he held? Would she be his mother? He couldn't fathom the ramifications, but something in the idea made him feel warm and safe deep within himself.

He noticed that the old man was indeed shivering. It had gotten colder. The lack of heat didn't bother his nanites much, but his cellular components did tend to stiffen and work less efficiently when it was cold. He cast about, then, for lack of any other option, he gathered dry grass and pine needles to spread over the prostrate man. That helped. The man quit shivering, and his breathing deepened.

Now Snake was content. He could do this. He could care for a human. His actions gave him a feeling of satisfaction and rightness. The man was an individual and deserved care. If Snake took care of him, that implied that Snake also deserved similar treatment. They were both individuals with intrinsic value. If he cared for the man, then maybe the woman would care for him.

He spent the night trying to balance out that equation. It was not susceptible to mathematical analysis, at least in any calculus that Snake understood. However, it did seem to make sense. He strained his memory, trying to recall the fragmentary memories of the dragon's human prey. They had felt the same way as far as he could determine.

By dawn, he was sure that caring for the old man made him more deserving of care himself. Besides that hope for personal benefit, there was an element of rightness about his actions. He felt that it was part of his job.

Taking the man to Abubecar had faded into secondary importance, although his programming required the action, he was prepared to offer as much assistance as he could to his captive.

THE ATV HAD to be abandoned as the forest grew thicker. The trees would allow no vehicle to pass. Michael regretfully left it behind. It had allowed him to get a good start and he was well off his own property and moving towards that of Chen.

He hoped to alert the man before he approached too closely. It was a good idea to knock before entering, so to speak. He, himself, did not look with particular favor on unannounced intruders, but then they couldn't approach without detection anyway. Chen would probably have his own warning system.

Killer and Flyx reported back to him at intervals. The fairy girl stayed much closer than the crow. She kept coming to land on his shoulder where she would tickle his ear with her long hair. When he'd laugh, she'd entreat him to carry her for a time, claiming that she was tired.

She was no great weight, and he obliged her whim. He was becoming suspicious that she was fond of him. He liked her. She was an amusing companion and surprisingly informed. She kept up a stream of lively conversation, making the walk less tiring.

Wold's sudden presence announced that they were close to Chen's home.

CHAPTER 20
RETRIBUTION

The ceiling of the room had water stains. Overall the place smelled musty. It obviously wasn't in good repair. The little weasel was a rotten homeowner as well as a thoroughly rotten host.

Sophie tossed restlessly on the bed. She hurt all over, but during the past few hours, she had regained a little equilibrium, a sense of herself that wasn't overwhelmed by pain and the desire for relief. She was able to think coherently for short periods.

The boredom and pain fog lifted sporadically when Darren entered her room. Once he brought her a sandwich. The bread was dry. She only nibbled a bit along one edge that did not seem so stale. She realized she must keep up her strength. She would escape as soon as she had a decent chance. If he thought that his tactics were going to make her accept him as a lover! Well, he had better think again. She was so angry with herself for falling into his trap that it didn't bode well for his survival.

Now that she could think, she was more angry with herself than with the small magician. He'd developed a means to influence her nanites without her noticing. They were still hers, she had checked their encryption, and it hadn't changed. How was he getting them to accept his commands?

Her thoughts were interrupted by another intrusion. Darren strutted in and walked over near the bed. Her pain faded as he approached. That was one good thing at least. He was obviously trying to condition her to respond favorably to him by rewarding her when he was present.

He was not much of a psychologist. Such an approach might work on someone who did not realize it was happening, but it only fueled her anger. It was insulting actually. The idea that she'd decide he was desirable because he inflicted pain on her when he left the room. It was a good thing she was perverse and stubborn.

The aspect that filled her with self-loathing was that she found herself looking forward to his presence. The desire was entirely too much like her desire for opioids when she'd been totally addicted. She was still an addict. There was no denying that, but she had learned to detest the feeling and her weakness. The combination bled over to Darren. She loathed him. Only a truly evil person would exploit someone the way he was trying to work on her. It placed him in the category of the drug dealers she'd known; men who dealt in human misery. He deserved to suffer horribly.

HER ATTENTION SNAPPED back to the little weasel. He'd said something. Best to pretend she was too groggy to understand. He couldn't learn that she was starting to recover to a degree.

"Wha...What did you ask?"

"Do you like me better now? You see, I don't want you to hurt. I'd rather reward you with pleasure. You just have to understand that I'm your friend."

This was too much. Sophie wanted to attack, but her nanites were as sluggish as she felt. It was almost as if some haze were in the room, interfering with her control. She tossed her head back and forth in denial. Darren didn't like that. As he stood to leave, the pain, which had faded somewhat, started to return.

"Still not ready to see how wonderful I am, huh? We'll see how much longer you can hold out."

The pain crashed down as he exited. She moaned, but then opened her eyes in surprise. That was it! He'd accidentally betrayed his means of control.

It was nothing he'd done in this visit; she'd visualized it as a haze interfering with her nanite control, but it wasn't. She had to tune her internal radio sense. As she did, she discovered an unusual low-amplitude background signal. It was on a frequency she usually did not monitor, and she'd previously missed it entirely.

The signal was not on the nanite-control frequency, but as she extended her sense, it blended with that frequency to produce two additional signals. One was higher and one on a lower band than usual.

There was a set of commands overlaid on the lower frequency. They were confusing her nanites. Although they were not supposed to be sensitive to that frequency, the tiny, semi-autonomous machines were picking up the commands through resonance or maybe because the main signal was heterodyned. Regardless, some aspect of the commands leaked through.

He was using that leakage to bypass her nanite security. It was spotty and faded out at times. That explained why her nanites were still her own. His control was only partial, but it was enough to keep her in nanite induced pain, and the fog kept her from breaking free. Now, if she could just figure out how to block the heterodyned signal, that would get rid of his nasty control. Once free, she'd make quick work of the nasty, little rat.

The interfering signal was weak. That implied that he either couldn't broadcast very strongly or that the actual source was shielded or distant. She carefully inspected her internal radio sense. It had been easy to widen up the bandwidth to receive the interfering signal once she'd thought of it. To widen the transmitter bandwidth was a little more difficult and would take more power; power she didn't feel able to generate, given her weakness.

Maybe she should focus her effort on the actual frequency Darren was using. That would take less power than covering the entire band. It would normally be a simple task for her to create a second transmitter.

Now it was almost impossibly difficult. She worked slowly, making sure the fog didn't mask her commands. Darren could not know what she was doing. She suspected that he didn't receive at all. He'd shown no response when she had transmitted in his presence. The only thing he'd responded to was the pain she'd caused by ripping the skin on his fingers.

Her nanites responded sluggishly, but accurately. Gradually the transmitter was built, using iron from her blood and other minerals. She'd have to remember to eat carefully until she replenished her body.

Finally, it was done and ready to be tested. It broadcast on the exact bandwidth Darren was using. She didn't have the energy to finesse the situation. She merely overwhelmed his signal, simultaneously sending commands to her nanobots on their normal frequency and also on Darren's.

There was a moment of confusion. Then the pain in her neck and shoulders faded, first to a dull ache, then the knots released entirely. She felt fine. The fog was gone. This was great! She'd almost forgotten what it was like to be whole and pain-free.

There was a click at the door, and it swung open. Sophie's eyes widened. She hadn't expected to be rescued, so when Flyx slid through the crack, she was surprised. Her nanite swarm hadn't provided its usual warning. Incapacitating her swarm was another thing to hold against Darren.

The fairy hovered in mid-air and looked over her shoulder through the crack, then flew near to whisper, "He's coming this way again. What shall I do?"

Sophie grinned with wolf-like intensity. Her expression must have startled Flyx. The small humanoid flinched. "What?"

"It's not you, Flyx. I'm going to make that evil little man wish he'd never been born. You just hide behind the headboard of the bed and stay safe."

Darren pushed the door open with a puzzled look. "I thought I'd closed that."

He looked suspiciously at Sophie. "You couldn't open it, who did?"

Flyx had followed Sophie's instructions and had hidden, but she hadn't been convinced that Sophie was able to fight. She suddenly shot out of her hiding place, flew straight towards Darren's face, then fired her most potent spell. It struck him precisely on the point of his large nose.

There was a loud snap. Darren screamed, then grabbed at his face. Blood poured between his fingers. He released his nose and looked at his bloody hand in horror, then at Sophie as if to ask her for help.

Sophie burst into laughter at the expression on his face. She shook her head at him, still laughing. "You're going to have a scar from that. Your nose doesn't look so good. Flyx, hit him again, please."

Flyx was now hovering near the door, and she obligingly shot a bright spark at Darren's posterior. He leaped at the impact and slapped at his behind with his free hand, trying unsuccessfully to hold his nose with the other.

He couldn't do the two things at once. His nose began to bleed even more than before. He caught at it, making the blood spurt through his fingers. He turned pale at the sight, then his eyes suddenly rolled upwards as he keeled over on his back in a full faint.

His head impacted the wood floor with a loud clonk. Flyx looked surprised, then proud. She landed by Sophie on the bed and said, "That's the best two spells I've ever made. Nobody messes with my Michael's wife."

She suddenly looked embarrassed as she realized what she'd said. She tried to recover by modifying her statement. "I mean that Michael's my friend, and I..."

Sophie gently touched the fairy-girl arm with her index finger. "I don't mind, Flyx. He's very lovable. I understand fully."

A rush of wings came down the hall. The next moment both Wold and Killer sailed through the door, Killer a little behind. Killer landed silently on the chandelier as Wold dropped to the floor, instantly reverting to his brown man form. He bent over Darren and inspected him, then gingerly felt his throat with a finger.

"He is still alive. He'll recover in a bit." He turned to Sophie. "Dear Lady, how are you? He didn't harm you did he?"

This was wonderful. Sophie laughed in relief, then found herself with tears in her eyes. "Oh, Wold. He hurt me badly." She paused, assessing her physical and emotional state. The sense of relief was immense, masking what aches remained.

She looked at the three unlikely rescuers. "But, really I've taken no permanent harm as his prisoner. I had just started to free myself when Flyx arrived. I can deal with him now."

Her expression changed as she looked at the recumbent Darren. He wasn't going to enjoy her judgment.

Once again she paused. Her nanites had alerted her to another presence. Michael was coming and bringing someone with him.

There was a loud crash down the hall. She giggled. Michael had his blood up and was not going to be polite. If a piece of furniture got in his way, it was probably going to be destroyed. His steps pounded closer to the door.

She was smiling at him when he entered. His eyes focused on her and he stopped short.

"My God, Sophie. You gave me such a fright. Are you okay?" He glanced down at the recumbent form of Darren. "Who's this? Is it who I think?" He lifted his sword in threat.

"Yes. This is Darren the Magnificent. You don't have to do anything. Flyx took him out quite nicely."

Michael looked at the fairy, who preened a bit under his gaze.

She said, "I cast my most powerful spell at his nose. Then he fell down. I rescued her for you, dear Michael."

Michael had the grace to blush a little, then looked apologetically at Sophie and shrugged somewhat ruefully.

"She's been a real asset. She very courageously attacked the vampire queen and, well..." He looked even more embarrassed. "She helped save me from that unspeakable creature. Now she's saved you. We need her as part of our household."

Sophie smiled again. "Yes, Flyx is a brave-hearted girl." She turned to the fairy and bent down, so their heads were on the same level. "Flyx, you're welcome to live with us as long as you want and when you want."

Michael glanced down at Darren, frowning. Just at that moment, both Chen and Gwen entered the room.

"Sophie!" Gwen exclaimed.

Chen nearly stumbled over Darren's body, then looked down. "Wow! What happened to his nose? That's going to leave a scar for sure."

He looked up as Sophie, Flyx, and Michael laughed.

"What did I say?" he asked, holding his hands out-spread in question.

Darren chose that moment to moan slightly. Sophie frowned at him, then focused her senses on the unattractive little man.

"Hmm. He trapped me rather neatly, but now that I have the time to assess him, he doesn't have much in the way of magic. His nanite swarm is sparse and only loosely integrated. He isn't capable of much power. His ability is mostly accidental, even though it is effective because it's unexpected. He's probably more dangerous to untalented people than to other magicians. I think that a few changes are in order.

She pondered possible punishments, then pulled Darren's nanite swarm away from him. Stripping him of his power would be punishment enough.

She integrated the freed nanites into her swarm and changed their encryption. They were hers now.

"I've got his external nanites. I think I'll make a couple of changes to his body. Just a minute."

This time she sent a nanite probe into Darren's body. She found a cobbled up radio transmitter. From the looks of it, he'd probably created it accidentally, and it probably hadn't worked well. That might account for the weak signal.

The miracle was that it had several parallel outputs that broadcast the same signal on multiple frequencies. That was how he'd managed to heterodyne commands to her nanites below their encrypted frequency. He used that mode automatically. Why he probably didn't even know how his spells worked.

Sophie made a wolf-like grin. Her nanites were disassembling Darren's transmitter. They reassembled a heavily shielded and efficient device that automatically warned nanites away from him. When they were done, she pulled them back to herself.

Then her eyes were drawn to his injured nose. It was still bleeding slowly. She sighed disgustedly then sent a small cloud of nanites to rebuild the wound, leaving a distinct scar as a reminder to him every time he looked in a mirror.

"He's no longer going to be able to use any magic. I wanted to flay the little wretch, but now I think that being one of the common folk and having to work for a living will be a better punishment."

Gwen added, "If he survives. The common people hereabouts have grudges against him. He's seduced many of the women against their will. He may not live long enough to walk out of the area."

Michael growled, "That's his problem. Let's get him on his feet and send him out of here. It won't be pleasant to be out tonight. There's a storm coming. He won't be able to find shelter with the locals, that's for sure."

Chen nodded and added, "We're going to have to stay here. The north wind has picked up. The sky is purplish black on the horizon and fully overcast overhead. If it weren't so early in the season, I'd expect snow from this. As it is, I think it's going to rain or maybe sleet. It'll be cold and windy. Are you sure you want to send him out tonight?"

Sophie sighed again. She wanted revenge. The old Sophie would have taken it without thinking. Something in her had softened due to Michael's love. The others were looking to her to pass judgment since she was the offended one, but she couldn't or wouldn't be as cruel as her initial impulse desired.

"Let's lock him up for tonight and then send him out tomorrow. We'll give him food and warm clothes, too. His life is now changed. He'll hurt no one else with magic. I hope he learns how wrong he was."

Wold made a hooting sound from deep within his chest, then spoke in a creaking voice. "I doubt that he'll thank you for the kindness. I'll watch him tonight."

He looked down at Darren, whose eyelids were fluttering.

"You, Mr. Magnificent! Get up and come with me."

ONCE DARREN WAS locked in a storage closet, they searched until they found Jack. He'd been locked in a bedroom and had been relatively comfortable. Darren had even fed him regularly. The man wasn't automatically bad. Sophie thought that he held some animosity against women. He apparently had been utterly unsuccessful at establishing a relationship with any woman before the change in the world.

Aside from some mice, the place had no other occupants. The kitchen was well-stocked, so the group had a good meal at Darren's expense.

Outside the wind was blowing at gale force. The gusts rattled the windows and whistled around the gables and eves of the building making an eerie keening sound. It looked as if Chen was going to be proven wrong in his assumption that it was too early in the season for snow. The clouds were low and threatening with no let-up in sight, and the temperature was dropping alarmingly.

Chen had gone out to check and now came inside, beating his cold hands against his legs to stimulate the circulation.

"There's some sleet in the wind already. If the temperature drops any farther, it's going to turn to snow."

Despite her anger with Darren, Sophie felt that she'd been correct in not putting him out in the weather. However, she had suffered enough at his hands not to trust him, even locked up as he was.

"Michael, is there any chance Darren could escape or do some harm?"

"No. I've asked Wold to continue to keep an eye on him. I agree. We don't want to risk him having some way to escape into the house. He might have weapons stored that we haven't found. No sense giving him another chance at us."

Sophie nodded. "I'm still nervous about him, but I'm ready for him now. He wouldn't be successful, even with a weapon, and I won't be gentle if he tries anything."

After supper, the four adults sat by the fireplace in the great room to discuss what was to be done about Abubecar and Jack's sister.

Michael was still aggrieved and didn't bother to cover up how upset he was. "Sophie, I'm hurt that you didn't wait for me. Look what happened! You were captured by a man who is barely any type of magician at all. I know you've always been stronger than your opponents, but there are other forms of attack. What if this Abubecar can do things that you've never suspected and aren't ready for?"

"You're right. I'm sorry, Michael. I should have waited. Now that we're together, though, I think that we should be enough to handle the guy." Sophie waved her hand to include the other two.

Chen shook his head in doubt. "I don't know. He frightens me. The last time I spoke to him, I got the impression that he only let me go because he felt I had nothing of value. He seemed very strong."

Sophie shook her head. "Yes, but how strong is the question."

Gwen answered, "We may not be as strong as you, Sophie, but I'm positive he is stronger than Chen and I together.

Maybe stronger than you. I don't know. I'd have to see you both simultaneously to assess your relative strengths."

She thought about that for a bit, then said, "He's unlikely to allow us that luxury. I'll admit that Darren gave me a bad time. His attack was on such a low level that I didn't sense it until it was too late and he had weakened me so much I could barely muster the force to escape. However, I had figured out how he did it when Flyx came through the door. I don't think he would have held me much longer."

Michael shook his head. "Maybe not, but it was too close for my liking. What if Abubecar can beat all of us together?"

She didn't like the tone in his voice. It betrayed self-doubt. Michael was usually so confident and easy-going. Now he was worried and, she suspected, feeling guilty and responsible for allowing her to be captured.

"Dearest, we have resources beyond the four of us. We have the Chimeras and maybe the fairies. Once the weather breaks, both Killer and Flyx will go to their people and bring back as much help as they can. Both groups are good resources, and both can help in a fight. And, we have Wold."

The four looked at each other. Wold was a strange creature. Neither Michael nor Sophie really knew how capable he might be. The owl-man seemed to have no nanites and no discernible magic. Despite that, he always accomplished what he set out to do, often in a way that implied magic was responsible. Not for the first time, Sophie considered that Wold might be a left-over creature from the old world; the pre-nanite magic world.

Michael had his own version of natural magic that usually manifested in good luck and a way of seeing through people and their actions. Maybe Wold was similar. Maybe he was a...she thought it over, trying the taste of the concept on her tongue. Perhaps he was a brownie or something like that; a true paranormal creature. There was no use asking him. He wouldn't answer. She'd asked him before about his origins, and he'd become very reticent.

Gwen interrupted her train of thought. "Chen has his trolls. They could be some help."

"Yes. They are kind of slow and most wonderfully stupid, but I can direct them to an extent. Their one virtue is that they can bite really hard. If they were to enter his mansion, they'd create havoc. They try to eat everything, at least when they're not having sex and reproducing." Chen shook his head deprecatingly.

"Aside from that, I can't figure out exactly what good they are. I've tried to set them up as guardians for my..." He looked at Gwen. "Uh, our property, but they are easily distracted. I have to keep on them to get them to stay on even the simplest task. That could be something I can do to keep Abubecar busy."

He brightened. "Besides, if Abubecar kills some of them, it will be a favor to me. The ugly little things reproduce too quickly for comfort."

Michael focused on Sophie. "It's late, sweetheart. Why don't we get some sleep? Maybe we'll think of some additional things in our dreams. Besides, no plan survives the first contact with the enemy."

She reached for his hands. "Then we'll have to improvise, won't we?"

THE STORM WAS still raging in the morning, and it had turned absolutely frigid. A couple of feet of snow had fallen during the night, and it was still coming down.

CHAPTER 21
COMPASSION

The wind had shifted to the north in the early evening. Sometime during the night, it had brought clouds. Now the clouds were thick, and sleet mixed with snow was falling. The wind was roaring through the trees.

It was nearly dawn, but there was no sign of light. The clouds were too thick. Snake checked his charge. The human was still breathing, at least.

That was good. What was terrible was the clouds were now releasing the first thick flurries of what would probably turn into a major snowstorm. Snake raised his neck and head from the ground to look upwards. There was a ragged vee of geese heading south on the storm wind. He could hear their mournful honks, first faintly, then louder as they came overhead.

Something about the sound brought a memory to the front of his mind. The image wasn't properly his; it had belonged to one of the humans the dragon had consumed. Snake inwardly flinched at the thought. True, he'd been part of the dragon, but now he was his own creature. He had changed during his travel, and he felt like he no longer knew what he was.

The sound of the geese evoked an incomplete mental picture. He inspected it. The scene was of a group of humans, a family, he thought. They were sitting at a table laden with food. There was a turkey on a platter, and the room was warm with light and good feelings. Snake flinched again. He knew nothing of such things. His existence was composed of varying degrees of pain. He recognized that sensation at least. He was intimately familiar with it.

The picture spoke faintly to him, telling a tale of a loving family relationship that he could barely comprehend. He moved his head from side to side, unconsciously trying to see more of the image to make sense of it. He made a slight rustling sound as he lowered his head back to the ground, then lay still, thinking.

The man that the dragon had consumed had been part of a family. Did the other members miss him? Snake missed those parts of himself that Abubecar had taken. The sensation was akin to direct pain, less intense in one way, but laden with sadness.

IT HAD BEEN wrong. The dragon had killed and consumed the man without any consideration for the man or his family. On the one hand, Snake understood the dragon's need for energy and chemical components. He was its descendant in a sense and had the same requirements, but...but...the man and his family. Snake felt an overwhelming sense of guilt that translated into shame. He coiled around and thrust his head under his body in misery.

That action didn't help. Snake shut his eyes tightly, then tried to compare his feeling of loss and pain with what the man must have felt. It was wrong; wrong to hurt another sentient being. He had to consume to live, but he could restrict his consumption to plants despite their lower energy level. They weren't sentient.

He inspected the picture again. There was a woman there. She was the mother of the children. She looked happy as did the children. He thought of Sophie, her face grimacing with effort and concentration as she destroyed the dragon that he had been part of. He had feared her then.

He wondered how his constituents had been lucky enough to escape her wrath. He was glad she hadn't pursued him.

Another picture came into his mind. Some of his nanites had recorded her expression as she looked at the man who had accompanied her. Her face was glowing with an expression that he recognized. It was similar to that of the mother in the picture. It was, he thought, what humans called love and it betokened a willingness to do things for others; to sacrifice for them. A feeling of kinship with the old man swept over him. The two of them were living creatures, and both could suffer. For his part, he'd mostly suffered, but now he wanted to find another feeling, one that was the opposite of suffering.

The picture of Sophie's glowing face came through his mind again. If she would just look at him in the same way. He had convinced himself that she was his mother. She was responsible for his existence, even if she hadn't intended it and even if it had resulted from an act of painful destruction.

The thought came into his head slowly. He and the old man were alike in many ways; not in form, but in the ability to suffer and feel the lack of suffering. He had no words for that concept.

If he cared for the old man, he then had a...what was it? A moral claim perhaps? He had a right to be considered as worthy of proper treatment in turn.

His mind leaped ahead to the conclusion. He would be worthy of love. Surely the woman would see that she was his Mother! She created him. She was responsible. He wanted her to love him and comfort him. She would ease his pain.

There was an element of doubt still in him. He understood the concept upon which he was fixated was not rational, but he thrust the uncertainty out of his mind. That was what would happen. He was sure. His tail twitched. He felt a new feeling; one he'd never felt in his brief existence. He felt concern and empathy for the man beside him.

Snake pulled his head from under his body and moved closer to the old man, shoving the grass and needles aside, trying to contact the man's body with his own. At the same time, he increased his metabolism so that he produced more heat than before. He could get by with low body temperature. The man could not and would need extra warmth in the storm.

High above, he heard the last faint honks of the wind-blown flock as it scudded southward. The wind rattled the trees. Thick flurries of snow descended to land softly on the ground, rapidly building up around the two.

THICK CLOUDS STILL hid the sun, although the snow and wind had stopped for the time being. Now the cold was an enemy that could prove fatal to the human. Snake was able to adjust his metabolism so that the cold's only effect on him was a slight slowing of his movements. Not so the old man.

The man was shivering again despite Snake's best efforts. He pulled away but discovered that the dry needles he'd hoped to find were now covered by snow. He writhed around searching and in the process, noticed that he was able to pile the fluffy flakes into mounds. That would help keep the wind off at least.

He circled the man, using his long body to bulldoze snow over the grass that covered the prostrate form. Once he'd worked a high mound over the man, he shoved his head deep inside and slithered tightly against the man. The insulating blanket of snow dulled the bite of the wind, and the pine needles and grass kept the direct cold from contacting the man's flesh.

Snake lay still, working to increase his internal heat production. After a time, he noticed that the old man no longer shivered. This would have to do until the old one woke up. He didn't know what they'd do then.

THE OLD MAN had been awake for a while. He had made small movements, but then lay still. Finally, he said, "Snake? Is that you around me? You're really warm. You're keeping me warm."

Snake moved slightly. "I keep warm. You. Snow much. You in grass. Snow. Wind stop. Get up, if want. You, man."

The human didn't respond at once. After a time he said, "Snake thing, You kept me alive. I was too tired last night. I probably would not have known it if I froze to death. That might have been for the best, though. I'm not good for much anymore."

The man rolled on his side, then breathed deeply. "Asleep in a snow bank with a snake creature. What an odd thing to do."

Snake was silent.

The man pushed at the snow with his arms and then sat up. "Whew! It's cold out here. I've got to get up. Can't stay here, but it's so cold. Brrr!"

Snake moved then, stretching his body and pushing the snow away from the man in arcs as he writhed.

It was cold. The temperature had dropped even more while the two had laid under the snow. The man was surely going to freeze. He'd die, and Snake would have failed at his task. That couldn't be allowed to happen.

"Man, lie. Snek cover. You. Snek find something keep warm. Stay here. Snek come back."

"I've got to relieve myself first, but then I believe I'll follow your directions. It was warm where I was, and it's too cold out here."

Snake watched as the man stood partially shielded by a tree and performed a biological function. It seemed wasteful. Snake could recycle the water he consumed. Running it out on the ground and losing the stored heat was a bad plan, but apparently something the man felt he needed to do.

Once the old man had finished, he lay back in the depression and Snake covered him again.

"Stay. Snek come you. Not long."

The man answered, his voice muffled by the snow. "If it's too long, I'll be frozen. I hope your master won't be unhappy if you bring in a frozen corpse."

Snake had no answer for that. He moved off, his mind mulling over the concept of failure. Abubecar would not forgive him. It might be that Abubecar would be angry that he'd taken so long already. His thoughts slowed, buried in a sudden spasm of fear.

The magician had already taken almost one-fourth of his nanite population. He was much slimmer than he had been when he had fallen into the human's trap. How much of his swarm could he lose before his mind became incapable of thinking at a high level? He didn't know. He wondered how he was able to think as well as he could. His processing ability was, as far as he knew, rooted in the synchronized action of all of his nanites. His memory was distributed throughout his swarm, each individual nanite contributing its own share of data that was stored in its limited memory bank.

He stopped, raised his head, and looked back. The snow he had piled up covered the old man completely. Maybe that would provide enough warmth.

As he turned back to his search, a sudden thought struck him. What if his nanites had recognized the danger of Abubecar's attacks and compensated by moving the thinking part of his mind deep into his body. If his processing was now centered in his head as was the processing of all of the higher biological life that he'd encountered, it would carry both good and negative implications.

If Abubecar took more of his substance, he wouldn't lose thinking ability, only memory storage. On the other side of the equation, he was now worried that he could be more easily and more severely damaged by an injury to his head. He dwelt on that idea for a time, thinking of what it might mean to him if he were to engage in combat. He now had to protect his head, something that he had not worried about before.

Did this mean that he was becoming more of a biological entity? He didn't know. His body was still a combination of nanites and living cells gleaned from prey. How would he survive, if he decided that he could no longer hunt if it involved killing possibly sentient prey? He paused. That would mean death for him or at least a gradual fading away of his ability to hold his nanite swarm together.

Humans killed and ate, though. Could it be acceptable to eat lesser, non-sentient creatures?

He couldn't worry about that at this time. He had a legitimate excuse, and he was doing his best to follow his orders.

Besides, he wanted the old man to live. He had to keep him alive to deserve consideration in his own right. How could he expect the woman—he deliberately changed his thought—his Mother to care for him if he didn't succeed? He moved through the snow, questing for a solution. As he moved, he whispered, "Mother. Snek want good. Please. Help."

THE STORM PICKED back up as he moved through the trees. The wind howled, and the snow again fell so thickly that it was impossible to see much. Snake continued searching although his body was beginning to suffer from lack of heat. He was approaching the point where he would require additional chemical energy to function well.

He moved through the trees and discovered a clearing. It contained mostly lumps that were snow-covered bushes. As he poked his head into one, he found a rabbit. He lunged and caught it before it could run.

The creature cried out as he held it in his jaws. He shivered. The cry was one of fear and pain. He almost let it go, but then thought of the old man. If he didn't eat, the old man would surely die. He bit down and then swallowed the still quivering mass.

That was better. His nanite-based digestion quickly broke the creature down and began to convert the chemical compounds into energy that he could use.

He slid through the snow blindly, but then stopped, his nose against a solid wall. It was a human dwelling.

Snake moved quickly around the building. It was deserted. There was an opening above him. He raised his head and slid through. Inside there were pieces of glass on the floor. It was a window that had been broken sometime in the past. He quickly investigated the cabin. It was small, but there were a wood stove, a store of wood, and blankets folded neatly on a bed. This was perfect, but how was he to get the old man here?

He left a trail of nanites in the snow as he returned to where the man was buried. They would mark the house's location. The return journey went much faster. He no longer had to search, but instead traveled quickly back to the place where the old man slept.

To his immense relief, the old one was still alive, although he was shivering under the grass and snow. Snake moved close to release more heat.

Now began another problem. The human could no longer walk and, in fact, wasn't making much sense in his speech. Snake began to worry. Had the man reached the point of no return? Was he too cold and would he die?

In a sudden rush of concern, Snake flattened his body. It took more time than he thought. The living cells and bones he carried within had become fixed in position. His nanites worked diligently to move them as he gradually flattened to the point where he could carry the human on his back without worrying about the man falling off.

The new configuration meant that his forward motion was far slower than before. He didn't like that. Another disadvantage was that the increased surface area meant that he now was losing heat at a far faster rate. He moved through the blizzard as quickly as he could, the semi-conscious man cradled on his back.

It seemed to take forever, but he finally reached the cabin. He was momentarily at a loss when he stopped below the window. The man would not fit through the hole.

A door! He suddenly remembered that human dwellings had a large entrance. Around the corner and there it was. It was shut, and he couldn't get it open. He rolled the old man off his back into the snow, then slid back to the broken window, regaining his normal body shape as he moved.

Once inside, he inspected the door. The lock was puzzling until he realized that he only need turn a knob. The door opened. The man's body was close. Snake latched onto the nearest foot with his teeth and pulled, sliding the man inside. He pushed the door shut with a coil of his body. The cabin seemed warmer already. The broken window was on the side away from the wind, and only a few snowflakes drifted through the shattered glass.

Snake knew what the blankets were for. He dragged them over the man and himself, then began to release as much heat as he could. The man stopped shivering after a while.

Snake allowed the time to pass. His mind was not given to sleep, but he found himself thinking of the woman. He corrected himself again. She was his mother, not just any woman.

Mother would be pleased that he had saved the old man. He wondered what that would be like. His fragmentary memories of humans seemed to say that it would be delightful. She would say nice things to him and she would...what? He didn't know. She could give him food and make sure he wasn't in pain or damaged. That would be nice.

He wanted such treatment with all of his essence. He must escape from Abubecar in some fashion and find Mother. The thought of going against the magician frightened him, but Mother would make it better.

He drifted waiting out the hours until the storm should cease, thinking slowly of how beautiful it would be to deserve and receive care.

Outside the storm raged on.

CHAPTER 22
PLANS

Sophie did not like to admit it, but her capture by Darren had shaken her confidence. She was unwillingly thrust back into her old self-image of an addict and a failure. Michael's presence helped and rationally she knew that she was a different person, a deserving and strong woman who had beaten her addiction and every opponent she'd faced since that time.

"Michael? Are you awake?"

The light coming through the window showed a dim gray. It must be late morning, but the storm was still blowing outside. They would not be going anywhere today.

He rolled over and groaned a little.

Sophie snuggled close, inhaling his distinctive scent. Something about his odor was comforting along with being slightly arousing. She slid her arm over him and rested her head on his shoulder before asking again.

"Are you awake?"

"Ugh. How can I not be with you jumping on me like that?"

"I wasn't jumping. I was only getting close for warmth."

"It is cold out, isn't it? Pull up the blankets a bit more."

They rearranged the blankets and then held to each other, basking in their shared warmth.

Michael moved his hand gently over her front, feeling the bulge of their unborn child.

"I would like to wait until you're over this pregnancy before we confront Abubecar. I don't want you to undergo unnecessary risk."

"We can't wait! He's already a threat to anyone who encounters him. It's going to be months before I deliver our baby. Abubecar could decide to attack the common people or maybe even us in the time between now and then."

"I know, but..."

"I'm fit and able to move now. If we wait and he forces the issue, I'll just be bigger and less able. We have to do it now."

HE SIGHED, WEARILY. "I know you're right, but I couldn't live without you. We'll have to be extremely careful in our approach."

"I know. I've spoken to both Flyx and Killer. They each believe their people will help."

"Even if they do, I'm not sure they'll be much good against him."

She thought it over. The fairies were able to cast simple spells; more pranks, really. Still, that might be helpful as a distraction. Despite Killer's self-adopted name, he wasn't much use in a fight. He could serve as a look-out and messenger though. That was probably the best use of the crows.

Wold would be a real help. She'd seen him take control of some problematic situations even though he'd never demonstrated any truly powerful spells other than his shape-shifting.

The Chimeras were out of this. Cisco would want to help, but he was needed at their estate. Besides, he was more likely to need help than to provide any significant assistance. She smiled as she recalled the small, mutant dog's bravery in one of her early battles.

That recollection led to the thought of Cal. She'd set out to avenge his death, but he hadn't been dead, only changed. His location now was unknown, but if she could find him, the great Were-bear that he'd become would definitely be useful unless he couldn't be persuaded to assist. He had changed in more than his shape. His thinking was now strange...other than human. She hadn't seen him lately. He might have become more alien in the interim. He couldn't really be counted on. Of course, there were other Weres as well, but they were, as a general rule, unwilling to help humans. It was likely that they'd think this was strictly a human battle. They couldn't be counted on either.

Michael pulled her close, holding her tightly. "What are you thinking about?"

"Just wondering what help we can really expect."

"Me too. We're going to have to wait until the weather breaks to find out. I think we should try to find Cal. He would be useful if he felt like it."

She smiled. "That's just what I was thinking. It would be great, if he would bring some other Weres, too."

"Don't count on that. They keep to themselves."

Michael sounded discouraged, but then he spoke in a more cheerful tone. "We could maybe convince them that Abubecar is a danger to all life, not just people. Besides we've got Gwen and Chen."

She laughed. "Don't forget Chen's trolls."

"Yeah. The trolls. Maybe they will bite Abubecar at a critical time, but I doubt that he'll have any difficulty dealing with them. Would you?"

"No. I'd set their metabolism down to such a slow pace that they'd become almost statues."

"You wouldn't kill them?"

"I don't think that would be necessary. I could, of course, but why waste resources?"

"I doubt that Abubecar will be so considerate."

She rolled over to face him. "We'll just have to make do with whatever help we can get. Meanwhile, we have to wait until this storm dies and I have an idea of how we can pass some time."

He laughed and bent to kiss her.

THEY HAD A late brunch. Darren's kitchen was clean and functional, in glaring contrast to some of his slovenly habits. They ate biscuits with gravy and sausage, pausing to converse and listen to the storm rage outside.

The afternoon was long, and conversation lagged. Each of the four became silent, choosing to dwell on the potential problems they might face. Michael stood moodily by a window gazing out at the storm while the other three sat quietly near the fire.

They'd heaped wood on the open fire, and it was cranking out enough heat to keep the humidity in the dank house at bay. They listened to the cold wind whistling around the eves, seeking ingress in any crack, without speaking. The threat of the wind and cold seemed to seep into their bones bringing discouragement with it.

At last, Sophie stood, stretched, then said, "Abubecar has just about beaten me without even lifting a finger. My mind is making him out to be superhuman, and I know he's not. I'm going to take a nap. Maybe I'll have a better attitude if I get some rest."

Michael nodded and walked quietly to the bedroom hall; a visible cue that he would nap with her. Gwen and Chen looked at each other, then Chen said, "We'll watch the fire for a while longer. Maybe we'll think of something that we've overlooked."

WHEN SOPHIE WOKE, it was evening. The storm had blown itself out. Now the sky was showing a spectacular sunset, although the colors were muted as if they'd been washed out by the snow.

Michael looked out the window, grunted, and said, "We'll be able to travel tomorrow. What is it to be? Will we head towards Abubecar's land, or will we send for help first?"

"Send for help, I think. Let's not get in too much of a rush. If we can enlist assistance, we will need to give them time to get here and then we'll have to assign roles to each group."

"Yeah. That's a good idea. The stuff Chen told us has me very worried about Abubecar. He may be more of a challenge than we've ever faced."

"I'm about in the same place. I...well, Darren damaged my confidence." She turned and embraced him, holding on tightly. "Michael, I can be beaten. I thought that I couldn't, but I've learned differently. We can't afford to lose to Abubecar. He's becoming a real threat to the people in the area and even to the magicians."

He hugged her back. His strength made her feel secure.

"I won't let anything happen to you. You're too important to me."

"I know. You to me, too." After a silent moment, she added, "I've been thinking. We need some kind of Magicians' Code. Some set of rules that we all swear to that will ensure the safety of commoners. We can't allow ourselves or others of our kind to run roughshod over fellow humans."

"Or, over other intelligent creatures either," he added, nodding in agreement.

"We'll have to get everyone to swear to agree and then set up some kind of enforcement mechanism if this is to work. I don't really know how to go about that, Michael. You're experienced at managing people. Can you figure out how to do it?"

"Well, much as you said, I guess. We can appoint a governing council. Maybe the more powerful magicians. We can have limits on the length of service and hold elections or..." He stopped, then shrugged and continued. "The details can be worked out. Let's have a conclave of all of the magicians we can find and let them jointly decide. That is if we can take care of the current problem first."

THE GROUP, INCLUDING Jack, Flyx, and Killer had a late supper. Wold took food to Darren and stayed there. No one had ever seen Wold eat and it was normal for him to absent himself during mealtimes.

The dinner conversation avoided talk of the conflict to come, staying on light topics. Afterward, everyone sought their own bedrooms to sleep or toss on their beds making and discarding plans.

THE NEXT DAY dawned clear and cold. Killer woke everyone early. He was in a rush to be off looking for others of his kind. Once the door was open, he rose quickly in the cold, dense air, circled once, cawed, then headed eastward in a straight line.

They watched until he was out of sight. A faint caw came through the still air as they turned to go back in.

Flyx, on the other hand, was reluctant to leave. She said that it was too cold but then admitted that she could adjust her internal temperature to compensate. After some delay, wherein she repeatedly looked at Michael, she, too, was off.

Instead of flying high, she threaded through the trees, staying hidden in the upper story branches.

Michael asked, "Do you think she's worried about an attack? Maybe an eagle or something? Or, is she staying low because it will be easier to find other fairies?"

Sophie thought about it, then poked his ribs. "I think she's staying low because she's trying to think of an excuse to come back and see you again."

He snorted. "That little fairy does seem to have a fixation on me. I'm glad I'm already spoken for."

"You dummy! She's far too small for you."

"Yes, there is that, but she's awfully cute. You have to admit that."

"I know. If you were her size, you'd never get any peace."

He laughed. "Peace or another spelling?"

She snorted in mock disgust. "Not from me, anyway. Not after that wisecrack."

They reentered the house, arms about each other. They would wait for two days before assuming that their emissaries had failed in one way or another.

CHAPTER 23
SNOWBOUND

The old man liked the cabin. He showed more energy than Snake though he had. Perhaps it was due to pure enthusiasm. Some cardboard had been placed in the broken window, and the stove was now lighted and beginning to throw off heat, driving out the cold.

"I could live here quite happily," the man said.

Snake considered, then asked, "What eat?"

"Right now, I'm planning on heating some soup." When Snake looked around, wondering, the man pointed at a shelf. "In those cans up there. Don't you know about canned food?"

Snake was somewhat taken aback. "What?" he asked, then felt embarrassed that he had displayed a gap in his knowledge.

The man smiled kindly at his captor. "Humans learned to preserve food long ago. That's one of the things that made us the rulers of the Earth; storing food to prepare for times when there might not be any available."

Snake rather diffidently asked, "You teacher. Students? What teach?" The idea had taken root in his mind. Perhaps the man could teach him more about some of the things that bothered him.

By now, the soup was in a pot and starting to heat on the stove top. It smelled...interesting...like nothing Snake had smelled in his present form, but the odor tweaked some of the captured memories in his memory bank. They seemed to speak of warmth and family. He sucked in air to gather more of the scent.

"Smells good, doesn't it? Will you be wanting some, or do you even eat, Snakie?"

"Snek, me. Not Snakie."

"Snek? Are you sure you don't mean snake?"

Snake wasn't at all sure. He belatedly realized that he had made a mistake in his pronunciation. To correct his self-chosen name now seemed foolish. It would demonstrate that he had erred.

He stirred uneasily, then repeated, "Snek, me."

The man seemingly paid no attention and concentrated on stirring the pot. Then he said over his shoulder, "I was a philosophy professor. I was most interested in the definition of consciousness. If I were still interested, you'd be a good subject. What are you, Snek?"

THIS WAS PUZZLING. "Snek? That what mean?" Then, "Oh, no. Snek make mistake. Mean structure. Yes?"

"Along those lines, yes. You don't look like you're completely flesh and blood. Are you some kind of robot?"

"Snek not know robot. You right. Not all biologic. Snek swarm of bots. Dragon bots. Bad dragon. Mother rip up. Bots scatter. Form body be live. Snek got bots and biological cells. Bones. Prey bones make hard."

The man looked horrified. Snake couldn't fathom why until the man asked, "So you're some kind of monster then?"

"No a monster. Me. Snek. Me. Bots outside Snek warn danger. Snek bots in you. Bots in you make better. Snek. Try be good."

"I'd forgotten that, but you're saying that I've got your nanites inside me. Am I going to be absorbed into your body?"

"Not. Yours. Snek give. Care you. Bots make you health best bots can."

The man looked stunned.

Snake added, "Not make too much. Old. Too much bad. Not fix. Snek master, he..." He trailed off.

What would Abubecar say about Snake making the man healthy? What did the magician plan to do with a human, anyway? It couldn't be anything good. He started to say more, but something in his programming, an over-riding inhibition, kept him quiet. He hadn't known about this before. Abubecar had partial control of his programming and it apparently extended to telling anyone about the magician.

"Snake, I can see that you're a thinking creature. Based on your conversation, you are intelligent, possibly as intelligent as a man, but you are woefully lacking in knowledge. You're almost a baby in that respect."

That was it! He was a baby. He needed Mother.

"Yes. Yes! Baby. Days from dragon. Snek travel. Eat animals. Get more bots. Think about Snek. Me. What me."

"You don't know what you are? You are some kind of artificial intelligence. That's what I think."

"Maybe. Snek not feel. Not same you. Thoughts center..." Snake stopped in shock. He was used to thinking of himself as a distributed nanite swarm. He had believed that his processing had changed as a result of Abubecar's assaults. Now it was evident to him. His structure had changed and was in the process of changing more.

"Snek think," he said slowly. "Think be like man. Thoughts in head not in bots. Memory in bots. Snek change to biologic. Maybe Snek die?"

"If you are biological, you can most certainly die. If you are a swarm of nanites, can you not die also? Do you not worry about destruction?"

"Snek no thought like that." He made another attempt to warn the man about Abubecar. This time he was more successful.

"Afraid master. He take bots. Hurt. Pain. Memory gaps. Forget. Want help."

"That's awful," the man said. He had turned away from the stove and was looking at Snake with a funny expression on his face. "I'm beginning to believe that I feel sorry for you, Snek. Based on that alone, I think you are a living creature and not a robot. Now I've got to ask myself how close to human are you? Will you become closer as you change? This is an interesting question. I wish that I had known you back when I was actively studying consciousness."

Snake tentatively asked, "Think Snek have mother? Want much mother. Help. Too much hurt."

The man didn't answer immediately. He dished up his soup and sat down on a chair, then slurped some from the edge of the bowl, all the while keeping his eyes on Snake.

"I don't think you had a mother originally, but if you're asking if you might find someone to care about you, about your existence, your physical health, your mental state, then I would have to say that it is possible. I'm fascinated by your thought processes."

"Man care Snek?"

"Well, I hadn't considered it like that. I believe that I do. There is self-interest, of course. I want you to be healthy, because you have been taking care of me and, despite my age and poor health, I find that I still want to live. You've given me something to be interested in, and I haven't had that since my last daughter died."

The man drank more soup, then carefully placed the bowl on the floor. "Yes, besides self-interest, I find that I am beginning to like you, Snek. You are a conundrum, a puzzle that tantalizes me, but besides that, you are innocent in a rather charming way. I do think you deserve consideration; someone to care about you."

Snake was overcome. It was a new experience, but not unlike a variety of pain. It hurt in a way but also felt good. He felt warm inside.

"Mother make feel good? Snek feel good now."

The man sniffed and looked down. "I'm not your mother, but I believe you are feeling something akin to emotion; a biological state of being that mediates behavior in a non-rational way."

Snake raised his head in alarm. He sensed a sudden sending; questing. While he had thriftily gathered up all of his nanites and brought them into the cabin with him, there were others outside belonging to the plants in the area. A signal came from them. It was faint, but he understood it. Abubecar was using the web of nanite-endowed creatures to signal his impatience. He wanted Snake to return.

He could not bring the man back with him. It was too cold. The man would die. It would be better if he left the man here in this cabin to fend for himself. What would Abubecar do to him, if he took that action? If his master was angry enough, he could destroy Snake with a minimal effort.

It was at this point that Snake made another mental advance. The concept of deliberately misinforming Abubecar came to his mind. He'd never before considered deception in quite that fashion. He had used a form of deception when hunting, but to deliberately tell a falsehood? That was something he had never considered.

"Master call Snek. Bring human. Snek found you. Man. Not worry what he do you. Now do. Snek fear. Master destroy Snek if no human. You be safe in house."

The man leaned back. "That's the most human thing you've said so far! You have a sense of empathy. This is wonderful. You've developed to the point that you can identify with another being. That is a human attribute and one that is near the root of cooperative behavior for my species. I'd even go so far as to say it is a necessary attribute for civilization. My, my!"

"Not understand. Snek. Man stay. Snek go. Lot snow. Maybe Master no angry. Tell man die. Snek drag man. Too cold for man. Yes. Man die. Snek leave in snow. Snek say."

"Won't he know from your nanites? Don't they store your memories?"

Snake was dismayed. He'd forgotten that his memory was distributed in all of his nanobots. If the magician stole part of Snake's essence now, he would have access to the contents of the nanite memories. A solution came after a moment.

"Bots erase memory. Snek forget you. You safe that way. Only..."

"Only, what?"

"Only, Snek forget man. Snek want Mother. Man make understand what like. Snek not want forget."

"Snek, humans dream. That is we have thoughts that play through situations that are not real – situations that have not happened. We imagine what the situation would be like and how it would make us feel. Can you tell your nanites that you imagined our meeting? Tell them that I was not real, but only a series of thoughts that you had. If you can do that, then your Master might not know you lied to him."

"Try. Must leave fast. He impatient. You safe in house?"

"Look along the wall. There is enough food to last me for some time. Snake, I'm old. I did not expect to live this long. You've given me something to think about, and if death finds me soon, at least I will have been entertained."

Snake pushed the door open a crack, slid through, then turned to stick his head back in. "Tell not truth be bad? Snek not want be bad."

"Ah. That's a difficult question. In this case I think that you are telling a lie for a good cause. That means that you are not being bad. Instead you are risking yourself to help someone else. That type of act is commonly thought of as good."

"Goodbye, man. Take care man. Want be well."

"And I, you. Make your nanites forget me. I think you'll be okay if you do. You are a good creature, Snek. I won't forget you."

Snake turned and slid into the deep snow. Behind him, he heard the door shut.

He replayed their conversation as he traveled. He could lie by falsifying the data in his nanite memory, but he didn't want to do it until the last moment. The memory of being treated like a worthy and good Snek was too precious. He wanted time to savor it.

Meanwhile, there were miles to cover before he reached Abubecar's lands. He could practice imagining. The old man had given him a feeling of what it was like to be cared for, and he wanted more of that. He carefully reconstructed the moment that had made him feel so good. The feeling wasn't as intense now, but it still created a warmth that he'd never thought he would feel.

He couldn't think of how to escape his captivity. Once free, he would seek out his Mother. She would care for him. His attachment to the woman wasn't rational. He knew that but persisted, since the thought felt right. If she treated him as he hoped, that would be...maybe it would be like the warm moment, but more intense. He wondered what that would feel like. Would it be nice? He thought it would, but he couldn't decide how nice. The only real aspect of his thinking was that he desired it to be true.

Snake's body vibrated, creating a sound that was somewhat like a sigh as his leathery sides rustled against the icy grains of surface snow.

CHAPTER 24
PREPARATION

Neither Killer or Flyx had returned by the next morning. Gwen was optimistic during breakfast, while Chen seemingly took the part of devil's advocate.

"The crow will find other crows. They're everywhere," Gwen said as she was sipping her tea.

Chen shook his head negatively, his mouth temporarily full of toast. He hurriedly gulped, then began to cough. Michael pounded his back.

After a moment, Chen regained his breath and gasped, "Got a crumb down the wrong way."

Sophie passed him a glass of water, and he took several swallows.

"There. That's better," he said in a more normal tone.

Gwen was concerned but hid it behind mock anger. "You dunce! You'd better be careful. Now that I've found you, I want you to be with me for years, not just a few weeks."

Chen looked at her with some amazement in his eyes. "You really do care for me, don't you?"

"I won't if you keep gulping your food. It's dangerous, and it's also impolite. What do you want? Our new friends will think your manners are awful."

Michael laughed, then said, "It's okay. I do things like that all the time. It's always tempting to talk with your mouth full when you've got an idea that won't wait."

Chen nodded, then said, "The problem for Killer is not finding crows, it's finding the right kind of crows, er...Chimeras. They aren't so common as all that."

Sophie sighed. She knew perfectly well that most of the Chimeras that had been created in the Hazelton lab were dogs and cats. They were more numerous than the uplifted crows, and, unlike the crows they were long-accepted pets and were now distributed among the human population, most having chosen families to live with.

The crows, on the other hand, were likely to be nearly anywhere. That posed a problem when it came to locating them. The odds were that Killer would find some of his folk, but would they know where others were? She revised her hope for aid from that quarter downwards.

FLYX WOULD HAVE a different problem. She undoubtedly could find others of her kind. Fairies seemed to have some sort of inbuilt compass when it came to their King. Flyx's difficulty would lie in convincing the others to join in the attack.

The fairies were standoffish at the best of times, not caring much for humans. Flyx was unusual in that regard. Sophie smiled a little, looking out the side of her eyes at Michael. If Flyx ever figured out how to increase her size or decrease his, she would have competition for her husband. It was funny in one way but somewhat tragic in another.

She shut her eyes in sympathy. What if she'd never met Michael? Or, worse yet, what if she'd met him, but he was involved with another woman? That would be painful. Flyx seemed to be handling her infatuation better than Sophie would if she were in that situation. All-in-all, the fairy girl was exceptional in more ways than one.

Sophie sighed again, shaking her head negatively. If anyone could convince the fairies to help, it would be Flyx. Her desire to please Michael would keep her on point long past the average attention span of most of her kind.

Michael interrupted Sophie's musing.

"I think I'll check the weather. It looks clear from in here, but I'm going out to look around anyway."

She nodded. "You're just anxious. Our two messengers will probably be back soon with plenty of help."

"You're such an optimist, dear. Sometimes I wonder if anything bad ever happened to you."

Michael instantly saw that his quip was a mistake. He knew about her horrible start in life and her addiction. She'd told him almost everything about the events leading to their first meeting in the Hazelton offices.

Her face must have shadowed in pain, despite her trying to hide her feelings. Michael instantly reached across and took her hand.

"Don't worry, baby. My old Granny's gift is all I need, and right now it is telling me that everything will turn out fine."

She nodded soberly, appreciative of his effort at cheering her. Her mood wasn't due to his statement, though. She was, in fact, predisposed to worry.

What if a hawk or an owl had taken Killer? What if something had happened to Flyx. She might have had problems with the weather. Her small body might be frozen at the base of some tree, covered by snow. They would never know what had happened to her—only that she never returned.

Chen looked back and forth between the two, assessing the situation. Then he stretched and said, "I'll go out with you. We should check the temperature, at least. It might be too cold to set out, even if it is clear. The temperature usually drops without cloud cover to keep it warmer, you know."

Gwen added, "You go with Michael. I'll stay here with Sophie where we can stay warm."

She made a mock shudder.

Chen laughed. "That's just like you. Love your comfort more than me, eh?"

"No. But there's no reason I can't have both comfort and you. Is there?"

Both the men laughed and headed for the door.

Gwen turned to Sophie and asked, "What are we going to do with Darren? It doesn't seem right to turn him out in this bad weather, despite his bad behavior."

"His behavior has been rotten bad. Really, though, I've thought about it. I wouldn't place him in the truly evil category. His magic isn't very powerful, but even so, it allowed him to change his life. Judging from the way he looks, he's never had any success at building a relationship. His magic must have seemed like a miracle to him. It would have been better if he hadn't used it to try to bed every woman he met, but strangely, I can't blame him too strongly for his actions. I could see an unattractive woman doing something similar."

Gwen frowned and started to say something, but Sophie interrupted.

"But! But, I also can't forgive him for trying to force me to give in. His power would be irresistible to someone without magic. That would make his actions less forgivable. The village girls probably were convinced by him despite their better judgment."

Gwen nodded as she continued.

"I've thought about it and, since I was the one most recently offended, I think I have the right to judge and sentence him."

"What will Michael say about that? He was furious on the way here. I thought he'd probably kill the guy instantly."

Michael was sometimes headstrong and impulsive, but he also had a kindness about him that she loved. He was not the kind of man that would rush in and kill someone in cold blood. In a fight, though...

"I know. He's made it clear to me that it's my call. So...what I think is that I'll strip most of the swarm away from him, but leave a few to take care of him. I'll reprogram them to ignore his orders and act autonomously. That will stop his magic. He'll remain healthy, but any women that he desires in the future will have to desire him also. He won't have any influence over them, other than his behavior. He'll have to figure out a way on his own to settle with the people he's offended."

"Yeah! That's a good idea. Can I be the one to tell him that he will have to earn any trust and consideration he gets? I'd like to see his face when he realizes he might not survive the next few weeks," Gwen enthused.

"That's fine with me. I've already given his swarm the orders. He's neutralized now. You can tell him whenever you want."

"Oh! But you didn't have time...I see! You did it while I was talking, didn't you?" Gwen's face was somewhat disapproving as if she was having difficulty believing that Sophie could strip another magician's power so quickly and easily.

She nodded. "That's what I did."

"How can you do that? I mean I can barely handle my own nanites. I can't imagine how you could control another swarm." Gwen looked worried as if she expected Sophie to start on her next.

"Gwen, I'm directly responsible for most of the magic that exists. As far as I know, I was the first human to figure out how to create an internal communication link with the nanites. Before that, I was well on the way to becoming an accomplished hacker. After the change, when Wiindigo broke free, I was the one that splintered him into bits."

It wasn't quite the truth, but Gwen didn't need to know about the drugs, Cal, and the rest of it.

Gwen nodded, taking a moment to think about that.

Sophie added, "Besides, I plan on only interfering with other magicians when they use their powers to injure other humans."

That still didn't seem to be enough, so she added, "Look, Gwen. I'll show you how to encrypt your personal swarm so that it will be protected. No one else will be able to slip a command in."

She stopped, then said, "They won't unless they have a technique like that of Darren. He bypassed my encryption in a truly original way. The saving grace was that he wasn't aware of how he did it. It was just a result of his poor level of control."

Gwen nodded. "I'd like to have a better encryption method. I'm not really sure what that means though. Can you fix it so Darren can't get to me?"

"Well, he's neutralized now, so that's not going to happen, but I can fix it so that similar magic won't have any effect. Now that you raised that possibility, I better show Chen, too."

"That's really nice of you."

Sophie noticed Gwen's eyes straying to her midsection. She was noticeably pregnant, mostly because she was so slim that the bulge showed as if she was much closer to term than the first trimester.

Gwen blushed when she realized that Sophie had noticed her eyes, then she smiled tentatively and said, "I meant to ask you. How do you feel about it?"

"You mean about being pregnant?"

"Yes. I never...uh, never consciously wanted to have a baby before. I was sure that it wasn't for me. My run-in with Darren just confirmed that. I know that I had some void that needed to be filled so that I'd feel complete. Darren exploited that, and I felt besmirched, violated. Now I'm...I guess I've changed. It seems...it seems...like something I'd like. Like something I really should do."

Sophie nodded encouragingly. "I'm fantastically happy about it. You don't know, but I had a terrible life before the world changed. I wasn't a good person. I was never able to find a decent man. I finally found one, and I'm so lucky. He loves me despite knowing every flaw I have and those I used to have. I want to have his baby. I want this baby," she said, gesturing at her abdomen.

Gwen nodded. "I was afraid of men. I actually thought that women were safer, but Chen is so gentle and sweet. He's funny, too. He makes me feel at ease. Not overwhelmed. I never worried about being pregnant. You see, I never had relations with a man before him. Now, I'm not so sure about it. I'm starting to worry about not being able to have a child. I think I really want one."

"Trust me. You do. It's the most marvelous thing. I can't wait until I can feel the baby moving."

"Does it slow you down? Do you worry about fighting and being too slow or having the baby be hurt?"

"No. Any fighting I do is not physical. It's strictly based on my nano-magic. I haven't worried about those things."

"Good. I was worried about exactly that. Now, I guess I'll just worry about getting pregnant."

"Why worry about that? You're in control."

Gwen looked shocked. "What do you mean?"

"Your nanobots can make sure you avoid pregnancy, and they can also make sure that his sperm finds your egg and it implants correctly."

"Oh, my God! You mean I can do that?" I had no idea."

Sophie was dismayed. Gwen had far less control over her internal nanites than she'd thought.

"Wait a minute. Can you follow me here?"

She gently took control over some of Gwen's nanobots.

Gwen said, "Yes. I can feel that. What are you doing?"

"Teaching you how to handle this type of thing. I'm directing a few of your nanites to monitor your ovaries and uterus. Look, all you have to do is to instruct them to..." Sophie stopped. It was harder to describe than it was to do.

"Let me just set it up for you. The next time you two get together, you'll be ready, and it'll happen. Here. Wait a minute. Ah. That's it. You're all set."

Gwen's eyes were round. "Really? I sort of followed what you did, but then I got lost. I don't think I'm ready for that level of control, but I kind of understand it."

Then the brown-haired woman's eyes began to water. She sobbed for a moment, wiping at her cheeks as she tried to regain control.

"Sophie, tha...thank you. I don't know how I can make it up to you. I was afraid that you'd be some kind of authoritarian, uh, I don't know what."

Sophie laughed. "You mean an awful witch?"

"Well, I guess so. I'm not very practical with my magic. I'm an artist and using my powers for art is what I really like."

She paused, then smiled a sweet smile. "I'm going to get pregnant. Chen will be so happy. I can't believe it. You know you're right. It is wonderful, and the funny thing is, I'm not afraid at all. I thought I would be, but I'm not."

There was a bang as the door flew open and the two men came back into the dining room. Both women jumped at the sound, then turned quickly to see the men.

"God, it's cold out!" Michael beat his hands on his sides dramatically.

Chen stripped off his coat, then said, "I don't think we'd better leave today. Even with magic, I fear we'd be frostbitten within a few minutes."

He looked at Gwen, and a puzzled expression moved over his face.

"What's up, Honey? You look like you have some secret that you're dying to tell."

Sophie and Gwen laughed simultaneously with a sort of guilty laugh, increasing his puzzlement.

Gwen shook her head, then dissembled, "It's nothing. We were just having a girl-to-girl talk. I'll tell you later, in private." She winked at Sophie.

Michael looked back and forth, then fixed his gaze on his wife's face. "I see that my little witch has been busy, Chen. You're probably in for some kind of surprise."

Chen looked nonplussed, then said, "I hope it's a good one."

Michael nodded, "It probably will be. She really only does good things. Except to bad people that is."

Gwen still looked embarrassed, so Sophie changed the subject.

"What about the cold? You said it was too cold to leave?"

Chen looked at her blankly, then seemed to remember his statement.

"Oh. Well, yeah. It's terrible out there. I checked the thermometer on the tree by the door. It's twenty-two below. We can't travel in this."

Michael backed him up. "No way. We'll have to wait until the cold spell breaks. Even with my nanites, I was cold. And they were trying to raise my temperature the whole time we were out. Do you think it's possible to exhaust their energy if they put out too much heat?"

"I'm not a physicist, Michael. You know that. You're probably more familiar with their energy storage abilities than I am. I can get them to use all of their stored energy as heat, but I don't know how long that would last. They'd have to have more fuel pretty quickly, I guess."

"Well, each one is limited, but they can convert chemicals to energy quickly. The problem is getting the fuel to them. You wouldn't want them to start converting your molecules for energy. You'd probably have to eat a huge meal to provide enough to keep them going for long in this kind of cold."

"I suppose it wouldn't make me get fat. They'd use the calories."

"Yes, but you're supposed to be eating for two now. I don't think having your nanites use the extra food would be good for our baby. We need to feed him."

Sophie smiled. "Her. I've told you before. She's going to be a girl."

Michael looked disappointed. "Well, I keep hoping you're wrong and it's a boy. Maybe you're wrong, but..." He brightened, "If it's a girl, I don't care. She'll be just as wonderful as you!"

Gwen looked back and forth at the two of them, then laughed. "I can see that you have a great relationship. You remind me of how I feel when I look at my man."

Chen said, "My goodness, girl. You're embarrassing me. Can we talk about something else?"

Michael rescued him by saying, "You know, I think we need better clothing. I came so quickly, and the weather turned bad so fast, that I don't have anything suitable."

He looked at Sophie and said, "Neither do you, dear one. I wonder if our host has anything that would work for us?"

Gwen said, "We can look around, or maybe we should just ask him."

At that precise moment, there was a small gust of air that caused the fireplace to pop and flare up. Sophie glanced toward the door just in time to see it move a tiny bit.

"Michael! Someone was listening at the door." She stood, thinking about going into the hall, but her nanite swarm, covering the room and, in fact, most of the house, sent her no signal that anything was out of place. She could feel her eyebrows lift slightly. It was puzzling. Maybe the gust had pushed the door open. She checked her swarm again. There was no one in the hall now..

Michael made a small snort with a wry grin on his face. When she looked at him, he said, "Sometimes things have a way of working out. We can look around for some additional clothing, but I suspect that the problem will resolve itself by tomorrow morning."

His attitude seemed too caviler. Sophie frowned at him.

"What do you mean by that?"

Gwen echoed her, "Yes. It's a rather cryptic statement. Do you know for sure we'll find warmer clothing somewhere?"

"Well, no, but it's been my experience that sometimes odd things happen when Wold is around."

Gwen asked, "That little man? What is he anyway?"

"Ah. Now that I cannot say for sure. It's certain that he won't answer a direct question either."

Sophie tried to clarify. "He manages our household for the most part, but he...I think he's a truly magic being of some sort. He can do things. Things I can do, but I need my nanites, and I can't sense any surrounding him. When I try, there's just a blur with a bit of static."

Chen leaned back and stretched his feet towards the fire, making a satisfied groan. Then he said, "I'm going to stay right here for a bit. That cold has gotten into my bones, and I want to wait until I warm up completely before I go looking for anything. By the way, has anyone checked on Darren lately?"

Michael said, "Wold has taken that responsibility, so I'm not worried about Mr. Magnificent."

"Trust him that much do you?" Gwen asked.

"Yes," he responded.

Sophie sighed. She'd decided while the others talked.

"Gwen, let's you and I do some snooping. We can probably convince Jack to help. I've noticed that he finds it hard to restrain his curiosity. Looking in closets is probably something he'd enjoy."

Michael was agreeable. "You two go and knock yourselves out. I'll stay here with Chen, provided I can get another cup of tea. If you don't find anything, don't be too upset. As I said, I think things will be okay tomorrow."

Sophie sighed. "Well, I wish that Killer and Flyx would come back. I'm worried about both of them."

He shook his head negatively. "We can't do anything about it other than wait. I'm trying not to worry, but I think they'll be alright. They're able to take care of themselves."

Sophie shook her head in turn. There was nothing else she could do. She turned to Gwen. "Come on, Gwen. Let's go and look around. Maybe we'll find something."

The two women left the room in search of Jack.

"Sophie, is he always that smug?"

She was a little ahead and turned her head to address Gwen directly.

No, but he's right about Wold. Things have a habit of running smoothly around our house. Oh! There's a closet by the door. Let's check it first."

"That's a logical place for coats. Maybe there's something there." Gwen skipped ahead.

The closet was a disappointment. There were two coats there, but they were obviously Darren's. They were small and filthy. Sophie knew they were his from a few remaining nanites that he'd left on them. They wouldn't fit either of the men.

Sophie was reluctant even to touch the things, as was Gwen, although she might have been able to wear one.

The artistic witch touched one of the coats with her index finger, sniffed, and said, "I'd have to wash this filthy thing before I'd dare to let it touch my skin."

"Let's go on. We might have better luck somewhere else."

Jack needed no convincing. He was eager to do something; anything. He'd been bored and had not understood much of the adult-level talk. Running around, digging into Darren's stuff, something that Darren would surely dislike, was just the thing to alleviate his boredom.

They searched until near suppertime but had no luck finding the clothing they needed although they turned up a surprising amount of odd stuff. Darren was a collector of weird junk and seemed to have no rhyme or reason about where he stored it.

There was a stuffed moose in one room along with a variety of quilts, most of which were dirty. Books were mixed with tools and bottles of unidentifiable chemicals. All-in-all it was a mess that made searching a thankless and unrewarding job.

At supper, Michael reiterated that things would be fine. After eating and some discussion, everyone turned in. The light through the windows had faded as they talked and its passing seemed to bring on an oppressive atmosphere conducive to sleep.

SOPHIE STRETCHED AWAKING Michael. He grunted, rolled over to face her then smiled.

"It's always a wonderful thing to wake up and see your face next to me. It's like I never lived until I met you."

She poked him in amusement. "Living or not, we've got to get going. I've got a bad feeling about that Abubecar. The sooner we take care of him and his evil, the better, I'm thinking. I wonder if he's allied with Wiindigo in some fashion."

Michael's face grew serious. "Now that's something I'd rather not think about. I hope you're wrong. I was about to say that I'm content just lying here under the warm blankets and looking at you. Now you've ruined the atmosphere, and I'm going to have to get up."

He struggled to find the edge of the blankets while Sophie laughed.

"You big lazybones. You would lie here all morning if I let you. Wouldn't you."

"You've got me pegged. It's comfortable here." He lay back and pulled the covers up again. Then tried to kiss her.

"No. You're not getting out of it that easily. Let's have breakfast and try to think what we're going to do that will be productive. I mean what can we do that will have an effect."

"Ah, well. No rest for the wicked, I guess."

He tossed the blankets back, shivered, and got up.

"It hasn't gotten any warmer. The room is cold."

Sophie was also shivering. She pulled on her clothes, then said, "I've got to get some hot coffee. That should help."

Michael opened the bedroom door, started to step, then paused with his foot in the air.

"Look at this! I told you things would work out."

"What is it?"

"Looks like cold weather gear to me."

He bent and pulled up a heavy parka.

"Here. This is your size, and there are pants to go with the coats, too. Oh, and mittens also. Looks like someone went to the store. The things are brand new."

Sophie scrutinized the garments. "They are new, but I can't find a label on them anywhere."

"Nor likely to find one either. They were probably made last night. I have no idea of how, or where the fabric came from. I'm also not going to ask. Wold wouldn't answer anyhow."

She shook her head. "You're right. He'd just bow and walk off."

There was a shout from down the hall. Chen and Gwen had found similar garments outside their door.

CHAPTER 25
LOSS

As Snake moved through the snow, he ordered his nanite swarm to store a completely false memory of the old man's death. He wasn't sure what would happen when he activated the command, so he hesitated for a time, thinking of their conversation.

Perhaps he was developing into a good Snake. He hoped so, lingering for an additional moment, reluctant to act. Then he activated the order to his nanites, implanting the memory of the old man's death.

He was struck with a horrible sense of loss. He'd failed the old man. He'd allowed him to die. The man had been the only creature of any sort that had thought of him as an independent and deserving being. He had liked that. Now, he could not speak to the man any longer. It hurt in a way he had never suspected. Death was final, and it had separated them. He felt guilty and remorseful. How had he failed to keep the man alive? He'd known that the man was old and frail. Why hadn't he done a better job?

The man had died. Now Snake had no human for his Master, and he had no...he paused, changing the thought, then continued, no friend to tell him he was becoming good. He flattened into the snow with anguish.

Finally, he began to move. Although he wanted to go elsewhere, Abubecar's commands mandated that he return to whatever punishment the magician would choose. As he pushed the snow aside, he whispered, "Mother. Help. Me, Snek. Please."

His progress was slower than usual. The snow had become crusted on top, and the necessity of breaking through it slowed him. His system was running low on power also. He needed to take time to hunt, but he didn't have the desire. The guilt he felt about the old man seemed to weigh him down. His forward progress became slower and slower.

A large deadfall loomed ahead.

At some time in the recent past, a forest giant, an amazing white pine, had fallen to a storm. The tree was upwards of one hundred and ten feet in length, and when it fell, its roots had pulled the earth upwards, leaving an opening into a sheltered space.

Snake hesitated. He should continue on, but he needed both rest and food. Abubecar's command seemed distant in both time and space. He raised his head to scan the area.

THERE WAS NOTHING but snow-covered trees and bushes. The ground was buried under at least two feet of snow covered with a hard, icy crust. There were no animals to be seen, and he could not sense any nanites other than his own. He lowered his head and slid into the hole.

The hole was shallow and partly filled with snow, but there was a dark crevice in the back. Snake poked his head through and found that it opened to a long space under the tree's massive trunk. Branches had broken and driven into the ground when the giant had fallen and these now served as supporting trusses for the mass.

There was a sudden snarl from the other end of the space. Snake flinched in alarm, then surged forward. It was a lynx.

The big cat had made its den under the tree. Snake had failed to sense it, because he was so distressed. The lynx knew it was outclassed. It turned and started clawing, searching for an exit through the hard crust of snow between some branches at the far end of the unbroken trunk. It failed to find an immediate exit and turned to throw itself at the intruder.

Snake overwhelmed the cat, crushing its skull with a single bite. This was food that he desperately needed. He paused for a moment to consider the life he had just taken. The lynx had lived by hunting. Now it had died to feed him. Surely it had valued its life in the same way he valued his. Was it wrong for him to kill in order to survive? His mind failed to provide an immediate answer.

However, the lynx would have injured him if it could have. Now it was dead. He pushed his misgiving away and consumed the body. His nanites instantly went to work converting the biomass into energy and molecules that would repair damage incurred during his travels.

He was aware of the process, but there was a new component; something he had never experienced. The act of digestion made him feel warm and content. Was this what organic creatures felt? He coiled into a tight series of curves and lay still, thinking.

The old man had died. He was responsible, and he suffered as a result. The lynx was dead, but despite feeling some regret for the animal, he was now feeling physically better. Perhaps that was a significant difference. Then a thought came to him. What if he had eaten the old man? He was physically capable of that.

The idea was shocking though. He'd never considered it. The dragon that had given him life had killed and eaten humans. Fragments of their memories were his heritage from that violence. Killing a human seemed wrong. Humans could think on a high level. They had a level of self-awareness that the lynx did not.

He wanted to be accepted by Sophie and have her treat him with consideration. He had much of the mental ability of a human. If his physical appearance was discounted, he was a thinking, feeling being just as humans were. That seemed to mean that he and humans were kin of a sort. Killing the old man would be distressingly similar to killing himself. That was the source of his feeling of wrongness.

He imagined facing Sophie and having her reject him for his physical shape. He thought about trying to emulate a human, but he was so used to his body now that changing it seemed deceptive. She would not like him if he deceived her in such a way. That would be like telling a lie for personal gain.

Maybe she would see that he was himself, a being with personal feelings and deserving of consideration. He was Snake. That's what he was. He would not change that.

He became conscious of another source of discontent.

The human language was more difficult than he'd thought at first. His knowledge was in bits and pieces. The actual speaking of the words was subject to strange and sometimes contradictory rules. He'd made a mistake with his own name, and hadn't known it until the old man had pointed it out.

The old one had been polite and had not ridiculed him about his pronunciation, but the fact that he'd named himself, "Snek" by accident was embarrassing. It seemed to mean that he was incapable of speaking correctly.

He rebelled against the feeling of embarrassment. He'd called himself, "Snek," so "Snek" he'd be from now on.

In a way, that was a good change. Snake was a generic name used for a particular class of reptile. He wasn't one of those. He was, as far as he knew, unique. Maybe having a unique name was what he needed. He could define himself as anything he wanted.

He wanted...he wanted what he had imagined: someone to care for him.

Now he was Snek, and he would do what he could to deserve the treatment he wanted. That made the most sense. It seemed reasonable that Mother would want him to be good. She could be violent and destroy, but he'd also sensed a special feeling between her and the man. The feeling lay in the few nanites of hers that had accrued to his swarm in the fight. They carried a different message about her nature. She was dangerous, but also tender and loving.

Snek yearned for tenderness, even though he suspected his understanding was incomplete and could be in error.

His thoughts dimmed. The warmth from digestion was good. His organic components were rebuilding themselves and needed rest. He sank into a twilight disturbed only by a feeling of sadness about the old man.

The sunlight filtering into the lynx den grew reddish and gradually faded. Snek was unaware. He lay still, unmoving in the cold, allowing the slow liberation of energy to repair and feed his cells and nanites.

CHAPTER 26,
DEPRESSION

The clothes fit. They were warm. Supplies had been packed and distributed, and now the group was ready to move. Wold and Jack were staying at Darren's house for two reasons. First, Sophie thought that Darren still needed watching. True, she'd disabled his magic, but she didn't trust the weasel-like man. Secondly, she was unwilling to allow Jack to come with them into danger. He would be a distraction that she was starting to believe she couldn't afford.

Wold was unhappy about staying, but performed his usual punctilious bow, turned and slipped back inside without saying a word.

Not so Jack. "I want to come. She's my sister, and you might not know how to find her. I've been there, I could..." His voice trailed off as he saw Sophie's expression.

She shook her head sternly, silencing the boy. "Jack, you have to stay here with Wold. Now, listen to me! You do not want to make him angry. Trying to follow us will result in punishment, and I can't imagine what he will do. You follow orders and obey him. I want no argument. You stay here."

She felt guilty, making Wold out to be some kind of monster, but there probably was a shred of truth in her words. Wold had little tolerance for what he viewed as incorrect behavior and she'd still not figured out all of his resources.

The disappointed boy backed to the door, preparing to wave as they left, but then he cried out and pointed. "The fairy! There she is."

If it could be said that a flying creature was limping, Flyx fit the description. She fluttered slowly forward, her right side held lower than her left. When she saw them, she sped up a little, but it didn't last long.

As if with her last energy, she arched downward and ceased flying a few feet from Michael's arms, forcing him to drop the pack he was holding to catch her.

"Dear Michael, I thought I'd never see you again. I don't deserve to see you. I failed in my mission."

"Are you hurt, Flyx? What's wrong?" Michael was concerned as were the other three adults.

"A HAWK STRUCK at me. It had some of the dark nanobots. I think it was controlled by the powerful magic that has been pushing the fairy-folk out of our territory."

Sophie inspected the tiny girl. Her side was torn and leaking blood. The injury was treatable. She pushed some of her nanites into the wound where they went to work knitting tissues back together.

"You'll be better soon, Flyx. I've given you some of my healing nanites. They're fixing the wound."

"Thank you. That is kind."

Flyx glanced at her somewhat dismissively, then turned back to Michael and said, "I found my people, but I couldn't get them to help. They are afraid. I don't understand. Fairies have never been afraid before."

Sophie leaned close and asked, "What do they fear?"

"They fear the black magic; the power. It first pushed us to the south and then to the east. Things went wrong for my folk since I've been with you. Some have disappeared, and a few have changed right before the others. They have become something else; something the black magic desires. I saw one. It was with the hawk that struck me. It wasn't a fairy. It had horns!"

"What? Horns? You say it had been a fairy, but the magic changed it?" Michael asked.

"Yes. It had an evil look and laughed when I was hurt. I hexed the hawk. The feathers fell out of its tail, and it lost control. Without tail feathers, the bird couldn't fly straight and crashed into some branches. The other fairy thing struck at me with a curse, but it was weaker than my magic. I fended it off, although it took most of my energy."

The wound was fresh, but Sophie wanted to make sure. "When did this happen?"

Flyx moved then gasped in pain before she answered. "At dawn. I was returning as quickly as I could. I had to fly a long way to reach the new Shee. Then I talked and talked, but it was no use. They wouldn't come."

Michael looked up at Sophie. "She's too weak to come with us. She'll have to stay here with Wold and Jack."

As if he'd been called, Wold appeared beside Sophie. "Let me take the fairy. I will make sure she's fed and rested."

Michael passed her to Wold, but she clung reluctantly to Michael's sleeve."

"Michael, don't go forward. The magic is bad there. It's strong. If it can change a fairy, it is too dangerous. Please give up the rescue and stay with me where we may be safe."

Sophie shook her head. "No, Flyx. This Abubecar is causing too much trouble. I'm beginning to suspect that he's associated with Wiindigo. If he is, then nothing is safe. We have to confront this threat and neutralize it."

"Oh, Sophie, keep Michael safe. I…" As if realizing what she was about to admit, Flyx colored a bright pink and turned her head to Wold's chest.

"Don't worry. I'll keep him safe." Sophie grinned at Michael.

He looked a little embarrassed, but then added, "We'll all be safe, Flyx. Don't worry about us, just get yourself healthy quickly."

Wold moved through the door with the fairy.

Michael said, "Now, where were we? About to leave, I think."

Gwen had been watching silently. Now she said, "The fairy was truly frightened. I'm beginning to worry about this mission."

Chen nodded in somber agreement.

Sophie realized that she needed to say something, but what? She wasn't a true leader, she was…she had been a nothing. She was an addict. She…stopped, startled. Where had that self-doubt come from? Her thoughts had spiraled downwards into a funk almost out of control. How had that happened?

She probed with her nanites.

"There's something. Wait, I almost have it. There. Michael! I sense other nanites in the area. They're few and seem to be hidden or trying to hide—hard to detect."

Her eyes widened in alarm. "We're being attacked! Are any of you feeling depressed or are your thoughts out of control in some way?"

Chen ignored her question. "I'm tired of this. I think I'm going to go in and get back in bed. It's no use attacking that guy. We won't get far."

Gwen looked at him in astonishment. "Chen, darling, what's happened to you? This isn't like you."

He replied, "I'm serious. We're wasting our time."

Sophie drew her swarm tightly around the four of them, then sent an arrow of energy at the nearest source of negativity. There was a flash in midair as the energy struck a clump of nanobots and destroyed them.

Chen looked surprised. "What was I saying? Oh." He rubbed his cheek reflectively. "You're right Gwen. That wasn't me talking."

The two looked at Sophie, their eyes wide."

Gwen spoke for both of them. "If he can do this to us at this distance, how powerful is he? I mean really?"

Sophie had no answer. She looked from the two to Michael, seeking reassurance. Her gaze caught him by surprise, and she saw an expression of something resembling dismay on his face.

He noticed that she was looking at him and rallied.

"He might be more powerful than we think, but so is Sophie. She's gathered an immense nanite swarm. You guys have seen only part of it. The last thing that contested her was a dragon formed of Wiindigo nanites. She ripped it to shreds and captured almost all of its nanites. I'm betting on her." He finished with a fake grin that he apparently hoped would be taken as sincere.

Sophie felt constrained to demure. Abubecar was an unknown, and, as such, should never be taken for granted. Over-confidence was just as dangerous as no confidence.

"We'll have to be careful. Maybe we can convince him to modify his behavior, and we won't have to fight it out. Or, maybe he will refuse, and we'll fight, but if we are alert, we should have a chance to determine how strong he really is. If he's going to be too much for us, we will retreat and think of something else. You know it doesn't have to be all or nothing."

The other two cheered up somewhat as she spoke. It might have been partly because of Michael's cheer leading or perhaps her more thoughtful response. She couldn't decide. The only thing she knew for sure was that she had a familiar feeling. It was like knowing that you were out of drugs and were almost down from the last high. That was when the fear started. You knew you'd do anything for the next pill, but you didn't know what it might be; what shameful thing you'd be forced to embrace.

She felt the muscles in her shoulders tighten in a way that they hadn't since she'd discovered how to get her nanites to cure her fibromyalgia. It really didn't matter what she'd said to her friends. She was going to free Jack's sister and make Abubecar pay for killing the rest of the boy's family. She might start with talking, but she was sure that it would go to open war almost immediately.

A new sense of resolve hit her. She turned to the forest and said, "Let's get going. It's a long way."

THE GOING WAS hard. The crust on the snow made walking difficult. She wished they had snowshoes or skis, but those items hadn't been available. They hadn't thought of them anyway.

She was tempted to use her nanites ability to create an ionic flow to levitate her over the snow, but the other three couldn't do that. It wouldn't be fair to them. Besides, the feat exhausted her nanites' energy stores quickly. That was something that she had to conserve. She'd probably need all of the energy they could carry in the coming conflict.

The two men took turns breaking the trail. Crunching through the crust took a lot of effort, and they tired quickly. It wasn't much better slogging through the snow in their tracks. It was by no means a level path. If she failed to step where they had stepped, her foot often sank in several additional inches in the unpacked snow. She'd almost fallen twice. Now she was careful to step precisely in the leader's footprints.

Gwen was having just as much difficulty. The artist wasn't particularly physically fit, and she was breathing heavily before they'd gone a mile.

Sophie abruptly stopped. This wasn't going to work. They would begin to sweat and get too cold. The situation could turn deadly in a few moments. She pushed her senses out. Something was different.

After a moment it came to her. The always present crosstalk of nanites was absent. Usually, the plants and animals carried a nanite load that was typically small and dedicated to keeping the hosts healthy. Those nanites continuously broadcast a low power signal that she could always pick up. She'd grown so accustomed to it, in fact, that its absence now was shocking. Did that mean that they were in a place where the plants were all natural? Were there no animals here?

She extended her swarm ahead of her and probed. Nothing. This was frightening in some strange way.

"Stop. Michael, stop. There are no nanites here. None at all! I don't know what that means, but it's not right."

"What do you mean? "Chen was puzzled.

"You know that all plants carry their own nanites. They talk back and forth. I can't sense anything here. It's like a vacuum."

He looked around. "Uh, well I kind of knew it. I think I've mostly ignored weak signals. I thought they were static or something."

"No. When the world changed, both Wiindigo's nanites and Hippocrates' spread. They covered the land in a few days. The Wiindigo nanites are wild. They become dangerous when they clump together and form an AI.

Wiindigo-based intelligences always come to the conclusion that natural life is theirs to exploit and destroy at will. There are fewer of the Hippocrates nanites. They are the ones that usually inhabit plants and lesser animals. I don't know where Hippocrates himself has gone—a self-created dimension or pocket universe I think. Anyway, the nanites he left behind are helpful, but they never clump and never form a significant intelligence."

Gwen asked, "Why is that? Why doesn't he help us? It seems like he could get rid of the Wiindigo nanites."

"I don't know that either. Wiindigo is Hippocrates child in a way. Hippocrates created a seed AI and smuggled it out of the confines of the development system. Maybe Hippocrates wants to see what will happen without his interference, whether humans can deal with Wiindigo. He once told me that natural intelligence was to be valued and protected, but now I wonder if he's testing us in some way that I can't understand."

Gwen made a face. "That's more than I wanted to know. I don't think I want to be tested. But, we've gotten off the track. What about the lack of plant nanites here? Why does that bother you?'

"Well, it may be that...oh, I don't know...maybe Abubecar has captured them or something. If he has gathered all of the plant nanites and converted them to his own use, that could mean that he's got a monster swarm at his beck and call."

Chen asked, "Even if they're Hippocrates nanites? Can they be converted to hurt us?"

Sophie looked at Michael for support. He shook his head affirmatively and explained. "In one key way a nanite is a nanite. The main difference is the programming. We created them with enough memory storage to hold a bit of personality. Their command set allows them to be effectively programmed for bits of tasks. When you direct your swarm to do something, you've got to have the task broken into bits that each nanite can accomplish."

Gwen seemed dubious. "Well, how can I get mine to create my art? I don't break it down into bits. I see the completed picture in my mind."

Michael shook his head, indicating that he had no answer. He made another try at explaining.

"I can't direct mine. They protect me for some reason and generally make sure I'm safe and healthy, but I can't do the things that Sophie can. I don't know precisely how she does her magic. I think, however, that she has formed an AI mind in her swarm and it parses the job that she wants done and directs her nanites. You guys probably do much the same."

Gwen looked stunned.

Chen glanced at her, then said, "Yeah. I think that's what I've been doing. It's kind of like running several game characters at the same time. I view it as having a group of helpers. I just can't always get them to do what I want. My trolls for example. Getting them to do something is like herding cats. They get distracted easily. My magic is the same. If the job is easy, I can do it quickly. If its hard, sometimes I get weird results; not what I expected. Sophie has much better control than I do."

He looked lovingly at Gwen, then said, "Sophie also has better control than Gwen. I think we're pretty good, but we've obviously got a long way to go."

Gwen started to speak, but Chen interrupted her. "Still, Gwen is amazing. Before we left, she decided my ugly, little trolls could use some work. She cast a spell that decorated them. Now they are all rainbow colored. Still, ugly, but with pretty colors." He laughed, inviting the others to participate.

Gwen wasn't to be distracted. "But, what does this lack of plant nanites mean? Is it something really bad?"

Sophie sighed. She couldn't put off her friend. "Well, I think, mind you, I could be wrong, but I think that Abubecar may have pulled in all the nanites in the forest from this point on. If he has, that means he's got a huge swarm to work with. I don't know how large it is and it's anybody's guess how well he can control it. Anyway, I'm thinking that we're moving too slowly. We need to do something else to reach him."

Michael grunted, "I've been thinking the same. Let's turn back. We should have skis or something. Anyone of you know how to cross-country ski?"

Chen shook his head, then said, "How about snowmobiles?"

Michael grunted as if he'd been struck, then said, "I didn't think of that. There are two at my estate. We'll have to get them. I'm so used to trying to conserve gasoline that it never occurred to me. I think there's enough gas to get us there, though."

Sophie's heart sank. It was a long way back to Darren's, then they had to get to Chen's, and from there, it was another long journey back to their home. It would take days, and the snow and ice wouldn't be any better on the way back than it was going forward.

"Michael, how are we going to get back there?"

He grinned wickedly. "Not all of us need to go. We'll leave these two lovebirds at Darren's home with Jack. You have enough power to lift yourself and me, right? We can fly back quickly. Once there, we'll make sure our nanites are recharged, then we can come back on the snow-machines. Simple, huh."

It was, but the prospect was depressing. It would take a long time and much effort. All the while, she was sure Abubecar would be increasing his level of control over his nanites and gathering more. She had no idea what his ultimate goal was, but it couldn't be good. Giving him more time was a bad thing.

They retraced their steps, but it seemed to take forever. Sophie was tired before they'd gone back a kilometer. She was used to being fit, but now she was cold and hungry. Maybe her pregnancy was responsible, she didn't know, but she wanted something to eat.

Michael was carrying some food in his pack. Sophie increased her pace. He'd gotten a ways ahead, and that angered her. He wasn't paying attention. Just a few strides more and—her ankle twisted as she broke through the crust. She fell and landed by a birch tree.

"Damn it! Ouch, that hurt!" Her ankle was sending waves of pain.

Michael turned back and was by her side in three steps.

"What happened?"

"I turned my ankle on a branch under the snow. I'm not hurt otherwise."

"Is it badly sprained? Can you move it?"

The ankle would move. It felt tender and twinged when she moved her foot, but it would probably do. Walking on it might even help with the swelling.

"I think I'm okay. My nanites are already working on it. Help me out of this hole and let's get going. Oh, and can you give me some of that jerky? I'm starving."

He laughed, then pulled her out of the snow. She hopped on one foot for a moment, wobbling, then he caught her arm and steadied her.

The jerky was good, and Michael stayed close, helping her when the going got tough. Even so, she was utterly exhausted when they reached the house.

CHAPTER 27
TWO STEPS FORWARD, ONE BACK

No one was in a mood to continue. The consensus was that the conditions made travel too dangerous. The four headed to the kitchen for something warm. Gwen and Chen lingered over hot tea while Michael, out of a sense of concern, checked on Flyx.

The fairy girl was already healing. Sophie's treatment had worked to good effect. Michael cautioned her to rest. Her flight muscles had been torn. Now they were knitting, but he thought she should remain in the large basket that Wold had made into a bed for her.

When he finally made his way to their suite, Sophie was already in bed. She'd taken a hot bath and now was waiting for him.

"What took you so long? If I didn't know better, I'd be jealous of that fairy."

"No. She's a spunky little thing, and I'd hate to see her crippled. She's healing well. She wanted to get up and join in. Apparently, she thought we were having a party. Celebrating coming back in out of the cold."

"You know she's got a crush on you."

"Yeah, you told me before. Well, you've nothing to worry about. She's too small for me. I need a full-sized woman for—"

She interrupted him with a laugh. "That's enough of that. I'm finally warm. If you want to get in bed with me, you'd better not be cold. I'll kick you out of the covers."

"I think I'm pretty hot." He suddenly realized what he'd said and looked embarrassed. "I mean...you know what I mean."

"I think you're pretty hot, too. Maybe you'd better get in here and snuggle up so we can be hot together."

This time it was his turn to laugh.

After a while, they lay back, talking lazily.

Michael sighed, then said, "I told Wold about our plan to get the snow-machines. He said he had a better idea and that I should give him some time to work it out. When I asked him what he was going to do, he just said, "Wait.""

THAT QUESTION AGAIN. What was Wold? Maybe Michael knew more than he'd told. "Wold is rather unusual, isn't he. What is he exactly?"

"You know, I don't have an answer for that. He showed up at the door one day."

"This was before the change, right?"

"You know, I never thought about it like that. It was. You've been with me constantly since we first met. Uh, well, except for a few times."

"Yes, like those vampires. What happened there?"

"It was a mess. I shouldn't have gone by myself. I didn't have any trouble with the majority of them, but the queen..."

Here he trailed off with an unhappy look on his face.

"What about the queen?"

"Uh...She couldn't get through my armor, so she did her best to seduce me into removing it. Sophie, I hate to admit it, but I was about to do just that. Flyx saved me. She hexed the queen right on the ass. Really zapped her, too. That distracted her so that I could break free of the enchantment. She came around a building, and I took her head off, then we got out of there and headed back. You know the rest."

"You should take that lesson to heart. You're brave and strong, and I know you love me, but you still have weaknesses. Especially for that fairy."

He laughed. "I owe her big time. I wish there was something I could do for her. She looks at me with a kind of hopeless longing. It makes me feel sorry for her."

Sophie shrugged. "Life's tough. She'll get over it when the right fairy guy comes along.

"I wish that would happen soon. Now let's get some rest. It's almost dark, and I'm getting sleepy."

"Okay. I love you."

"And, I love you, too. Don't worry about Flyx. It's unbecoming and unrealistic."

"If something happens to me, keep her close. She may not be your size, but I rather trust her to keep you from doing anything too foolish."

He mumbled something sleepily and rolled over. She pulled the covers close and snuggled against his broad back. Life was good or would be if she didn't have the issue with Abubecar hanging over her head. She worried about what he was doing and whether he was now strong enough to defeat her.

She tossed around for a while, unable to sleep, thoughts of Abubecar torturing her.

The cold lurked in the corners of the room, sending cold fingers across the floor, but the two were warm under the covers beyond its power. At last, Sophie fell into a deep sleep interspersed with worrisome dreams.

WOLD GENERALLY WAITED to pull his magic off in the morning. He wasn't present when they got up, but as they were finishing breakfast and wondering if the cold would break, the sound of the snow-machines' engines grew louder and louder.

Sophie stopped eating and looked at Michael. A moment later Chen heard it.

"Is that what I think it is?" he asked.

Gwen nodded. "It must be the snowmobiles. Where's Wold? Did he get them? How could he? He's too small to drive one."

The engines came to a stop outside. Then they could hear the front door slam followed by some talk. A moment later Wold came into the kitchen followed by Alehandre and Polly, both of whom were wrapped up in heavy winter gear.

"Whew!" Polly said as she pulled off her mittens. "It's so cold out there I was sure I was going to freeze solid as a Popsicle."

Alehandre said nothing but walked stiffly over to the fireplace where he began to remove the frosted winter clothing he was wearing. Bits of frost landed on the warm hearth where they evaporated in small puffs of steam. When at last he was free of his coat, he beat his arms against his sides in a manner reminiscent of the chicken dance. Then he paused to shiver dramatically before looking at Polly meaningfully.

"Ah, Polly, I was so cold I was sure my heart would stop and my blood freeze. It was only the fact that I had to make sure of your safety that kept me going. I could not bear the idea of you being cold."

Both Gwen and Sophie's mouths dropped open in surprise while Michael made an effort to keep from snickering. Chen's response was more measured. He covered his amusement by asking, "How did the two of you conceive of such a crazy notion as to come after us on the snowmobiles? Especially in this weather?"

Polly simpered at Alehandre, then answered. "We were at home, snug as bugs in a rug when Wold showed up as brusque and officious as ever."

Everyone looked at the small brown man. He bowed formally in response.

Polly continued, "He told us you needed the machines and since he cannot touch them himself, brave Alehandre volunteered to bring one to you. I could not in good conscience allow him to go by himself."

Alehandre interjected, "She's very caring."

She continued with an aside to Sophie. "You know how flighty he is. I had to make sure he remembered where he was going so that he could come back to me. All-in-all, it seemed better if I came along to keep him on the right track." Then she laughed, self-consciously, and added, "Besides, I've never ridden a snowmobile before, even though I always thought I'd like to try one."

Michael couldn't hold back his mirth any longer. He tried mightily, but then exploded with a combination snort and laugh. He made another effort to get control, then said, "You've got that one crossed off your bucket list. How did you like it?"

She nodded, "Yes, it's off my list. I thought it was fun, at least until I started getting cold. Then it became a chore. I don't mind telling you that the last few miles were awful. I thought we'd never get here. Thank goodness that Wold kept flying back and urging us on,"

Michael turned to Wold. "We were going to get the machines. Why did you get these two old ones to bring them here."

Wold bowed again, then stepped forward three precise steps. He blinked his eyes, giving a fleeting impression of his alter owl form.

Michael, the situation is worse than you know. Time is important now, and you would have taken too long to travel to your home. I took it upon myself to get the only two who could bring the machines quickly. If I could have done it myself, I would have."

Sophie asked, "Yeah. What is that? Couldn't you have driven one and at least left Polly where she'd be safe and warm?"

Wold swiveled his head to look directly at her. "I cannot touch such things. They are..." He paused, seeming to shudder slightly. "Inimical to me. I can't bear contact with iron in any form. Those smelly internal combustion engines are unnatural devices. No."

His head turned again, taking in the rest of the group, then his eyes came back to focus on her. "I could not bring them to you alone. I take responsibility for putting the two at risk. It had to be done, just as we must proceed against Abubecar quickly."

Alehandre who was looking at Polly with an expression that seemed to imply his stomach hurt. Polly was smiling back with a slightly flustered look. The two had become a couple, as unlikely as that was.

Sophie nodded in acknowledgment. "At least they made it with no harm."

Alehandre took that moment to stumble and fall to his knees.

"I fear my feet may be slightly frostbitten."

Michael jumped up and began to unlace the man's boots. When they were off, Michael held up a sock, scowling. "Alehandre, you should know better than to wear cotton socks in such weather. They are damp and look at your toes! They're half frozen. You're going to find it hard to walk for quite a while."

Alehandre querulously replied, "Those socks have served me well, besides they were all I could find."

Polly placed her hand on the lanky man's forehead. "Don't worry, Dear. I'll take good care of you. We'll have you right as rain in no time."

Sophie wasn't sure if Alehandre's nanites were up to the task of healing frostbite. She probed, without moving from her seat by Michael.

The man's internal nanobots were disorganized, but some were actively working at saving the cells in his toes. She directed a small part of her swarm to help. The microscopic machines clustered on his bare skin and began reconstructing cells that had been destroyed by ice crystals.

"Alehandre, I want you to go to bed for two days. Stay warm and stay off your feet as much as possible. Above all, don't get them cold a second time. Between your nanites and some I've just given you, you'll be fine. It will take at least two days, though. Polly, please make sure he keeps his feet warm and doesn't walk any more than he has to."

Polly nodded. The older woman's nanites had once been part of Sophie's swarm. She'd given them to her out of compassion and gratitude for Polly's help in the initial struggle with Wiindigo.

In the intervening time, Polly had changed from a fragile old woman to a healthy senior. She appeared twenty years younger than her actual age, which was, Sophie though, somewhat north of eighty. Perhaps Polly and Alehandre would make a good match. It was apparent that they thought so.

Wold brought the group back on point with a hooting sound.

"They'll be safe here. Unless you fail, then there will be no haven for anyone. You must prepare and go quickly." Having gotten their attention and delivered the message he wanted, he stepped back against the wall, almost blending into the woodwork.

Michael asked, "Alehandre, did you bring extra gasoline? You will have burned at least half of the tanks getting here."

The skinny magician nodded. "Wold made me fill some spare tanks. It was cold, and they were heavy. It was all I could do to lift the frigid things, but I persisted heroically and they're—"

Michael stopped his dramatic recitation. "Great! I'll top off the tanks before we leave."

He turned to Sophie. "Dearest, we are going to have to take on this threat. Do you have any reservations about it?"

She did. "I've been worried about Abubecar. I don't know anything about him but what I've heard and that's been precious little, but something tells me that he's going to be...he will be difficult."

Gwen said, "I've told you all I know about him. Isn't there something, some old saying about how knowing your enemy isn't as important as knowing yourself?"

Chen said, "I'm not sure about that bit of wisdom, but Sun Tzu speaks to that in The Art of War. He said that if you know both your enemy and yourself, you shouldn't fear the results of many battles, but if you know yourself and don't know the enemy, you'll lose half of the time."

Sophie was dismayed. That wasn't what she wanted to hear.

Chen continued, "Of course, knowing yourself is better than not knowing yourself. He said that if you don't know either the enemy or yourself, you'll always lose,"

Gwen grunted, "That's not quite what I was hoping for, but at least we know ourselves. Right?"

Michael cheerfully affirmed, "Right! We know what we can do. We'll have to go carefully and try to figure out what he can do as we approach. Now, I've known Wold long enough that if he says something is urgent, I believe him. We'd better get going."

Dressing for the outdoors seemed to drag out, giving her time to worry.

What if Abubecar had more nanites than her large swarm. One nanite could nullify another in a direct battle. They all had the same structure and, assuming they were fed, the same level of energy. If he had more, then he could counter hers and still do damage. If he knew some odd attack that she hadn't experienced or thought of, that was a problem. Just like Darren.

Oh! That was a good thought. She could use his heterodyne stealth attack. Maybe Abubecar wouldn't notice until it was too late.

Still, she felt like she had before the change. She'd been a loser, an abused drug addict. Only two men had ever treated her decently. First Cal, and then Michael, who had fallen in love with her at first sight. That was a miracle. Still, how could she face such a powerful man? She was weak. She knew the seeds of her addiction were still there, buried in her personality somewhere. Darren had almost brought them back to life. The others would help. Maybe that would be enough to get her through.

But...

Doubt slowed her movements, and she lagged behind.

Michael brought her back to reality. "Sophie? Are you ready to go? We're all dressed, and the machines are ready.

CHAPTER 28
ADVANCE

Both machines were idling, their exhaust rising in the still, cold air. Sophie climbed on behind Michael. Chen and Gwen straddled the other machine.

Michael briefed Chen. "Slow for turns and watch out for low-hanging branches. The machine can tip if you go over a hidden deadfall. We'll move slowly until you get the hang of it. It's not too hard. Ready?"

The engines roared, and they headed towards the thick wall of forest. The roads were mostly overgrown; their surfaces so irregular that it was easier to thread a passage between the trees, following animal trails when they were available. Care had to be taken to avoid places where the trees were so thick that the machines could not fit through.

Sophie clung to Michael's back, her face deep in her hood and partially buried against his parka. She shifted when he did, but otherwise paid no attention to the physical aspects of the ride. Her mind was elsewhere.

The plants and trees and what small life lived in the area seemed to be without nanites. This was definitely abnormal. Trees, especially large ones, always attracted a population of nanites as did animals. A tree's population was sparse, limited by the energy the plant could spare.

The nanobots worked in a symbiotic manner, repairing damage while gathering excess energy to fuel their own needs. Animal swarms were usually proportional to the animal's size. Mice had few, while a bear might have almost as many as a human. The nanites in animals were autonomous, still not under conscious direction. The animals benefited by the general benevolence of the nanites. The tiny machines were structured and programmed to repair damage on a cellular level. Only when a higher intelligence directed them did they become harmful.

Humans could direct them, although most people did not have the ability. The so-called magicians had varying degrees of control.

There was another possibility, too. When the nanite population in a particular area reached a critical density, they could form their own conscious AI. If they were unmodified nanites, it could take either a benevolent form or possibly an evil one. If the nanites had been part of Wiindigo's massive swarm, the AI that formed was always malevolent.

THAT HAD BEEN the source of the dragon that she'd last defeated and was, she thought, the form of the vampires that Michael had encountered.

She had been sloppy with the dragon. Some of its substance had escaped. There had been so many nanites in its swarm that she couldn't capture them all. Her own swarm had grown when she'd captured that of the dragon. The constant acquisition of nanites had increased her capacity. Now she felt she could deal with a far larger number of nanites.

She pushed her face harder against Michael's back. There was always something bigger and better. No matter how good you were, it was a safe bet that someone else would be better. It had better not be Abubecar.

She'd allowed him to become a monster in her mind. In truth, he wasn't a good person, from what she'd heard. Killing Jack's family and enslaving his sister weren't the acts of a decent human. He needed to pay for that. The possibility of him allying with Wiindigo was bothersome. That was the one thing she feared above all else. It could raise the oncoming conflict to a level that she couldn't imagine.

The fact that there were no nanites in the forest they were passing through seemed to imply that Abubecar had gathered them to himself. If he took every nanite over hundreds of square kilometers, he would be immensely powerful. That wasn't possible. Was it? She tried to put the idea out of her mind, but it kept popping up.

She circled around to her original idea; the one that she and Michael had discussed long ago after the dragon's demise.

Would it be possible to create a virus? The nanites were relatively simple, and each had only a small memory store. A virus that would propagate through their radio communication system would have to be tight and economical. The goal would be to remove the commands that predisposed the individual nanites to form a Wiindigo supermind. She hadn't paid much attention to the Wiindigo programming previously. It had been enough to merely co-opt any enemy nanites she found, wiping their memory banks wholesale and then shoving her command set into the vacated space.

She forced her attention outward. It wasn't entirely true that there were no nanites present. There were a few, scattered here and there. Her swarm located one on a tree trunk. A subset of her nanites attached to it and pulled it back towards her, drifting on a gust of wind.

"Michael! Stop! Stop! Now. I need a moment."

The snow-machine coasted to a space between two trees and idled. He turned, twisting his torso and leaning so that he could see her. She shook her head and held up a finger, signaling him to wait.

The captive nanite was immobilized. It was calling for help, but the cross-talk from her swarm drowned out the weak signal. She focused, bypassed its security, and read the code contained in the memory.

There it was! A small subset of code was grafted onto the normal nanite operating instructions. It was to seek out other nanites with identifiers that had a specific sequence, then link with them. The accumulation that would result would inevitably create an AI with Wiindigo's characteristics.

It would hide and grow until it was large enough to attack humans. There was no limit on growth. In that, it was like cancer. If allowed, it would link all the nanites in the world, converting the wild ones to its own image. If that happened, all biological life was forfeit. It would leave nothing living, stealing all molecules to create more of its own nanites.

She suspected that it would eventually create a means of space travel in an attempt to dominate and consume other worlds. Suddenly, the thought of Hippocrates crossed her mind.

As she considered the benign AI, another thought wove itself into her consciousness. This happened so smoothly that she would not have noticed, except that the feeling was alien. It was structured differently from her normal thoughts.

It occurred to her that that parts of the virus would have to be stored in different nanites. When an accumulation began, the virus would assemble and become active when the intelligence level ramped up. That way it could strike at a critical stage, converting all of the accumulated nanites simultaneously into a non-aggressive form.

The idea was sheer genius. How had she thought of it? It would result in nanite accumulations that could be considered organisms that would automatically work towards better conditions for biological life. The result would be to gradually increase the productivity of the world and increase intelligence in humans and higher animals.

The strangeness of the thought suddenly clicked. Hippocrates had disappeared into a self-created pocket universe. Apparently, his isolation was not total. He'd inserted the thought into her mind, so he was monitoring events on Earth.

A second thought or rather a feeling popped into her mind. It wasn't a sequence of ideas, but a pure feeling of approval. It was Hippocrates! She knew it. If he was willing to intervene, even a tiny bit, that gave her an advantage. She wondered if he regretted the creation of the seed AI that he'd loosed in his initial attempt to escape confinement. The seed had developed into Wiindigo—something that Hippocrates hadn't seemed to anticipate. Of course, that was before his IQ had spiraled off the charts.

"Michael, you can go ahead now. I've got an idea I'll be working on, so don't disturb me, please."

He leaned the side of his head against her forehead and said, "Okay, but the going is getting harder. The snow is deeper here, and there is some kind of mist on that hill across the valley."

She opened her eyes and looked around. He was right. The far side of the valley had thin tendrils of mist sliding through the trees.

"Just go. We've got to deal with this, mist or no mist."

He gunned the throttle. The machine slid through the snow, circling around Chen and Gwen, who'd passed them, then stopped to wait.

She put her head against his back again, concentrating on forming the right pieces of code. It would take several modules, each of which would be contained in an individual nanite's memory. They had to be self-assembling when enough nanites had accumulated to form an AI.

She designed a trigger based on the AI's intelligence level. When it reached the point that it had an element of self-identification, the virus would activate. Once activated, it would propagate and spread rapidly through all the associated bots in the swarm converting them to a benign form that was more Hippocrates than Wiindigo. The reaction would continue until there were no more unconverted nanites.

She had just finished composing the second to last module when the machine stopped again.

Chen and Gwen had stopped beside them. They were on the edge of a bluff that dropped steeply towards a frozen-over lake. There was a house on the far side.

She looked more closely. No. It wasn't just a house. It was a mansion on the order of Michael's and perhaps even grander. Someone had built it without care for the cost. The grounds were partly overgrown now, although she couldn't see well. A mist obscured the place, thinning at times, then flowing so thickly that it came far out onto the ice.

Chen asked, "Do you think we can cross the ice on these machines? Is it thick enough?"

Michael grunted making an ambiguous sound. "Ugh. I don't know. It's been cold enough, but it's early in the season and it hasn't been cold long enough. I'm worried about falling through. Let me go down and check the thickness."

He stepped off the machine and slid down the slope. There was a brightening glow as he reached the ice from his suddenly manifested sword.

He swung and chopped for thirty seconds, then poked the sword down into the hole repeatedly. Apparently, the ice was thick enough. He waved them down.

Chen started his machine forward, traversing diagonally across the hillside, which had a sparse growth of birch. He and Gwen descended partway, then he made a swooping turn and came back on the final leg down to the lake.

Sophie watched, then scooted forward. The machine seemed huge to her, but she'd driven it before, just not down a bluff. She followed in Chen's tracks.

All went well until she reached the turning point. She swung around, but the heavy machine fought her attempt to turn back uphill. It slid downward with increasing speed. Straining with all of her muscles, she wrenched the steering back uphill, but the machine started to tip.

There was a clear gap through the sparse birch just to her right. She steered for it and quit fighting the machine's weight. It slid through the trees, accelerating, bumped over some hidden rocks, then lifted in a low jump, landing with a bang on the wind-swept ice.

It slid outward across the lake for some distance, then crunched to a halt against a long snow drift. She turned it and calmly motored back to where Michael was standing.

"Wow! Are you okay? I didn't know you could ride like that," he shouted.

She snickered. It had been fun after the initial fear.

"Yeah. I thought I'd take a fast way down. Want to go back up and try it with me? It was fun."

He caught hold of the handlebars as she stopped.

"No. I think I'll pass. You scared me to death. You didn't really do that on purpose did you?"

"No. The machine was so heavy that it was like it had a mind of its own. I saw the gap and made the best of it."

"I'm glad you're so fast thinking. Now let me drive again. You can continue to rest until we get across the water."

They started towards the far shore, which was perhaps a couple of kilometers distant. The mist swirled and thickened, seeming to advance to meet them.

CHAPTER 29

SNEK

Snek shuddered with shock. He had been drifting, allowing his thoughts to float in a happy fantasy where he was near Mother. She had given him food and had been kind to him. Then something had happened.

He was no longer in the lair. He was moving through the deep snow. His Master had summoned him while he dreamed and his nanites had responded without his knowledge. They had taken control of his body and started moving through the snow.

The realization made him frantic. It was as if his body had isolated itself from his mind. He was trapped inside and could not escape. He attempted to move, but the nanite-controlled body continued slithering through the snow, now moving around a tree, now under a bush.

He ceased trying to break out and retreated into thought. He could see and hear. The sound of the ice granules against his skin made a soft susurration. He could feel the movement also.

Snek wasn't totally isolated, but his voluntary motion was out of his control. He wondered at this. He had thought he was all nanite with only some organic components. If that was so, then only some of his swarm were rebelling to follow Abubecar's directions.

Snek probed carefully. The nanites in control of his motion were locked with new encryption. It must have been part of the sending, intended to enforce his compliance. The control pathway was the same, but the opening code had been changed.

His old code had been part of him from the beginning. It was the native encryption in all of the Wiindigo nanites. He'd been remiss not to change it. That was a mistake he wouldn't make again, assuming that he was able to break free.

Even if he were able to regain control of his motion, would Abubecar allow him to retain that control? The magician might simply destroy him. He was afraid to break out, yet the sensation of being captive in his own body was yet more fearful.

The first code he tried failed. He generated others in rapid succession trying for a brute force exploit. None worked. His Master was a strong magician and arrogant. That arrogance meant that he was proud. Snek had seen that without fully realizing what it meant. Now he reconsidered.

HUMANS WERE AT least partly motivated by pride and—he did something that he had never done before. He jumped to a conclusion without thoroughly analyzing all of the data. He used his Master's name as the code and...it worked! He was back in control.

Snek continued moving forward, luxuriating in the feel of being himself again. He hadn't known it would be so horrible to be taken over. The knowledge gave his existence a dimension that it hadn't had before. He'd known he could cease. His nanites could be stolen, decreasing his substance. The biological parts of him could die. He had not known what horror was until this moment. Being a prisoner in his own body and being forced to watch passively while it obeyed another's control was purely awful.

Now the sending came again. He paused, feeling the impulse flowing into his nanites from the thinly spread network. The signal wasn't overpowering and would not have been successful in taking him over if he hadn't been unaware. He felt a sense of longing, thinking of his beautiful fantasy, but then it wouldn't do to engage in that kind of dreaming again. It only made him vulnerable.

Snek lifted his head above the snow. It was difficult to tell exactly where he was, but he thought that he still had more than a day of travel to reach Abubecar's dwelling.

He flinched. There was an overtone of anger to the sending. He began to move as quickly as he could. It would not be right to make his Master wait. There would be a punishment.

The hours went by. Snek had made good time, finding that the snow had crusted over in some places and was strong enough to allow him to glide on the surface. That was quicker than burrowing under the crust. When he did that, he encountered various obstructions such as deadfalls and those slowed him.

He was now at the outskirts of Abubecar's land, and he'd found something interesting, something not right. There were footprints here. Some humans had passed recently. They had broken a trail.

Snek followed, searching for any nanites that had become separated from the humans. They either had kept their swarms under tight control, or they had no nanites whatsoever.

In the first case, they would be powerful magicians, and he was dubious about encountering them. Caution would be required. If it were the second possibility, they were of little interest, except that he might be able to capture one and return with it to Abubecar, thus fulfilling his mission orders. That might mean less punishment.

On the other hand, it would mean the death of the human. This was something that he didn't want. He mulled it over as he traveled.

The tracks appeared to be made by four humans. Two were men, he could tell from the size of their feet, and two were children or women. Snek lifted his head to trace out the direction they were headed. There was a place in the snow ahead where something had happened. They had stopped to rest by a birch tree.

He investigated, then stiffened in excitement. One of them had fallen. He could sense a nanite that had been left on the birch trunk. He approached, then paused.

The nanite was familiar. It was...it was one of Mother's! Snek began to shake with an emotion he could not understand. He carefully pulled the nanite into his swarm and left it in the care of the few that he had inherited from her at his beginning.

Mother was here! He should warn her about Abubecar. He started to follow in her footsteps. She was moving away from the magician's territory, and that was good.

He had traveled only a short distance when the summons came again. This time it was far stronger as if Abubecar had developed an amplifier. Snek stopped dead, then turned. The summoning was too strong to be ignored. He had to return to his Master.

A surge of regret washed over him leaving behind a feeling of sadness; something that was becoming too familiar. Warning Mother would not be possible. Besides, if he went to her, he would only lead his Master to her. He could not imagine what would happen then, but it would not be good. She might even be hurt. That was something he would not tolerate.

He began to move towards Abubecar's mansion on the lake. As he pushed the snow aside and wormed through the thickets, Snek analyzed the single nanite he'd obtained.

Getting through its encryption should have been impossible, but the other nanites from Sophie's swarm that were now part of his system had given him the key. Once in, the code structure was different in some significant ways. If he were to implement those changes in himself, would that make him closer to her or would it damage him in some manner?

There was no way to tell except by testing. A small clump of nanites on his surface would suffice as a test group. A few changes to their programming and...there. It was done. They didn't act any different. They were still part of him.

Encouraged, he converted more, creating a larger and larger colony of Sophie programmed nanites. They retained their memories. He was careful to maintain that aspect. Losing part of what made him Snek was not a good idea. It had taken too much hard thought and suffering to reach this point. Change caused by forgetting was an unacceptable loss and potentially uncontrollable.

A hill rose ahead. Snek recognized it as the one on the southeast side of the lake. There was a steep incline on the other side, then the lake lay between him and the mansion.

He shuddered, making a sighing sound. Regret and trepidation for the future slowed him. He glided to a halt, raised his head, and looked back. There was no sign of rescue.

He had hoped. Mother was back there. Snek whispered, "Help. Please. Mother. It's me, Snek. Help, please."

There was no answer. His head slumped into the snow, then he started the climb up the hill. It took only minutes—far too quick to Snek's mind. Navigating the bluff down to the lake was easy. He allowed gravity to pull him almost straight downward, only deviating a minimal amount to bypass inconveniently placed birches.

He slid onto the bare ice, cleared near the shore by the wind, and began to wind across the vast expanse. His progress was slower. He wasn't built for travel on frictionless surfaces. His body pushed against the ground as he wove forward. Now, the bare ice made a poor surface to push against.

Snek's thoughts were bleak. It was highly likely that Abubecar would do away with him, merely ripping his nanites away for use elsewhere. He'd failed at his task and had returned late. The sendings had been fraught with threat. He returned again and again to the idea of fleeing. It would be so easy to turn and go far away.

Every time this thought came up, the counter thought followed. He could not run. He carried the seeds of slavery within him. Abubecar's control of most of his nanite population kept him moving forward. If he could only figure out how to break free.

He had converted a large percentage of his nanites by changing their code to match that of Sophie's bots. That had given him hope that his Master's commands would also be changed, but it had failed to work. Snek wondered why Abubecar's control had not wavered.

The nanites that were directly involved in his movement had taken the new programming, but somewhere he was missing something. He was still Abubecar's slave.

The mansion was close. On this side of the lake, snow had drifted into long ridges covered with a brittle crust. He was able to slide over the ridges more quickly, and his body left a winding, grooved track as his weight broke through the thin surface layer of the drifts.

He paused and lifted his head, but the urge to continue forced him to drop it immediately. There was no time left. He had to escape.

Snek searched his body. He'd always accepted that it worked and had never wondered how. Now, desperate with fear, he traced the commands from his mind through the nanite communications network to his muscles.

There it was! He hadn't understood how Abubecar was influencing him until now. Some of the nanite code relating to their communications had been changed. It was not an optimal place to graft on a control module, and that was why he'd never considered the possibility.

He began to work at reprogramming the thing. It was like a virus in that it seemed to have a life of its own. It resisted his attempts to change it. He pushed and destroyed it in one nanite, but the nanite then malfunctioned, and he had to kill it to get it to quit.

The problem occupied his mind until he found himself at the lake door to the mansion's kitchen. There was a dog entrance there, and he slid through, noticing as he did that he had grown thicker and presumably longer since he'd left. Now he barely fit through the door, even though it was designed for a large dog. The Holden's had owned some Huskies. He'd seen pictures in the living room. The dogs had run away or been destroyed by Abubecar as non-essential.

Snek slid through the house until he reached what had been the gathering room. There was a large fire in the fireplace that created too much heat for him to feel comfortable. Abubecar stood near the hearth, looking out the window.

Snek stopped, coiled, and waited.

After a few minutes, the large magician said, "So, you come back late and without any human. I should have better servants than you. I could use your nanobots for other tasks. I have a lot to do."

He turned to look at Snek. "You saw that I've pulled in all the nanites I could find. You must have noticed that there were none in the woods."

Snek moved his head from side to side. He'd never spoken to Abubecar. His first attempt at human speech had been to the old man. The memory brought a brief pang of grief and a sensation of failure. The man had been his friend, and he'd allowed him to die.

Abubecar raised his hand to send a curse at Snek but then dropped it back to his waist.

"Maybe you didn't notice. You haven't impressed me with your intelligence." He moved closer and looked at Snek's eyes.

The feeling was that of being invaded. Snek wanted to blink, but could not. After a moment, he was released. He lowered his head and turned it away.

Abubecar said, "I see you allowed the human to die. That is failure. You've earned punishment, but I'm going to delay it. You haven't escaped my anger, though. You can count on suffering later, but I haven't the time to attend to you properly. Someone is sniffing around on the outskirts of my property. I can sense them. There is a magician, and the signal seems doubled or cloudy. Maybe it's more than one magician."

He turned back to the window and continued speaking, although his voice was now softer as if he were conversing with himself. Snek remained still, hoping not to attract attention. Punishment later could always become punishment now. Any delay was good. He needed the time to try and break the virus code to free himself.

Abubecar clasped his hands behind his waist and muttered, "I've instructed my nanites to work at discouraging the invaders. It hasn't worked. They're still out there somewhere."

He turned to Snek. "I want you outside. Go patrol along the lake shore. My senses are acute, my nanites are alert, but I want you out there too. If anyone approaches, attack them. Kill them and bring their bodies to me. Now go and don't disturb me. My swarm requires instructions. It has grown, and it offers me much power."

Snek backed away fearfully. The man's speech didn't make much sense, but he now sensed Wiindigo's presence. It was familiar to him, almost like coming home. He'd started life as part of a Wiindigo dragon. There was no way to disguise the feel of the energy. Abubecar's nanites were vibrating with it.

The feeling repelled Snek's reprogrammed swarm, making him fearful. He slid quickly out of the mansion, through the snow that covered the lakefront patio and deck and then onto the ice. A few minutes later, he was two hundred meters away. That was as far as he dared go. He paused, then turned and began to patrol back and forth, guarding the lakefront.

Above him, the sky turned dark with a mist of nanites. Snek felt that he should flee, but the virus code still held him. The looming swarm seemed uninterested in his motion, so he continued patrolling, working at breaking the virus' control as he glided back and forth.

When he reached the other end of the estate, he paused and looked around, scanning out over the ice hopefully. There was nothing there. He dropped his head and started slowly back. As he moved, he whispered, "Mother. Help me, Snek. Please."

By the time he had reached the southern end of his self-defined patrol, he had made a breakthrough. He stopped before turning back and analyzed his insight. A feeling of triumph flushed through him. That was another new sensation. He'd had minor victories before, but they'd merely involved capturing food. This was an intellectual achievement. He'd figured out how to defeat Abubecar's virus.

It took a few minutes to start the process, but once started, it went quickly. He'd created a tiny bit of code that acted as a key to the locked virus. Insert the key in the right place, and the locked code opened. Once opened, he changed one single byte at the heart of the virus disabling it. He could wait until later to work at removing the inert code.

He created a tool, a small program that carried out the necessary actions without his direct supervision. It worked amazingly well. After watching it for a few milliseconds, Snek returned his attention to the external world.

The mist was darker around the mansion. Those were Abubecar's nanites; a huge swarm. Snek wanted nothing to do with it. It was better to flee as far and as quickly as he could before Abubecar realized he was free and took steps to recapture him.

The ice on the lake made for slow going, so he slid up on the edge of the shore. He looked out over the lake from the higher elevation. Still nothing, but despite the lack of physical assistance, he felt that Mother had inspired him in answer to his plea.

"Thank you, Mother. Me. Snek. Thanks you for the help."

With that utterance, he began to move southward as quickly as he could.

Sometime later, Snek stopped. Something had happened. Something momentous. There was a powerful sending. A recall. Abubecar was summoning all of his swarm close. It was powerful and an evil thing. Snek found himself turning back before he realized what was happening.

He struggled for a moment and then overcame the urge to return. Instead, he opened his senses and concentrated on what was happening to the north.

Abubecar was being attacked, and he was enraged. That much was clear. Someone was attacking him from the lake. Snek was torn. Should he continue his escape, or should he go back and see what he could do?

Then there was a flash in the sky from the north. Some terrible energy had just been released. It gave off a brilliant white light that gradually subsided. Snek was paralyzed first by the electromagnetic wave that accompanied the burst and then with the sudden realization that only one source could be responsible. Mother!

His doubts disappeared instantly. He must go and help her. She could put an end to the evil magician. Snek would never have to fear after that. She had helped him with inspiration. He must, must, must help her with the struggle. It would be dangerous for him, but it was necessary.

He raced back northward.

"Snek come. Help Mother."

CHAPTER 30
EVIL INTENTIONS

The lake was wider than it appeared. Either that or the mist was deceptive. It blew in strands and clumps, obscuring the far shore, then clearing to display the mansion in astonishing clarity.

Sophie's unease became intense. Finally, she couldn't put up with it.

"Stop, Michael," she shouted in his ear.

The machine coasted for a bit and came to a halt. Chen and Gwen pulled up alongside.

Chen looked at Michael. "Why are we stopping here?"

He shrugged. "Sophie wanted to stop."

Gwen chose that moment to speak. "I'm feeling nervous. There's something about that mist. Do you notice that it has retreated ahead of us?"

Sophie looked back. The mist had formed a valley into which they'd ridden. Now it extended behind them and was closing in the path they'd taken. They would shortly be surrounded and covered by it.

She probed at it with her radio sense. Suddenly her mind blanked in fear at what she had sensed.

"It's nanites! Wiindigo nanites! Abubecar has allied with Wiindigo. There are too many. He's too powerful. Go back!"

The machines roared, spun, and headed for the opening. The mist closed in, moving more quickly. It was evident that they wouldn't get clear.

Sophie was quivering inside. Her prior experience of abuse and addiction rose up in her mind. She wasn't strong enough to fight this. She couldn't think. The image of Michael saying he loved her and the thought of her baby came into her mind.

She'd fought drug dealers and Wiindigo. She'd beaten her addiction. She knew how to fight, and Michael and the baby were reasons to put aside her fear. She made a growling sound in her throat, then launched an attack on the mist.

It recoiled, moving in a massive swirl as if a strong wind had blown a gust into its middle. There was a momentary opening, but it closed quickly. She struck again, creating a large dome-shaped space around them. The mist circled around the circumference, swirling along the icy drifts as if it were an angry creature.

GWEN HAD BEEN cowering back, but now both she and Chen began to attack. Chen's sending caused chunks of mist to cease moving as if they were paralyzed, while Gwen created colorful bursts that disrupted the mist's attempts to thicken. She transformed one section into a rainbow of colored tendrils. The color faded, but as it did the tendrils drifted down in confusion to settle on the ice.

Sophie was peripherally aware of Michael's armor from the glow it cast. He was ready to combat physical threats and, what was better in her mind, he was fully protected against the mist.

She concentrated and began an elaborate routine to bypass the attacking nanites' security. Once in, she switched them off, and they fell like clouds of dust to the snow-covered ice. The mist thinned, then suddenly withdrew back towards the mansion. She continued neutralizing the nanites, then realized that there was nothing left to fight.

Abubecar had pulled the majority of the swarm back to the mansion. He'd be better able to control them when the distance was less, and his signals were less attenuated. Now the shoreline appeared to be an impenetrable black cloud that showed swirls of movement at the junction of ice and land.

She pushed on Michael's shoulder, and he drove slowly forward. The other two followed after a moment. Sophie looked back. Chen looked determined, while Gwen was pale and gasping. She wasn't as strong as Chen and the effort had greatly tired her.

The mist concentrated as they drove forward. She looked to the side and saw an odd track in a drift. It seemed like a giant snake had wound its way across the surface, leaving a depression in the hard-packed snow. She shrugged it off. Whatever it was would wait. The mist was billowing higher and higher directly in front of them.

Suddenly it coalesced into an image. It wasn't there, and then it was; formed of mist, but with a surprisingly solid look. Her lips moved, "Abubecar."

The magician might be powerful, but he was not original. He'd formed the mist into a cartoon-like character; a turban-wearing caricature with a spade beard and an ornate staff.

Lightning crackled around the staff as the cartoonish image leaned far forward, grimacing, then shot a bolt of all-too-real electricity directly at them.

Sophie raised her arm in a warding motion. A thin wire composed of nanites from her swarm interposed between them and the bolt. The lightning struck the wire, blowing it into a cloud of nanite debris as it followed the line to ground itself against the ice.

There was a cracking sound and water poured through the resulting gap, flooding over the thick ice. Both snow-machines died, victims of the static burst.

Sophie could hear Gwen yelling at Chen to get up. She glanced that way. He'd been thrown off his machine and now was convulsing on the ice. Gwen jumped off the machine and grabbed him, sending a healing spell as she did. He stopped shaking and sat up.

She couldn't afford to watch them. The magician was raising his staff for another strike.

She reached deep within herself for strength, then grabbed almost a fifth of Abubecar's swarm, forcing the nanites to form an eagle. The bird stooped at the giant magician's head with claws outstretched.

Abubecar turned with a shout, his face contorted in anger. He tried to strike the eagle with his staff. The bird avoided the strike and ripped off the turban. It flew out of sight over the mansion, trailing a long stream of fabric behind it.

The giant figure tried to catch the fabric, but it slipped through his fingers. His arm lengthened rapidly in pursuit.

Sophie didn't pause. She struck before his grasping hand could reach the bird. This time she sent a flaming arrow of nanites into Abubecar's back. He hissed like a steam jet. The point of the shaft stuck through his chest, and a splatter of blood arched away from it as he spun toward her, his eyes glaring.

"You'll pay for that, Bitch. You have no chance against me. Against us!" His voice modulated downwards into a deep bass with an unpleasant overtone.

She recognized that sound. She'd heard it before in her first battle with Wiindigo. The AI had taken over the man. Abubecar and Wiindigo were now one entity. The stakes of this fight were far higher than she'd realized. If she lost, the world lost.

She snarled in acknowledgment. Nothing like a little more pressure to bring out her best effort. Abubecar's mouth opened to say something else. Before the words came out, her nanites slammed a massive piece of lake ice into it. His head blurred and became misty.

Her eyes blinked at the sight.

Oh, no. He's all nanites. There's no biological part there to damage. I'll have to attack them directly. Physical attacks won't work.

His head reformed, confirming her realization.

He opened his mouth again, and a swarm of hornets shot out, flying directly at her.

There was a golden flash. A glow surrounded the four on the lake. Michael's nanites had extended his protection to cover all of them. The hornets glanced off the golden force-field in all directions. They lost their shape and became wisps that merged into the nanite mist that circled around the four.

She looked at Michael. He was not holding his sword. Instead, he had a strained expression and was holding his hands out, as if he were pushing the golden shield against the hornet swarm. He had suddenly learned how to control his nanites, but it looked like he was tiring quickly.

Abubecar waved his arms, bringing the cloud of nanites down upon them. Michael was gritting his teeth, trying to hold his force-field.

Sophie's mind was blank for a moment. She needed time to think, time to figure out a better attack.

It looked like Michael's field was fading. The clouds of nanites were darker and closer. She had to do something now.

She forced half of her swarm into a tight ball and shot it into the Abubecar swarm's center, simultaneously closing her eyes and turning her head away. There was a blinding explosion that glared through her eyelids. Everything went black for a moment, then streaks of light flashed in the darkness.

Sophie opened her eyes to a different landscape. Part of the mansion had been destroyed. The entire lakeside facade lay in ruins. The energy had scattered the clouds of Abubecar/Wiindigo nanites, creating a thick dust of inactive nanobots that slowly drifted down, blackening the snow.

Her heart sank. Half of her own swarm had been destroyed.

Abubecar had disappeared, but that didn't mean he was defeated. Wiindigo had proven to be very resourceful in the past. She had to make sure he was beaten.

The sky lightened as the mist dropped in swirls of dust. She looked at her companions. Both of the lesser magicians were unconscious. Chen had been thrown by the explosion and was lying in a heap against one of the inert snow-machines. Gwen was twenty meters farther out on the ice, lying on her back, her arms outspread.

Michael was crouched down. His armor was intact, but he had his hands on his eyes.

"Michael! Are you hurt?"

He replied calmly, "The next time you're going to set off an atomic bomb, warn me. I'm mostly okay, but I can't see anything. I think my nanites are working on my eyes, though."

He lifted his head and looked at her. His face was red, burned by the light and his left eye looked terrible. It was covered with blood and charred black. No. The blackness was a film of nanobots working to repair the damage.

Michael couldn't see. He'd be no help until he could. She had to go after Abubecar alone. There was no time to waste.

"Stay here and get your vision back. I'm going into the mansion. I've got to finish this fight now before he recovers."

"Wait. I'll be better soon. I don't want you going in without my help." He raised his hand to stay her, but the effort was marred by the fact that he extended it in the wrong direction.

"No. I've got to get him. You stay."

She turned back towards the mansion, pulling the remains of her swarm tightly against her body. She didn't have Michael's inbuilt armor, but she could still protect herself.

It was difficult climbing over the wrecked lakefront to reach the patio. She took her time, not wanting to waste energy by having her swarm levitate her. Energy was at a premium now. She'd need every Joule she could retain.

There were nanites in the dust that had not been destroyed. They had been at the higher levels of the mist cloud and farther away from the EMP burst. It took her a little more time to capture them, but it was worthwhile. When she had crossed the patio, those she had gleaned reinforced her swarm. She wasn't at her former strength, but she was close.

The ruined mansion opened in front of her like a cavern. It was dark inside. She thought she should be able to see some light from the windows on the other side of the house but then understood that the darkness was a cloud of nanites. Abubecar's power had not been destroyed. There was a massive swarm inside the remains of the building.

It took all her will-power to enter. Once inside, the swarm sheared away from her, leaving her in a space of her own. Small attacks came at her like knives sticking through the walls of a paper sack. They came to nothing. When one of the pointed things touched her swarm, it was instantly absorbed, becoming part of her defense. She kept her mind tightly focused; a loss of concentration now would be fatal.

The darkness began to fade. Sophie was capturing nanites as quickly as she could. Once they were part of her swarm, they merged with her shield.

Abubecar was hidden somewhere in the rooms ahead. She must go forward until she found him.

A sudden sound behind her made her spin. Michael was standing there. His left eye was sealed shut under a now glowing patch of nanites, but his right was clear.

"I couldn't let you have all of the fun by yourself."

"You idiot! I'm doing fine. I'm almost back to full strength. You should have stayed back there. Gwen needs help. And Chen."

"They'll have to wait. Where's Abubecar?"

"He's somewhere ahead. The darkness is his swarm. He's up there waiting."

"Let's go, then. I may not be able to see so good, but I can still use my sword." At those words, the weapon came to life, materializing out of the air in his right hand.

She moved forward, stepping over broken furniture and a section of roof that had fallen into the room. The high vaulted ceiling tilted at an odd angle overhead. It looked to be on the verge of falling into the room, and she hurried her steps. It would be safer once they were in the undamaged section of the house.

There was a groan, and the ceiling sagged more. Bits of plaster fell around her, one slamming against the nanite shield that covered her head. The shield shook as more of the mass struck it. The nanites flexed as they absorbed the shock.

She entered the darkness of the next room. Abubecar's swarm was thicker there. She stopped. It looked like red eyes were floating in the mist of nanites. The hair rose on her neck as the eyes moved independently through the murk, inspecting her.

Behind her, Michael choked out a warning. "Watch out. The queen!"

She turned to see him in the embrace of a beautiful, dark woman. His eyes were wide open as the woman whispered in his ear. Her tongue licked at his neck causing the nanite armor to glow more brightly there.

Sophie raised her hand to shove the woman away with a nanite-powered push. Her action was interrupted by the mist. It seemed to jump to the attack all at once.

She was surrounded in a swirling torrent of black nanites. Sharp points jabbed at her randomly, keeping her defense working. She could no longer see Michael. She stepped towards where she thought he had been and stumbled over something hidden in the darkness. When she recovered, she'd lost her sense of direction. She turned about slowly, capturing nanites as she moved.

There was a lighter area ahead. She moved toward it. That must be the way out. Michael was there, and he needed help. It brightened as she approached.

She went through an opening, and the nanite-created darkness stopped. It wasn't bright in this room, but enough light came in that she could see. A large man was standing by a fireplace. She remembered Cal. Before he had become a Were-bear, he'd been an equally colossal man. The person she now faced made Cal seem small.

He turned to her with a scowl.

"You've caused me trouble and pain. Yes, pain, although I thought I couldn't feel that any longer. I should thank you for showing me that I'm not as powerful as I thought, but the pain puts all thoughts of thanks out of my mind. You're going to suffer and then die for your insolence. I will not be disrespected any longer by anyone."

He struck at her with his swarm. The darkness flew in from all directions, and she was pulled back and forth violently as the swarm tried to break through her defense.

She gathered her strength and waited it out. After a moment, the attack waned. That was the sign she wanted. She shot a burst of energy directly at the man-shape. It flared into flames that surrounded and covered him. The mist wavered and faded. He screamed, a sound that rumbled through the house and morphed into the dual base and overtone that she knew was Wiindigo.

The flaming form staggered, then, with an apparent huge effort, it did something—something she did not understand in the slightest.

The room seemed to flicker rapidly. There was a sensation of vertigo. Her heart pounded so quickly it felt like it was going to burst out of her chest. Her stomach heaved, and she looked down in horror. A wave of incredible pain washed over her, then centered itself in her lower abdomen. Each heartbeat caused a throb of pain to radiate upwards.

Her belly was growing huge. It felt like it would explode every time her heart beat. At the same time, her energy was fading. She was so tired that she could barely remain on her feet. Whatever he'd done was horrifying. She bent with a spasm as the remains of her last meal spewed across the wood floor and carpet. The odor increased her nausea, and she retched again, then a third time.

Her internal nanites should have prevented the illness, but they seemed inexplicably slow. Then she understood that they were working. It was just that her time sense seemed to be distorted. The nausea faded away.

She dragged her eyes away from her growing belly and looked up.

The door through which she'd come was suddenly clear of mist. All of the Wiindigo nanites were engaged in this unexpected attack. They were swirling around her in a strangely regular pattern.

The open door provided a view of Michael, still in the woman's arms.

Then Flyx zoomed into the room behind the two. The fairy instantly cast a hex that caused the woman's nose to explode. The view faded as the nanite mist swirled thickly again, but she thought that Michael had freed himself and was swinging his sword.

Abubecar's bass voice echoed in the room. "I can't beat you directly, but my muse showed me how to speed up personal time. We're locked together in a warp. You can't escape until I will it. I'm keeping you here until you give birth. When you do, you'll be vulnerable. You won't survive past that moment."

He laughed, a vast, evil sound. His face suddenly appeared before her, looming out of the swirling mist.

Sophie flinched as the understanding of his threat struck her. She gasped with pain. Her womb was contracting. A sudden gush of thin fluid caused a hot sensation along her legs. A part of her mind screamed that she had to get her pants off. The baby would be trapped inside. That could not be allowed to happen.

All thought of the conflict disappeared in her urge to protect her baby. She ripped at her coveralls with hands that were shaking too much to operate the fastenings. In desperation, she used her nanites, now more responsive, using part of the swarm to pull the fabric into shreds. The next contraction was immensely painful, but she felt a sense of accomplishment. The baby was coming. She instinctively squatted.

Abubecar loomed over her again, his hand carrying a long, curved sword.

She bent her neck in submission. He had won. The baby was coming out. She had no strength left to concentrate on anything but that. If only she could get it out before the sword fell.

He laughed again, cruelly, then unable to resist, taunted her. "I'll let you see your child for a moment before you die, but I'll own the child afterward. Its life will be hell. I will use it as I will, and I'll keep it alive to torture and torture again. You should not have challenged me, but your death will be just the barest beginning of the revenge I will have."

She heaved, every muscle taut, and the baby slid free, landing partially on the carpet. It instantly gasped, then screamed.

Abubecar spoke again. "Look. It's a girl. That's wonderful. Think how I will torture her."

Sophie screamed in anguish. "Michael!"

She had to do something, but she was so tired. She looked around for help, searching for anything to use as a weapon.

SNEK WAS TERRIBLY afraid. The conflict within the mansion was destroying the building in its violence. He moved closer and looked through the broken window into the lounge. Abubecar was there facing the woman. His woman, the mother who had caused his existence.

Abubecar had done something, and the two were blurry. Mother's stomach was growing quickly. She was about to give birth. This was a sacred moment. He had to help. The magician couldn't be allowed to hurt Mother, no matter the consequence to Snek. He slid quickly through the opening.

SOPHIE SAW MOVEMENT past Abubecar's looming legs. A giant snake slithered into the room. She looked up. Abubecar's arm raised the sword high for the killing stroke.

Time seemed to freeze. The snake coiled then lunged at Abubecar with a cry.

"Not hurt Mother!"

It struck the upraised arm with its fangs, coiling around the man's body at the same time. Abubecar staggered from the impact and the snake's weight. The snake's tail brushed across her shoulder, knocking her to the floor beside the screaming baby.

Abubecar wrestled with his attacker for a moment, then the snake ripped its head downward and back, severing the sword-holding arm which fell to the side. The sword skittered off across the wood. Blood shot from the torn shoulder. There was a flash creating an impression of blackness filled with red eyes.

She blinked, then opened her eyes in time to see the snake fly across the room, strike the wall, then writhe randomly as if its spine were broken. The placenta slid out and across her leg at the same time.

In some strange way, that final act of birth cleared her mind. She could now concentrate on the battle. The snake's attack had given her the time she needed. Abubecar was fumbling with his remaining hand for the sword. The red-eyed mist was coalescing around him again.

It was time to act.

Sophie made a massive effort, taking more will-power than she thought she had. Her previous struggles with opiate addiction paled in comparison. Gasping, she propped herself up on her left arm, trying to avoid the baby. Her hair hung limply, dripping with sweat. She raised her eyes and glared at Abubecar through strands of wet hair that stuck to her face.

He'd recovered the sword and was straightening, looking over his shoulder at her.

The virus she'd created was ready if only there were enough power left in her swarm. There would have to be. There was no choice.

Her eyes lost focus as she grafted the code onto a carrier wave and heterodyned it into the magician's swarm, bypassing all of his security as smoothly as a knife slicing through warm butter.

Abubecar stood bolt-upright and stopped moving. He looked surprised, then horrified. His body began to blur. His nanites were losing their ability to cooperate as the virus took hold and propagated through the swarm. He started to dissolve, clouds of nanites flowing off into swirls of unformed mist.

Sophie ripped ruthlessly at the nanites, scattering them. Her system couldn't absorb that many at once. Without glancing at the shivering snake, she jammed a mass of nanites into it.

Abubecar's swarm closed about him, and his face suddenly took on more solidity. He opened his mouth, to say something, but Sophie struck viciously at his head.

There was a disturbing sense of doubling as she struck. Then she understood. Her child was joining in the attack. She almost lost her concentration in her astonishment, but her anger flared again, and she steadied.

Together the two of them ripped the head off the magician's body, then tore it into microscopic bits, separating every cell and every nanite. The enemy swarm lost all cohesion, part of it floating away on the wind that blew through the ruined mansion, part of it coming into her possession.

Sophie was still propped on her arm, but she felt much stronger. Her belly no longer hurt. She looked for her baby, expecting to see it still lying against her legs. The child was not there. She jumped up, frantic. What had happened to her baby?

A small blond girl child, physically about three years of age stood beside her. Sophie's mind stalled for a moment, then she understood. Abubecar hadn't stopped the time warp at the precise moment of birth, the way he'd planned. The snake's attack had disrupted his plan. Now, both mother and child had healed and grown.

Sophie reached for the girl, and the girl smiled lovingly at her.

"Mommy. I'm glad we beat that bad man. I didn't want him to hurt you."

"My baby! You're—you're beautiful. And you can talk!" She couldn't think of what to say.

The girl snuggled against her. "I'm not a baby. I'm Mercy. I named myself."

There was a noise behind them. Sophie turned to see the snake sliding across the floor. She raised her hand in defense, then stopped.

"I know you. You were part of that Wiindigo dragon. Now you've changed. I sense...I sense nanites in you that are like mine."

Mercy said, "The snake saved us. He wants to be my brother."

SNEK MOVED CLOSER. Mother had helped him. That meant she must care for him, but he was suddenly full of reluctance. He was afraid to find out what came next. What if she didn't care for him? What if it had been an accident and she'd meant the nanites she sent him to destroy him? He was frightened but irresistibly drawn to her.

He slid even closer, screwing up his courage. He had to know. Had he become deserving of care? Would she be his mother?

"Mother. Snek afraid. Pain. Snek stop Abubecar. Bite arm. Please care Snek. Snek try good. Snek learn good. Please?"

There was the sound of running. Michael came charging through the door, armor glowing and sword raised. He struck the door jamb on the way through, breaking the wood and sending him off balance. When he recovered, he stopped, dumbfounded at the sight of his beloved Sophie holding a small blond girl in one arm and stroking the head of a giant snake that was coiled loosely around them both. He lowered his sword and stood, trying to comprehend the scene.

Flyx flew in, landed on his shoulder, then turned to look at the dust pile that had been the vampire queen. She took a lock of Michael's hair in her hand and twisted it gently.

"That ugly vampire woman won't bother you again, Michael. I hexed a wooden stake through her heart. I'm really a powerful fairy."

Always quick, even though he did not fully understand what he saw, Michael had calmed enough to respond. He laughed. "And a very good one, Flyx."

Then he asked, "Sophie, what the hell is going on, and who is this girl? And, above all, what is that snake thing?"

Sophie turned to look at him, her face shining.

"Dearest, meet your daughter, Mercy. This is Snek. He...is her adopted brother. He will make sure no harm will touch her."

CHAPTER 31
RESOLUTION

The mansion was on the verge of collapse. They looked, but the only evidence they could find of Abubecar was a slime of cells on the floor and walls. Sophie and Mercy had indeed ripped him to pieces.

Snek knew where Abubecar had held Jack's sister and they looked. It was in a part of the building that still stood, so they hoped she'd be there, but there was no sign of her. Holding Mercy in one arm, Sophie closed her eyes and tried to sense some trace of the girl. When she opened them again, they were dark with anger.

"We're too late, Michael. He killed her. There are a few of her nanites scattered in here that he missed. Their memory tells the story. She's been dead for a day."

He put his arm around her, pulling both her and Mercy close. "We'd better check on Chen and Gwen. Your blast hit them hard."

Snek led the way to an exit at the end of the hall. Outside, it seemed warmer than it had been. The sun was high, and the wind had dropped. The snow crunched underfoot as the group worked their way around the ruin and down to the lake, Flyx flying close to Michael.

Both Gwen and Chen were on their feet, holding each other and talking. When she saw them, Gwen said something to him. The two started forward to meet the group.

Snek's belated appearance startled the two. He'd slid under the snow, then popped his head and neck out next to Sophie.

Gwen raised her hand to attack.

Sophie cried, "Wait! This is Snek. He saved me. He's mine, my creation, my unexpected child."

Snek felt a warmth surge over his body at those words. He had finally found Mother, and she accepted him. He was happy.

They righted the snow-machines and made haste back to Darren's house. The clear sky promised a cold night. Snek followed as quickly as he could, reaching the house some hours behind them.

The three of them were snuggled in bed, covers piled warmly over them, Mercy in the middle.

SOPHIE COULDN'T QUITE reconcile her feelings. This was her baby and had been born just a few hours ago. Now she was a small child. There had been no time to bond with her, no time to enjoy her babyhood. She pulled the little girl close. Mercy looked up at her and traced the lines of her face with a small, soft hand.

"I know, Mother. I was within you for months. When things happened, it was confusing, but I grew quickly. I think my mind grew quickest of all. I'm still your baby, even though I'm a little girl. Never fear, I love you."

Michael's eyes widened in response. Sophie saw his reaction and understood.

Mercy was something unprecedented; a child with an almost adult mind. She'd been born and had become a child in a matter of seconds to him. Now she carried out adult-level conversations.

Michael put his arm over both of them and pulled them close. Then he said, "I hope you'll learn to love me also."

Mercy wriggled around to face him. "You big Silly. Of course, I love you, Daddy."

He stroked her blond hair, experimentally, as if he couldn't quite believe she was his little girl.

Sophie smiled, then remembered something.

"Michael?"

"Yes, what?"

"Flyx is out by the fire. I think she's sad."

He knew what she was getting at. "I can't help that. You're mine, and now we are a family. I think Cisco will be pleased, but I can't help Flyx."

"Maybe we can help her."

"How. What do you mean?"

"I've got far more nanites in my swarm than I can deal with on a practical basis. I gave a mass of them to heal Snek. This precious child has taken others. She's going to become very powerful. I can tell."

"But, what about Flyx. I mean, I'm glad that Mercy will be powerful and Snek...well, he'll take some getting used to, but Flyx? She needs to find a mate among the fairy-folk."

"No. What I mean is that, if you're willing, and only if, I can take some of your genetic code and create a fairy-sized version of you. Don't worry, it won't hurt, and he'll be completely independent of you."

He looked nonplussed. "Uh, will this be like giving birth?"

She laughed. "No. Nothing nearly as painful."

She knew he'd give his permission without waiting for him to speak, so she took action. There was a blur in the air, then: "Look. Here he is. The fairy version of you."

There was a thump on the bed by Michael's feet, and he looked down. A small, winged version of himself looked back at him.

"I never realized I looked so large," Michael-the-fairy said. "Handsome too, I'd say, if I were a human."

Sophie said, "Here, I'll open the door. Fly out to the main room and look for another fairy there. I think she'll have some things she will want to discuss with you."

The room empty again, Sophie lay back.

"He's an independent creature. Your attitudes influenced his outlook, but they do not control him." She touched his face, then added, "You know that the fairy-folk started in precisely this way. They are created things. Not by me, but somewhere there is a magician or magicians who understand their power well enough to create them. Also the other mutated humans; the Weres, the vampires, and maybe some others that I don't know. Cal was the first Were. Wiindigo created him by accident. Now there are more. Someone evil must have created the vampires. They are not a good thing to unleash on the world. We'll have to investigate that sooner or later."

Mercy asked, "Mommy, what are 'pires?"

Sophie laughed. "So, little bug, you don't know everything yet. I was wondering."

Mercy snorted and said, "I know what you talked about while I was inside you. At least during the last part of when I was inside you. At first, I didn't know anything but warmth, but then I knew you were making me. It made me feel good to be wanted in that way."

Michael gently kissed the child's cheek. "You need not worry about being wanted. You're exactly what we dreamed about. We've both loved you since before you were even started."

There was an outraged hooting from down the hall. Then quiet, followed by a discrete knock on the door.

Sophie said, "Come."

The door cracked open, making a narrow entrance. Wold slid through, then bowed his characteristic formal bow.

"Those crazy fairies. Flyx had a fit when a fairy that looked like Michael showed up. They've been flying around in a kind of dance ever since. They knocked over three lamps followed by a candle. The curtains caught on fire, but not to worry. I've put them out. The fairies went out the dog door. Cisco opened it for them. I don't know where they are now."

A dry, small voice interjected, "They flew up and headed south. From their scent, I believe they were thinking about creating a little fairy."

Cisco reared up on the bedside and asked, "Can I come up? You guys look so nice and warm. I could use a good cuddle too."

The door creaked as it opened farther. Snek's head appeared above the foot of the bed.

Cisco eyed him warily as he spoke.

"Mother. Mercy. Michael. All safe. Me, Snek. Watch. You sleep. Me watch by fire."

Snek slid back out.

Cisco snorted, "Of course all is safe. I'm here." He puffed out his chest and held his head erect. "Nothing can get by me."

CHAPTER 32
MERCY

The early flowers were in bloom, and the birds were busy, singing, staking claim to their territories, and courting. The midday sun was bright, only intermittently obscured by white, puffy clouds scudding northeastward on a light breeze. Bees were flying over the flowers in the warm sun. It was a great day to be outside.

Mercy was lying in a hammock near the lake. She'd been reading but had put aside her book, just to listen to the day.

The hammock stirred a bit, and she trailed a hand out to rub it along Snek's smooth, dry back. He was lying in the grass beside the hammock. She couldn't go far without him coming along. He took his task to watch over her quite seriously.

He was unique; an AI creature accidentally formed by her mother, Sophie. He had leveraged himself up in intelligence to the point of sentience. He'd been influenced by the little he knew about Sophie and had gradually come to view her as his mother. This had been the source of a great struggle within him as he tried to comprehend the difference between good and evil.

He'd developed his own, personal sense of morality and compassion as a result. When he'd finally found Sophie and contributed to her victory over the evil magician, Abubecar, she had recognized what he was and had accepted him as a sort of surrogate child that she'd created.

He had been Mercy's constant companion for the past four years.

Her parents had tried, but so far they had failed to have another child. Something about the time-warp that had accelerated Mercy's birth had left a permanent effect on her mother's body that Sophie's nanites couldn't seem to counteract. Still, Mercy felt lucky to have Snek as her...well, brother wasn't entirely correct, but she thought of him in that way. He was always willing to do what she wanted, and she felt secure due to his presence.

Now the wind had picked up slightly, carrying the call of a loon from out on the lake. Mercy sat up in the hammock and looked at the weald that grew thickly around the estate. The old forest had been thick before the change in the world. Now, with the nanites that existed in symbiosis with the trees, it had become mighty in a way that befitted a forest that was centuries old.

EXPLORING THE PATHWAYS in the wood might be fun. She'd been going into the woods since she'd arrived home immediately after her birth. The time-warp Abubecar had used to attack her mother had not ceased at Mercy's birth but had continued for a time after. During that moment, she'd grown from a baby to the physical size of a three-year-old while her mind had matured beyond that point.

Now, at the actual age of four, she looked like a seven-year-old and behaved more like she was in her teens. She'd wondered if she was ever to find a boy who would be interesting. Her father absolutely set his foot down at the idea of her hanging around with older boys. Young men, he had called them, were too old for her. He didn't think she was prepared to deal with them.

Mercy laughed silently to herself. She could easily deal with any man. Even an accomplished magician would not be able to defend himself against me. I learned from my mother in the moments after my birth. Now, I've grown more powerful.

In answer to that thought, her nanite swarm, spread over acres of the estate, quivered and reported. There was no threat anywhere.

She jumped out of the hammock. Snek lifted his head a little, looking at her inquiringly.

"C'mon, Snek. Let's go explore in the woods for a while. I'm bored."

Snek said, "Snek hungry. Maybe find something to eat. Okay."

She skipped away towards one of the paths that led into the trees, Snek following.

There were birds building nests and lady slippers to find. She found mushrooms among the trees. The path wound back and forth, gradually moving away from the mansion by the lake. Mercy continued, her thoughts flitting from one thing to another.

Here was a clump of raspberry bushes. She'd remember those. They had no berries as yet, but later in the summer, they'd be ready to pick.

There was a sudden rustle in the bushes and a cotton-tail rabbit dashed down the path in front of her. Snek lifted his head in interest. He was fastidious in his eating habits. Killing things seemed to cause him some type of moral pain, but still, he had to eat, and live food was what he required.

They continued for a while. The forest grew thicker, and vines grew into the trees. Mercy had not been this way before. She usually turned back at what she knew was the edge of their estate.

Now, a feeling of wanderlust had struck. She was unsatisfied with herself and wanted something to make her feel better. It was one thing to be intelligent when solving problems, but having a more-or-less young adult mind captured in a child's body was sometimes bothersome.

What would it be like, if she found a young man out here? Say, maybe fifteen or older. She thought of what she'd say. He'd have to be handsome, of course. She'd impress him with her wit and intelligence.

Maybe he'd see her as more than the child she appeared to be.

It was a pleasant fantasy. When she stopped to look at another mushroom, she realized that Snek was no longer immediately behind her.

She sent for him, using her radio sense. He had found a fresh deer track and was hunting. She'd ignored him when he turned off the trail some minutes ago. Now he was about to attack. Now, he'd killed it.

She smiled. Deer were numerous and pests. It took some doing to keep them out of the garden. Even her nanite defenses weren't always up to the task. The deer had their own nanites, and they seemed to cooperate in helping the animals get into the choicest vegetables.

Snek would take a few minutes to feed, then he'd be on her trail again. Maybe it would be fun to get far ahead of him. He was so careful to stay near her, it would do him no harm to have to work at it for a change.

She ran down the trail, observing the woods. The trees grew thicker here, and the ground was softer. She was headed to a wet area. It would be best to be careful and not get into a boggy place. Her nanites could lift her over the ground, but that required more effort than she liked. She slowed, walking more carefully.

The path she was following had gradually narrowed and then finally disappeared. Snek would be on her trail by now. Still, the forest here was kind of spooky. The vines were thicker, and the undergrowth grew high, obscuring what view the lush trees might have allowed.

The thought of meeting a Were-creature passed through her mind. The Weres were not all as friendly as her mother's friend Cal, the Were-bear. Some were dangerous. They wouldn't bother her, though. She could easily turn one into a giant frog or whatever she wanted. Besides, her nanite swarm provided a warning.

She checked her swarm, just in case. The nanites were spread out from her. Those on her trail extended back to the estate, but those ahead of her were only a few hundred yards away. They were now reporting a disturbance of some kind off to her left and behind some higher trees.

Mercy looked over her shoulder. Still no sign of Snek. She shrugged. He'd have to catch up on his own time. She walked towards the disturbance, curious about its nature. Her nanites hadn't reported on that. It wasn't some animal, they would have told her that, or if it were a Were-creature. There was nothing there, just some mist that hovered under the thickly standing trees.

She stopped and looked. The mist had the unmistakable feel of the enemy—Wiindigo. The evil AI was widely distributed across the land. It resided in wild nanites. When they accumulated into a dense swarm, their communication ability increased and the individual units formed a distributed AI. Wiindigo was the result.

Her mother had explained to her that Wiindigo was the child of Hippocrates, a benign AI that was mostly not in the world. Wiindigo had no regard for humans or any other life for that matter, while Hippocrates respected humans and kept tabs on them from his own pocket universe.

Hippocrates had told Sophie that he wanted humans to develop on their own. Her mother thought that he was hoping they'd grow into worthy companions for him.

Wiindigo, on the other hand, would casually destroy all humans, and all life on the planet, if it thought such an action would help it grow. It often tried to accumulate enough nanites to become dangerous, but always it had failed. It would reach a point where its presence became known, and either her parents or other magicians with nanite manipulating power would destroy the accumulation.

The mist flowed thickly, suddenly growing opaque and casting midnight-like darkness under the trees. It began to glow, a nauseating greenish color. At times clumps became visible.

Mercy watched, unafraid. She felt that she could handle this relatively small bit of Wiindigo if she had to. She jumped, startled.

One of the clumps had manifested a red eye that had blinked when she saw it.

The mist swirled even more tightly, then began to take discrete form. A giant man shape was starting to appear between the trees. This was far from what she'd hoped for in her fantasy.

Instead of a handsome young man who would engage in an entertaining conversation with her, this thing was massive, lumpish, and showed little evidence of charm or intelligence.

The mist drew back a little, revealing the shape of a huge ogre. It was still forming, the nanites in the fog condensing and filling the gaps in its arms and body. It looked at her, its eyes glaring balefully as it licked its lips.

The thing was immense with bulging muscles that were probably big enough to break trees in half. She might, after all, be in some danger.

She started to retreat, then caught peripheral sight of motion in the higher branches of the trees. Snek was up there. He had sensed the ogre and was slipping through the branches silently, moving to a vantage point behind the huge creature.

Mercy had forgotten how large Snek was. Now her perspective of him was distorted by the immense size of the Wiindigo ogre. Snek wasn't small compared to it, but he was vastly outweighed.

He coiled around a tree trunk, then slipped over some branches to hang poised above the ogre's head. He looked at her, awaiting her signal.

Mercy felt reassured now that her guardian was present. Between the two of them, they could surely deal with the creature.

The ogre looked at her, then slowly came to a decision. It moved forward menacingly. A ropy drool of saliva slid out of the corner of its mouth, followed by a long black tongue, which licked the thick lips in anticipation. The creature's actions seemed to show that it viewed her as a tasty snack rather than a threat.

That was insulting. She was far more potent than she appeared. Besides, she had help.

Mercy raised her arm, then pointed it at the ogre. Snek understood and moved to a better position for attack. His jaws opened wide, stretching. He'd increased the size of his fangs. They were usually unobtrusive, but he could make them larger when necessary. He seemed to think that this was one of those times.

If Snek was even a little worried, shouldn't she be also? The ogre took another step forward. It was now so close that there was no alternative. She couldn't outrun the thing. Once it began to move, it would bulldoze through the trees and brush at a deceptively high speed. She'd have to wind her way through the obstacles, and the ogre would catch her. It would have to be dealt with now.

She gathered her power about her and waved Snek to attack. Snek would distract it, then she'd capture its nanites.

The End

CHARACTERS

The All-Powerful but missing AI: Hippocrates
The EVIL AI: Wiindigo – can manifest as anything
The EVIL that might turn good: Snake/self-named as Snek

The GOOD POWERS:
Sophie Monroe
Michael and Sophie's daughter: Mercy
Michael O'Keefe
Polly Kincaide – lives with M & S and cooks.
Flyx the fairy (and her kind – ruled by a King)
Wold the owl/brownie
Cisco the chimera poodle
Other chimeras: Killer the crow
Cal the were-bear
The Neutral but possibly friendly:
Gwen
Chen – gamer learned to be good at magic – generally neutral, but interested in Gwen. Afraid of Abubecar.
Chen's Minion Trolls
The Comic Relief: Alehandre d'La Blancia

The BAD seduced by The EVIL:
Abubecar – captured the Holden estate where he resides after having killed all of the family save Linda and Jack (who somehow escaped)
Linda Holden – his mind-controlled paramour
Darren The Magnificent
The catalyst: The Holden's youngest son - Jack Holden

ABOUT THE AUTHOR

Eric S. Martell set out to become a scientist when he was five. He was attracted to psychology and earned a Ph.D. in that discipline. When personal computers came along (way back in prehistory), he became adept with them and spent years in software design, creating everything from early childhood learning software to military training modules. He has been trained in various types of energy healing, has lectured on the law of attraction, made a living investing in and selling real estate. Eric is a black-belt in Tae-Kwon-Do, pilot, scuba diver, jazz guitar player, outdoorsman, and addicted to both science and science fiction.

He started by writing a book about his real estate experiences and a second one that deals with the spiritual aspect of selling. He then turned to writing science fiction-his true love. His books are carefully researched and offer both believable science and compelling characters set against realistic action. His science fiction books cover alien invasion in an apocalyptic setting, political structure, space travel, advanced weapons, quantum physics, hunting, war, romance, time travel, and alien worlds.

He's been published in a series of anthologies and has several full-length science fiction novels available. His writing goal is to provide his readers with stories they cannot put down and he takes readers' suggestions seriously.

Notices about new books, free short stories, opinion posts, and preview pages for many of his books can be found on his author blog at http://EricMartellAuthor.com. He can also be found on Facebook at ESMartellbooks.

BLOG INFORMATION

If you enjoyed this book, please follow my Author Blog at EricMartellAuthor.com for information about my other books. You'll find free short stories there, occasional preview pages for new novels in progress, and blog posts about things that I find interesting (most lately Artificial Intelligence).

I welcome comments and enjoy discussions with readers.

You can also follow me on Facebook at ESMartellbooks. My Twitter handle is @emartell.

I can be found on MEWE and GAB. You can also email me directly through my Author Blog.

LINK FOR AWARD-WINNING CYBER-WITCH:

http://bit.ly/Cyberwitch

LINKS FOR MY TIME-TRAVEL STORIES

Heart of Fire Time of Ice
http://bit.ly/HeartofFire

Paradox: On the Sharp Edge of the Blade
http://bit.ly/ParadoxBlade

All the Moments in Forever
http://bit.ly/Moments

LINK FOR THE GAIA ASCENDANT TRILOGY:

The Time of The Cat
Second Wave
Confederation
http://bit.ly/GaeaAscendant

LINK FOR MY ANTHOLOGY:

http://bit.ly/Asterats